THE CALLING
THE MAKING OF A VETERAN COP

A NOVEL BY LT. DAN MARCOU

Holt, Michigan

Thunder Bay Press, Holt 44842

*I dedicate this book to my
most important backup officer
and the love of my life,
Vicki*

CONTENTS

INTRODUCTION

There has always been, and will always be, an intense public interest in police work. The reason for all the interest in what cops do is, to put it quite simply, police work is intensely interesting. There have been many thrilling, heart-wrenching books written about police work. Some of our favorite characters in books, on television, and in movies are cops. There are Columbo; Dirty Harry; Riggs; and Walker, Texas Ranger, to name a few.

I am venturing to give you one more book about cops. The slight difference is that this is a novel written by a real cop, about a fictional cop named Daniel McCarthy. It will take place during McCarthy's formative years, and it will chronicle McCarthy's first five years in the challenging career that is law enforcement. I hope it gives you a sense of police work that may be slightly different and, hopefully, as engaging as other police stories you have enjoyed in the past.

I like to describe police work like a roller coaster ride. There are highs and lows. There are slow times, suddenly punctuated by moments of tear-producing laughter or sheer terror. At times, you wish someone would let you off. When the ride is finished and you do get off, you are very glad you took the ride but not quite sure you would take it again.

When my son was very young, we used to love to ride roller coasters. We had a roller coaster motto that went like this, "The higher, the faster, the upside-downier, the better." That motto fits for a career in police work also—as long as you survive.

Hop on! Enjoy the ride.

PROLOGUE

The screaming and breaking glass caused Dan to sit bolt upright in his bed. A moment ago, he'd been sleeping soundly, and now he was wide awake and the fear was back. He knew it well. "Whiskey night," whispered his older brother Bobby, when he sensed his little brother was awake. Dan crawled out of his bunk and found his gun belt. Bobby whispered frantically, "What do you think you're going to do with that? He'll kill you!"

Dan ignored his brother's warning and resolutely strapped on his gun. Dan sat down on the stairs and slowly lowered his butt off the top step, sliding to the next and the next and the next, until he was sitting quietly, unnoticed on the bottom step.

His mother was no longer screaming. Now she was crying. She was holding her prized matched set of crystal candleholders. They were shattered. "Why do you have to be so mean?" she sobbed.

"Mean my ass!" said his father, pulling back his right fist as he brought his left into a boxer's guard. "I'll show you mean." His mother, already on her knees, dropped her broken treasure, as she covered her head.

Dan pulled his revolver from his holster. The fear was overwhelming. He hated the fear. He wondered if he would become brave some day. He wanted so much to not feel the fear. He wanted to sleep all night one night and not feel the fear.

His father walked towards his cowering wife. Dan aimed his revolver at his father. It was all that he knew to do. His father was huge. Dan was not only much smaller than his father, but he was overwhelmed by the fear. "Dan, don't do it," whispered his brother Bobby from the top step.

Dan took steady aim at the chest of his father, who stepped within reach of Mom, cringing into a ball on the floor before this monster. Dan's heart pounded like a steel drum in his ears. The fear! He hated the fear. He squeezed the trigger. Bang! Bang! Bang! Bang!

"Open the door!" Bang! Bang! Bang! Bang! "La Claire Police Department—open the door!"

Dan brought his gun down. His mother sprang to her feet and swung the door open. "Thank God you're here!" said mother in her whiskey night voice. It was only in the middle of the night that she sounded like this.

"Get the hell out of my house!" shouted his dad in his whiskey night voice.

"Sir, calm down. We're just here to help," said the muscular young officer. He was as big as his dad, but Dan noticed the muscles. He had muscles like Superman, but no cape.

"Help my ass! You better call for some help if you come into my house without an invitation! Get out!" bellered dad, as he lunged at the young cop. The cop, fresh from "the Corps," stepped quickly out of the way and the rest happened too fast for Dan to comprehend. Then his dad was taken out the door.

The house was quiet. Dan slid his gun back into its holster. The fear was slipping out of him gradually, like the air from the slow leak in a balloon.

The fear, which was so much a part of his young life, was melting away, thanks to Superman-without-a-cape. No four-year-old should know such fear. A four-year-old should fear the dark, fear the monster under his bed, and the coat tree in the corner at night. The monster should not be real. The monster should not be "Dad."

The young policeman returned to the house to talk to Dan's mother. He was the first to notice the little boy sitting on the bottom step. The serious look on the young officer's face was immediately replaced by a broad smile. "Howdy, pardner. Is that a six-gun you're packing?" smiled the officer, noticing the genuine Lone Ranger pistol the little boy had strapped to his hip.

"Are you going to be a cowboy when you grow up?" asked the officer, as he wiped a tear from the little boy's cheek.

"Nope. I'm goin' to work with you," said the little boy, smiling, happy that the fear was almost gone.

"Well then, you'd better put this on," said the officer, while he set his eight-point hat on his young backup-in-waiting's head.

The smile somehow managed to get bigger and the little boy ran off, surprising the policeman with his speed. The boy climbed up onto a recliner and stood still, with his hands on his hips as he looked at himself in the mirror.

"I'm thinking we *will* be working together some day," said the cop. "I better introduce myself, young man. My name is Compton. What's your name?"

"McCawty," said the youngster. He still looked in the mirror while he adjusted his hat just-so.

"Nice to meet you, Mr. Cawty," said Compton innocently.

"McCawty!" said the four-year-old with an intensity in his eyes that Compton thought must have been practiced and learned in another life.

"Meet Danny McCarthy, Officer Compton." said Danny's mother, who was smiling now at the little one she realized had come to save her. "Danny McCarthy. If this little guy says he's going to work with you someday, you might as well clean out a locker for him right now."

Compton laughed. He finished gathering the information he needed and soon forgot the encounter. It would blend in with the thousands of calls he would handle over the years.

But four-year-old Dan McCarthy would not forget. That night lit a flame in the little boy that would become a passion. He wanted to grow up to be Superman-without-a-cape. He wanted to be someone who could help melt the fear away. He wanted to be a cop.

CHAPTER 1
MCCARTHY'S FIRST DAY

The worst part of being a rookie is that you know you are a rookie, and everyone else knows you are a rookie. For some reason, the worst thing that someone can say to you is, "Are you a rookie?" The positive thing about being called one is that you get used to being insulted early in a career where being insulted is an everyday occurrence.

When Dan McCarthy got into the patrol car for the first time, it was almost overwhelming. There were buttons for red lights, spot lights, the siren, the public address system, the radio, the radar. The car was equipped with a shotgun, camera, binoculars, preliminary breath-testing unit, life jacket, first aid equipment, and a teddy bear.

McCarthy hoped that before he had to get out on his own, he would have the opportunity to learn from a master—an experienced white mouse to help him through the maze that is police work. He hoped Officer Stanley Brockman was the "master patrolman," who would teach him to be the kind of officer McCarthy had dreamt of being since he was four years old.

Brockman was a ten-year "veteran." Boy, did that word sound great to McCarthy. McCarthy longed to be referred to as a veteran. This word triggered a whole series of thoughts and fantasies. "I can see the headlines," thought McCarthy. "Officer McCarthy Saves Another Life." "Officer Dan McCarthy Thwarts Robbery," "McCarthy Selected Officer of the Year."

Suddenly Officer Stanley Brockman slid into the driver's seat and shook the rookie out of his daydream. "Rookie!" Brockman said, in a tone both disdainful to McCarthy and entertaining to Brockman.

"Dan McCarthy is my given name," Dan recited. "You can call me Dan or McCarthy."

"Are you jerking my chain, kid?" asked Brockman, looking at Dan as if he were an alien. "Rookie . . . I will call you rookie until you are not a rookie anymore. I might even call you rookie then, if I think if makes your ass tight."

"Yes, sir," answered McCarthy, trying to hide his emotion, for he was truly pissed.

"Oh-oh. I guess I made the rookie mad," said Brockman, seeing the look in McCarthy's eyes. "Boy, rookie, I hope you are not more dangerous to me when you're mad, cuz you are already dangerous. You're fucking dangerous, all right. Dangerous to me, cuz you're a rookie! Listen, rookie! I hear you're a college boy. I want you to forget everything you think you've learned, because you know nothin'. Now you're in the real world, this is the only school that matters—the school of hard knocks. That degree of yours and a dime will get you a hot cup of coffee. If you take that degree into a bar fight, it will get your ass kicked. Now, all I want you to do is keep your hands off everything, keep your mouth shut, your eyes open, and maybe you'll learn something." So beginnith the lesson.

"Rookie"—there was a time no one ever called McCarthy a name that he didn't like. He wouldn't allow it. No, he wouldn't stand for it. Those days were over. McCarthy would have to tolerate such abuse and worse if he was to make it in law enforcement. There was a time, when to call Dan a name that was deliberately meant to anger him, was calling out McCarthy. Then the fight was on. Now he had to take it.

Then McCarthy wondered about the rest of Brockman's statement—the part of "forget everything you think you've learned . . ." Brockman was referring to. Was it just everything related to law enforcement? Should he pretend to not know how to read? Should McCarthy ask Brockman to tie his shoes for him and change his diapers? Dan was having second thoughts about this guy. He was hoping to be partnered with the law enforcement equivalent of Yoda. McCarthy was not sure who Brockman was the law enforcement equivalent of, but it definitely wasn't Yoda. "Never mind that," thought McCarthy. "It's official. You're on patrol," McCarthy thought as the Brockman wheeled the squad car off the ramp and onto the street.

Patrol to the new officer is like a Sunday drive. A rookie doesn't have "cop eyes" yet. Cop eyes allow a person to see beyond the façade that a city street is. Brockman was constantly swinging the squad car around, and making contacts for God knows what reason, while making comments like, "Did you see that?" or "There's that son of a . . ." McCarthy did not yet look at the street from a cop's point of view. He was eager to learn. He was determined to learn!

During each call and stop, Brockman made the contact and Dan merely served as the backup officer. Later in the shift, while patrolling on Highway 41, a black pickup suddenly veered to the left, crossing the centerline. Dan yelled excitedly, "Did you see that?" Then Brockman glanced as if annoyed at his unwelcome shadow and accelerated to gain ground. The veteran quickly caught up with the vehicle and hit the squad's overhead lights.

Instead of pulling to the side of the road, the driver seemed as if he did not see the lights and continued traveling up the highway, occasionally drifting to the centerline and back to the roadway's edge. Brockman hit the siren and the whine shocked the silence of the night. This brought the occupant of the pickup back into this world all too suddenly. The pickup's driver hit his brakes hard and the truck abruptly stopped, partially on the shoulder and partially on the roadway. The driver had stopped on a hill, creating a terrible hazard.

As Brockman exited the patrol car, he saw something which the rookie didn't. He yelled, "Stay in the car!" The passenger was climbing out of the truck while it was still in reverse. The driver was clearly as drunk as Otis of Mayberry ever was. The fact that his vehicle was rolling backward escaped the driver's consciousness. The movement of the vehicle coupled with the twelve-pack of beer the driver had consumed before driving, made it impossible for him to accomplish anything, except to tumble from the cab of the truck. He landed hard on the seat of his Levi 501's, and there he sat.

The pickup now seemed to have a mind of its own. It rolled driverless toward the squad, and Brockman deftly moved the squad out of the path of the truck. "Thank God, he didn't let me drive," thought McCarthy, as he watched the driver sit blissfully on the ground,while the front wheels of the truck ran over the drunken man's legs.

The truck continued on its course in a circling pattern across the lanes of traffic. Somehow, other startled drivers managed to miss the unmanned black Ford. Other vehicles noisily marked their passing with the screeching of tires. The truck finally came to rest in the ditch on the opposite side of the road and injured no one. Or did it?

Brockman ran to the truck and slipped the gear into park. He pushed on the emergency brake to make sure the errant vehicle's careening days were over. Dan ran to the driver, expecting the elderly gentleman's legs to be crushed and useless. The driver was still sitting motionless right where he landed. Dan noticed a dazed look in the driver's eyes, as if he was watching a documentary on an imaginary television. There was a perfect dirty tire impression across both pants legs.

The rookie asked, "Sir, are you all right?"

The driver turned toward the rookie and a smile broke slowly across the elderly man's face as he said, "What did you stop me for? I wasn't speeding." The man did not appear to be injured, but as a precaution, he was taken to the hospital. The old "stunt man" did have some bruises, but nothing was broken. The gentleman was charged with operating a motor vehicle while intoxicated.

He was taken to the La Claire Police Department, where he was processed by Brockman, while McCarthy watched. The driver was given a breath test and found to have a blood alcohol content of .24, which was more than twice the legal limit.

When the old man, whose name was Roy, was told his blood alcohol content was .24, he laughed and proclaimed, "See! I had to drive, cuz that's sure too drunk for a man of my age to be walking about town." Roy was clearly his own best audience, because this response kept him laughing on and off for quite a while. Each time he would say to himself, "too drunk to walk," the laughing would start all over again.

Roy was released later that night to his adult daughter. Officer McCarthy sent off a closing goodbye to Roy's daughter, "I'm sorry for the way this has inconvenienced you, ma'am."

Roy's daughter stopped and smiled, "Thank you for your kindness. I'm sorry for my father's behavior. He's a good man, but he has never quite grown up." She left with Roy in tow.

Brockman had a quick critique of the rookie's performance. "Next time, kid, get your head out of your ass. Your first night was almost your last night. If I wouldn't have yelled, that truck would have flattened your ass. Yeah, and what was that comment about being sorry for the inconvenience? We don't have to be sorry for shit. You're not a goddamn social worker! You're a cop! I got a bad feeling about you, rookie."

Yeah, well, fuck you, Brockman," was the thought McCarthy wished he could express but somehow turned it into, "Yes, sir, I will keep trying." McCarthy thought Brockman knew as much about communication, as McCarthy knew about police work. McCarthy then thought, "Well, in about five years or so, I will be a veteran and poor Brockman will still be a prick. I know I'm a dumb rookie, but Brockman doesn't have a clue that he's a prick."

And so ended Officer Dan McCarthy's first day on the job.

CHAPTER 2
A FRIEND FOR LIFE

There are many ways to make a friend for life. Some people sit next to each other in the first grade and share a Twinkie on the playground. Some people play high school football together and win the big game in overtime against Crosstown High. Others might share the awkwardness of braces. Others still, may be the new kids in a strange school. Cops often become friends for life when they share an intense moment together.

While Dan found that he loved being a cop, he found the work difficult. There was so much to learn. Stanley Brockman was the officer McCarthy primarily worked with, and Stanley outwardly acted as if he disliked McCarthy and disapproved of everything he did. It seemed to McCarthy as if Brockman wanted the rookie to fail and would find a way to make him fail. To Brockman, McCarthy was always "rookie" or "The Shadow," never "my Partner."

The shift came, however, when Dan saw himself scheduled to work with a younger, but experienced officer, Randy Stammos. Randy was about four years older than Dan. McCarthy had a good feeling about Stammos, even though he had been unusually quiet around McCarthy. As Stammos wheeled the patrol car away from the station, Stammos acted as if McCarthy wasn't in the car. McCarthy did not have a problem with this attitude. Dan found it easier to work with someone who did not notice he was around than it was working with someone who didn't want him around.

When Stammos interacted with the other officers, it was clear he was well-liked and well-respected by everyone around. Stammos still had very little time for the new kid on the block. And yet there was a clear edge that Officer Stammos had over Brockman, in McCarthy's eyes. Stammos did not seem to care one way or the other if Dan succeeded or failed. That, to McCarthy, was much more acceptable than the attitude of Brockman, who openly seemed to love the idea that he was better than this know-nothing rookie he was riding with.

Then came the call over the radio: "255, respond to a violent domestic at the Hendersons'." Randy responded, "10-4, I'm 10-76 (en route)." "Great," said Stammos to himself. "Those assholes are at it again."

Dan asked hesitantly, "Who are the Hendersons?"

Randy said, "If you've never been in a fight before, you're going to be in one now. They always fight with each other, until the cops get there, and then they fight with the cops. They have both been arrested for battery to a police officer. Well, have you?"

"Have I what?" questioned Dan.

"Have you ever been in a fight?"

"Oh, yeah." This was true. Dan had brothers and had grown up in a tougher part of town. He had boxed, wrestled, and studied the martial arts. He had a black belt in tae kwon do and had also studied aikido, hapkido, and some judo. He did not like to fight, but the thought of the physical job of a police officer made him prepare himself for the inevitable. He was 5' 9' and 165 pounds. He lifted weights, ran, and was in the physical condition of a professional athlete. Fighting was not how he wanted to prove himself worthy of this profession. McCarthy just knew that it was one of the realities of the job. What he lacked in size, he more than made up for in skill.

As the squad car pulled down the long driveway, McCarthy spotted the Hendersons in the turnaround of the driveway, between the house and the garage. Old Man Henderson was on his knees. The patriarch was being pounded mercilessly by his son Harry. Harry's brother, Perry, staggered about, laughing and cheering.

Old Lady Henderson and her daughter immediately ran toward the squad, yelling, "Do something before he kills Dad." Their concern was immediately understood by both officers, and the officers' quick movements reflected the urgency of the situation.

When Perry's retarded consciousness became aware of the officers' arrival, he laughed even harder and shouted toward Harry, "Look—it's the cops!" Perry then stumbled backward and sprawled over the hood of a conveniently placed parked car. He landed on his back and conceded to himself that this was where he was going to spend the night. He just lay there, laughing like the village idiot without a village, looking at the sky, and taking an occasional swig from his bottle.

It appeared Randy and Dan could concentrate their efforts on Harry tonight.

When Harry saw the officers running toward him, he stopped pummeling his father and bolted. Stammos wasted no time. He was on a dead run after Harry. Dan paused to ask Old Man Henderson, "Sir, are you all right?"

The bloody elder of the Henderson clan looked up at Dan and answered with unbridled sincerity, "Fuck you, you worthless piece of shit!" spitting out blood. Dan detected the odor of twice-kreusened beer.

McCarthy decided, from the comment, that Henderson would live; so Dan joined the pursuit. When Dan caught Randy, Stammos appeared to be calling to Harry to come out of a large bush on the edge of Henderson's property. The moon was behind a cloud, and since there were no street lights in this area, it was as dark as a bat's family room. The area's only light was Randy's flashlight. The rookie circled the bush, to cut off any possible escape. Suddenly, there was a crashing sound, as if a large buck deer was scared out of its bed. This sound was instantaneously followed by the thud of two bodies striking together and the sound of the wind being pushed out of Randy's lungs as he was sandwiched between Harry and the ground.

Dan ran around the large bush and with the aid of his flashlight, he could see that Harry was on top of Randy, trying to pound him into the alfalfa. Randy was blocking as many of the blows as possible, but he was finding it difficult to recover from the suddenness of the assault. Dan turned his flashlight off, because it only aided the accuracy of Harry's blows, and in the darkness took Harry by the chin and peeled him off Randy. Harry fought hard to break McCarthy's hold and punch someone, anyone, in the process.

McCarthy delivered a punch, which served no purpose other than to sprain Dan's hand after it struck the drunken combatant's rock-hard skull. Dan immediately followed up the punch with a series of strong knee-strikes into Harry's guts, which caused him to finally crumple to the ground. Harry tried to get up again, but was ridden down by McCarthy. Then, working like a well-oiled machine, Stammos and McCarthy were able to maneuver Harry's huge wrists into handcuffs.

Harry was a big man. He was tall and possessed a jail yard "buff," from jail-time weightlifting. He was mean, for no particular reason, and he was now going to jail. He would scare most any man who faced him. He could definitely hurt, maim, and even kill, if given enough alcohol, the opportunity, and the victim. Motive was not a requirement for any of the Hendersons.

Harry Henderson did not know that he played a crucial part in helping McCarthy become a "veteran." It did not fully happen that night, in that struggle. However, a bond was built between Randy and Dan. They fought the beast together, and together they had won. After leaving the jail that night, Randy extended his hand to McCarthy. McCarthy placed his hand in Randy's and they shook hands. For the first time, McCarthy felt the pain from his sprained hand. The adrenaline pumped into his body during the struggle had kept the injury a secret until now.

Randy looked directly into the young officer's eyes and said, "You saved my butt out there, kid. I want you to know that you have just made a friend for life. I don't call lots of people friends, but when I do they are stuck with me forever, if they'll have me as a friend."

"That's OK with me," answered McCarthy with a smile, concealing the pain in his hand for the moment.

"If there's anything I can ever do for you, just let me know," Randy said in a manner that McCarthy knew made the statement more than just words.

"Teach me to be a cop. I want to be as good as you are. A respected veteran, just like you." McCarthy had answered without even having to think.

"It's a deal, kid. What do you prefer being called?" asked Stammos.

"McCarthy. Dan. Anything but rookie, if you don't mind." said McCarthy.

"Sure, McCarthy," said Randy.

"Can we do one other thing?" asked McCarthy.

"Sure. You call it, McCarthy," said Stammos.

"Can we go to the hospital. I think I better get my hand x-rayed," said McCarthy, comparing the size of his right hand to his left.

"Sure," said Stammos. "And here is your first lesson. Never hit a Henderson in the head." They both laughed.

Stammos turned the squad around and headed toward the hospital. McCarthy shared his first of many hearty laughs as a cop with his new "friend for life," Randy Stammos. It would also be his first of many visits as an officer to the emergency room. Brockman was right about one thing, at least. The school of hard knocks did exist.

In the process of teaching McCarthy the skills he needed to be a good cop, Randy learned as well. He learned that they worked well together and could be a team in the truest sense of the word. Randy would not let this young cop fail. If Dan wanted to be a good cop, Randy was going to help make it happen.

Randy saw to it, personally, that Dan learned what he needed to know to be a success. The rookie helped Randy get home safely after one close call. In return, he gave back a gift most priceless. He slowly, patiently, and personally, turned the rookie onto the path toward being a veteran.

CHAPTER 3
MICHAEL MALARKEY

There comes a time for every new copper to be "on his own." The first night alone is beyond exciting. This part of a policeman's life contains a series of firsts. Officers will sometimes remember their first pursuit or their first felony arrest. Sometimes officers have many firsts all at once. Until many firsts are experienced, the baby cop is uncertain of his or her ability. As McCarthy left the line-up on this, his first night alone, his intestines were tied up like a birthday clown's balloons. The cause was the excitement and uncertainty of driving alone into the unknown.

As Dan slid into his cruiser he thought, "I now know what freedom smells like." It smelled like a smoke-free patrol car without the odor of Stanley Brockman's "Ode de French Whore Cologne." On the other hand, he would miss the gentle but firm guidance he received from Stammos. McCarthy theorized that Stammos was the anti-Brockman. He was the antidote for the venom poured into him by Brockman.

As McCarthy wheeled his squad about on his beat, the radio crackled, "All units respond to a report of a man having chest pains in the area of Highway 41 at one of the payphones. This came in second-hand. He was on the phone with a friend and said he was experiencing sharp chest pains. The phone then went dead. Check all the payphones along Highway 41. We have no better description."

When the call ripped McCarthy away from his thoughts, he was on Highway 41 just outside the entrance to Gibbon Park. He remembered there was a payphone in the parking area of Gibbon Park, so he swung his squad into the entrance and could see there was one car parked near the phone. Then McCarthy's heart bounced. The car was initially blocking his view; but as he approached, he saw a large man lying motionless between the car and the payphone. "255, I have that subject. There is a man down by the payphone in the main parking area at Gibbon Park.

Send me a backup immediately and an ambulance 10-33 (emergency fashion)."

McCarthy had worked for an ambulance service through college, so he was a trained Emergency Medical Technician. He looked the subject over and saw no signs of life. He listened for the exchange of air after tipping the man's head back to open up his airway. McCarthy detected nothing. The man had no pulse and no respiration.

McCarthy went immediately into action. "Sir, are you OK?" he yelled. At the same time, he continued to try to find any sign of a pulse. McCarthy found nothing but saw that the man's color was still good, indicating that he had not been down too terribly long.

McCarthy began cardiopulmonary resuscitation by forcing air into the man's motionless deflated lungs. The officer checked again, fruitlessly, for a pulse. When he found no pulse, McCarthy felt for the proper landmark on the chest of the man, positioned his hands and began the chest massage, counting out loud, "One, and two, and . . ." After each sequence, McCarthy would blow two more breaths into the man. He would then reposition his hands and continue with the massage.

As McCarthy could hear the sirens from the ambulance approaching, the man let out a loud gasp, as if he had just awakened from a very bad dream. After the gasp, this poor man began breathing on his own. McCarthy stopped the CPR and stood by, monitoring the man, until the ambulance screeched to a halt very near McCarthy's squad.

As the EMT ran up, McCarthy yelled to him, "Male, about 50-55, experienced a cardiac arrest and had good color but no pulse or respiration when I got here. I did CPR for about five full sequences and he is now breathing again. The arrest was not witnessed, so I do not know how long he was without oxygen before I began CPR."

"Thanks! We'll take it from here," said the young attendant.

Like many victims of sudden heart attacks, the man was obese. Dan assisted the ambulance attendants loading the suffering man into the ambulance. This was Dan's first call for service alone, and he had performed, to his mind, rather well. He had stayed calm and maybe even saved a life. With that call answered, he felt as if suddenly it was official. He was an adult, doing the serious work of an adult. There was no question about the fact that this was a life and death situation for the large man, and Dan McCarthy had been there for him. People could count on him for their very lives. His world would never be the same as it was before.

Dan then told the dispatcher that he was back in service. Dan thought for a moment that the terminology of the job seemed strange. When a cop is busy with a call, he lets the dispatcher know, "I'm out of service." When the cop is done and doing nothing, he lets the dispatcher know,

"I'm back in service." McCarthy thought that it probably should be the other way around.

With that mental debate complete and settled, McCarthy returned to patrol. Police patrol is the sanctioned act of looking for trouble. The better an officer gets at developing his "cop eyes," the more trouble he finds. There are police officers that are purely report-takers. They manage to spend an entire career hopping from call to call. They respond to a burglary call to have a lady show them where her jewelry was. This cop will look and see the jewelry is gone, and then complete a report. That will be the successful completion of the call.

This cop will then see a man who wants to tell him that someone smashed his car window and removed his hunting rifle from the back seat of his car. The officer will diligently put into writing the fact for all to read that this poor man lost his hunting rifle and had his car window smashed all on the same night. This officer will take the complaint without so much as an "I'm sorry" or a "tough break."

These officers will respond in minutes to the places where crimes have been committed and take the stories of those who were there when it happened. They have no passion to find the criminal before the crime, during the crime, or after the crime. It does not cross their minds. They say things like, "Little cases, little problems. Big cases, big problems."

Report-takers are beloved by the community. They are the ones that take advantage often of the free coffee and donuts that the community lovingly offers cops for their service. They say things to younger officers like, "A good cop never gets cold, wet, or hungry." Sometimes they even discourage other officers from doing their job. If an officer has a good night, this guy will corner the officer in the locker room, and say, "What are you trying to prove? Are you bucking for stripes? You know they'll expect that from us every night. Lay off." This type of cop is what is called a "ROD"—retired on duty.

Dan was determined to be what is sometimes called a "5 percenter." This is the opposite of a ROD. This is a cop who gives 100 percent every night. This type of cop doesn't just take reports, he initiates them. He develops in his career a long string of self-initiated successes. He checks out the suspicious man in the alley and, through stop-and-frisk techniques, finds the crowbar on the suspect and recovers the stolen jewelry from the burglary the man had just committed. He's the cop that can outthink, outrun and, when needed, outfight the career criminal. The 5 percenter can do these things 100 percent of the time. When this cop takes the complaint of a theft, he'll check the neighborhood for witnesses. Sometimes he will find other crimes and sometimes he will find someone who has a key piece of information which leads to an arrest.

Dan wanted to be a 5 percenter with all his heart. As Dan returned to his beat from the "man down" call, all of these thoughts were passing through his head. He suddenly spotted a car stopped in the driveway of a restaurant. The driver was clearly not going to move until McCarthy was gone. As the squad passed the driver, McCarthy saw "the look" on the driver's face. It was the first time Dan had seen the look. McCarthy recognized the look as an extremely unnatural and even uncomfortable facial expression but, being a rookie, McCarthy did not recognize its significance.

The general public is unaware of the physical indicators that good cops pick up on. They are as subtle as the light odor of cachet but readily detected by the veteran officer. These are very much like the signs the old frontier scouts picked up on that made them realize in advance that big game or danger was near. A veteran cop sees them and acts on what he sees without thinking. Dan was not a veteran yet.

Officer McCarthy turned around and as the driver finally pulled out of the driveway and headed down the road, Dan followed him. This obviously made the driver visibly nervous. He continually watched the rearview mirror, and the car began to drift back and forth in the lane. Then, because the driver was paying more attention to the patrol car behind him than the road, the nervous driver ran through a stop sign and nearly had an accident.

Dan hit the lights of the squad and the nervous driver swerved abruptly to the side of the road. Dan contacted the dispatcher. "255, I will have a traffic stop, B16-259, on 41 near Sunset."

"10-4, 255," replied the gravelly voice of Hix, the dispatcher on duty that night.

After calling in the stop, McCarthy cautiously approached the driver of the vehicle. The young officer scanned the interior of the car for anything unusual, but the car was empty, except for the smiling driver. A smile much too big for the occasion.

Upon reaching the driver's side, McCarthy greeted the driver. "Good evening, sir. I'm Officer McCarthy of the La Claire Police Department. You just ran through that stop sign back there. Are you new to the area?" asked Dan.

"Why, yes, officer. I am sorry about the stop sign," the driver answered in a saccharine-sweet manner that to a more experienced cop would have set off alarms. Dan did not pick up on the insincerity. He was new to the world of police work and was not used to being lied to with a smile.

"May I see your driver's license?" Dan inquired further.

"I'm sorry, officer, but I left my wallet in my other pants," answered the man with the smile as he searched for a wallet, which he'd already claimed was not there. Once again, McCarthy did not notice. "It's at home. I can take you there, if you want."

"No, that won't be necessary. I'll need your full name," said McCarthy, with pen and notebook in-hand.

"Michael Q. Malarkey, officer, sir." answered the driver, with a smile that was now so large McCarthy could have counted the driver's teeth if he cared to.

"What's your date of birth?" asked McCarthy.

"7-4-68, sir," said Malarkey. "I just live a few blocks from here. I can take you to my house. I can clear this up in no time," offered Malarkey with his toothy grin.

"Oh, that won't be necessary," answered McCarthy, as he returned to his squad to verify the driving status of Malarkey and check him for warrants.

"255, I would like to run a 10-27 and 10-29 on Michael Quixote Malarkey, who is a white male with a DOB of 7-4-68," queried McCarthy.

After Dan called in the check on the smiling miscreant, Hix, a long-time cop, subtly acknowledged the transmission curtly with the response, "10-4, it sounds like a lot of malarkey to me, 255." This warning was lost on young McCarthy.

After a few minutes of waiting, Hix came back to say the driver was "not on file," which meant the information was wrong. To a seasoned officer, this is a no-brainer. The man was lying. A veteran would have known immediately to summon backup and continue the investigation, because "Malarkey" had something to hide. Rookies don't know this on their first night alone. It has never happened to them before.

Much of what happens to young officers is so foreign to them that it can be compared to a small child seeing an escaped tiger lying on the grass. The child has never seen a tiger and does not know the tiger is lethal. The child may even approach the tiger and say, "Here kitty, kitty, kitty." To all those that know what a tiger is, this seems incredible. If the child survives the encounter, it will never mistake a tiger for a kitty again. Like the child, the rookie learns hard and fast how dangerous the unknown can be . . . when the rookie survives his or her mistakes, that is.

Dan approached the driver again and explained, "Sir, there seems to be a problem. The dispatcher says your license is not on file."

The driver then sighed heavily and explained nonchalantly, "Oh, that has happened before. I was born on July 4, but there was a typo on my license, and it's listed as July 5. It creates confusion all the time. If you run my license July 5, it will come back as valid." The driver smiled his toothy grin again and suggested amiably, "Officer, I live two blocks from here.

I can show you where I live, if you follow me, and my license is in my other pants just inside the door."

Now this story to anyone with more than five hours on the street would sound absurd. To Dan, who had been out on his own now for four hours and fifty-nine minutes, this sounded reasonable. He smiled and returned, "Sure. Go ahead, I'll follow you."

As Dan got into his squad, he radioed to Hix, "255 will be following Mr. Malarkey to his residence. He states he has his license there."

"10-4. It's a nice night for a drive, 255." Hix replied, his voice dripping with sarcasm. Hix was someone who had learned the hard way. He could predict what was about to happen and felt, "Why shouldn't the rookie learn the hard way, too? He who learns hard, learns best. Besides, look at me. I learned the hard way. I don't have any stripes or awards to show for it. All I have is more time on suspension than most people around here have time on the street." Yes, Hix knew exactly what was about to happen. The rookie was about to learn the hard way in the school of hard knocks.

As the driver pulled out, the youthful officer followed at a safe distance. Suddenly, after traveling three blocks, the driver accelerated full-out. The rear end shifted left and right. The tail lights began to get smaller and smaller. Dan, stunned by this turn of events, fumbled as he accelerated, hit his lights and his siren. He then grabbed the mic, screaming into the mic, "255, I have a 10-80 (high speed pursuit)! The subject is fleeing southbound on 41 at a speed of 80 plus."

Hix blandly came back, "Gee, that's a surprise, 255." He then dispatched other units to start heading in 255's direction.

Most police cars are high-performance vehicles. Cops are trained in pursuit driving. This is where the rookie had the edge. The fleeing vehicle was a beater, and the driver was over-driving his skill level. He fled south on 41. The vehicle traveled out of the city of Le Claire. Once out onto the open country roads, Malarkey, or whoever he was, hit 100 miles per hour. He was about five miles outside of Le Claire and suddenly McCarthy saw the brake lights light up and the front end of the car dig in, while the back end began to shift back and forth. McCarthy had to brake hard to avoid a collision as the pseudo-Malarkey turned sharply off onto a side road, "255, Malarkey is now eastbound on Dyerson Road!" It suddenly hit Dan like a load of fresh manure on a hot humid day. "Malarkey? You stupid rookie! He told you his name was Malarkey and you believed him." Dan then replaced the mic and continued to steer.

"10-4 on that last transmission, 255," was Hix's immediate response. Dan then realized he still had his mic keyed, and he had confessed to everyone in the county that he was a stupid rookie. Every officer, commander, dispatcher, and all those in scanner-land knew Dan McCarthy, at four hours and fifty-nine minutes into his first shift on patrol alone, realized that he was still a stupid rookie. The car continued speeding eastbound on Dyerson Road.

Suddenly, the vehicle's rear end fishtailed wildly to the left and the driver left the road. He cut his lights and cut up an old farmers' logging trail, which had heavy shrubbery lining it. Without hesitation Dan was behind him, still in pursuit. As McCarthy heard the scraping, screeching sound of the branches on the sides of his unit, Dan thought, "I wonder if this is damaging the squad. I wonder if I am suppose to damage the squad." This thought was fleeting. It was replaced . . . no, knocked down and stomped right out of his brain . . . by the dominant thought in total control of every fiber of his being. "I Must Catch Michael Malarkey!"

Dan radioed, "I am in the woods southbound away from Dyerson."

"On foot, 255?" asked Hix.

"Negative. I am still in the squad, on a dirt road." answered McCarthy.

The chase cut through the woods and then came out on a meadow. The vehicles traversed the meadow. One was running with no lights, and the other had red lights and siren on for the benefit of God, nature, and to serve notice to Michael Malarkey that this rookie was going to chase him to hell, if he had to.

Without warning, the Malarkey vehicle slid to a stop and the driver was off to the races on foot. Dan exited his squad, sprinting the moment the squad stopped, and joined the chase on foot. As McCarthy ran past the abandoned car, he noticed it was badly overheated and steaming. Horrors! He saw the Picasso-like markings on the side of the vehicle, which were made by the branches on the wood trail. He thought, "I hope my squad doesn't look like Malarkey's car." This was again, a fleeting thought replaced by another, more urgent mental fixation. "Forget about the squad! Catch Michael Malarkey!"

The suspect was about 5' 10" and 170 pounds. Dan was smaller, but had trained for years for this moment. It was his first physical challenge, but this thought had not occurred to him. He only wanted to "Catch Michael Malarkey." Dan matched the suspect stride for stride across the meadow and then through a freshly plowed and fertilized field.

The suspect had long hair and looked like pictures of Charlie Manson before he grew his beard. He was a recreational smoker and as his chest began to heave and legs began to feel like logs, he began to realize that it was not going to be as easy to outdistance this rookie physically as it was mentally.

The suspect continued to run toward a farmhouse on the land that the chase brought them to. It was the only farmhouse visible. Dan stayed with Malarkey but could not gain on him. McCarthy now realized it was much more difficult running in a gun belt and squad shoes than it was in shorts and Nike's.

Malarkey reached the house, swung open a door, and slammed it shut as fast as those words could be said. The lock clicked and Dan stopped. Now he started thinking like a cop. He positioned himself on a rise behind the house and was able to see the whole house. McCarthy panted into the radio, "255 to dispatch. The subject just ran into a white farmhouse on Dyerson Road. Have the squads keep their sirens on, and I will talk the first unit into the driveway. Please have that unit give other units the address of the farm."

Dan could hear the approaching sirens and talked them into the right driveway. In a manner of minutes, he had four officers on the scene. One of them was a tall sergeant named Dave Compton. Dave was a veteran officer, whose human essence contained a strong serving of natural-born leadership. He arrived at the scene and took command. He did not need stripes on his sleeve. People looked to him as a leader before he became a sergeant. McCarthy knew Malarkey was as good as caught, now that Compton was on the scene.

As Compton ran up to McCarthy's location, he was in a crouch and kept a berm between himself and the house as he covered the ground. He quickly and quietly positioned the arriving officers to prevent the suspect from fleeing the house.

As Compton reached McCarthy, Dan was regaining his breath and composure. In hushed tones McCarthy explained to Compton, "Sergeant, a man, who said he was Michael Malarkey, fled from me and I chased him to a field over there," said McCarthy, pointing a finger back toward where his squad was still parked. "He dumped his car because it overheated, and then he ran on foot. I chased him to this house. He ran in and locked the door. He is still in the house." McCarthy said this while hardly taking a breath, and each word came out as if it was in a race with the last word spoken.

"Does he have a weapon?" asked Compton, cutting from the chase to the chase.

"I never saw one," replied McCarthy, who felt silly for not including this information with his report to the sergeant.

"Compton to dispatch," said Compton over the radio. "Any luck on finding that number to this house?"

"There is no phone listed for the residence," answered Hix.

"10-4. I'll be making contact at the residence," Compton reported to the dispatcher and to the other officers at the scene, simultaneously.

Compton approached the house after he positioned the other officers around it. He pounded on the door and immediately a tall, thin man with long hair came to the door. The thin man was wearing briefs in a U.S. flag design, which caused Compton to glance disparagingly toward the man's nether regions. This man was a holdout from a community co-op in the Haight-Ashbury district, circa 1970. His hair was long, ratty, and hung down to his shoulders.

This hippie wannabe knew the law. Before Compton could say a word, the tall man began his diatribe, "You can't just come into my house in the middle of the night. You need a warrant. I know the law. I'm study-ing law at the university. Do you have a warrant?" The co-op leader made this statement in a manner that made it clear he was happy with his words. He was satisfied that, in this little game of chess . . . Check!

Compton answered without hesitation in his command voice, "Not now, but I will have. In fact, please don't send him out. I'd rather get the warrant and come in and search this happy home of yours, confiscate your stash, and arrest everyone in the house along with your buddy. So what's it going to be?" Checkmate!

The co-op leader immediately changed his expression and passed from hippy barrister to scared kid. "Please wait a minute, sir. I'll be right back."

In less than a minute the side door swung open and Malarkey exited on a dead run. McCarthy had the angle on him this time, and literally executed an open field tackle within fifty feet of the door. Malarkey's resistance was immediately overcome by Dan as he whipped on a leg lock. The pain caused Malarkey to stop squirming and snap his hands behind his back in an urgent acknowledgment of submission.

The grimace on Malarkey's face told everyone that his fight and flight were over. McCarthy put the cuffs on his adversary with the speed and adroitness of a rodeo cowpuncher.

After the handcuffs were on, Dan spoke to the suspect in a calming voice, "Now the chase is over. The fight is over. The lying is over. We got off to a bad start, but that is over. We are now going to get along just fine. I am going to ask you some questions. You need to understand your rights. You have a right to remain silen . . . Do you understand these rights."

"Yeah," Malarkey said, as he spit out some dirt he'd taken in when he hit the deck.

"Do you want to answer some questions? I would like to start all over again. This time I would like to get the truth from you, sir," said McCarthy in a remarkably quiet tone of voice, considering the circum-stances. McCarthy had let up all the painful pressure on the leg lock, but maintained the hold itself on the suspect.

"Yeah, I'm sorry, man. My real name is Rob Brownell. I lied because I don't have a license, and I'm sure there are some warrants on me. I think my PO (parole officer) wants to talk to me, too." This was said as McCarthy released the leg lock and straightened out the suspect's legs. "Thanks, man! That hurt," Brownell added as the hold was released.

"I wish it wouldn't have been necessary, Rob. You have not been too cooperative up to this point, you'd have to admit," explained McCarthy as he completed his search of the prisoner.

Dan stayed with Brownell, while Officer Dooley of the La Claire Police retrieved McCarthy's squad. When Dooley returned with the squad, Dan assisted Brownell into the back seat, carefully cushioning his head.

McCarthy then said to everyone gathered, "Thanks a lot for your help, everyone."

After the other officers were returning to their squads, Sergeant Compton approached McCarthy and said, "This is your first night alone, isn't it, kid?"

"Yeah, he sure pulled a fast one on me. I feel kind of stupid." McCarthy said, dropping his eyes to his feet in embarrassment. As he did this, he noticed for the first time that his boots were covered with mud, or manure. He could not tell the difference.

"Listen, kid. Some cops think the good thing about this job is that after a while you learn to trust no one. Then this sort of thing doesn't happen to them. The bad thing about that is after a while you *don't* trust anyone. That goes for your wife, your kids, everybody. Don't beat yourself up because you believed someone. You'll learn to develop your instincts. It doesn't happen overnight. Even when that happens, every once and a while someone who has lied their entire life is going to come up with a lot of malarkey and you're still going to fall for it. You learn more from your failures than you do from your successes. Regardless of all that, you still caught the bad guy."

McCarthy looked up from his filth-covered boots and smiled at his sergeant.

"Hey! Nice tackle! You're going to be all right, McGrew!" said Compton.

"Thanks, Sarge," answered McCarthy, whose smile now covered his face.

"There is a character in a poem I liked when I was a kid called Dangerous Dan McGrew. Did you know that, kid?" said Sgt. Compton.

"Yeah," said McCarthy, obviously cheered by a sergeant who knew how to inject the positive into nearly every situation.

"I would like to call you Dangerous Dan McGrew, but the character ends up getting shot; and that's a bad omen for a cop. Let's call you Dyno. You hit that guy at a dead run like a little stick of dynamite, going off.

Can I call you Dyno?" asked the sergeant, who had just become McCarthy's favorite sergeant for life.

"You're the sergeant!" McCarthy said with a large smile on his face from the compliment. He liked the name Dyno. He liked the fact that he had caught Malarkey in spite of his naiveté. The smile generated by Compton disappeared, however, when McCarthy took a closer look at his squad car. In the light of the driveway, scratches were visible on both sides of the squad.

"They'll buff right out!" said Compton, reading the look on the rookie's face.

McCarthy ran checks with Hix on Mr. Rob Brownell. It made the squad damage a little more tolerable when it was discovered that Brownell had no license, but more importantly he had outstanding warrants in two states. One for armed robbery and the other for delivering controlled substances.

After receiving confirmation on the warrants, McCarthy told Compton, "Sorry about the scratches on the squad. I chased him up an old logging trail over there," McCarthy said, gesturing in the direction Dooley had come from when he retrieved the squad. "Don't worry about it, Dyno. Like I said, the scratches are not deep, and they will buff right out. It looks worse than it is." Compton continued, "I think we named you right, Dyno. This is your first night alone, and already you've saved your first life, had your first car chase, foot chase, felony arrest, and damaged your first squad. I have one critique for you, though, McCarthy."

"Yes, sir, what is that?" asked McCarthy.

Compton then put his hand on McCarthy's shoulder and leaned toward his right ear. He paused for a second and said under his breath, "Until you get some dust on your locker, I'd keep that 'stupid rookie thing' a little more private than you did tonight. When you feel a need to remind yourself that you are a stupid rookie, take your thumb off the mic."

"Good advice, Sarge. Thanks," said McCarthy with a smile and an instantaneous blush.

CHAPTER 4
FOUR AT A TIME

To a cop working the night shift, "bar time" is "prime time." Much of what happens during the night, happens the hour before and the hour after bar time. It is the climax of the drinking man's evening. He has to find the girl . . . or he realizes someone else gets the girl. Tempers flare and fights break out, since reason has long been washed away by the alcohol.

The drunks then drive home, if they make it that far. Sometimes they turn a parked car into a mass of twisted metal. Sometimes they kill a family on its way home from a wedding, a birthday party, or even a family vacation. When the drinkers do make it home, they are often angry and looking for a fight. That's when their wives suffer and the domestic disturbances get called in. "Bar time!" The bewitching hour for police officers.

Tonight's bar time would be no different. Randy and Dan were patrolling, when a blue, four-door Ford with two occupants caught Randy's attention. "Follow that car, Dan! The passenger gave me the look," Randy said abruptly.

"What's the 'look'?" Dan puzzled as he made a U-turn and began to follow the vehicle down McGruder Boulevard.

As McCarthy followed the car east on McGruder, Randy explained, "It's the look a guy gives you when he knows he's carrying dope, revoked, wanted, or even has a body in the trunk. It works like this. He sees a cop and then he thinks, "What if the cop stops me? He'll run a check on me and arrest me on a warrant, and he'll see the hundred pounds of dope I got in the back seat. Then I'm goin' to prison for twenty years, and I'll be the bend over toy for a guy named Rocko, whose breath smells bad. The guy thinks that, and then voilá, the look."

Dan asked, "You can't stop a guy just for the look, can you?"

"No way!" proclaimed Randy. "You have to have a reasonable suspicion to stop someone. Something they did, or didn't do, that would lead you to believe they are committing, or about to commit, a crime. You can stop them for a traffic violation, no matter how minor, too. We play by the rules. That's what makes us the good guys. A cop that doesn't play by the rules is as bad as the bad guys—maybe even worse. Boy, this guy isn't going to give us a reason."

The driver was following every traffic law. There just was no reason to stop him other than one cop's gut feeling that he was up to something—because of "the look."

"255, respond to a 10-16 verbal domestic on 1238 Main Street," interrupted the radio.

"We're en route," responded McCarthy.

"So much for the look. They're dirty, though. I'd bet my life on it," Randy hypothesized. This was said more for his own benefit than McCarthy's.

The domestic was handled quickly. It took very little investigation. The argument was at the Arnetts' home. Louie Arnett was supposed to come right home from work and bring burgers for the family. Instead he stopped for a beer, or two. The hamburgers were stone cold by the time he got home. Marge Arnett was upset and yelled loudly at him, which caused the neighbors to call.

When Stammos and McCarthy arrived, Louie was trying to shove the cold hamburgers down Marge's throat as she was pinned down on the dining room table. Marge was squirming to break free, as she choked on the burgers. McCarthy and Stammos could see the struggle and hear Marge's sobs, muffled by a mashed Big Mac, through an open door. The two officers entered the house without knocking and rushed to Marge's rescue.

Louie was pulled off Marge and quickly handcuffed. After a statement was taken from Marge, McCarthy took some pictures of the burger mash and the tipped-over furniture as evidence. Louie was taken to the county jail, where he was tucked away for the night.

Louie's only statement was, "The bitch wanted burgers, and she got her burgers. What's the fuckin' problem with that." Then he ended his comments with, "I want a fucking lawyer." This last statement was said with great disdain and precision, with each word pronounced slowly, individually, and correctly.

After finishing her statement, Marge packed some things for herself and the children. She said, "I have lived with that monster too long. I'm through!"

After Randy and Dan cleared from the jail, Randy said, "Swing back to McGruder and see if we can spot that car again."

Dan, who was already heading that way, said, "Got ya, Randy."

Almost immediately upon reaching McGruder, the car was seen coming onto that street from the parking lot of Lorcan Enterprises. The car had its lights off and now there were four occupants, instead of two. It was 2:30 a.m. and Lorcan had been closed since 5:00 p.m. The cleaning crew did not work past 10:00 p.m. Randy immediately got on the radio and reported, "255, we'll be stopping a blue Ford with four occupants on McGruder near Lorcan Enterprises. Send us some backup."

McCarthy hit the overhead lights and the car's driver immediately pulled to the side of the road. As McCarthy cautiously approached, he noted there were four people in the vehicle and now all of them had the look. Even the rookie could see it.

"I'm Officer McCarthy of the La Claire Police Department. You were stopped for having no lights on. Keep all your hands where I can see them. I will need to see identification from each of you, please," said McCarthy. "I will direct you one at a time to obtain some identification. Please make no movements other than those you're told to make. Keep your palms up."

McCarthy cautiously collected the identification from everyone inside the car, while Stammos stayed in a position of cover. As a man in a trench coat in the back driver's side leaned to get identification, McCarthy's flashlight saw the end of what appeared to be a barrel sticking out from under the man's leg.

McCarthy drew his weapon instinctively and barked, "Occupants of the car put your hands on your head, interlocking your fingers. Do it now!" Stunned by the suddenness of the command the four in the car immediately slapped their hands on their heads into the position ordered, as if they had been in this position before. "Eyes forward," McCarthy barked. "Now don't move!" Stammos followed suit, drawing his weapon and maintaining his position of advantage over the occupants.

McCarthy pulled the gray metal barrel out from under the leg and discovered it was a pry bar with shiny fresh scratches on it. He showed it to Randy. Randy's comment was "Bingo!" The bar had obviously just been used to burglarize something. The most likely spot was Lorcan.

McCarthy then called to the driver, "Driver! With your left hand toss the keys out the window of the car." The driver did so awkwardly. "Now put your hand back on top of your head! No one move!"

Stammos got on the radio as the first backup unit was arriving. "Check the security of Lorcan. This vehicle just left with their lights out and we have a pry bar on one of them."

The first backup unit to arrive was Sgt. Compton. After hearing Randy's transmission, he expertly swung his squad around. He headed quickly and silently to Lorcan.

Within three minutes, the radio came alive. "Be advised, 255, you have a burglary here. The rear door is ajar and has been pried on," reported Compton in a calm voice that somehow also communicated the urgency of the situation.

By this time, McCarthy and Stammos had plenty of backup. There is nothing a night shift officer likes more than catching a burglar. From the transmissions on the radio, it was clear that McCarthy and Stammos were onto something that everyone wanted a piece of. That was OK with McCarthy and Stammos. There would be plenty of work to go around.

McCarthy ordered each man out of the car, one at a time. He hand-cuffed and searched each one, borrowing handcuffs from the other cops arriving at the scene. By now there were five officers assisting at the scene of the stop.

Each suspect was carefully searched by McCarthy. The leader of the group, David Proctor, had Lorcan checks on him and a signature stamp from Lorcan's owner. This would have allowed Proctor to forge and cash the checks with impunity nearly anywhere. It was quite literally the proverbial "blank check." Sgt. Compton assigned Dooley to handle taking the complaint at Lorcan. The company manager was called to Lorcan to talk to Dooley.

All four career criminals were transported to the county jail and held in separate interview rooms. For McCarthy, it was all so much at one time. Compton assisted by dividing up the labor. He arranged for Stammos to handle the interviews, while McCarthy continued at the scene of the stop. This was a challenging project for the rookie.

The car was eventually searched. McCarthy found a loaded .357 revolver on the passenger's side of the vehicle. The trunk was full of office equipment from inside the small company. All the cash on hand from the company was in a bank bag, shoved under the driver's seat.

This investigation did not end at the scene. It was like most investigations that often are like a snowball rolling downhill. It constantly was picking up speed and the case was getting bigger and bigger. Due to the obvious need to follow-up on the case, Compton contacted the Detective Division; Sgt. Hopkins and Joe Darnell were assigned to the case.

They obtained search warrants on Proctor's home first, and it was a treasure trove of information and evidence. The detectives discovered these four had been working together since Proctor had gotten out of prison four months earlier. His specialty was to pick a business whose payroll checks he could easily turn into cash. One of the others in the car, Butkus Joplin, was found to have done time with Proctor. Joplin was a fence for the office equipment. He would steal the office equipment, while Proctor went after checks and anything that would help him in passing the checks.

Proctor would steal company uniforms and coats bearing the business logo. It would then be simple for him to cash a payroll check while wearing a uniform from the business.

The driver was a professional driver. Joplin and Proctor had been inside Lorcan the first time the car was spotted by Stammos and McCarthy. The driver remained cool. He continued calmly on his way, drawing the officers away from the burglary in progress. The only mistake he made was to exhibit the look. Then, as luck would have it, Stammos and McCarthy were called away to "The Big Mac Attack."

The driver then returned to Lorcan to pick up Butkus and Proctor. The passenger in the front seat was a nineteen-year-old with numerous juvenile contacts. Like any good businessman, Proctor was training new blood. The nineteen-year-old was along to learn. The warrant on Proctor's residence was the most lucrative. He was tied into thirty-four burglaries by items found there. Proctor's MO (modus operandi) was to dress like an employee in the business whose checks he stole. He would then cash the checks he would write to one of his many aliases, and in most cases no one would look twice.

When a man in coveralls covered in paint comes into a large grocery store chain and asks to cash a payroll check from a drywall and painting business, he doesn't get a second glance. The checks were never higher than $250. Cash twenty-five checks in one town in one day and you've just made $6250, in one day, the easy way.

Stammos and Sgt. Darnell conducted the interviews and were able to convince all involved to confess, except Proctor. That made it better. Proctor was had . . . "Dead Nuts." There was no need to have a statement from him. A statement would have made him seem penitent in front of the judge at sentencing. The judge dropped the hammer on him.

Proctor received a sentence of ten years. He filed an appeal attacking the grounds for the stop. One year after the stop, the Appeals Court in the State of Wisconsin upheld the stop, stating the stop was the result of "just plain old-fashioned good police work". This brought a proud smile to the faces of McCarthy and Stammos.

McCarthy and Stammos knew their partnership was special. It was one that would definitely pay dividends. It would also give them challenges that are best faced standing beside a tried-and-true friend. The more time they spent together, the bigger the challenge they could handle. Slowly, they became a team and moved together as surely and smoothly as the pistons on a fine Italian sports car. Together, they would become the criminal's worst nightmare . . . two highly motivated cops that loved catching bad guys.

CHAPTER 5
LOUIE AND MARGE: ACT TWO

If someone were to have asked Dan McCarthy on the night of the Lorcan burglary, "Who was the most memorable person you met tonight?" he would have answered "Dave Proctor."

But the memory of Proctor faded. As years passed, the memory of Proctor would be filed away with the thousands of other ne'er-do-wells that would find themselves secured in the handcuffs of Officer Daniel McCarthy.

The most memorable person met by Dan McCarthy on that fateful night would ultimately be Marge Arnett. After she was nearly choked to death by a Big Mac, Marge had separated from her husband, Louie. She filed for divorce and obtained a restraining order against her husband. A restraining order theoretically makes it impossible for someone to contact another person in any way. Although these documents make it easier to prosecute the abusive husband, they do not fully protect the victim against a goal-oriented assailant.

Louie did not take the separation well. He was like most other wife-beaters. They look at their wives as property. They will not lose control over their property, and they do not fathom that they cannot have their property any time they wish.

On this night, one month after the hamburger incident, Louie had spent much of the night in his favorite bar telling all who would listen, what a bitch he was married to. Louie, who surrounded himself with people of the same ilk, was encouraged by his drinking buddies to take back what was his.

At 12:30 a.m., Louie tossed down his last beer. He threw down a handful of coins on the bar and left the tavern. He drove to "his home" and parked in front of the house. Louie walked up to the front door and unlocked it. He was surprised that his key still fit. He quietly entered. He could hear laughter in the living room, where Marge was playing a game of Chutes and Ladders with the boys.

Louie walked through the kitchen and saw Marge sharing a laugh with his two young sons. "It will be too bad that they have to see this," he thought. "Fuck it. She made me do this and they should know what kind of woman their mother is." He then cut the phone line with a steak knife and the monster was free to roam. There would be no cops ruining his plans tonight.

With rationalization out of the way, Louie burst into the living room and the laughter was swallowed by sudden silence floating on a dark cloud of fear. Marge and the children froze, consumed by their shared terror of this man. Marge tried to get up from the couch, but Louie hit her hard in the face with his large fist and knocked her back onto the couch.

The two young children watched terrified, as their father ripped their mother's dress from her body. She was dazed from the punch but was able to scratch him hard on the face, drawing blood and leaving proof that she had not consented to what he was about to do to her in front of their young sons.

Louie pounded her hard and repeatedly, as if she was a tough piece of meat rather than the woman he pledged to make happy just eight years earlier. He yelled, "Open your mouth, bitch. I've got something for you." He beat her until she followed his commands. He then forced himself on her in every way possible. The graphic, surreal scene had two small witnesses. The children would never forget the scene of the naked beast forcing their mother to her stomach and then crawling a top of her. He then began thrusting and grunting in pleasure. Their beautiful beloved mother answered each thrust: "No . . . Please . . . Dear God . . . The children . . . stop . . . oh God . . . help . . . uh . . . uh . . . uh . . . dear God please help."

As the naked, sweaty demon grunted and thrusted, he became a memory that would wake the children up in the middle of the night in a cold sweat for the rest of their lives. A naked, thrusting, sweating beast, incapable of human qualities. Then suddenly he seemed to explode. "AAAAARRRGH!"

The children were frozen. They watched without making a sound. They hoped they were invisible. As much as they loved their mother, they feared they would be next. They would never recover from the savagery visited upon them by their father.

After Louie satisfied his lust for dominance over this poor creature, he slumped on top of his sobbing, humiliated "wife." As Louie slowly rolled off his whimpering naked possession onto the floor of the living room, he lay guiltless and satisfied for a few moments. His children managed to crawl behind a recliner in the same room. They were hiding from the monster, shaking and surrounded by their fear. He slowly stood himself up and walked up the stairs of "his house" and went to sleep in "his bed."

After about one hour, Marge was able to throw her tattered clothes about her beaten, bleeding body. She made it to the phone, but it did not work. She could not find the children. They were afraid to come out of hiding, for they were old enough to know that their mother was the one who brought out the monster. They reasoned that if they hid from her, the monster would not find them.

One month after the Lorcan burglary, while patrolling alone on a Wednesday at 1:30 a.m., McCarthy saw a figure staggering down a poorly lit sidewalk. From behind, the figure looked like a drunk. Almost immediately this perception was replaced by the reality. It was a woman. Her clothes were shredded like a shipwrecked heroine in a B movie. Her face was swollen and smeared with her own blood.

McCarthy radioed to dispatch, "255, I'll be out with an injured woman. Send me an ambulance and some backup." McCarthy quickly hung up the mic, pulled the squad to a stop, and ran to the woman. When Marge saw the officer, she turned to him and began sobbing. At first she cried out of relief, and then relief was replaced by shame.

McCarthy gently assisted her to a seated position on a retaining wall. He ran to the squad and removed the first aid equipment stored there. He immediately began to apply pressure and bandages to her wounds. An ice pack was placed delicately on her cheek, which was visibly swelling.

Marge immediately responded to the kindness by slowly turning her head and making eye contact with her young rescuer. She seemed to recognize McCarthy and immediately the words came out, "He's at the house! He hurt me real bad! The children! You've got to get the children out! Get that animal out of my house, before he hurts my babies!"

The story came out in gasps and sobs. The woman was dazed and the humiliated victim of an especially violent domestic assault. This was the type of assault that would make headlines and shock a community to its core—if it was done by a stranger. Since it was done by an estranged husband, it would not generate much more than a snippet on Page 8, Section D of the La Claire Journal—that is, if it was reported at all.

Backup arrived and shortly after that, an ambulance. While Marge was being attended to, McCarthy asked Officer Gary Carpenter, another young officer, to come to the house to attempt to find the monster that did this. The house was only two blocks from the spot Marge was being attended to by ambulance personnel.

McCarthy, feeling the children were still in danger, wasted no time going to the house. When the two officers arrived at the house, Carpenter asked, "Do we need a warrant?" McCarthy responded quickly,

"No, this is an exigent circumstance," a term he learned from his criminal law instructor in college. Normally police need a warrant to enter a house, which constitutionally is a person's "castle." Officers don't need a warrant when an emergency exists.

"Shouldn't we ask the sergeant, or call a district attorney at home?" queried Carpenter, who knew McCarthy was just as new at this as he was.

"It isn't too exigent, if I have to call someone and ask. There are kids in a house with a man that just hurt that woman in a way that I have never seen a man hurt a woman before. I'm going to take him to jail before he hurts anyone else. Besides, we have the wife's consent to go in." Carpenter nodded and followed McCarthy.

The lights were on downstairs and the front storm door was closed, but unlocked. A bloody handprint was visible on the inside of the storm window, left during the painful retreat made by Marge minutes earlier. The inside door was an ornate antique oaken door, with a brass knocker, and it was standing wide open. Both officers entered the home cautiously and quietly after telling dispatch, "We're going in."

The living room was in disarray. A Chutes and Ladders board game and its pieces were spread across the floor. A large plant was on its side with dirt spilled from its pot. Shreds of cloth matching the wife's dress were lying in tatters on the floor. There was blood on the carpet, and the coffee table in front of the couch was smashed and in splinters.

McCarthy and Carpenter found the children still shivering behind the recliner. The children saw the policemen and the oldest boy, who was holding the younger brother as if to shield him from the dangers of their world, knew the reason for the officer's presence immediately.

"He's upstairs," the child said, pointing with one hand and still shielding his brother with the other.

The officers led the children outside the front door, where Officer Dooley was just arriving. The children were placed in his safekeeping. Dooley was a big cop with an even bigger heart that began to ache immediately upon seeing the look of devastation etched in the faces of two such small children.

McCarthy and Carpenter returned to their hunt for the monster. They quietly climbed the stairs. As they approached the top, they could hear that Louie, after having satisfied his need to own Marge again, was sleeping the sleep of contentment. The drunken bully was as loud and obnoxious asleep as he was awake.

The officers were on him and he was in handcuffs before he could shake himself out of his contented slumber. "Police Officers—you are under arrest!" were the first words Louie heard.

"What!? What!? What did I do? I didn't do nothing. You come into my home. I'm sleeping and you arrest me for nothing," protested Louie.

McCarthy then read Louie his rights. McCarthy found that this act helped suppress the urge to beat the hell out of this piece of shit. After successfully reading the Miranda Warning and repressing the urge to personally mete out justice to Louie, McCarthy said, "Mr. Arnett, you are under arrest for false imprisonment, aggravated battery, violation of a restraining order, and first degree sexual assault."

"Sexual assault? Who did I sexually assault?" protested the drunken thug.

"Your wife," McCarthy replied, his voice communicating surprise at the question.

"Bullshit. That bitch invited me over. She's playing a silly-ass game. She asked me over. She wanted it! I gave it to her and that's that! Besides she's my wife, and this is my house. Get the fuck out of here. You need a warrant," growled Arnett defiantly.

"I want to file charges against her. Look at my face. She scratched me," whined Arnett.

Louie was taken to jail, where he belonged. This was only temporary, because this crime was a domestic crime (small "d" and small "c" to so many in a civilized world). The injuries, the viciousness, and the very real danger that the victim was in, was identical to any other brutal rape. The danger of the victim being victimized by the attacker again was very real, but the court would treat this situation much differently than any other rape. Marge had the misfortune of being married to her rapist.

Louie apologized, sought treatment, and pled guilty to a misdemeanor battery charge. Louie and Marge loved each other in a strange way that would become all too familiar to Officer McCarthy. McCarthy could not call it an unusual love, because he would see it too often. Siamese twins were unusual. Domestic violence and the strange love that binds the participants together was not unusual. There were far too many cases of it to describe it as isolated, unusual, or out of the ordinary.

McCarthy would spend his whole career trying to keep men, women, and their children from killing each other. Sometimes he would succeed. Sometimes he would not. Lessons learned hard are lessons learned best. Louie and Marge were teaching the young crusader a lesson on domestic violence that would be fitting material for a Master's thesis in sociology. McCarthy would meet Marge and Louie again.

CHAPTER 6
STOP SHOOTING!

It was 3:30 a.m. on one of those nights when the town was still bustling. Then bar time comes, and everyone just disappears. The radio had gone quiet, and it was the time of day that earned the police car the name "the prowler." A cop was free to prowl and find what he could find.

Dan had been an avid hunter prior to becoming a cop. He no longer felt the need to hunt. This job seemed to satisfy the primal urge to stalk the dangerous game. Except this was not a game. The people being hunted could fight and sometimes shoot back. McCarthy thrived on the excitement of not knowing what might be waiting around the next corner. He was quickly becoming a creature of the night.

From about 3:30 a.m. to 5:00 a.m., many night shift officers took their lunch break. Dan rarely did. He would take a sandwich in his squad and eat it whenever he felt like it. He called the time between 1:00 a.m. and 5:00 a.m. "prime time." That was when trouble walked the streets. It stayed in the shadows, but it was there. McCarthy could sense it. He was out to find as much of it as possible.

McCarthy pulled silently up to Farley's Bar on Lincoln Street and walked around it, pulling doors. Suddenly the silence was broken by the squeal of tires and an accelerating motor. Dan instinctively ran back to his squad and as he reached it, a beige Chevy Impala slid to a stop at the intersection in front of him and the young driver's eyes met McCarthy's. The driver immediately accelerated north, away from McCarthy and then took the first turn east, in an obvious effort to lose the officer.

McCarthy jumped in his squad, shut the door, clicked his seat belt, put the squad in gear, accelerated, and radioed-in the pursuit, all in a smooth, furious few moments. Upon reaching the intersection where the youth had turned, there was nothing. The Impala was gone, swallowed up once again by the shadows.

McCarthy stopped, rolled down his window, and could hear nothing. "He must be close," thought McCarthy. He then slowly prowled the neighborhood for his prey, up and down, back and forth, checking side streets and alleys. Suddenly something caught his eye in an alley that he had just passed to his right. As soon as he backed up to enter the alley, the driver of the Impala put all his weight on the accelerator, causing the Chevy's rear end to whip back and forth wildly like a trophy northern pike just feeling the hook. The chase was on.

The suspect had pulled in a line of parked cars and shut his lights off. What McCarthy had seen was the faint cloud of exhaust fumes in the darkness. The months on third shift had sharpened his night vision. It had sharpened all of his senses.

McCarthy hit the lights and siren, but the driver ignored them. A passenger was turned all the way round in the seat and was watching McCarthy constantly. McCarthy could tell by the passenger's animated movements, he was either urging the driver on or pleading with him emphatically to stop. "255 has found the vehicle. I have a 10-80 (pursuit). We're heading westbound on Rubicon," shouted McCarthy.

"10-4, 255," answered dispatch calmly.

McCarthy then reminded himself to calm himself. He knew he thought better, drove better, communicated better, and fought better when he calmed himself. He did some abdominal breathing, learned in his years in martial arts. During the next transmission, McCarthy sounded like a different person. His voice was quiet, understandable and controlled. "255, the subject is now heading north on Lincoln Street at 70 mph. I can see there are two suspects in the vehicle. They look like teenage males and the vehicle is a beige Chevrolet Impala. The plates are Wisconsin H-Henry 55-662, that's H-Henry fifty-five thousand six hundred and sixty-two."

As the vehicle reached the interstate, Stammos caught up with the pursuit. The two squads could do nothing but follow. As the fleeing vehicle careened up the ramp, it raised clouds of dust as it repeatedly skipped off onto the gravel shoulder and back onto the roadway. Once on the interstate, the driver accelerated full out. McCarthy keyed the mic again and, in as calm a voice as he could muster, reported, "The subject is eastbound on the interstate at 100 plus miles an hour." Traffic was light on the interstate. McCarthy was amazed at how suddenly 110 miles per hour seemed no different to him than 70. It was like a drive in the country. That was about to change.

After traveling about four miles on the interstate, a state trooper appeared ahead of the pursuit. The two troopers' squads with lights on tried to stay in front of the fleeing vehicle. Then one of the squads moved to the side of the Impala. McCarthy could see they were trying to box the suspect in and slow him down. McCarthy followed at a safe distance. He thought he should let the more experienced troopers take over, since the interstate was their bailiwick.

The troopers' maneuver appeared initially to be working, since the speed of the vehicles dropped to about 65. Suddenly, the driver of the Impala jerked his vehicle to the left, ramming one of them, causing the trooper to slide off into the ditch line to the left. The young driver then accelerated past the remaining trooper, and the pursuit was on again.

McCarthy checked his mirror and could see the trooper in the ditch was all right. In moments, the trooper was back on the road in pursuit again. By the rate of acceleration, McCarthy could see that the trooper was now truly pissed. Stammos was directly behind McCarthy, who was now behind the first trooper.

The dispatcher broke into McCarthy's consciousness by reporting, "255, be advised that Wisconsin plate H55-662 is reported stolen from Dane County last night."

"10-4. He just rammed a state patrol vehicle. There appears to be no one injured. We are still eastbound on the interstate at milepost 43, traveling 95 mph at this time," answered Dan.

The stolen vehicle's driver slowed down gradually, and then abruptly crossed the median. He began heading deliberately eastbound in the westbound lane of travel on the interstate. It appeared he was doing this to cause a serious accident to aid in his escape.

The squads paralleled him and this maneuver only served to slow down the suspect. All cars seemed to see the danger soon enough to move out of the young maniac's way. The driver took the first entrance ramp he came to and used it as an exit. The squads were all able to stay with him by taking their ramp. McCarthy radioed, "He is northbound on 52 from the interstate."

The vehicle was now three miles from Booneville. It was a rural community twenty-five miles from La Claire. One mile outside of Booneville, McCarthy could see that the Booneville officer had set up a rather unique road block.

The Booneville officer was an elderly retired gentleman. He was a part-time police officer. He parked his squad, blocking the southbound lane of traffic, leaving the northbound lane open. The fleeing felon was currently in the northbound lane. The Booneville officer had his shotgun out and was down on one knee. As the vehicle passed, the Booneville officer opened fire. He fired first at the tires; and then after the Impala passed, the antique hobby cop fired through the back window of the vehicle.

McCarthy found himself instantly driving in slow motion through crystallized pieces of safety glass, which appeared to float in the air like the airborne seeds of a dandelion on a breezy summer day. McCarthy was immediately on the radio. "Stop shooting. Tell whoever is shooting to stop shooting." There was no response, since the chase was now so far out, McCarthy and Stammos could only hear each other and no one else could hear them. All the other pursuers were from other agencies, and they had their own radio frequencies.

McCarthy noticed after the shooting that there was only one head now visible. He thought that must mean one of them was hit. He pictured his young career ending suddenly with this young miscreant's life—just because some old wannabe out playing cops and robbers wanted to shoot the bad guy. McCarthy continued the pursuit and then thought, "Breathe."

At the same time McCarthy was losing enthusiasm for the pursuit, the suspect was apparently sharing the sentiment for different reasons. The young passenger in the stolen car was not dead at all. He had ducked his head when the shots were fired at the tires and was, therefore, missed by the buckshot that shattered the rear window.

From that point, the terrified passenger began to cry and plead with the driver to stop. Finally, the sobs had their effect on his buddy, who slowly came to a stop. As the stolen Chevy was swarmed by the pursuing officers, the occupants' hands immediately went up and the driver yelled, "Don't shoot! We're just two small children."

"I want your hands on your heads, interlocking your fingers, and do it now!" commanded McCarthy, with his weapon menacingly directed at the interior of the car. The two miniature bandits complied and then without further commands, slipped out of the car. "Down on the ground! I said, down on the ground," yelled one of the county deputies Dan did not know. The ne'er-do-wells were both ordered out and handcuffed by McCarthy. McCarthy placed one in his car and Stammos took the other.

The Booneville officer arrived shortly after the arrest. He got out of his squad and casually walked up to McCarthy. The Booneville cop had his shotgun slung over his shoulder. He proudly admired his handiwork. He appeared self-satisfied with the fact that he had just put nine .33 caliber double-ought buck pellets into the back end of a stolen car. He cared not that it was being driven by fourteen-year-old and thirteen-year-old car thieves. The Booneville Cop smiled and said, "Pretty good shooting, don't you think?" He then looked to McCarthy for acclaim that never came. He was greeted with silence. McCarthy was speechless.

McCarthy couldn't say anything. Shooting at this car was justifiable. Its driver was deliberately trying to seriously harm officers and the public just to get away. McCarthy knew also that, because the criminals were fourteen and thirteen, the public would have been outraged if one of them would have been injured or killed. When the public is outraged, new officers on probation are easy to fire.

McCarthy did not know whether to scream at the Booneville officer or thank him. So McCarthy did neither. He transported his prisoner back to La Claire. He would have liked to have smacked the punk kid responsible for all this, but he wouldn't. He gave him a ride to the Juvenile Detention Center, where they were both locked up for the night. They would be on the run again before a fortnight passed.

McCarthy headed back to the station and began writing his report. By the time he turned in his paperwork, it was time to go home to his wife, daughter and son.

McCarthy went to bed, but sleep would not come. Each time he closed his eyes, he saw the shattered pieces of the back window of the stolen car floating in mid-air, as he drove through the mist-like pieces of glass at about 100 miles an hour.

Dan had experienced a massive adrenaline pump, and he discovered there is no restfulness for quite some time after one of these physiological chemical storms. Dan decided not to waste his time in a vain effort to sleep. He slipped out of his cool, comfortable sheets and slid on his tattered Ray Nitschke jersey, socks, his Nikes, and he was ready to run. Since he had so much energy, he decided to put it to good use.

Within minutes McCarthy was on one of his favorite trails running through the Wisconsin woods. When he returned home, his curly-haired little pal, Nate, was awake. "Hey, Nate. Let's go to the yelling house!" The blonde bundle of energy shot into his room to change his clothes. He loved the "yelling house." It was in the "far park," a longer drive in Dad's car than the "near park," which was across the street. These accurate monikers were affixed to these childhood landmarks by Nate to easily distinguish them from the rest of the possibly less enjoyable locations that he might be dragged off to by adults. Dan got Christa and the three of them were off.

At the far park, Dan followed, with Nate at a dead run. Nate's balance and speed were disrupted by the uncontrollable giggle, caused by the excitement of going to the yelling house. It was not really a house at all. It was an old band shelter in which every whisper echoed. To a three-year-old whose father sleeps during the day, it is the greatest fun in the world to have a place where he can make as much noise as he wants. Dan told his son that at the yelling house he could make all the noise he wanted, as long as he was running.

As Dan pushed his daughter, Christa, in the stroller, she smiled enormously. She found that watching her brother was all the entertainment in the world she needed at this point in her life. Moving fast in her stroller and watching her brother, her two favorite things to do, almost caused a sensory overload of fun that was nearly more than she could bear. At last, she could hold it in no longer and she giggled and squealed, which echoed magnificently in the acoustic barrel that was the yelling house.

The running and laughter finally wound down, after all three were exhausted. Dan returned home and turned over his two progenies to his wife. "Sure. Get them all wound up for me and then you crawl into bed," said Victoria, as Dan kissed her ear lobe.

"Stop that! You know that tickles!" she squealed, trying unconvincingly to act angry.

"Why don't you take the kids to Grandma's, and then you can join me," suggested Dan, as he moved his kiss to a spot that he knew did not tickle his beautiful young mate.

"Grandma's! Grandma's! Grandma's!" yelled Nate, running in a circle.

Christa saw her brother was excited, so she followed suit. Something good would come of this excitement for sure, she thought. She then squealed her approval, "Boompa! Boompa!"

"Quiet down, Nate. You're not at the yelling house," said Dan sternly. "Now look. You have Christa all wound up."

Nate kept his momentum going circularly, but now he repeated in a whisper, "Grandma's. Grandma's. Grandma's."

Christa, who was now in her high-chair moved her arms up and down, mimicking her big brother, who she adored, "Booma! Boompa!"

"I'll take them to Grandma's, but don't count on me coming back, Daniel McCarthy," scolded Victoria in mock anger. "I just might make a day of it."

While Victoria transferred the custody of the children to her parents, McCarthy threw pizza in the oven. He was taking it out as Victoria returned home. "Pizza for breakfast? I'll never get used to this," said Victoria, as she looked longingly at the bubbling cheese while Dan sliced the pizza.

"It's not breakfast for me. This is supper. It's my second favorite thing I like to nibble on after work," said McCarthy, as he took a piece and fed it to his pretty young bride.

As she tried to take a bite, a section of cheese and tomato slid off and fell onto her white blouse. "I'm sorry," McCarthy said, as he tried to wipe the stain off the blouse.

"I'll get the stain out," said McCarthy, as he unbuttoned the blouse.

"I've never seen you so worried about a stain before," said Victoria playfully, as the blouse was slid off her shoulders, revealing she had removed her bra. Then she threw the blouse to the floor and moved slowly into her husband's arms. She looked into her husband's eyes. Both could feel the warmth of the eternal flame, which was their love igniting into a blaze. Victoria said quietly in almost a whisper, "You know this pizza is too hot. The only way pizza should be eaten in the morning is cold. Let's eat it later, after it gets cold."

"Is anything good hot in the morning?" asked Dan innocently.

"As a matter of fact . . ." Victoria pressed her lips hard against Dan's, as she unbuttoned his shirt. She slid it over his broad shoulders and softly kissed his muscled chest. Dan picked Victoria up into his arms, as if there was a threshold to be crossed. They kissed again, and he carried her to their bed, never losing contact with those warm, soft, loving lips. He set her down softly, and then stood over her and looked upon her beauty. He could not decide what he loved most about her. Her soft blonde hair revealed a hint of red when in the sun. Her eyes, which twinkled when she laughed; sparkled, when she loved; and made her look like Bambi, when she cried. Her body belonged on a pedestal in the Athenian ruins. Her heart turned the beautiful work of art that was "Victoria" into a masterpiece. He sighed deeply at the thought of how lucky he was.

"Are you sighing because you are getting tired of me?" asked Victoria, who was puzzled by her lover's hesitancy.

"You couldn't be more wrong," Dan answered, as he slid next to her and kissed her as if it were the first time. The two lovers melted together and became one.

As Dan lay next to his beautiful blonde wife later that morning, he found himself gazing once again at his wife as she slept. She was as pretty as a poster girl and twice as nice. She was real. McCarthy could hardly believe that a few hours earlier he was in the middle of gunfire and careening cars. Now he was in the midst of warmth and love. His mind then purged itself of thoughts, concerns, and memories, as Dan McCarthy listened to Victoria's slow rhythmical breathing McCarthy wrestled with impending slumber to conjure up one more mental communication, "Thank you, God, for my life, for my family, and for my wife." With that he surrendered to sleep.

CHAPTER 7
BROCKMAN TAKES A NAP

Most of the third shift officers started their day with an unusual energy that would look out of place anywhere else, considering it was 11:00 p.m. For a third shift officer, this was his 9:00 a.m. Third shift was an interesting mix of officers. Most of the shift was comprised of young men, who did not have the seniority to move to another shift where a person could sleep at night. There were some older officers who chose to stay on third shift because of the action, and it allowed them to spend more time with their families.

Then there was Brockman. Some said he stayed because it had the least number of supervisors. Some said it was because no woman would sleep with him anyway, so why go to bed at night. Some theorized it was to attempt to ensure that every new officer could learn how to be as obnoxious as he was. The truth was—no one knew why Brockman stayed on the night shift. He did not let anyone get close enough to understand what made Stanley Brockman tick.

The reason could well have been that the Brockman that used to exist wanted to keep the Brockman that now exists hidden from the light of day. Brockman was a man who was embittered by the job.

Job-related stress takes its toll on many professions. People are taught how to manage their stress. Cops have to manage levels of stress higher than can be imagined by people outside the profession. Police experience the same kind of stresses as any other person, such as financial problems, difficulties in interpersonal relationships, deaths in the family, etc. For some reason, law enforcement officers kill themselves three times more often than bad guys kill cops. No one had any idea how many times Stanley Brockman had almost "enhanced" that statistic.

In the workplace, however, they have to deal with stresses unique to the profession. Brockman had been around long enough to see exactly too much. Why, in one day of his career, he started out the day by cutting down a teenager who'd hanged himself because his parents grounded him. The last call of the same day he thought would be a breeze. He knocked on a door to talk with a resident who was unreasonably angry about a utility bill. Instead of breezing through a simple call, he was met by a 300-pound grandmother wielding a butcher knife. In a split-second, he pictured himself shooting the woman and being crucified in the press. He then pictured himself doing nothing, and the woman in this scenario burying the knife into his throat. Brockman did neither. He stepped back away from the attacking woman and fell down the steps, breaking his clavicle. The woman went back into the house and was arrested later, after Brockman was rescued. The humiliation caused by his being injured on the retreat from a 300-pound grandmother was more than most could tolerate. What really hurt Brockman was the self-doubt caused by the knowledge that he could not make a decision when his life depended on it.

It was impossible to know if the impact of this very bad day was the reason why Brockman seemed to hate everybody, especially McCarthy. After McCarthy learned about Brockman's history, McCarthy suspected this was why Brockman seemed angry all the time. This was why it was hard for the young officer to return the hostility Brockman so deserved. McCarthy thought, "Brockman injured more than his clavicle during the fall. Brockman suffered a compound fracture of his confidence."

McCarthy was taught in the academy that a cop has to be like a power-lifter. If you go into a weight room, not one with shiny equipment and mirrors without finger prints on them, but a really dirty weight room, with Olympic bars and free weights lying all over, you'll find power-lifters. These guys have huge arms and can lie down on a bench and, in most cases, bench-press 200 pounds more than their body weight. This comes from years of training the body to manage greater weights than most people would ever attempt.

Cops have to be the power-lifters of stress. They have to handle stresses that most people never have to think about. They see the things on a regular basis that if they even experienced it once would send some people to a therapist for the rest of their days.

Brockman had experienced most of what a street officer could experience and then some. Those that knew him said he was not always so bitter. He used to be a pleasure to work with. He had been passed over for promotion a number of times. Citations and commendations were few and far between for everyone, because the administration at the time felt, if you gave too many out, they wouldn't mean anything to those who received them. Therefore, those who received them were usually special people in special positions. Brockman knew the job and did well on the tests, but "didn't interview well." His positive attitude was faltering anyway, and then came the broken clavicle.

After that, he was done trying. He was done trying to get ahead. As far as Brockman was concerned, to get ahead in this job depended on two things, "Who you know and who you blow." Soon, two words you would hear from Stanley Brockman every day of his life were two words firmly entrenched in the vocabulary of every burned-out cop, "Fuck it!" It was his answer to every challenge that faced him. The reason he could say fuck it was because its was all "Booshit!"

Stanley Brockman was on a slippery slope. Bitterness was his constant companion. Bitterness camouflaged the pain. It seemed to anger him more to see anyone else in a good mood. Brockman would go out of his way to spread discontent, short-circuit enthusiasm, and make everyone as miserable as he was.

Stanley especially hated "rookies with college degrees." The rookies still loved the job. They had their whole future ahead of them, and Brockman envied them to the point of hatred. McCarthy could only feel sympathy for Brockman in return. In their time together, McCarthy learned a great and valuable lesson from Brockman. If he was not careful, he could become Stanley Brockman in twenty years.

Brockman did not know it, but he had become a criminal's "dream cop." He would rather drive by than investigate. He would call in sick when he wasn't. He was slow to arrive on all types of calls, especially trouble calls; because then he would not have to do the paper work involved. He would always say, "A good cop never gets cold, hungry, wet, and never, on any occasion, volunteers for a call." Stanley on most nights was a ROD (retired on duty).

If you were any type of criminal, you wanted Stanley Brockman to be the man on the beat. It increased your odds for success considerably. Stanley was a report-taker, and any cops who let the job get to them could become like Stanley Brockman. McCarthy would not let that happen to him, *ever*!

It was 3:00 a.m. on a Tuesday night. McCarthy was driving second half of the shift. Rather than spend the shift belittling and complaining about his rookie partner, tonight, Brockman had chosen to ignore McCarthy. Brockman, in the ultimate act of disregard, had now dozed off. Brockman was the only partner McCarthy had that slept. McCarthy hated it. He wanted to drive to the station and ask Sgt. Compton to take a look at his partner. McCarthy was not old enough, established enough, and brave enough to do it. That was about to change.

At 3:01 a.m. McCarthy was skimming through alleys checking businesses silently with the squad's lights out. As McCarthy rounded the corner of Shock Electric, he saw the figure of a twenty-year-old man next to the rear door. McCarthy could see the man was prying at the door. At the same moment McCarthy realized the dark figure was a burglar, the burglar spotted the squad. The criminal bolted. McCarthy was stunned momentarily by the sudden and drastic change in the status quo. The pause was ended by McCarthy exploding out of the squad like a thoroughbred from the gates at Churchill Downs. The chase was on.

As McCarthy began distancing himself from the patrol car, he thought of his obnoxious, unfriendly, currently useless partner. He turned and yelled to Brockman, "Foot pursuit!"

At that moment, Brockman was climbing into bed with his dream girl, Sandy. Sandy was a clerical person who was stunning. She had blonde hair, ample breasts, and dressed to show them. At this moment, she was wearing a clinging flesh-colored nightgown that was a wrap-around and opened from the front. She gazed longingly at Brockman and was about to reveal the mystery that he believed all male members, and maybe even a couple of female members, of the La Claire Police Department wanted solved. Brockman wanted this question answered. "What denomination are Sandy's nipples? Were they quarter-sized, half-dollar-sized, or, 'Bingo,' silver-dollar-sized?"

Then Sandy began to slowly step out of her nightgown and suddenly the bed jerked convulsively. She stopped her sensuous striptease and Brockman pleaded, "Keep going. Please don't stop."

Sandy's head tilted and her face became distorted and showed anger and disgust with her admirer. She then yelled, "Foot pursuit!"

As Brockman was startled awake, he discovered he was alone in the squad. The door to the driver's side was standing open. In the darkness, he could not recognize where he was. He attempted to get out of the squad, but he felt a tightness in his pants that made it difficult to maneuver quickly. He limped to the driver's side and spotted the damaged door at Shock Electric. He looked about, saw no one, and froze. Stanley Brockman knew that his career was in the hands of his partner. "Damned rookie!" Brockman said out loud. Brockman was like any other slug in any other workplace. He could not understand anyone else's enthusiasm for their job, and he hated that. He even hated it more when their enthusiasm toward work made him work. Brockman jumped into the squad and began driving. He didn't have a clue where his partner was.

"Damned rookie," repeated Brockman to no one, but now in a more concerned tone of voice. Brockman was concerned more with his own career than the safety of his young charge.

McCarthy was staying with the male stride for stride. As McCarthy pursued the felon, he mentally processed as much information about the burglar as possible, in the event he lost him. The man was about twenty, with brown hair down over the collar. He was skinny and kind of looked like Mick Jagger. He was wearing blue jeans and a DARE T-shirt. He had high-cut Nike shoes. "I can catch this guy; he's panting and wearing high tops. They have to weigh a ton," thought McCarthy. This thought, however, caused him to notice the weight of his duty belt bouncing on his waist with every stride he took.

Then McCarthy thought, "His hands! Watch the hands! The hands kill! What does he have in his hands?" One hand was empty; the other still held the tire iron that he had been prying on the door with. "Watch that tire iron," thought McCarthy.

The foot chase had cut around to the front of Shock Electric, and both the pursuer and pursuee were out of sight of the then-sleeping Brockman immediately. The crook cut across a four-lane, divided highway and between two businesses. McCarthy was following, trailing by about fifty feet.

McCarthy looked up and down the highway for help, but there was no one. You could fire the proverbial cannon down the street without hitting anyone. McCarthy hoped that he would see Brockman spring to life and swing the squad around Shock Electric, but there was nothing. The radio was silent and no one had called in a thing yet.

McCarthy did not want to break his stride by radioing in yet. He had hoped Brockman would do it. The suspect stumbled and got back immediately to his feet, and McCarthy was now right behind him.

As the agile rookie sprinted behind his prey through the bowels of the industrial park that Shock Electric was a part of, Brockman's excited voice finally came over the radio, "255, we're in foot pursuit! Shock Electric."

McCarthy could not help but think this was funny. He felt more affinity at the moment with his fleeing adversary, than to Brockman. He yelled to the suspect, "Do you hear that? 'We're in foot pursuit,' he says."

The suspect could not help but turn, while still running and ask rhetorically, "What!?" At the same moment, McCarthy began to swing around to the suspect's right side. He did not want to tackle the suspect, because he still carried the tire iron. McCarthy could see the suspect was wearing down. He also had developed a slight limp after the fall. McCarthy ordered him to stop again and the frightened felon, instead of stopping, continued to run, only slightly faster. To someone watching this it might have looked like a scene from *Wild Kingdom*, where a cheetah is closing ground on an injured gazelle.

McCarthy made his move. He cut around to the right and took hold of the arm, which held the crowbar. McCarthy locked in on the right arm

and elbow, but the fleeing felon still firmly gripped the potentially deadly crowbar. Once McCarthy had the elbow and wrist firmly in his grasp,
he popped the elbow sharply. This caused the arm to straighten and
elbow to lock out painfully. This sharp maneuver involuntarily opened
the suspect's hand and the crowbar flew out of it and bounced off
McCarthy's knee. McCarthy felt nothing at the time; there would be
time to feel the pain later.

McCarthy then swung the criminal in an arch down to the ground.
When he hit the ground, the suspect skidded to a stop. The Mick Jagger
look-alike was placed into a painful armlock that immediately ended his
resistance. McCarthy yelled, "Police, relax. It's over. You're under arrest."

The exhausted ne'er-do-well felt the hopelessness of the situation
coupled with personal exhaustion and answered in gasps, "OK! OK! OK!"
McCarthy let up on the pressure and smoothly applied the cuffs as if he
was born with handcuffs in his hand. Click!

McCarthy recited from memory, "You have a right to remain silent . . ."
Dan then began to step back out of the parallel dimension a policeman
steps into during these intense moments. He now could hear the confusion on the radio. He could hear the sirens of other squads responding to
assist. Brockman had called in the foot pursuit, but had given the wrong
direction of travel. He was directing converging units to the area to the
rear of the business. McCarthy's transmission broke in amongst the chatter on the radio, "255, I have the suspect 10-95 (in custody)."

McCarthy searched the suspect as the ne'er-do-well lay catching his
breath on the ground. It was clear by the cash the lawbreaker had on him
that Shock was not his first burglary this night. "Hey, buddy, are you
hurt?" asked McCarthy.

This concern shocked the twenty-year-old felon, who had been
involved in the criminal justice system since he was nine and had stabbed
his brother over whose turn it was at the joy stick while playing a video
game. "Yeah, my knee is kind of sore. I think I hit it pretty hard when I
fell."

McCarthy then inspected the knee and asked, "Do you think you can
walk?"

"Yeah, I can walk. I just banged it up," answered the suspect.

"What's your name?" asked McCarthy.

"Mitchell. Billy Mitchell," answered the burglar.

"Well, Billy. I'm Dan McCarthy. As you know, you are under arrest.
Now, you ran because it is your job to get away. I caught you and disarmed you, because it was my job to catch you. I know it hurt a little
bit, but now that's over. I want you to know we're going to get along
fine, OK?"

"Sounds OK to me," answered the puzzled criminal.

"I want to ask you some questions. I explained your rights to you. Do you understand your rights?" asked McCarthy.

"Yeah," was Mitchell's answer.

"Would you like to answer some questions right now?" McCarthy then added, "Man you're fast. I don't think I'd have caught you if you didn't fall."

"Yeah, I'm sorry about all that. I'll talk to you. Shit. You got my ass anyway, man."

McCarthy assisted the man in getting to his feet. They began walking back to the squad, and McCarthy picked up the tire iron. McCarthy realized, as the two began to walk back toward Shock Electric, that his knee pained him fiercely, but he hid the pain from his prisoner.

By the time the two arrived back at the squad, Billy Mitchell admitted burglary was his intent at Shock Electric. Billy also told McCarthy that he had broken into Caball's Bar and Hardin's Restaurant within about four blocks of McAllister's Bar. Mitchell claimed he was working alone. "I like working with people I can count on," Billy added with a laugh, "so I always work alone."

McCarthy could empathize with Mitchell tonight. Brockman had let the rookie down tonight. It was the kind of mistake that could have gotten McCarthy killed and Brockman fired. The thought of working alone every night he was scheduled to work with Stanley Brockman was a very tempting option to Dan McCarthy right now.

McCarthy waited for an opening on the main radio channel, which was cackling with activity. "255, I have one male in custody. He states he also was involved in the same activity at Caball's Bar and Hardin's Restaurant. Please send squads to those two locations to check the security."

Almost immediately a squad arrived at Hardin's and then at Caball's. Then came the transmissions, "10-4 on the burglary at Hardin's," and, "Be advised we have a burglary at Caball's also."

When McCarthy reached his squad, he eased Mitchell into the squad, taking care to protect Billy's knee from further injury. After shutting the squad door, McCarthy turned his attention to Brockman. Brockman started to give directions to the younger officer, but stopped abruptly when he saw the look in McCarthy's eye.

When McCarthy was angry, his face lost its normal warmth. The smile disappeared and McCarthy's amiable countenance was replaced by a persona of frightening intensity. His hazel eyes turned a dark gray. He had a blood vessel on the left side of his forehead that seemed to be the carrier of the suppressed anger. It looked now like it was about to burst.

"No. Say nothing to me right now," McCarthy said, turning his eyes away from Brockman while he held his hand up as if he were signaling a Chevy to stop at a busy intersection. "You will stand by here for the owner and take the incident complaint. I will get a written statement from Mr. Mitchell and handle the evidence I found on him. Then I will write up the report. I will talk to you later."

McCarthy turned to walk away, paused, then turned back toward Brockman. With the command voice of a ten-year sergeant, he ordered, "Don't you ever call me rookie again. Tonight, you let me down. You let your department down. Hell, you let yourself down every day of your life. I very well may still be a rookie, but tonight, you lost the right to call me rookie."

McCarthy turned and walked back to the squad. He got in with Mitchell and asked, "How's the knee? Do you want to see a doctor?"

"No way! It's just scraped. I can't afford a doctor, even if I need one," answered Mitchell, still surprised by this young officer's genuine concern.

As they drove to Central Station, McCarthy nonchalantly mentioned, "You know, a guy who commits three burglaries in one night, obviously has done it before. How about we take the time to clean your closet?" suggested McCarthy, looking at Mitchell eye-to-eye via the rearview mirror.

"What do you mean, clean my closet?" queried Mitchell.

"Tonight I can write the report and tell how cooperative you were. You can give me information on other burglaries that I know and you know you have been involved in. Then the judge sees them all at one time. One contact. I can tell the judge that you came to me with this information to clean your closet—to make your life right again."

McCarthy knew judges like people to admit and feel sorry for what they have done. If a bad guy goes to the wall and shows no remorse, the judge is more likely to hammer the jerk at sentencing. That's why, when a cop says, "Do yourself a favor and talk," in reality that's true.

Mitchell didn't know this. He just knew he was being treated with an ounce of respect. He knew he had been caught by someone he feared and respected. He knew he was run down, spun down, and disarmed by a cop who clearly did not do it by accident. The same cop then treated Billy with more care and concern than he had ever received. He trusted this cop; and before he could think about whether it was good for his case or bad for his case, he was hearing himself say these words, "Yeah, I'll tell you. It's not as many as you think."

At the station, McCarthy took Mitchell to an interview room. He removed the cuffs, and as Mitchell rubbed his wrists, as all criminals do after the cuffs are taken off, he asked McCarthy, "Hey, what was that thing you did with my arm? Are you in the martial arts? Are you like a black belt or something?"

"Or something is right," replied McCarthy. "The most important thing I learned in the martial arts is that to get respect you give respect. Tonight and whenever we meet in the future, I will treat you with respect and I ask that you do the same with me. My name is Officer McCarthy. Dan McCarthy. You can call me Dan."

"McCarthy? I've heard that name before. Isn't he like a detective in a TV series?"

"Yeah, that's right," McCarthy answered. "Can I get you a pop?" McCarthy asked with a smile.

"Sure, I'll take a Pepsi. If all you have is Coke, I'll do without."

"Wow, that's the same way I feel about it. We have Pepsi," chuckled McCarthy.

"That's something we have in common." They had more than the mutual appreciation of Pepsi in common. They both were young, intelligent, and had potential. They both were from the poorer streets of La Claire and had consciously chosen their career paths. Both had an amiable disposition, but could be dangerous to an adversary. They smiled now, but there was no mistaking the fact that they were adversaries. Both suspected that they would meet each other again.

"Has anyone ever told you that you look like Mick Jagger?" asked McCarthy, as he set the can of Pepsi down in front of Mitchell.

"Yeah, all the time. Except he makes more money than I do, but I get more pussy than him," said Mitchell, as he opened his can of Pepsi. They shared a laugh, as the officer laid a pen and a statement form in front of Billy. Billy took a long swig from his Pepsi.

"Man, that tastes good right now." Billy then picked up the pen and started writing immediately.

Mitchell ultimately admitted to thirteen burglaries. McCarthy then talked him into getting some treatment for his injured knee. After the knee had been cleaned, McCarthy transported Mitchell to jail, and as he was being led to his cell, he turned to McCarthy and held out his hand. The two recent combatants shook hands and Mitchell said, "Thanks." He paused for a second and then said, "I don't know why I just said that to you." Mitchell then limped down the hall toward Receiving in his bright orange jail jump suit. McCarthy watched Mitchell turn into his Receiving Cell.

McCarthy thought, "I'll meet him again." McCarthy was right. Billy Mitchell would help McCarthy become a veteran.

Later that night, as McCarthy was writing his report, Brockman approached him. There was none of the arrogance and anger that had been his trademark behavior in the past. He politely laid his portion of the report down on McCarthy's pile of paperwork.

"Say, McCarthy . . ."

McCarthy held up his hand and stopped Brockman from saying whatever he was about to say. McCarthy had decided it was his turn to talk. "Listen Brockman, this is a time for a monologue, not a dialog. You listen and I'll talk! Since we have met, you've treated me like a piece of snail shit. I would feel bad about that except you were just being fair since you treat everyone like a piece of snail shit. You let me down tonight. You were asleep and I could have gotten seriously hurt. You wouldn't have had a clue as to where to send the ambulance. I could go to the Sergeant and make a complaint. It might cost you your job and it might not. I won't though. Instead, all I ask in return is that from now on, when I'm around, you treat everyone around you with the respect they deserve. That's me, the other guys, the suspects . . . everyone! If you do that, I will never tell a soul how truly worthless you were tonight. If you don't improve, the deal is off, and I will be telling this story for the rest of my career."

Brockman stood silently for a few moments. He looked different to McCarthy. McCarthy, being the optimist he was, thought maybe that meant some wonderful transformation was taking place in the heart and soul of Stanley Brockman. A grinch-like transformation. "Fair enough, McCarthy. It won't happen again," answered Brockman.

From that point on, McCarthy did notice Brockman tried. He couldn't just stop being Brockman, but he was definitely a kinder and gentler Brockman. He stopped calling McCarthy a rookie, and everyone noticed he acted differently. Stammos said, "Lately, Brockman is a lot nicer than he used to be. He's now just acting like an ass, instead of an asshole. That's an improvement for Brockman."

McCarthy learned that, in this world of police officers, it did not pay to let things go unsaid. One thing that would serve an officer well on the street and among an officer's peers would be a reputation that command-ed respect. McCarthy realized this and would be heard to say often throughout his career, "There is a fine line between fear and respect. I'll accept either and demand one. It's your choice." Respect was important to McCarthy. He felt you can't get it unless you give it. It's better when people are motivated to do your bidding out of respect than out of fear. McCarthy wanted to motivate people because of the respect he earned. This was much preferred by him.

He would discover that, in the real world, sometimes fear gets you by.

CHAPTER 8
"THE BRAWL"—A MATTER OF LIFE AND DEATH

McCarthy had just begun his shift. He had just reached the downtown area and noticed a well-known personality, Ricky Cantwell, at the corner of Third and State. Cantwell turned away from traffic, cupping his hands to block the breeze while he lit his cigarette. McCarthy drove on by, trying not to make eye contact. It appeared that the lighting of the cigarette was an attempt by Cantwell to cover his face. Dan thought there might be an outstanding warrant for Ricky.

McCarthy passed and looked in the rearview mirror. He noticed that Cantwell lit his cigarette and appeared relieved to see the squad pass without McCarthy looking twice at him. Cantwell was especially relieved, because he knew he was a wanted man. He also knew the young officer behind the wheel of the squad. He was happy the officer did not notice him, because he had things to do and people to see. Tonight was not a good night to go to jail. Cantwell continued on his way, unconcerned after seeing the squad continue on.

McCarthy contacted dispatch, "255, 10-29."

"255, go ahead," came the immediate response.

"I'd like a 10-29 on Ricky R. Cantwell."

After about three minutes dispatch called, "255, we have an active warrant for that subject for possession of a dangerous drug with intent to deliver . . . no bond, body only."

"255, that subject is walking east on State Street from Third Street. I would like a backup," McCarthy answered.

"I can be there in about one minute. Where do you want to meet?" piped up Stammos immediately.

"I'll cut him off from the west and you come in from the south on Sixth. We won't give him a chance to run," directed McCarthy.

"10-4," responded Stammos.

Cantwell walked nonchalantly up State Street smoking his cigarette. He had no idea he was going to wake up in jail the next morning. McCarthy wondered how people could live like Cantwell. They were always in jail, just out of jail, or about to go back to jail. They couldn't hold a job. Their lot in life was to give grief, pain, and sorrow to everyone who loved them. They did nothing notable other than sleep, eat, have sex, do drugs, and commit crimes. Cantwell was a small-time dealer. He sold drugs to support his habit, have sex with crack whores, pay his rent, and eat. Those are listed by priority.

McCarthy had parked his squad out of sight and was following Cantwell on foot from the west. When he was within striking distance, McCarthy radioed, "Now, Randy."

Stammos pulled up right in front of Cantwell, cutting suddenly across his path.

Cantwell threw the cigarette and then turned sharply to run west. McCarthy was on him and used Cantwell's own spinning momentum to spin him back, dumping him over the hood of Stammos's squad.

"Police, relax, you're under arrest, put your hands behind your back. Do it *now!*" In one short sentence, Ricky was told everything he needed to know. Ricky wasn't ready to relax, though.

Ricky tightened his arm and tried to break free of McCarthy's grip, but McCarthy quickly locked Ricky's wrist in a painful gooseneck configuration, which caused Ricky to grimace and cease his fruitless efforts to escape. McCarthy rewarded him by letting up on the pressure and the grimace disappeared from Ricky's face. By this time, Stammos was on the other arm and, in short order, Ricky was handcuffed. McCarthy said, "Thanks, Randy."

"Anytime, Dyno," said Randy. The two had grown to work well together. They had had a jerky start, but now were working together like pistons in a high-performance engine.

During the search of Ricky, McCarthy found eight small bindles of cocaine equally filled with about a 1/4 gram for sale. Ricky had $1,500 in cash on him. McCarthy wondered why every "scumbag" had more cash on him than McCarthy had ever seen at once in his whole life.

Ricky was transported to the county jail. Cantwell had run because he knew he would go to prison if caught with the cocaine. He had already used every lame-ass excuse a judge would buy. He had already gotten two, "One more time and you're going to prison, young man!" speeches. There would not be a third.

This had been the third time Cantwell had met the young McCarthy. Once at the scene of a battery, Cantwell was arrested by McCarthy. Ricky tried to swing on the young officer, but had been spun with his own momentum neatly to the ground and placed tightly into a hold that made him resist no further. That night, he asked McCarthy, "Where'd you learn that shit?"

The next time they met was in court, when Cantwell was found guilty on the charge of battery, which McCarthy had arrested him for. The public defender had gone into depth in his cross-examination, attacking McCarthy for over-reacting and throwing his client brutally to the ground. He discovered that McCarthy had a black belt in tae kwon do and also studied in aikido, hapkido, and judo—styles of grappling and joint manipulation.

When asked if he studied all those styles so that he could abuse his authority, McCarthy explained, "The aikido, judo and hapkido were for me to better control resistive people, without resorting to higher levels of force. The tae kwon do was to be better able to win, when I could not get a controlling hold on someone. I am a police officer who is 5' 9" and about 165 pounds. This is a physical job that requires that I be able to serve and protect others. I always wanted to be a police officer; and I figured if I can't protect myself, how could I expect to protect someone else?" The public defender's strategy to attack McCarthy failed and Cantwell was convicted.

The third time Cantwell and McCarthy met was about a month after the trial, when McCarthy was booking a prisoner and Cantwell was a trustee in the jail. Cantwell said to McCarthy, "Hey, McCarthy. You chop-sock-eyed anyone's ass lately?" Cantwell kidded, as he made a childlike karate-chop demonstration.

McCarthy smiled and replied, "Well I haven't chop-sock-eyed anyone since . . ." He paused, looked at his watch, and finished, "What time is it right now?" Then McCarthy added, "How long you have to serve?"

"One week, with good time," Ricky chirped.

"You behave yourself this time, Ricky, 'cause we've got to stop meeting like this."

"If it wasn't for guys like me, guys like you would have to get a real job, Officer McCarthy." This answer pleased Cantwell and made him laugh at himself.

The response pleased the young McCarthy. He realized that a criminal just recognized him and called him "Officer McCarthy." The young McCarthy did not know why it pleased him so much that a criminal recognized him as "Officer McCarthy," but it did. He almost felt guilty by the welling of pride inside himself that it generated.

Now Cantwell was under arrest again via McCarthy in their fourth meeting. Ricky was on his way to prison and he knew it. They always know it, because judges say things like, "The next time I see you in front of this bench . . ." Judges think this scares criminals, when all it does is makes criminals more desperate in their dealings with officers. Cantwell would have run, fought, or killed, if he could have gotten the opportunity; but he didn't get the opportunity, and even he was relieved.

Prison was not even guaranteed. There was always the possibility of another shot at probation, treatment programs, or, as a last resort, Cantwell could find Jesus. They always find Jesus. McCarthy always thought that a criminal claiming to find Jesus to get out of jail, was God's real intended sin, when he wrote the Commandment; "Thou shalt not take the name of the Lord thy God in vain."

The criminals also could get the real luck of the draw—Judge Alice. Judge Alice liked criminals more than policemen. She shed tears for criminals she had to send to prison, but never a drop for the victims the criminals put in the hospital. Police referred to her court as going to see "Alice in Wonderland." You always wonder whether you would get Alice or the wicked queen, when you went to "Wonderland." Regardless, judges who told criminals, "The next time I see you in court you're going to prison," only created a dangerous situation for the next cop that had to lay hands on the guy.

As Cantwell headed back toward the receiving area of the jail, he paused and turned to McCarthy and said something McCarthy would hear often in his career. "You know, if I had to get arrested, I guess I would just as soon get arrested by you." Ricky knew he had lost every battle with this young officer, but he'd never lost his dignity.

"Thanks, that's the nicest thing anyone has said to me all day. Good luck to you, Ricky," said Dan.

At the station, Dan carefully dropped a small amount of the white powder into a field test packet. He then cautiously popped the glassine ampoules inside in the proper order and "shazam!" He saw the robin's egg blue color develop in the pretty pink liquid that told him Ricky was an "honest" drug dealer that handled a good product. This was good cocaine. To cops, the colors were as welcome as a beautiful sunset.

After weighing, packaging, and placing the cocaine securely into evidence, McCarthy wrote his report. Dan enjoyed writing his report. It was his way of debriefing what happened and deciding if there was anything he could have done differently. This arrest could not have gone smoother. He felt good that he could count on Stammos and the others on his shift for help. Randy's lunch tonight is going to be on me, thought McCarthy. That is, if we get time for lunch. With that thought, McCarthy turned in his report to the desk sergeant for review and enthusiastically hit the street again. There would be no lunch break for Officer Daniel McCarthy on this night.

It was 2:00 a.m., and the dispatcher reported, "An ambulance was called to the pool at the Holiday Inn. The EMTs are now asking for police assistance with an unruly crowd there."

Officer Carpenter was dispatched and McCarthy immediately chimed in, "I'm close. I'll back him up." Carpenter arrived first, and when McCarthy entered, he saw a man bleeding badly from a laceration on his forehead. Carpenter was busy keeping back several drunken people, while the EMTs were trying to attend to the man's injury.

Dan McCarthy worked his way over to Gary Carpenter and asked, "What happened here?"

Carpenter responded, "The ambulance was called because this man hit his head. A group of his friends were going to throw him in the pool and they dropped him on his head. He's with this group of auto mechanics here for a conference. He doesn't want to press any charges. The ambulance personnel called us because the crowd is less than supportive."

McCarthy could see that Carpenter, the EMTs, and he were the only sober people in the place. The majority of the mechanic's group was on the next level, which overlooked the pool. There was a party in every room on the upper level, and the group was yelling and jeering at the officers. The liquor they had consumed had washed away any sympathy that they might have had for their injured friend.

As McCarthy looked in wonder at the stupidity that alcohol conjured up in people, the hotel uniformed security officer came jogging up to McCarthy and Carpenter. "Something needs to be done about that entire group. They have been nothing but problems since they got here. The other motel guests are checking out left and right because of the problems. What are you going to do about it?"

McCarthy could see that they would need more help and responded, "We'll stay right here for now. We are going to get this ambulance crew out of here first and then get some more help, before we deal with that crowd."

This answer did not seem to satisfy the security guard, who clearly wanted the entire crowd of 100-plus drunks immediately hustled out of the hotel. He wanted it done by these two young officers ten minutes ago.

With that being said, McCarthy and Carpenter began to move the bystanders around the pool to allow a path for the ambulance attendants to get out. The group on the level overlooking the pool was hanging over the railing, yelling for help in a mocking manner. One rough looking female was heard to yell to Carpenter and McCarthy, "Hey, Osifer! Yeah, you, rookie! Come on up here, and I'll make a man out of you!" To add effect, she lifted her T-shirt and bared her large, sagging, darkly-nippled breasts. She had one in each hand and lifted them up alternately, as if she was juggling.

Naked breasts were just the kind of encouragement this crowd need-ed. The volume of hoots, laughs, and cheers climbed a few hundred deci-bels after the breasts were juggled. Then the forty-plus-year-old barfly squeezed her large breasts together, while she licked one nipple slowly and completely. She then blew a kiss to the officers.

The nearly all-male crowd moved out to the railing on the balcony above the pool and roared its approval in one voice. McCarthy, at the same time, radioed to dispatch, "We have a large disorderly crowd here. We will need more officers to assist us. Send us whatever you have avail-able and tell them to step it up." McCarthy wondered how many cops had been injured in the past during riots which were started by a woman tak-ing her clothes off.

McCarthy could not hear if the dispatcher replied, because the crowd noise was too loud.

"Oh, my God, no," was all young Dan McCarthy could say, when he saw that the security guard had decided to go to the second level by him-self to accomplish God knows what. Now he was in trouble. About five male mechanics were bouncing him amongst themselves. One was wear-ing the guard's hat and was talking on a phone yelling, "Send more secu-rity guards! Make it snappy!" The request for assistance to help the tor-tured minimum-wage employee would go unheeded. Help would not be forthcoming, because the phone receiver that the mechanic was using had been torn from the hotel room phone.

McCarthy grabbed Carpenter by the shoulders and talked right to his face with the urgency that the situation called for, "Get this ambulance crew out of here right now and then come back and help me if you can. I have to go up there now and try to get him out of there. When you get outside, find out if dispatch got my request for more units, and tell them we need them now! This thing is bad and it's only going to get worse."

The two officers then separated. McCarthy worked his way up to the game of security-guard rugby and pulled the man out of the circle. "Get out of here now!" McCarthy said into the guard's ear.

"He has my fucking hat!" the guard argued.

"Get out of here now! The hotel can bill them for the hat, along with the phone and every thing else they break before this thing is over. Now move!"

The guard saw the intensity in McCarthy's eyes and immediately left. McCarthy could hardly believe what happened next. The group of five individuals now began to maneuver around him. It was their intention to play a game of police-officer rugby with him.

"Gentlemen, my name is Dan. You guys came here to have fun and now it's getting out of hand. Someone has gotten hurt and I don't want anyone else to get hurt . . ."

Before he could finish the thought, the man with the phone and the hat lunged toward McCarthy. He dropped the phone, and before he could grab the officer, McCarthy took the extended arm and quickly put it into a wristlock, bringing the leader of the crowd to his tip-toes. "Relax, sir, you are under arrest!"

Just then a man stepped forward and said, "No he's not. He's staying here! Let him go, you fucking asshole!" McCarthy wondered if this was the second-in-command of this mob, but before he could contemplate the mob's chain of command any further, McCarthy could feel his prisoner being tugged from him and someone grabbing both of McCarthy's shoulders from behind. Mr. Second-in-Command then stepped in front of McCarthy and placed his left hand on McCarthy's chest, to measure the punch he was about to hit McCarthy with.

McCarthy had practiced this scenario too many times in his years of martial arts classes, to have to stop and think about it. Number Two took too long to measure his punch. McCarthy moved to hit him back first! The mechanics had tried to victimize someone who would never make a good victim.

McCarthy released the arrested mob leader with a hard push in the direction his friends were pulling hard on him. This sudden push caused his friends to lose their balance and fall backward like a scene from the Three Stooges. This gave McCarthy room to work. McCarthy then delivered two full-powered front-punches to the nose, then the chin of Mr. Second-in-Command, just as he was stepping forward to deliver his measured punch.

The first blow took him out of the fight and left him on one knee, dazed and bleeding from his nose and upper lip. The second blow came so fast that Mr. Second-in-Command would not be able to distinguish it from the first. He would always remember just one devastating punch that knocked him senseless.

McCarthy then felt another drunk to his left rear who attempted to grab his left arm. This drunken mechanic wanted all of McCarthy's arm, but he only got part of it. The mechanic caught the elbow as McCarthy shot it directly back and up into the large man's chin. The man immediately slid down the wall, to a seated position, where he would sleep off the rest of the fight.

Most members of the crowd realized that what was happening was more serious than they had planned for this evening, and they scampered back to their rooms. The small group that was playing security-guard rugby chose to stand and fight.

The leader was now up again and came from McCarthy's blind side. He was larger than McCarthy and with his right hand grabbed

McCarthy's weapon. He yanked it hard, in an attempt to pull it from his holster. His left arm moved around McCarthy's neck and McCarthy felt it closing down on his airway. There was no time for fear and no time for thought. If this drunken, enraged idiot got McCarthy's gun, McCarthy's life would end on a balcony at the Le Claire Holiday Inn. The urgency of the moment was transferred into intensity. McCarthy ducked and spun under the leader's arm, breaking his grip on the gun, which stayed secured in its holster. The trained move brought McCarthy to the rear, with the leader's left arm in a rear-wristlock behind his back. McCarthy then ran the leader chest first into the wall, stunning him momentarily.

Those left standing in the hallway froze, mentally stunned by the suddenness and effectiveness of this young officer's defense. McCarthy had the leader secured against the wall and the pressure on the leader's left wrist kept him wanting to stand still for the time being. McCarthy keyed his shoulder mic and called, "10-78 (officers need assistance), 10-33 (emergency)! We're involved in a brawl!"

"Brawl? You fucking ain't seen a fuckin' brawl yet, you asshole!" growled the leader. McCarthy added pressure to the wrist, which caused the leader to move up to his tip-toes and wince. This calmed him for the moment.

"Give me your other hand! You are under arrest!" The leader slowly began to bring the right hand back toward the left one in response to the pressure and commands, but then another brave mechanic thought he saw an opening and quickly was on McCarthy from McCarthy's right side. Just as quickly, McCarthy delivered a snapping back-fist to the nose and mouth of the would-be assailant, dropping him immediately to his knees with a broken nose. This blow brought the man to his senses and he immediately turned and ran, realizing he had just attacked a cop. He also realized that this cop was going to win. He was escaping, taking the evidence of his crime, his broken nose, with him.

The movement of the back-fist caused McCarthy to loosen his grip on the leader. The leader, sensing an opening, broke away and spun quickly, putting both hands around McCarthy's throat. Once again, McCarthy sensed this man wanted to kill him. McCarthy was not about to let some drunken mechanic put his name on some marble wall. McCarthy threw an arm straight up in the air and pivoted backward and away, instantly breaking the grip of the leader. He then spun forward, driving his knee hard into the guts of the leader, doubling him over. McCarthy spun the belligerent mechanic into the floor and slipped into a figure-four leglock, applying pain at the same time he barked the command, "Your hands! Now!"

The suspect's hands shot back in the hope that the incredible pain he was feeling in his leg would stop. The cuffs snapped on, and instantaneously the suspect felt relief, but then it hit him. "I'm fucked!" he said out loud.

"No argument here," answered McCarthy, as his cuffs clicked quickly onto the leader's wrists.

By now McCarthy noticed that Carpenter was behind him, handcuffing Mr. Second-in-Command. The crowd had chosen to scatter rather than pitch in. "That was a good thing," thought McCarthy. Backup officers were now rushing up the steps toward McCarthy and Carpenter.

Months later, this case would go to trial. It would take two days of testimony, which would attack McCarthy's voracity and accuse him of overreacting and using excessive force. The defense attorney attacked McCarthy relentlessly over the facts of the case. McCarthy calmly told the story as he remembered it, which was as it had happened.

The mechanics would tell the story of an injured friend, a concerned crowd, and an overbearing, aggressive, mean-spirited McCarthy, who had lost his temper and spun out of control.

McCarthy and the other witnesses withstood the badgering and then the decision was up to the jury.

It would take a jury only thirty-three minutes to convict the mechanics.

As the courtroom cleared, the defense attorney for the mechanics approached McCarthy in the hallway. He offered his hand to the officer, and McCarthy returned the courtesy. The attorney then leaned toward McCarthy and said quietly, so that the communiqué could only be heard by the two criminal justice system antagonists, "You know, when those guys described the officer that did this, they claimed he was 6' 4". I was surprised, and they were embarrassed, to see you enter the court room all of 5' 9", 170 pounds."

"Thanks. 165," said McCarthy.

"What?" asked the puzzled attorney.

"I'm 165 pounds," repeated McCarthy.

"I'll let them know," laughed the attorney. "I'm glad your all right."

The attorney then leaned toward McCarthy and added with a whisper, "Hey, I'll deny saying this to you, but . . . way to go. I would have paid to see it."

As McCarthy left the courthouse, he realized he had won the fight on two levels. He had physically won it and legally won it, too. Everyone was convicted and no one had grounds for a suit, except for maybe him. He also realized that the attorney was just doing his job. It was nothing personal. This would help the young officer in future cases, because he would almost never take anything personal, neither when he was on the street nor on the stand. He would testify knowing he held the trump card—he held the truth. That would make him a better witness.

Mark Twain once said something like . . . the truth can get run over by a train and survive, but a lie will die of a common cold." McCarthy loved the feeling of being a "good guy." Most cops are just that, good guys. Even the women officers. They're "good guys." They all do what's sometimes the most difficult thing to do, day-in and day-out. That is, "the right thing."

An intoxicated attorney would one day confide in McCarthy that in law school he was taught to hope that, when their clients lie, they will lie as close to the truth as possible, making the case easier to defend. McCarthy would, from now on, have an advantage on the street and in court. He would always conduct himself within the law and tell the truth on the stand, even if it was difficult. He would not allow someone to bait him into becoming angry, either on the stand or on the street. Intense was acceptable, but not angry. That would not happen!

McCarthy remembered what one of his police science professors had said, "The man who angers you, conquers you." He knew that emotions can help you in a fight on the street, until you lose control of your emotions. That's when a cop loses, by being ineffective or excessive. Since the court case was merely an extension of the street fight, he realized he needed to be in control on the stand. The attorney, in those few moments in the hallway, gave McCarthy insight into the mind of a defense attorney's that he would never forget. The attorney had nothing personal against the officer. No matter how aggressively an attorney goes after an officer on the stand, the only time he wins is when the officer gets angry. The strongest approach is to stay professional and tell the truth. Then let the jury decide.

Telling the truth was very important to McCarthy. He spent twelve years in Catholic schools having this fact hammered into his young brain. He thought then that it was important to tell the truth. Now he *knew* it was important.

McCarthy learned much from the life-and-death poolside struggle at the Le Claire Holiday Inn . . . to live by the axiom, "The man who angers you, conquers you. Stay in command of your emotions."

McCarthy felt reaffirmed by the jury's decision to believe him. A jury was never needed to tell McCarthy what was true and what was not. There would be juries that would be swayed by the theatrics of a defense attorney and the lies of their clients. It would not change the face of truth, however. The truth can not be altered by a lie. The truth still exists in reality and in the mind of McCarthy. It even exists sometimes in the minds of the criminal and his attorney.

Over the years, attorneys, judges, and police officers would come to know that what McCarthy spoke was the truth, the whole truth, and nothing but the truth. He believed to lie, you would lose the most important life-and-death struggle of them all. That is to keep your honor alive. McCarthy would say in later years, "To win with a lie is how you allow your honor to die. Tell the truth, first, last, and always." McCarthy would always defend his life with honor and his honor with his life.

CHAPTER 9
LOUIE AND MARGE: ACT THREE

As soon as McCarthy finished his squad check and told dispatch he was clearing from the station, the dispatcher informed McCarthy, "255, I have a call for you. Give me a phone call to get the information."

"10-4," replied McCarthy through his collar mic, as he already was exiting his squad car to make the call from inside the station. He was instantly pumped for two reasons. He liked being busy and getting a call right out of the chute usually meant it was going to be a busy night. The second reason he was pumped was because calls that dispatch could not give out over the air were almost always interesting.

McCarthy hustled back into the station and phoned dispatch. The dispatcher told him, "A Marge Arnett wants you see her at 548 Sumner Street. She is having problems with her husband again and wants to talk to you and no one else. She thinks her husband is going to kill her. She says her husband is not there right now. Do you want another unit?"

McCarthy thought for a moment and replied, "Yeah, but have them stand by up the street, in the event the guy shows up while I'm inside. The woman's husband is Louis Arnett. He is very violent, and if she thinks he is going to kill her, then he probably is."

As McCarthy parked up the street from 548 Sumner, he scanned the area and could see the neighborhood was quiet. He wondered how many times Marge Arnett had moved, trying to find peace, trying to hide from the beast. "What a way to live," said McCarthy to himself.

As Marge answered the door, she looked nervously up and down the street. She saw the second car. McCarthy saw her concern and answered the question before it could be asked, "I wasn't sure what the problem was. That officer is here, so that I can listen to you without being interrupted."

Marge nodded and motioned for Officer McCarthy to come in. She led Dan into her neatly kept home. McCarthy thought, "I wonder how she motivates herself to keep the home so neat in the midst of such a chaotic life." Then McCarthy looked at a picture hanging on the wall, of Marge with her children. "She probably does it for them. So they have some order in their lives, and it is the one part of her life she can control," McCarthy thought to himself, as Marge motioned for him to have a seat in the living room, treating him as a friend she anxiously had been awaiting.

"Would you like a cup of coffee?" Marge asked, with a nervous smile on her face.

"No thanks. I don't drink coffee. Can you believe that, a cop that doesn't drink coffee?"

"I never heard of such a thing. Well, you're young. I'm sure if you work long enough at the job, you'll get corrupted," Marge said. When she stopped talking, McCarthy saw her lips tighten and then begin to quiver. Then she dropped her face into her hands and she began to cry quietly, but audibly.

McCarthy let her cry for a few moments, and then slowly asked, "I can see that you are upset. How can I help you tonight, Mrs. Arnett?"

"I am so afraid. I am afraid all the time. I am afraid every day. I can't live like this anymore. I thought he didn't know where I lived, but tonight I got a call . . . just breathing. It wasn't sexual. It was an angry breathing. It was him, and I think it's going to happen tonight. Can you stay tonight?" She reached over and took McCarthy by the hand.

As she leaned forward, McCarthy could not help but notice her robe fell open, revealing she wore nothing beneath it. Marge's maturity made her beauty even more striking. Now McCarthy wondered if it was fear that made her call him and only him, or was this all an act. He wondered if Marge, having dressed in this manner, while asking him to stay the night, was triggered by fear or lust. Dan wondered if he was being trusted or tempted.

He answered, "Mrs. Arnett, I cannot stay here all night, but I can take you to the women's shelter. You'll be safe there."

"No! I won't go there ever again. My children need a home. I want to stay in my home." Marge exclaimed, with a sincerity that made McCarthy feel ashamed that he thought she might be faking fear to arrange a tryst with the young officer.

McCarthy could not find the words to convince Margaret Arnett to leave her home tonight. He then asked her to dial 911 immediately if she heard anything at all that was suspicious. McCarthy told her that he would drive by the house as often as he could. The officer told Mrs. Arnett to turn the outside light on if she thought her husband was around and the phone did not work. This was the best compromise plan that could be worked out. "I am standing my ground. I will not run again," she proclaimed resolutely, albeit recklessly.

McCarthy left the home and told the dispatcher to notify him immediately about any 911 hang-ups, as soon as they came in. Dispatch could continue with the trace, but in the meantime they should tell him about it.

McCarthy pulled his squad up to the side of his backup officer's squad. McCarthy was pleased to see that it was Randy Stammos.

"What's up?" Randy asked, in his no-more-words-than-necessary style.

"She thinks her husband is going to come and kill her tonight, but she won't leave the house. I explained to her that we can't sit on the house all night, and we can't stay with her in the house. Randy, can you hustle over here with me if there is a 911 hang-up, or just hustle over if I call you? I think she's right about her husband." Dan did not have to wait long for an answer.

"Fuckin'-A," answered Randy. With Randy, fuckin' A was yes with an attitude. Fuckin'-A meant anything Randy wanted it to mean. If a pretty girl walked by, he would change the emphasis, "Fuckin'-AAA!" and that would mean, "That girl is sure pretty." If a woman passed who would not look good to a bachelor finishing his thirteenth beer at bar time, "FUCKIN' A" would accurately describe his dissatisfaction with her appearance.

While entering a bar fight and seeing the 6' 3" 240-pound trouble-maker tossing people around, Randy would quietly pause and whisper in awe, "fuckin' A" , which could be determined to mean, "Sometimes, when dealt with the enormities of life in all its facets, a man can feel so inadequate to live up to the responsibilities that he faces on a day-to-day basis," or, "Let's go tighten this Hulk up, before he hurts us real bad."

To Randy, fuckin' A saved time and usually said it all. People always somehow knew what he meant. Tonight it meant that he would be there for McCarthy.

Three hours later, a dark, foreboding figure stood outside Marge's apartment, leaning against a large maple tree. The man stayed expertly hidden in the shadow of the large tree. The cigarette's red ember was all that gave his position away, as he took one last toke from his Marlboro. He inhaled deeply, then dropped the cigarette to the ground as he exhaled.

His first step toward the apartment expertly stomped out the red ember, as he headed for the apartment like a man with a mission. He did have a mission. He knew now, at this moment, he could do what he came here to do. He was going to stomp out the red ember of life that existed in the heart of his "bitch-wife."

"Tonight," Louie Arnett thought, "I will kill this woman."

The knock at the door sent Marge's heart into her throat. She knew his knock like she knew the faces of her children. She knew she should not go near the door. She could not help herself. Even though it's a cliché, she was drawn to it like a moth to the flame. Domestic violence happens so often that the actions and reactions of the offenders and victims would almost be cliché, if not for the terrible tragedy that is the end result of this violence. It would be easy for someone outside looking in to say, "Don't go to the door. Call the police." In much the same way that the viewer of a horror movie wants to tell the baby sitter, "Don't check out that noise in the basement."

The big difference is that domestic violence is real drama played out nightly in thousands of homes across the United States. Most perpetrators in abusive relationships hold a Svengali-like control over those abused. Many abusers have programmed their victims to respond to them in a certain way, much like one of Pavlov's dogs. The victims often are truly helpless in their presence. Domestic violence is all about power and control.

Arnett knocked on the door, "Honey. Come to the door," said Louie, in his Prince Charming voice.

"Please, go away, Louie. You're not supposed to be here. The police were here earlier, and they will arrest you, if they see you," answered Marge, as she moved quietly toward the phone.

"Sweetheart, I haven't had anything to drink for a week. I have decided I am leaving the state. I'm getting treatment, and then I'm not coming back until I get my head on straight. I know I've done you terribly wrong. I want to make that right, but I have to get myself straightened out first. I have scraped up some cash, and I want to give it to you before I leave. Please open the door . . . just a crack, so I can leave this money for you and the kids. Then I'm out of here." Louie pleaded, with his voice laced with what sounded like genuine sincerity. "I love you, Marge. I think that is part of my problem. I love you so much, it has not been healthy. I know that now. Please open the door."

Arnett sounded so believable to Marge. She walked to the door to open it. Before she opened the door, however, she turned on the signal light and then picked up the phone. She did these things without thinking, as if part of her was struggling to stay alive and fighting an all-out mental battle with the part of her that was carrying her toward certain destruction.

She dialed 911, as she opened the door for her Prince Charming; but instead she found only the beast! The door swung open as if knocked in by a whirlwind. He was on her instantly, tearing the phone from the wall.

As she was knocked back, he slammed the door and locked it behind him. He knocked her backward on the couch and told her, "If I can't have you, no one will." He hovered over her, enjoying the power and control he held over her at this moment. He relished the fear in her eyes and was going to make this moment last.

Three hours had passed and, in between calls for service, Officer Dan McCarthy drove by Marge's house seven times. On the eighth pass, McCarthy saw it. The outside light was on.

McCarthy grabbed the radio, his heart pounding. "255, send backup right away to 548 Sumner Street. The light is on."

"255, be advised we were just about to call you. We received a 911 hang-up. There was a fight going and a woman yelled for help."

"255, I'm out at the residence," McCarthy said, as he hung up his radio. McCarthy then undid his seat belt, shut down his lights, swung open his door and quietly shut it, all in one, smooth motion.

"I'm 10-23 (arrival) at 548 Sumner," Stammos said. He pulled right behind McCarthy. McCarthy knew that, since Stammos had arrived so quickly, he also had to have been checking the area.

Both officers ran to the residence. Before knocking on the door, they peered through a break in the curtains on the picture window next to the door. Upon looking inside, Stammos and McCarthy saw Arnett wielding a large butcher knife. He was holding the knife overhead in a stance reminiscent of the movie *Psycho*. Marge was sprawled backward across the couch below the beast. She was bleeding badly from her nose, but Louie was almost ready to do his worst. Arnett was about to make good his promise that he made to Marge often, "If I can't have you, no one will."

"FUCKIN' A," said Randy. Then, as if this statement was the signal to activate a predetermined plan, both officers moved as one. They drew their weapons simultaneously. McCarthy front-kicked the door near the lock, causing the door to burst open and slam against the far wall.

"Police. Drop the knife!" yelled the officers in unison.

As the door opened, Louie froze. He mentally was unprepared for the suddenness of this interruption. All the color rushed immediately from Louie's face. He looked like a deer on the highway, caught in the headlights of an oncoming Mack truck.

After a moment of fear-induced indecision, Louie dropped the knife. His hands went straight up in the air and he began to cry, "Oh God, don't shoot. I wasn't really going to hurt her. Please don't shoot."

"Get down on the floor. Do it now!" ordered Dan McCarthy. Arnett moved immediately, inspired by the thought that tonight he had decided to kill, not to be killed. Arnett surmised by the look of his captors, that they could both kill. Louie was covered by Randy, while Dan approached.

Louie looked into Stammos's eyes and determined he was looking into the eyes of a man who not only could kill, but quite possibly hoped that Louie would do something that would give him the opportunity *to* kill. Louie was also a man who could kill and recognized the look. Louie broke off eye contact with Stammos, dropped his shoulders, and dropped his eyes toward the floor like a wild dog that was showing proper respect for his pack's alpha leader.

Just before reaching the cowering bully, McCarthy holstered his weapon. He then kicked the knife out of reach and dumped Louie facedown on the couch. The handcuffs clicked expertly onto Louie's two wrists almost simultaneously. McCarthy had practiced the skill of "speed cuffing," and could apply handcuffs on both wrists of any suspect in about one-half second in training. This time, the cuffs were both on, immediately upon contact.

Louie contemplated his predicament and knew instantly the mistake that he had made. He had relished the moment too long. He wanted to enjoy the look of terror on his wife's face while she knew that the knife was going to be buried deeply into her chest. He wanted her to know she was about to die and that her "loving" husband was going to kill her. Louie wanted her to have time to think how painful it was going to be, and then he wanted to make the death painful. Experienced homicide investigators will tell you that when a homicide victim experiences overkill, it is usually done by someone who formerly loved the victim. This incomplete homicide would have been one described as overkill.

"If only I would not have relished the moment so long," Louie said quietly to himself into the couch as he lay face down.

McCarthy heard the statement as a garbled mumble, as he safety-locked the handcuffs, so that they would not get any tighter during transport. McCarthy and Stammos had not only arrived in time to save Marge, but they kept Louie from committing a homicide; and instead he was being handcuffed for a relatively minor felony. This would ultimately lead to a plea bargain on a pocketful of misdemeanors. Arnett would be sentenced on all his charges to a lengthy probation and one year in jail, with work-release privileges, courtesy of Judge "Alice in Wonderland."

Ironically, Marge, who was still under the spell of this man, would approve of the plea bargain. She also did not want her children to bear the stigma of having a father in prison. Louie would be ordered, as a condition of his probation, to have no contact with Mrs. Margaret Arnett. Louie would get one more chance to reconcile his life, before landing in prison. If either of these vicious attacks would have been launched against a stranger, Louie would already be in prison. Because they were directed at his wife, somehow in the eyes of the civilized world it made it much less serious.

Yes, Louis Arnett told the judge, he was being treated for alcohol and was attending an anger-management program. He wanted to be a "better person" and "right the wrongs" he had done in his life. He pleaded to be given one more chance out of prison. He even used his Prince Charming voice in the courtroom. The judge gave him the chance Louie asked for. These pleadings were music to Judge Alice's ears.

After a light tap on the wrist, considering the circumstances, Judge Alice expressed hope for Louie's redemption but ended her speech with this stern warning, "If you come into my court one more time for anything, I will send you directly to prison!"

"Your Honor, I promise you'll not see me again," Louie said, with a believable sincerity. As he turned away from the Judge, Louie's Prince Charming façade faded into the persona his children and wife knew only too well . . . the beast.

CHAPTER 10
LOUIE AND MARGE: THE CURTAIN FALLS

It had been a year since Marge Arnett had been saved by McCarthy and Stammos. Her intermediate life had been uneventful. She seemed to be out of her life with Louie for good. The divorce had been final now for six months. She was seeing a man she had met at her new job.

The kids were clearly happier than ever. She always thought, "What will we do without their father? How will we make it financially without him?" She could now see that they all thrived without living day-in and day-out with a Jekyll and Hyde in the house.

The man she was seeing was the opposite of Louie. He was a professional and a gentleman. They had been dating for about a month, but she still had not spent the night with him. She was hesitant to get that involved with anyone yet. She felt that when she was ready, however, Boyd was the man for her.

Marge and Boyd had gone to dinner and a movie with the kids. The kids had just been put to bed. The couple sat down on the couch, cuddling close like a couple of teenagers. Boyd's eyes met Marge's and there was a long silence as their lips moved closer together. Then they kissed. Boyd's hand slipped gently to Marge's breast. Marge instantly took hold of Boyd's hand in protest, but then pressed it closer. She felt passion's furnace burning, as her heart pounded. Her nipples hardened, and once again she felt her womanly orchid blossoming, as if she once again was in the spring of her life. She knew she loved Boyd. She wanted to be with him for the rest of her life. He was a real man. He would never hurt her. Boyd would always protect her.

Tonight, she would make love with the man she loved. Tonight, she would be one with Boyd. She parted her legs shyly, feeling like a schoolgirl on prom night, and she took Boyd's hand and placed it between them. He immediately felt the moist welcome his beloved's sacred garden had prepared for him. He was moved to an overwhelming love for this tortured, sweet creature. He knew how hard this was for her. He would not let her down. Not now. Not ever.

CRASH! Boyd, who had experienced no violence in his life up to this point, froze in his place, but Marge recognized the noise immediately. The noise brought her to her feet instantly, but it was too late. It was the beast. He stood before them, a pistol in each hand.

"I have one for each of you cheating bastards!" Louie roared, holding the guns out at his sides. Boyd recognized immediately that something had to be done or they would die. He made up for his initial shock, and yelled, "Run Marge!" as he tackled Louie.

Initially the attack caught Louie unprepared. He hit his ass hard on the cheaply carpeted and unpadded floor. He recovered immediately, though, as the two rolled about on the floor. Louie managed to get to his feet again, but Boyd took him down again, gallantly fighting to save Marge and the kids. When the two landed, the weight of the two desperate men broke an end table into many pieces. Boyd took hold of Louie's wrists, desperately trying to gain control of the guns. Boyd was fighting to live and Louie was fighting to kill. The motive for each was life and death.

Marge ran to try to help Boyd. She stomped on one of Louie's wrists, until the gun fell out of Louie's hand. She gripped it like a gun fighter and thought of shooting Louie. She could not do it. She was not a killer. Not all humans can kill other humans—even when their lives depend on it. The jackal had married a lamb.

Marge then ran to the door and threw the gun as far as she could. She returned to the life or death struggle. When she reached the two men, she saw that the man she had learned to hate was on top and was pushing the muzzle of the gun hard against the chest of the man she learned to love.

"Oh God, please don't!" Marge heard herself scream. Marge watched the scene, as if she was viewing it frame-by-frame through a view-master.

Then the gun exploded. The report seemed to last for seconds, and the flash set Boyd's shirt on fire temporarily, as the bullet penetrated Boyd's guiltless heart. In that moment, Louie cut short Boyd and Marge's happily-ever-after.

Without hesitation Louie turned the gun toward Marge and yelled, "Like I said, bitch, if I can't have you, no one can. Now you and I both will die, and this is all your fault."

Marge dropped to her knees, covered the back of her head with both hands, and bent forward. This time, Louie did not waste time relishing the moment. The gun exploded a second time. The bullet tore through both of Marge's hands and skimmed across the surface of her skull, leaving a furrow. It lodged just beneath her scapula. For Marge, everything went dark immediately.

McCarthy had just cleared from a call. An elderly lady had complained that someone had stolen a lawn ornament. The lawn ornament was a flat wooden figure of the backside of a fat, little old lady bent over, tending to the garden. The little old lady (the complainant) felt strongly that the little old lady (the lawn ornament) was pilfered by "college students." She wanted to know why the La Claire police did not stake out her neighborhood, because this was the second lawn ornament lost in the neighborhood this week.

McCarthy had just begun rolling through the neighborhood to see if he could find the discarded ornament, when the call came in, "255, 10-33 (emergency) traffic."

"255, go ahead."

"Respond to 548 Sumner. A Mr. Louis Arnett is on the phone. He says he just shot his wife and her boyfriend; and if the police arrive before he gets the nerve to shoot himself, he says he will shoot the first officer on the scene. Use extreme caution."

McCarthy thought the last three words were unnecessary. McCarthy was very close, and less than a minute after receiving the call, he was calling, "255 is 10-23 (at the scene)?"

McCarthy removed the Benelli semiautomatic shotgun from the locking rack in the patrol car and immediately charged the weapon, causing the round setting on the rail to feed into the chamber. McCarthy clicked the safety off and approached the house, trying to keep a large tree between the house and him for as long as possible. As he scanned the front of the house, the front door swung open quickly and Louie emerged.

Louie held a stainless steel Model 66 Smith & Wesson revolver in his right hand. Before McCarthy could say a word, Arnett yelled so loud that his voiced echoed throughout the quiet neighborhood. "They're dead. I did it, and fuck them both!" Louie yelled, in his whiskey-inspired dialect.

"This is the La Claire Police. Put the weapon on the ground!" shouted McCarthy, as he sighted the shotgun on the center of the murderer's chest.

"Fuck you. You ain't gettin' out of this so easy. I'm a taxpayer and you're going to earn the money I pay you tonight, asshole!" As he started this sentence, he began to walk slowly toward McCarthy, who was now behind the tree, with only part of his head and the muzzle of his shotgun visible to Louie.

"Stop or I'll shoot!" ordered McCarthy.

Arnett stopped for a moment, still holding a death-grip on the revolver.

"Go for it!" laughed Arnett. "You'd be doing me a favor. I'm going to hell tonight; if you don't shoot, I'm going to send you on ahead."

"Don't do it. Put the gun down and we'll talk. I don't want to shoot you, Mr. Arnett, and you can't want to shoot me. You don't even know me. Maybe if you get to know me, then you might want to shoot me, but right now you have no reason. Come on, let's talk."

"Talk's cheap, kid. I've got nothing left to say. Here's a little something to remember me by . . ."

McCarthy saw the weapon moving, but not toward him. Instead, Arnett moved the gun to his own temple. The shot was muffled and the result was instant. It was something to remember him by, all right. McCarthy would be able to play back the picture in his head anytime he thought of it for the rest of his life. He could retrace the graphic path the bullet took, in and out of Arnett's head. He would remember the pink mist that sprayed out of the opposite side of Louie's head. He would flash back to the image every time he would turn a sprinkler on in the summer. He would be able to see Arnett's body slowly crumple like a house of cards, already lifeless as it hit the pavement.

McCarthy approached Arnett and checked for a pulse, as he called for an ambulance. By now Carpenter and Compton were arriving on the scene. McCarthy wondered what kept them. He felt as if he had been alone a long time, when in reality he had been there for 56 seconds. It was 56 seconds, but it seemed like hours. Compton and McCarthy entered the house. McCarthy quickly checked for a pulse on Mrs. Arnett. He thought, as he did, that it was hopeless, seeing the blood oozing copiously from the wound in her head. He was shocked. Not only was there a pulse, but it was strong and she was breathing.

Compton checked Boyd, and it was clear that he was gone. He had died the death of a brave man. Possibly the struggle with Boyd had shook Louie enough to cause him to miss making the killing shot he had hoped for when he shot at Marge. Boyd had not died in vain. He had saved the woman he loved. Marge was still alive.

McCarthy always carried Cling and four-by-four bandages with him. He could never quite shake free of the EMT in him. He applied them quickly to the wound on Marge's head, asking Compton to hold pressure. After bandaging her head, he moved on to Marge's severely maimed hands. McCarthy put a rolled up Cling in each hand, before bandaging, to keep the hands in a natural position. Her wounds were severe, but it appeared to McCarthy that Mrs. Arnett would survive.

When the ambulance personnel arrived, they loaded Mrs. Arnett into the ambulance.

Compton told Carpenter to stay with her and write down any statements she made, "Word-for-word. You got it?" directed the sergeant emphatically.

"Yes, sir, Sergeant," Carpenter answered, already following the stretcher out of the house. The Arnett boys were found in their bedroom closet. The older one was holding the younger one. They were old beyond their years. They had witnessed more violence in their few years on earth than most people witness in a lifetime. Their mother would physically recover, because she was a strong, determined woman. She would spend the rest of her life trying to bring normalcy back into the life of her boys. The odds were against them, but she was determined. She would need therapy for a long time. The therapy was not for the trauma of what had happened to her. She would always feel responsible for Boyd's death. If only she would not have fallen in love with Boyd. If only she would not have hoped that she might find peace and happiness with such a kind man. If only she could have shot the beast herself. If not for these "if only's," Boyd would still be alive. This would be the thought that would hound her the rest of her life.

After seeing the scene, McCarthy felt guilty for trying to talk Arnett out of ending his life. He felt guilty about not shooting Louie the night he had the knife. He felt angry about the system that kept giving Arnett probation and jail time, when Arnett belonged in prison. He wished Judge Alice could be there so he could show her the carnage that she did not cause but could have prevented.

Finally, though, he would realize that there was only one person at fault here: Louis Arnett. He was a husband who had looked upon his wife and family as his property. He had beaten and traumatized them, while he lived. He would haunt them after his death. The culture that nearly tolerated violence in the home and a judge, who felt more sympathy for suspects than victims, were his unwitting facilitators.

McCarthy would discover that Louie was not so unique. There are Louie's that live in every community and on many streets. Although they don't all kill, many are capable of it. They put many women and children in fear of their lives day-in-and-day-out. They are "domestic terrorists." They are more likely to kill someone in your neighborhood than any bomb from any follower of "Jihad." Like the Jihadist, they target the innocents. They terrorize their wives and children. Sometimes, to all others around them, they show the face of kindness and compassion, which actually hides the heart of the beast.

CHAPTER 11
THE REAL WORLD

After the Arnett tragedy, McCarthy came home and found himself unable to sleep. He could not stop replaying in his mind's eye the last few moments of Louie's life. He could remember the ironic smile on Arnett's face as he said, "Talk's cheap, kid. Here's something to remember me by."

The smile then turned suddenly grim, and McCarthy could see Arnett squeeze the trigger slowly, ever so slowly. Then came the explosion of the weapon. He could see the bullet enter the temple and a tuft of hair pop from the top of the head. The small divot of hair bounced on the ground only slightly before Arnett's lifeless body did. Sleep could not come with this surreal movie being played over and over again in the young man's mind.

Dan gave up on sleep and left the bedroom. His wife, Victoria, was in the process of trying to feed the children breakfast. Nate saw his dad awake and burst out of his chair, "Are you done sleeping, Daddy? Can we go to the park?" He was a four-year-old ball of fun. He was his dad's best buddy, bar none.

"You bet, Skate! If you help Mom with Christa, we will all go to the park," was the hoped-for response that came.

"Dan, you need your sleep. This will mess you up for the whole week." Victoria was always watching out for her husband. She never wanted him to be a cop, but she finally relented. Now she was bound and determined to make sure the life, the hours, and the job did not get the best of him. She wanted the best for her husband, the kids, and herself.

Christa smiled from her highchair, where she was wearing as much of her breakfast as she had eaten. She was a year-and-a-half-old, and McCarthy could not picture that this delightful little princess was headed for the "terrible twos." How could anything terrible come from a face that held such a beautiful and constant smile as hers?

He crouched down next to his little girl and said, "Come on, Christa, say it for me. Daddy's Gir-rell," he said in a sing-song voice. Christa could copy almost anything an adult said, syllable for syllable.

She mimicked perfectly, "Daddy's Gir-rell." This always brought an approving laugh and hug from her dad. He pulled her out of the highchair and immediately Christa shoved a piece of soggy toast into his mouth; McCarthy took a bite, as if it were a piece of French pastry. After seeing it was so tasty, Christa finished the rest.

After breakfast, the four walked across the street to the park. They lived in a quiet residential neighborhood. They had just managed to scrape enough money together for a down payment on their three-bedroom ranch house. The house was comfortable, but it was the neighborhood that sold the house. It was definitely the respite that McCarthy needed.

Nate ran ahead with the dog, a purebred Dalmatian that could have been named Pongo, but was actually named Jazz, who loved to run. It was four legs, a head, and two lungs. It was poetry in motion to see this sleek, muscled, black-spotted running machine in full-stride. The Dalmatian was a breed that at one time in history was a "carriage dog." It would run stride-for-stride with the horses and warn its master in the carriage, if highwaymen lay in wait—a fitting match for McCarthy. McCarthy loved to run, and he was always looking to outsmart the "highwaymen" of his day.

When the giggling group arrived at the park, Nate headed directly to the swings. McCarthy got an incredible workout, keeping his son's swing as high as Nate liked. It was as high as McCarthy liked it also, since the higher he went, the louder Nate laughed. That laugh was the medicine McCarthy needed right now.

Victoria held Christa in her lap while McCarthy pushed. Then Jazz began to bark, which was all part of the ritual. The dog felt less like a dog and more like a member of the family. When the family was swinging, Jazz felt he should be swinging, too.

Dan then picked up the dog and got into a swing. Soon the entire family was in motion. He looked over at Victoria. She had given up a job in banking to be at home with the kids. It was not what most "modern women" did, but McCarthy's little family benefited immensely by her revolutionary act, contrary to the women's movement. McCarthy looked at her smiling face. He never ceased to be moved by her beauty, which was only enhanced by the tender way she cared for their little family. "I'm a lucky man," McCarthy thought to himself. "May I never forget it."

Victoria McCarthy was a blonde Nordic beauty whose smile was a gift she gave freely. She passed the smile on to her daughter. Her light blonde hair, she passed on to her son. As they all laughed and swung, McCarthy thought about the Arnetts. He could not understand why Louie would bring such pain and suffering to his family, when all this joy was just a walk to the park away.

"Did you have a rough night, Sweetheart?" Vicki asked. She could not help but notice her husband had become suddenly quiet and serious, even as he swung.

"Yeah, rough." His answer was halting and told it all, "Love you."

"I bet you say that to all the women you've married and have had two of your children," said Victoria, who began to kick higher as she spoke, causing Christa to giggle even louder.

Jazz suddenly began to bark and wriggle to get free. Nate was off the swing and at a dead run heading toward the merry-go-round. This would require more pushing for Dad. As Dan ran toward the merry-go-round, he thought again how truly lucky he was. He was determined not to let the sadness he faced in the surreal world of a cop, infect the real world he lived in.

"Daddy, make it go faster," pleaded Nate.

When the kids in the park saw that McCarthy was about to give Nate a ride, they jumped off the monkey bars, hopped out of the sandbox, and sprinted to the merry-go-round. Dan McCarthy was famous at this park for his merry-go-round rides. This one would prove to be no disappointment for the kids either.

Two hours at the park was just what the doctor ordered. McCarthy crawled back into bed after wearing himself out. Victoria tucked him in and kissed him gently on the lips.

Nate jumped up on the bed and kissed his dad's cheek, quickly reciting, "Night, Dad. Love you, Dad," and then shot off to his next adventure.

Christa was lifted to the bed by her mother to give her dad a kiss, and for the first time on her own sang, "Daddy's Gir-rell." She was rewarded by a hug, a kiss, and a tickle. Jazz, still thinking he was one of the family, licked Dan on the cheek and nibbled on his ear, whining constantly his love for his master, until Dan had pushed the dog away, pleading, "Enough already!"

Victoria turned the fan on high, which was how a night worker keeps the noises of the day out of his room. The hum was soothing, relaxing, and the act of turning it on, for Dan, had been a loving ritual Victoria performed on a daily basis. There was love in all of this, and McCarthy felt it. He dozed off, with thoughts of his family on his mind. The dreams generated by the day in the park won the battle for McCarthy's mind, replacing the nightmares generated by the night at the Arnett's.

McCarthy was young and had already learned what some people never live long enough to realize. He had already learned that, in this world and probably the next, his family was the best and most important thing in his life. They gave him balance, perspective, satisfaction, and were his reason for living. Victoria came back into the room to give him one more unsupervised kiss. It was warm, soft and, to McCarthy, like her . . . sheer perfection.

Victoria looked into his eyes and asked, "Is there anything you want to tell me?"

McCarthy thought for a bit, and asked, "Do you remember the story of the Garden of Eden, where Eve and Adam were thrown out after they ate the apple?"

"Yes?" Victoria replied, in an inquisitive tone.

"What if they were never thrown out? What if Earth is the Garden of Eden and most men are too narrow-minded to see it?" asked Dan.

"I don't see a Garden of Eden," added Victoria. "I see a heavily mortgaged three-bedroom ranch with a lawn filled with runaway crab grass. How can a guy who works a job like you do, stay so positive? That theory takes even positive thinking too far," scoffed Victoria.

"You can't see it, because you got stuck married to me; I, on the other hand, have been given you. I definitely got the better end of the deal." Dan then kissed her one more time and laid his head back onto the pillow. With thoughts of the park, the children, Victoria, and his own personal Garden of Eden, McCarthy slept the sleep of the exhausted.

McCarthy would learn that he had the tools he needed to cope, always at his disposal. Those tools were his family. He would never forget that he needed to put things in perspective. He had little control over the world at large, but he did have control over his personal world. Even if the world at large was a mess, his world was pretty spectacular. He would never forget that he had to work in one world, but he lived in the other.

Like any young professional, McCarthy wanted to be successful in his chosen field. He realized that due to the job, the system, and constantly bearing witness to the ugliness of the world, some cops become bitter and cynical. McCarthy would learn that to be successful in his field, he would have to maintain a view of the world from the proper perspective.

McCarthy would grow to grasp that there were some things that he could not change, and there were some that he could. He would have to constantly strive to identify what he could not change and not let the frustration of this take away his ability to recognize the things that could be changed and the desire to change them.

Most of all, Dan McCarthy would know the difference between the surreal world where a cop patrols and the real world that he lives in. As much as possible, they must not collide. Try as a cop might, he or she is not always able to keep them apart.

CHAPTER 12
A COP'S CHRISTMAS STORY

It was December 23rd and Dan's wife, Victoria, felt it was not Christmas unless the family did some shopping together. She was a very efficient shopper and really had all the shopping done by the day before Christmas Eve, but she was a young wife and mother bound on creating Christmas family traditions. Christmas shopping as a family was to be one of them.

McCarthy was as thrilled about a shopping trip as most husbands, but he liked doing almost anything with the kids. Dan felt the children made everything fun. Nate and Christa were special. Nate was walking next to his little sister. She had just picked out a pair of socks for her grandpa and a jar of gift jelly for her grandma. She was proud of her choice, and felt she had chosen wisely. Nate loved to torment his sister in ways that did not hurt her, but succeeded in entertaining him.

McCarthy was nibbling on cashews and sipping a Pepsi, while Nate kept reaching for the jelly, telling Christa, "I want some. I'm hungry." She would jerk away, indignantly holding the socks and jam tightly to her chest, replying, "No! Don't touch-a me, Nafun."

For her size, the socks and jam were quite a load, but she insisted on carrying them. McCarthy could not find the proper time to step in and be the good father, because he had a hard time being stern at the same time as he was being so entertained. Victoria had stepped away from her "three" kids to pick out some wrapping paper.

Dan found a bench that was open in the crowded mall and sat down, while the kids were allowed to peruse the highly decorated section of the mall. They were watching the many intricate moving figures in the Santa's Village display. Nate and Christa were back to being best friends again, which they were most of the time, and McCarthy was watching Christa's face light up every time one elf, who had accidentally been wrapped in a present by another, would pop out of the package.

As McCarthy watched, a figure to his right caught his attention. As he focused on the leather-clad perennial criminal, McCarthy's heart began to beat harder and faster.

Billy Mitchell had gotten out of prison about one month earlier and already he was wanted for a string of burglaries. He had burglarized four churches. After stealing the cash and gold he could carry, he would leave his bizarre calling card. He would defecate on the altar inside each church. When a security tape from one of the burglaries was played at line-up, McCarthy was able to identify him immediately. McCarthy was surprised that he was out of prison so soon. Due to his unique MO, Mitchell had been dubbed "The Holy Shitter."

Mitchell was wanted on multiple felonies and now McCarthy had that wanted felon standing fifty feet away. McCarthy then realized he could not leave his children. He walked quickly over to the kids and took them by the hand, "Come on kids, I need your help." Since the whole night had been an adventure, they happily came along, excited to find out what was next.

McCarthy took the children over to the closest service counter and asked to use the phone. Immediately, McCarthy called 911 and Hix answered. "Hix, this is Dan McCarthy. I'm at the east Towne Mall outside Sam Goodie's. I am watching Billy Mitchell right now, and he has outstanding warrants for burglary and parole violation on him."

"Where is he right now?" asked Hix seriously.

"He's inside Sam Goodie's. It looks like he's staying for a bit. How close do you have someone?" queried the nervous father of two.

"I only have one unit available and that's Dooley. He's close," answered Hix.

"I'll stand by and point him out for Dooley," McCarthy said, as he made a face at his children, who were watching their Dad intently.

After hanging up, McCarthy identified himself to the lady at the service counter. "Ma'am, I'm Officer Dan McCarthy of the La Claire Police Department," he explained quietly, as he unfolded his wallet, showing his badge to the startled mall employee. "Can I leave my kids here for a few minutes? There is something I have to do."

"Certainly, officer. Is everything all right?" she asked, with concern in her voice.

"It should be, but please keep them here." McCarthy then turned to Nate and Christa, "Nate, hold your sister's hand and stay right here at the counter. Christa, stay with your brother. Daddy will be right back." Both children seemed to understand the importance of this request, and

McCarthy wondered if he was doing the right thing, as he walked to an area just outside Sam Goodie's to wait for Dooley.

McCarthy wasn't there for more than three minutes, when Dooley appeared at the mall entrance. McCarthy met Dooley and asked, "Do you know Mitchell?"

"Yeah, I've dealt with him before, but I don't know if I'd recognize him on sight," Dooley reported.

"How far away is your backup?" asked Dan McCarthy.

"Everyone is tied up. It's just you and me buddy," said Dooley.

As this conversation was taking place, Mitchell exited Sam Goodie's. He then saw Dooley, and quickly his head snapped back and away, as he tried to look nonchalant. He was now headed for the main exit of the mall.

McCarthy did not need to signal to Dooley. By using the telepathy that develops between cops, Dooley knew the man he was looking for was heading his way. Dooley cut off his retreat, stating, "Sir, I'd like to talk with you a minute, please."

McCarthy circled to the rear, making escape nearly impossible. McCarthy looked back at the service counter, where his children stood watching. Nate was still holding his sister's hand.

"What the hell am I doing?" thought McCarthy. "This is crazy. I'm not armed, I have no radio, I have no handcuffs." McCarthy's attention returned to Mitchell.

"What can I help you with officer . . . sir," Mitchell replied, in the courteous manner of a man just out of prison.

"You are Billy Mitchell?" Dooley stated and asked at the same time.

Picking up on the uncertainty, Mitchell laughed and quipped, "I'm Zach Mitchell, Billy's brother. I get this all the time. He's my evil twin. He gets in trouble and people always think I'm him. I have some identification here . . ." He began to search for a wallet in the manner McCarthy had learned to be wary of. It was the diversionary search.

McCarthy motioned to Dooley, indicating this was indeed Billy Mitchell. It was at this point that Mitchell noticed McCarthy for the first time. The recognition was written all over his face, and Mitchell knew his charade was up. Instantly he bolted and was caught by the arm by McCarthy; Mitchell's own momentum was redirected, taking him into the wall and stunning him momentarily.

McCarthy placed Mitchell in a wristlock, and instinctively reached for his handcuffs, but they were not there. By now, Dooley had quickly moved to the left side and placed the left arm behind Mitchell's back. Just as it appeared the arrest was going to be made almost without a hitch, another leather-clad figure appeared, yelling, "Get your mother-fucking hands off my brother!"

The man, Zach Mitchell, looked just like Billy and was immediately onto Dooley's back. Zach spun Dooley off Billy. Zach immediately stepped into a boxer's stance and was bouncing on his toes, doing his best impression of Mohammed Ali. McCarthy didn't hesitate to push off Billy, and after he had, Dan delivered a full-power, front-thrusting kick to Zach's belly. It knocked Zach back, doubling him up briefly, but Zach then just stood back up with even more resolve.

In these moments, Billy chose to run and was putting this plan into action, as he headed back into the mall. Dooley was already occupied. He shot a double-leg takedown on Zach, who was already on his way to the ground in Dooley's grasp.

Without much thought, like a beagle after a rabbit, Dan pursued Billy Mitchell. Billy had started his run slightly off balance and wasted time to turn around to see if he was being followed. At the same time as he did this, McCarthy hit him in the area of the waist, sending Billy sprawling hard onto the floor. McCarthy immediately moved into his favorite ground-control hold, the leglock. This hold caused no lasting ill effects but was very painful and nearly useless to put up resistance, when properly applied. Mitchell soon discovered, after a bit of initial squirming, that it was indeed properly applied. Dan reached once more instinctively for his handcuffs and once more was reminded that he had none.

"Stop resisting! I am a police officer! You are under arrest!" McCarthy said with authority. It was said as much for the sake of the crowd as it was for Billy. Billy may have stopped squirming out of respect for the authority of McCarthy or the effectiveness of the hold. More likely, however, he stopped squirming out of embarrassment. What soon became apparent to Dan McCarthy was that either the fright of the moment, or the double-stunning he took during the arrest process, had caused an accident. Billy must have had another church burglary planned for that evening, because when he was taken down by McCarthy, Billy had dropped a fresh load in his pants.

Now, since McCarthy had no handcuffs or radio, Billy sat in this position for what seemed an hour. In reality, it was more like three to five minutes. Time is distorted during times of uncertainty and also when you are subjected to horrific odors for long periods of time. McCarthy hoped that none of the crowd gathering would think he was the source of the odor. Eventually, Officer Jared Jackson excitedly pushed his way through the gawking crowd and paused to compute what was happening.

"I need cuffs on Billy!" panted Dan, as he added more pressure on the hold, in response to Mitchell's renewed attempt to squirm away before help arrived. Jared handcuffed Billy, and Dan took the opportunity to tell him, "OK, Billy. The fight is over. You have a right to remain silent . . ."

"You got a right to kiss my fucking pearly white ass!" interrupted Mitchell, angry as he realized he would be in jail for Christmas.

"No thanks, Billy. Anything you say can be used against you. You have a right to an attorney."

"My attorney can suck my dick!" yelled Mitchell, to the dismay of one parent, who had young twin girls in tow. The twins both looked at each other and covered their faces tightly, trying vainly to contain the laughter brought on by the dirtiest language they had ever heard used in front of their mother. Each child's attempt to not laugh thwarted the efforts of the other, and both simultaneously burst out in a giddy, childish laugh that seemed to enrage their mother. She spun both children around, and they covered their mouths to hide their laughter. It was right to try to hide the laughter, because their shocked mother led them away from the scene, chiding McCarthy for staging such a display in front of children at a mall during Christmas.

Billy and Zach were both led out of the mall to Dooley's and Jackson's squads. They had both calmed down—Zach, because he could not believe what he had done and now had come to his senses. Billy calmed down, because he realized he was a grown, sober man, and he had just shit his pants in front of about a hundred people. He wanted to get to jail ten minutes ago.

After placing Billy in the squad, Jackson returned to McCarthy. With his face distorted in disgust, he asked McCarthy, "Did he . . ."

"He most definitely did," answered McCarthy.

"I think we'll have to rename this guy. He should be the Unholy Shitter. That is some unholy shit in that man's pants. Thanks McCarthy!" Jackson exclaimed, in a sarcastic tone. "You don't get a Christmas card from me this year," Jared added, rubbing his watering eyes.

"Merry Christmas to you, too, Jackson," McCarthy said with a laugh.

"Did you hit him that hard or did prison life just loosen up his sphincter?" asked Dooley.

"You know, I'll just ask him." said Jackson. "That will be an ice breaker I'll use, when we interview him."

"I've got to get back to my shopping. I will do the paperwork on the arrest after I take the family home. Contact Sgt. Hopkins. The burglaries are his investigation. Thanks, Dooley. Thanks, Jackson," McCarthy said, giving each a firm, sincere handshake. "Merry Christmas, you guys."

"Thanks for the help, Dyno," said Dooley. "Merry Christmas."

McCarthy found his children right where he'd left them. The only change he could see was that, though they were still holding hands, each now had a large candy cane in their free hand. "Look, Dad," said Nate, holding the candy cane up as high as he could. "We got this from Gloria," motioning the candy cane toward the smiling lady behind the service counter. "She gave it to us while you were catching the bad guy. Her name is Gloria, just like the Christmas song . . ."

With that, the curly-haired child began singing like a choir boy, "Gloooooooooooooooooria in Excelsis Deo."

As Nate sang, Christa kept working on her candy cane, rocking her head back and forth to the music. McCarthy thanked Gloria profusely and filled her in on what had just happened. McCarthy felt that she had earned the right to know everything. She would have a story to tell at her family's Christmas gathering on Christmas Eve.

As Dan, Nate, and little Christa turned away from the counter, there stood Victoria, beaming. She was so happy she had created a family tradition that could be carried on, year after year—a family shopping trip. "Hi, Guys! Are you having fun shopping with Daddy?" Before they could say a thing, she added, "What did you do?"

Christa immediately felt it was most definitely her turn to talk and talk she did, without looking up once from the largest candy cane she had ever experienced in her short lifetime, "I bought socks, and jelly, and Nafun teased me some, and then we watched the elves." There was a short pause for her to take another lengthwise lick from her candy cane. "Then Gloria gave us candy canes and taught Nafun a song and I couldn't learn it, cuz it had hard words." There was a longer pause as McCarthy hoped on hope, because of the crowd, the commotion, and the song learning that he might have worked his parental misdeed in the dark . . . but then, "And then we watched Daddy fight with the men."

Busted!

CHAPTER 13
THE SHEPHERD

It was February in Wisconsin. February was usually the month of suicides and domestics. The month of "cabin fever." During a long winter, there is not much for families to do inside a house that has not already been done to death by February. Not everyone can ski, skate, or snowmobile. Not everyone wants to.

This winter had been different. It was a "warm" winter. It was warm by Wisconsin standards. During the daytime, the temperature climbed at times as high as the lower 40's. Some days the temperature spiked at 55 degrees. At night for the third shift officer, it dropped below freezing again. This is cold, but much preferable to below zero with wind-chill.

The snow that had accumulated was nearly all gone and there were openings in the ice on the Decorah River already. Fishermen were still venturing out onto the ice in certain spots, taking the risk that they would be one of the ones that would inevitably fall through every year, by pushing the limits in their search of the tasty Wisconsin winter fish, the crappie.

This night was slow. McCarthy and Stammos had worked one domestic, where the fight had started over the remote. The husband was in total control over the remote for the TV and when the wife finally got the remote, it was covered with an orange crumby layer caused by Cheetos fingers.

This domestic was all yelling and the neighbors called it in before it got worse. No one got physical, so Stammos and McCarthy separated the participants. After some deft mediation, all parties involved regained perspective and realized they were suffering from cabin fever. It was a unique domestic in that by the time Stammos and McCarthy left, the oral combatants were laughing at the fact that they had become embroiled in an argument over Cheetos on the remote.

The fact that the belligerents in this domestic were laughing and hugging each other before Randy and Dan had left, made it unique. Unique or not, this was much more satisfying than hauling one to jail. The neighbors had called and the police had arrived before anything was said and done that could not be taken back. People with cabin fever have been known to kill each other, or themselves, unless someone intervenes.

Ask any cop about cabin fever and the full moon. Cops will tell you those phenomena have an effect on some people that is as powerful and mind-altering as any illegal drug. After this call, which came in early, the radio was silent for McCarthy. He weaved in and out of the streets and alleys of his beat and all appeared well. He occasionally parked his squad and walked sections of his beat, pulling on the doors of businesses.

Nothing stirred other than the occasional barking of a dog. It was the type of night McCarthy loved. It was a crisp 28 degrees, warm for this time of year. The clouds were wispy and they passed in front of the bright three-quarters moon, as if God had pushed the fast-forward button.

On quiet nights, McCarthy could not help but think of God. McCarthy was a deeply spiritual man. It was not a "I have to go to church every Sunday and sit impatiently through the service" kind of spiritual. McCarthy could watch the wind blow tall grass lazily back and forth in a Wisconsin meadow and feel His presence. He could sit on his deck and listen to the chirping of a sparrow, and sense the Good Lord had done his work well. Even after McCarthy arrested a burglar who had broken into a church and had defecated on the altar, McCarthy could not help but think, "Isn't it sad how some men fail in their efforts to use the great gift of free will?" Tonight was one of those nights when McCarthy's thoughts were spiritual.

McCarthy continued patrolling. Occasionally, he would cut his lights and hug the curb, prowling through neighborhoods, watching, listening for a noise, a movement, anything that would break up the quiet of the night. He patrolled his business district, his residential area, his taverns, and found nothing. At 4:14 a.m., a bizarre noise broke the silence of this night. McCarthy rolled his window down and at a distance he could hear the cries of someone . . . or something. It was a howl that combined pain, fear, and an urgent plea for help. The noise was coming from a section of the river that was lined with boathouses. Boathouses are structures built on stationary platforms that float on barrels. They are anchored to large telephone pole-sized posts, buried deep into the river's bottom. As the water rises, the boathouses rise with it. As it falls, the boathouses fall also. They lined the shore of the Decorah River.

McCarthy got on the radio as he headed in the direction of the mournful cries for help "255, 10-33 (emergency) traffic."

"255, go ahead," answered the dispatcher quickly.

"I hear someone, or something, crying for help near the boathouses on the east side of the river. It is in the area of War Eagle Road. Send me a backup unit."

"255, we just received a call on that. The caller says that he can't tell if it is a man or beast, but it's definitely injured and needs help. We heard the howling over the phone, and he was calling from the west side of the river. Use caution," stated the dispatcher.

As McCarthy pulled into the area, the intensity of the howl had grown. It was clear that someone, or something's, life and death struggle was growing more urgent. McCarthy exited his squad, still unable to determine if the howl was from man or beast. McCarthy thought the howl-cry was the type of noise a teenager in a horror movie stupidly leaves the camp site to check out and never comes back. When they do find him, he is hanging upside down, dismembered, and attached to the ceiling of a cave wall, being held there by some unidentified, slimy, sticky substance.

McCarthy stopped. He was close now. He still could not differentiate the plea-for-help squeal as man or beast. Whatever it was, it was losing strength and sounded near death. "I'm 10-23. The noise is coming from the last boathouse to the north," McCarthy reported over his walk-unit, as he sprinted toward the boathouse. As Dan reached the boathouse, he ran down the plank to the decking that surrounded the house.

On the far corner of the boathouse, Dan discovered the source of the loud, sorrowful howling. It was a full-grown German shepherd, fallen through the ice near the boathouse. It was desperately struggling to climb out but could not, because it was being held back by the leash still attached to its collar.

When McCarthy reached the drowning K-9, the dog clearly turned its attention to the officer. Its mournful howl for help regained momentum, as if the dog was concerned that this ignorant human might not notice its plight. McCarthy loved dogs and had always had one since he was a child. McCarthy knew a dog could bite when it was afraid, and he hesitated approaching at first, worrying the dog might bite. This concern was immediately swept away by the look in the eyes of the German shepherd. This dog was clearly pleading for help.

Dan radioed one more time, "It's a drowning German shepherd and I am going to have to go into the water after it. I'll be at the boathouse on the far north end of the line of boathouses." Dan then said to the desperate K-9, "There. If this doesn't work out, they'll know where to look for us."

Dan then stopped and said, "What in God's name are you about to do? This is a dog! You are about to stick your neck out for a dog." Then he looked into the shepherd's pleading and terrified eyes. The story of the good shepherd came to mind. The shepherd would always risk his life for his flock, because they were a part of "His flock." Dan then proclaimed to no one that could understand him, "All creatures great and small," and thus ended the internal debate. Dan could see in the German shepherd's eyes that the dog was beseeching McCarthy to help. Its cries had turned to whimpers, now either because help was near, or because it was tiring and losing the tenuous grip it held on life.

Officer Dan McCarthy went to work, quickly, without obstruction. He had made his decision. McCarthy undid his gun belt and the stays that held it in place, in the same order he did after each shift, except now his movements were rapid, yet precise. He went to the edge of the platform around the boathouse and lowered himself into the water. He had swum in this river countless times in the past, and even in the summer the temperature of the water always caught him by surprise. The ice cold liquid he had lowered himself into took his breath away. The cold he instantly felt was penetrating and all-encompassing. He realized while treading water that there was a strong current, and he was swimming in an opening surrounded by a sheet of ice. The dog must have been chasing a rabbit across the ice and ran right off the edge of the frozen floor that covered the river.

McCarthy fought to keep himself beside the boathouse, as he worked his way to the dog. He knew that if he got swept under the ice in the darkness, this would be his last shift. He kept a firm grip on the underside of the boathouse decking, as he maneuvered toward the dog.

The water was beyond cold. There is no word that describes the coldness of Wisconsin water in February, when you are submerged in it. It is as if a million needles are being jabbed into you continuously, and the pain from this is all you can perceive. McCarthy thought that people experiencing this for more than a few minutes, where there is no hope of rescue, must truly welcome the relief offered to them by drowning.

McCarthy reached the dog and discovered the animal was being both saved and drowned by the leash. The leash had hooked on a nail on the underside of the boathouse. It was keeping the drowning dog from getting out of the water, but at the same time keeping it, in all of its terror and exhaustion, from going under.

McCarthy worried once again, what the dog's reaction would be when it sensed it was unhooked. Once again, the pleading in the shepherd's eyes convinced him all would be all right. "It's OK, boy. Help is here. I'm here to help," McCarthy said in a reassuring tone. His voice quivered drastically, since now his body was engulfed in an almost uncontrollable shiver that seemed to cause his bones to quiver like a section of industrial aluminum in a strong wind.

Dan worked through it. He unhooked the dog and felt it immediately begin to sink. It was alive, but limp. The dog was unable to assist in its own rescue. He had finally succumbed to the cold and was welcoming death at the moment life was once again being offered as an option. Dan held the dog with one hand, and the decking of the back of the boathouse with the other, as he worked his way back around to the location where he had entered the water.

As Dan reached the side deck where he had entered the water, he hooked the leash onto the deck to hold the dog in place. The leash had saved this beautiful German shepherd once, and it would save him again, because McCarthy could not climb out while holding onto the dog. McCarthy slipped out of the water, thinking this would be somewhat of a relief from the cold, but he was wrong. As the wind hit him, the cold, to his horror, intensified. He had thought when he was in the water that he had been as cold as it was possible to be. He now realized that, in life, for every bad there is the possibility of a worse.

After McCarthy reached the deck where the leash was hooked, he struggled to unhook the dog again. Dan was violently shivering. Every extremity that did not have the capacity to retreat inside his body was shaking, like he was on the verge of a grand mall seizure. Dan managed to free the leash and struggling, lifted the water-logged shepherd to the decking of the boathouse. The dog lay conscious, but limp, on the deck.

Just then, the heavy pounding of footsteps on the plank leading to the boathouse brought McCarthy back into the "here and now." For a time, he felt as if he were somewhere between this world and an unknown. Dooley rounded the corner, reached Dan, and in a winded and excited voice fired, "Are you all right, Dan?" He then dropped a knee to the large mass of soggy fur on the deck. "Is he alive?"

"Yes to both," answered Dan, his voice barely understandable, because it was coming from vocal cords that were shivering out of control. He then directed, "Get on the radio and ask for the cadet to get here quickly. He is in the jeep tonight. That will be perfect to transport this dog. Tell the cadet to turn the heat of the jeep on high! Have dispatch call the La Claire Animal Hospital on-call person and have them open the hospital right away. Tell them we are bringing in a German shepherd suffering from hypothermia."

McCarthy carried the dog to the end of War Eagle Road, where his squad was parked. As he arrived, the cadet was just pulling in. Cadets are young people who want to be cops. They have a tendency to drift toward the locations of interesting calls. On this quiet night, this call, with the painful cries of the shepherd in the background, had caught the attention of everyone with a radio or scanner in the La Claire area.

McCarthy gently placed the shepherd into the open area to the backend of the jeep. He reassured the dog that all would be well. The dog struggled to lift its head, and McCarthy was the recipient of a lick that clearly was meant to say, "Thank you."

The excited young cadet spun the tires of his jeep as he left to take his patient to the animal hospital on his mission of mercy.

Carpenter told McCarthy, "You need to get out of those clothes."

McCarthy said, "Not just yet. I'm stopping out at the animal hospital to make sure this dog gets in all right."

Upon arriving at the hospital, McCarthy was happy to see the vet was waiting. McCarthy was a little ashamed to think the vet might not come at this time of day because it was "only a dog." Of course, the vet would come. He'd become a vet because he loved animals, and animal emergencies were the only type of emergencies he knew.

McCarthy carried the dog into the hospital and set the dog on a table. The doctor examined the dog, which was, in the light of the hospital, a beautiful shepherd reminiscent of Rin Tin Tin. "The dog is suffering from hypothermia," said the doctor, still apparently engrossed by the examination of the shepherd. "It just needs to be brought back to its normal temperature slowly."

The doctor gave the dog an injection and then picked it up off the table. The doctor slowly lowered the shepherd to the floor. Dan McCarthy was amazed . . . the dog could stand. The magnificent animal was slowly led to a cage in another room, where the doctor had set up some space heaters around the cage. Blankets were in place for bedding in the cage.

The shepherd appeared very willing to go to a cage, now that freedom had only given him a brush with death. As the dog reached the cage, it suddenly stopped and looked toward McCarthy. The dog turned and slowly walked past McCarthy, brushing its entire body against the shins of Officer McCarthy, as if it were a cat. The dog reached the cage, paused, looked back at McCarthy, and entered the cage.

"Amazing!" exclaimed the doctor. "I am sure that means thank you very much, in the language of German shepherds."

McCarthy was speechless. It was the best, most sincere thank you he'd ever received. He had heard law enforcement was a thankless job, but that was not true. He would remember the warmth of that thank you for as long as he would remember the cold of the water.

CHAPTER 14
COMPTON

Sgt. Dave Compton was the kind of sergeant every cop hoped he could work for. After you had a sergeant like Compton, all that came after him would have difficulty living up to the model set by him. Compton always knew the right thing to say—the right thing to do. He never made a bad situation worse. If Compton was made into a word, placed in the dictionary, and given a definition, it would read: **Compton** a walking solution, looking for a problem.

David Compton would be a street sergeant until he retired and that suited him. He would never be promoted for a number of reasons. The main one was that when you wanted Compton's opinion, he would give it. Sometimes the unadulterated truth is too hard on the ears.

He did not waste his time forming answers to administrators in such a way that the words would fall easy on their ears. He just told them the truth that everyone knew but hesitated to tell the hierarchy of the La Claire Police Department. All members of the ruling class have a tendency to "kill the messenger" bearing truths.

The quality that so annoyed and vexed Compton's superiors, endeared him to the officers he "served." That was how Compton looked at his job as a sergeant. He didn't command his officers—he "served" them.

When someone screwed up, he would not beat around the bush. Compton would always tell them directly. This sergeant always did it in such a way that it was a learning experience. Compton never *acted* sincere. He *was* sincere. Compton felt he owed two things to the officers he served. He would say, "It is my job to tell them when they've done wrong, and, just as important, I need to tell them when they've done right."

Compton would also tell them, "I'm not here to be your buddy. I'm here to make you better. If I can be your buddy *and* make you better, all the better." If there was any new sergeant that wondered how to be an effective supervisor, all he needed to do was watch Compton. In short, Compton was a leader in the truest sense of the word.

Sergeant David Compton made people want to perform well for him. He wasn't afraid of work either. If all the officers were busy, he would handle a call himself. His exploits as a patrol officer were legendary. Compton always seemed to be in the thick of it. He found trouble before it found someone else. If there was a police-related headline in the *La Claire Journal*, Compton's name could usually be found in the first paragraph, just below the byline.

The men and women who worked for Dave, liked him. They trusted him. Even more important, they emulated the best parts of him. Many supervisors in the public and private sector are "do as I say, not as I do" supervisors. They hold their employees to standards they never held themselves to. No one knows that they do this better than the employees they supervise. It is hard to respect this type of supervisor.

Compton was a "do as I do" supervisor. He did not have to tell people to get back to work. People being led by him did their job, because it was expected of them. He expected no more of them than he demanded from himself. He let them know what was expected of them, and his people tried to live up to Compton's expectations. When they did their job well, Compton would smile, wink, pat them on the back, and say, "Good job!"

Like most of the best first-line supervisors, Compton had become somewhat a father figure. He was a veteran officer who had dedicated himself to patrol. He had over two decades in law enforcement. All of that had been spent in patrol. He had been in that Marines' "Ooh-rah!", as he would always say. People who knew him well said he was in heavy combat in Vietnam.

The story told was that his firebase was nearly overrun one night. He and what was left of his platoon established a small perimeter within the firebase and lasted out the long night. Dave Compton received a purple heart and silver star for his actions. Other people who knew him told the story. He never did.

The officers of his command almost thought they would hear the story from Compton at the Polar Bear Plunge. The Polar Bear Plunge is unique to states like Wisconsin. In February, someone cuts a large hole in the ice of the Decorah River. Donations for Special Olympics are promised in the name of volunteer plungers. Compton was a long-time supporter of the Special Olympics. He usually could get nearly the whole night-shift to plunge. This year, the entire shift except McCarthy plunged. The memory of his icy plunge after King, the German shepherd, was still too fresh in his mind to jump in again, when no living thing's life was at stake. He would watch.

When it came time for the police department to plunge, the night-shift went last and jumped in as a group. They were led by Sgt. Compton. You couldn't help but notice the scar in Compton's chiseled upper torso. He wore it as naturally as the small unobtrusive tattoo, "USMC," on his left upper, rock-solid arm.

After the plunge, all the plungers were in a large, heated tent, drinking coffee and eating chili. One high school kid, who had also plunged, asked Compton, "Where did you get that scar? Did a criminal shoot you?

Compton's simple answer was, "No son. I came by the scar when I was about one year older than you, in a small rural country in Southeast Asia called Vietnam."

"Were you a Marine?" asked the inquisitive young man, noticing the tattoo.

"No son. I am a Marine. Once a Marine always a Marine. Saying you were a Marine is like saying you were an American. You say I am an American and I am a Marine, Ooh-rah!" All the other young officers under Compton's command listened intently, hoping this young man would get the story from Compton.

"Did you ever kill anyone in Vietnam?" was the final question, asked and answered.

"I'm glad you asked that question." McCarthy and the rest of the younger members of the shift stopped what they were discussing and listened. "Whenever anyone asks me that question, I always take the opportunity to say a silent prayer for the people I fought with and against, who died. You see son, we were never really enemies. We were all just fighting for our country. We were soldiers, and there is a bond between soldiers that transcends death. Now, if you don't mind, I am going to observe that silence now in their memory." He bowed his head and closed his eyes. Without a word being said, everyone else in the group did the same.

Later that night at the La Claire Police Department, Sgt. Compton walked into the line-up room and sat down at the table in the front of the room, facing the assembled officers. "Have you all dried off since the plunge?" asked Compton.

"Fuckin'-A!" exclaimed Carpenter, speaking for the whole group.

"Some of you still look a little wet behind the ears to me, but that will pass. Listen up! I have to fill you all in on the homicide that happened earlier. The suspect's name is Brown, and he has admitted to being the shooter," said Compton, with a deathly serious look on his face.

Everyone sat up straight to listen to what Sgt. Compton had to say.

"Is he one of the Browns from over on Steele Street?" asked Officer Carpenter.

"No relation," said Compton. He continued, "The guy had three daughters and they were all beautiful. He told the detectives that, whenever a guy came over to pick one of them up on a date, Brown would answer the door holding a shotgun, just to make an impression on them."

"Tonight all three had a date. There was a knock on the door, and Brown answered the door with the shotgun, and the guy says to him, 'Hi, Mr. Brown. I'm Joe. I'm here to pick up Floe. We're going to the show. Is she ready to go?'

"Mr. Brown then called Floe, and let her leave, since it appeared that this was a nice guy. Fifteen minutes later, another guy knocks on the door, and Mr. Brown answered it. There is another young man at the door, who says, 'Hi, Mr. Brown. I'm Eddie, and I'm here to pick up Betty. Is she ready?'

"Mr. Brown let him go with Betty, since he seemed like a nice enough guy. After a few minutes, there was another guy who came to the door and knocked. Mr. Brown answered the door, and this guy said . . . 'Hi, I'm Chuck.' So Mr. Brown shot him."

Everyone at the line-up laughed. Officers genuinely liked Compton. He was a supervisor who always had a smile on his face, unless a serious tone was needed. He knew the job, and when he gave an answer to a question or made a decision, he was rock solid.

Compton tried to start out the officers' day with a laugh. The jokes were sometimes good, sometimes bad, but mostly pretty lame. Good joke or bad, the officers grew to look forward to them. If one of the officers got called out early, they would contact their beat partners later to see what they missed in line-up. They would copy down the missing persons, the new warrants, the new stolen vehicles, and somewhere in the mix of information, Compton's joke would be passed along. The good feeling about working on the shift spread with it.

"Seriously, there was a homicide in Madison. The suspect was from La Claire. His name is Richard Sprotsky." With the mention of this name, a large percentage of the officers nodded their heads in recognition. Most had dealt with Sprotsky in the past. His specialty was starting and finishing bar fights. His favorite technique was to palm a pool ball, tell a subject to step outside, and nail the poor sap who had mistakenly believed there was some honor in a bar fight.

Compton continued, "Apparently he started a fight and then finished it by burying his knife in the skull of a guy outside a bar on State Street in Madison. He killed a college kid in a fight, over who was next up at a pool table. They have not recovered the knife. Go get him guys! The little weasel is back in town. I know it." This energized the shift, and they started the night with a positive energy that few sergeants could generate, other than Compton.

The shift hit the ground running this night. Bar fights, prowler complaints, drunk drivers, and domestics were occurring on all sides of the city at once. Some sergeants would find a reason to stay inside every night. They would chain themselves to the desk until they made lieutenant. Then they would stay there until they retired. This was not the Compton way. He was always on the street within ten minutes of lineup. This night was no different.

About ten minutes after hitting the street, Compton called for a backup on the secured channel. The secured channel on the radio was a special scrambled channel that people with scanners could not hear. It was difficult for officers to understand each other, but when the radio message was sensitive enough, officers resorted to using it. The transmission sounded as if Compton was inside a garbage can, but the urgency of it was such that somehow everyone understood it.

"230, I've spotted Mr. Richard Sprotsky. He just entered the front door of the Sidekick Tavern. I want a unit to cover the rear exit on the alley side of the bar. Send me the next two units to the front and one more at the back. Have all units responding, approach silent."

Officers then responded immediately, "256, I'm a block away and I'll cover the back."

"255, I'll respond to the front with Officer Compton. My ETA (estimated time of arrival) is one minute," broke in McCarthy.

"233, I'll back 256 up in the rear," called Carpenter. "I should be just behind 255."

"Is anyone else clear?" asked the dispatcher. The dispatcher was aware that all other units were tied up, except Brockman. Brockman did not answer.

"234," said the dispatcher.

"234, go ahead, I'm at the pumps." answered Brockman.

"Brockman, you horse's ass," thought every cop and dispatcher working that night. Brockman would not volunteer for any call—not even to assist in the apprehension of a murder suspect on his beat. To Brockman, suckers volunteered. Now he would not only have to answer this call, but he would have to gas his squad tonight to cover his story that he was "at the pumps." That was all Brockman cared about. McCarthy could not help but take his mind off the seriousness of Sgt. Compton's request to think a hardly novel thought about Brockman. "Brockman is a prick!"

As McCarthy pulled up, he parked his squad down the street from the Sidekick. Sgt. Dave Compton was out of his squad and in a doorway. The doorway provided concealment. It also was situated perfectly to allow Compton to observe the front and side alley door of the Sidekick Tavern.

When everyone was in position outside the bar, Compton contacted the dispatcher, "Hold radio traffic on the main channel. Have all other radio traffic go to Channel 2."

The dispatcher answered, "10-4. All units except those at the Sidekick go to Channel 2."

Sgt. Compton then told everyone at the scene, "Hold your positions for right now. I do not think he noticed me. He is wearing a black leather jacket open at the front. He is also wearing a black and gray Grateful Dead T-shirt and torn jeans. That's him talking with the bouncer at the front door. We'll take him when he steps outside." As he spoke, Compton put his radio into its case and as smoothly, quietly, as a big cat stalking an elk, crossed the alley. He held his position at the corner of the tavern, which bordered the alley. He drew his duty weapon, which was a department-issued 9 mm Glock 17. It carried 17 in the magazine and one in the chamber.

Sprotsky shook the bouncer's hand and turned to walk away. His path was directly toward where the big cat lay in wait. Sprotsky's head was still turned toward the bouncer, who obviously knew Sprotsky and was still yelling his last farewells to him.

"Police! Don't Move! Get down on the ground, Now! Down now, Sprotsky!" Compton yelled this in a dominating command voice, while maintaining his cover position behind the corner of the tavern. Compton had a command voice any Marine drill sergeant would be proud to call his own.

Sprotsky's initial reaction was to freeze, as if he turned to a pillar of salt. His eyes had the look of a character in a horror movie who'd just discovered what was making the noise in the basement. The only movement that could initially be detected was that his lower lip had begun to tremble uncontrollably.

Then McCarthy noticed that the faded, torn blue jeans were regaining some of their old color in the crotch area. The stain was growing, and extending down the inner leg toward the knee. Sprotsky's lack of compliance was—*could* not move, rather than *would* not move. Compton's sudden and unanticipated entry into the criminal's world had put a fear into Sprotsky.

Sprotsky then slowly, as if his limbs were as rusted as the Tin Man of Oz, dropped to his knees, reached for the sidewalk and flattened out on the ground.

"Turn your head to the left," yelled Sgt. David Compton, as he held the muzzle of his Glock steady on the suspected killer.

"D-D-Don't shoot, m-m-man. I'm not armed," pleaded Mr. Richard Sprotsky, who just hours earlier had buried a knife into the head of another young man. The victim had just gone out on the town in Madison to celebrate passing his calculus final. Sprotsky, who had shown no mercy to the young college student, now begged for it for himself.

"McCarthy, cuff him! Carpenter, keep the sidewalk clear!" Compton ordered.

McCarthy moved up the sidewalk and holstered his weapon. McCarthy came down in a three point control hold while he maintained a rear compliance hold on Sprotsky's right arm.

McCarthy then noticed Sprotsky's expression on his face change, as if he had remembered he'd left the house on vacation and left the water in the tub running.

He suddenly reached his left arm under his body. McCarthy quickly reacted by putting a great deal of pressure on his compliance hold, causing pain to Sprotsky. The pain cannot injure, cannot be described, and needs to be felt to be understood. McCarthy snapped an order, "Give me your hand!"

Sprotsky could not hear the order, for he could not experience hearing, seeing, tasting, or any other of his senses, because he could only think of the pain. One phenomenon with the technique that McCarthy noticed was that when it worked, a suspect who had it done to them, would instinctively shoot their hand back toward McCarthy as if to say, "Please handcuff me quickly and stop the pain."

As soon as this happened, McCarthy let up slightly, taking the pressure off and immediately rewarding the man's compliance with relief. McCarthy quickly applied the handcuffs, wielding them "as ably as Arthur wielded Excalibur," is how Compton later put it.

Compton then holstered his weapon and assisted McCarthy in aiding Sprotsky to his feet. Compton changed from the arresting officer to Sprotsky's best friend, in the tick of a clock. "Rick, it's me, Dave Compton. I see I scared you a little bit. Let's get you out of here," he stated, as he hustled Sprotsky into the alley, out of public view. "McCarthy, bring my car over here and leave yours secured. You come with me. Carpenter, get a cadet to drive McCarthy's unit to the station. We don't want to leave it here. Carpenter, I want you to interview anyone Sprotsky talked to inside and get statements from them." While Compton was calmly giving these orders, he was conducting a search of Sprotsky. Compton removed a brown bottle containing cocaine, which was on a chain around the suspect's neck. There was a silver spoon attached to the black cap of the bottle. He had about $650 in cash on him.

Cops always marveled at how, no matter what kind of existence the dregs of society live in, they always had more cash on them than most cops had in the bank. Inside the right sock of the suspect, Compton felt something and instinctively yelled, "Knife," to alert all officers of the higher level of threat. Compton pulled several evidence bags from the side pocket in his tactical pants. He carefully put the wallet, containing the cash, in one bag, and wrote on the bag "right rear pants pocket."

He slid the brown bottle with cocaine, spoon, and chain into another bag and labeled it "around neck." He then set the bags on the hood of the squad, which had been brought over at his direction. Compton took gloves from his glove packet on his belt and placed them snugly on his hands and carefully removed the knife from inside the right sock. Later, it would be discovered that this was the murder weapon. The victim's blood and hair were on the knife, along with Sprotsky's own blood.

During the autopsy of the victim, a tip of a knife-blade was found broken off and stuck deeply in the skull of the victim. The knife recovered by Compton would be found to be missing its tip. The fracture on the knife matched perfectly, according to experts, the fracture of the tip left in the victim's skull.

As Compton finished his search of the suspect, he transported Sprotsky to jail. He took him to an interview room and carefully collected and packaged each article of clothing. Rick, who had breathed his last breath of freedom as a young man, stepped into a jail uniform.

Compton then advised Sprotsky of his rights, and stated, "I'm not going to waste a lot of time with small talk, Rick. I know, you know what this is all about. I know, you know, we know what you did. I am just going to give you the opportunity of telling us why you did it. If you went to State Street with the intent of killing someone, that's one thing; but I don't think that's how it happened. I'm guessing something got out of hand tonight, and you are as sorry as can be that it happened. I'm giving you the opportunity to tell us how sorry you are for what happened."

"I am, man. He was never supposed to die, man." The words came out like they were fired from a tommy gun. Sprotsky obviously had used some of the coke already, before he was arrested. "The guy was bigger than me, and all I wanted to do was scare him. I let my mouth write a check my ass couldn't cash again. You know how I am, Sgt. Compton, sir. The next thing I know he is on me, swinging, and I meant to hit him back with my fist. I did it kind of automatically and I stuck him with my knife.

The next thing I know I can't even get my knife out of him. I had to pull real hard and then it came out. It made noise like I was cutting up a deer or something. Then I just ran and ran. I came back here to score some coke and get laid one more time, before I'm gone to Waupon for life, man. You got me before I got laid," Sprotsky lamented, as his eyes dropped down, and the coke-inspired energy seemed to drain out of him.

A look of deep regret formed on his face as he sighed, ending his statement by repeating in an almost somber tone, as if he realized what he did not experience he might never experience again. "You got me before I got laid."

By the time a detective was called, Compton already had a signed and taped statement from Sprotsky. Sprotsky even thanked Compton for being so kind and understanding. He appreciated that Compton got him out of the sight of the crowd after Sprotsky wet his pants. "You scared me, man!" explained Sprotsky. The criminal is a strange person. A criminal often is not the least bit embarrassed by being arrested for rape, robbery, or murder. In their world, they have a need to protect their secret . . . that they feel fear.

Compton felt a cop should take his case as far as he could, before he turned it over to a detective for follow-up. This created hard feelings in the minds of some detectives, who looked at the officers on patrol as a subspecies.

On all serious cases, a detective would be called in to follow up. Most of the cases need more follow-up than a patrol officer could do in a shift. Some officers would hold a suspect and not even try to interview the suspect until a detective arrived. Compton never needed to call a detective to interview one of his suspects. The only reason a detective would need to be there, would be to take notes on Compton's technique. Compton would always leave an interview making two things. He would make a good case and a new friend.

McCarthy new that when he watched Compton work, he was very privileged to be watching a master. He thought tonight he saw, in a matter of moments, Sgt. Dave Compton strike fear in the heart of a murderer. He rapidly shifted gears, after getting compliance, and treated the murderer with respect. He allowed the "scum of society, a shit bird, a dirt bag," by all systems of measurement, to retain his dignity. The criminals would tell Compton things that they would not tell a priest.

McCarthy had watched a master at public relations on this night. Compton had become, over the years, a master of communications. He could get people to do what he wanted them to do and say the truth, which was what he wanted to hear, under the worst conditions. When there was no time for the establishment of mutual respect, then Compton could immediately strike fear into the heart of anyone. Sometimes, fear was good enough.

McCarthy would never forget the night Sgt. David Compton made the cold-hearted, cold-blooded murderer wet his pants in public. It was Rick Sprotsky's last act as a free man. He would be sentenced to life for the brutal bar fight stabbing. He would never be free to pee in public again. He would never kill again. Then in an instant, Compton became the killer's best friend. He became the killer's confessor.

At a pre-shift line-up some time later, Brockman was sarcastically chastising Sgt. Compton about arresting "poor Rick." Brockman continued that "poor Rick would never get high again, and, for Christ's sake, you could at least have waited to let him get laid one more time. He'll never get laid again."

Brockman was just wrong on one point. Prison was not so restrictive that Sprotsky could not experience the rush of cocaine. He was under the influence of the same rush when he buried the knife into the skull of his victim in Madison.

Compton answered the second point by stating that Rick would get laid again. Sgt. Compton stated, "Rick will just have to change his perspective on what constitutes great sex. He will have to think out of the box so to speak. It is kind of like Rick is a football player whose coach has just changed the position that he plays. Rick entered prison a tight end, and now he will be a wide receiver."

After the burst of laughter following Compton's adlib, using Brockman as his straight-man, Sgt. David Compton released his young charges out onto the streets of La Claire. Compton was a man that anyone could respect, fear, love, but not hate. He was too good a man for anyone to hate.

There were two important things Compton did for the young officers. The first thing that he did was to set an example for them to follow for the rest of their lives. An example of a real man, a real husband, a real father, and a real cop. The second thing he did was to see to it that they started nearly every shift laughing. Compton would say that laughter was the medicine for the body and soul.

McCarthy did not want to just be a good cop. He wanted to be as good a cop as Sgt. Dave Compton. It would not be easy, but McCarthy was very patient, very determined, and Sgt. Compton was very good. Possibly as good as it gets.

CHAPTER 15
SHOTS FIRED, OFFICER DOWN

Every police officer knows that there is a possibility they could be seriously injured or killed, in the line of duty. No officer truly believes that it will happen to them. Officers train from the beginning of their career up to retirement to prevent that from happening. No matter how much officers, mentally or physically, prepare for armed confrontations, many officers are killed in the line of duty each year. None of their family members knew that the last night they went to work would be the last time they would see their beloved father, mother, husband, wife, brother, or sister again.

Each time an officer dies, they leave behind a litany of regrets for things done and undone. "Oh my God, we argued about nothing before he left" or "I didn't say 'I love you. Be careful.' I always say I love you and be careful!"

On this particular November night, McCarthy started work as enthusiastic ever. Everyone was still pumped about the Sprotsky arrest. Compton started line-up, as usual, by announcing, "Did you hear about the terrible tragedy in Colorado. Four attorneys in a Dodge mini-van going over the Rockies crashed through a guard rail, and the vehicle plummeted over 500 feet, killing all four of them."

Carpenter immediately volunteered to be the straight man tonight and interjected, "So what's the tragedy, Sarge?"

Compton snapped back, with the timing of Jerry Seinfeld, "The Dodge mini-van holds eight." The laughter was instantaneous, and after Compton saw that he had started his young troops off right, he gave out the stolens, wanteds, missings, notes from upper command, and the extra attentions that made line-ups necessary.

As everyone gathered up their gear to hit the street, McCarthy asked Carpenter, "Did you know that was coming? Did Compton tell you to say that?"

"No. I swear, I just walked right into it," exclaimed Carpenter, shaking his head. "I thought I was being clever."

The first call of the night was a large underage drinking party. McCarthy always wondered why kids felt the need to be so blatant, while breaking the law. So often, they would congregate in a house by the hundreds in a quiet neighborhood, as if they wanted the police to show up. McCarthy concluded the arrival of the police was affirmation that the party was a success.

When McCarthy and Carpenter approached the house, the music could be heard from a block away. McCarthy and Carpenter approached the back, while Stammos, Compton, and Brockman approached the front. Compton had decided to take extra people, because the house in question had repeated violations.

As Compton pounded on the front door, it was opened by a seventeen-year-old kid dressed like Elwood Blues, who obviously wasn't expecting the La Claire Police Department, since he had a freshly tapped beer in his hands. Instinctively, he tossed the beer and slammed the front door.

In moments, the back door burst open and the first Blues Brother ran right into McCarthy's arms; the rest of the party-goers slammed into a large overweight kid in a homemade toga, carrying a lit "bong," who had stopped in the doorway when he saw police out back. He also slammed the door. Then all the lights went out in the house, and the hundred-plus house guests spent the next forty-five minutes wishing the police gone, while the youths attempted to find a safe place to hide.

In that period, Sgt. Compton worked on getting a search warrant for the house. He obtained it by calling dispatch, which in turn arranged for a conference-call with an assistant district attorney, a judge, and Sgt. Compton. Telephonic search warrants had made getting a warrant in the middle of the night easier than getting one in the middle of a business day. The judge was on-call, so he or she was always available and there was no waiting.

The fact sheet of the warrant was then taken to the judge to sign, and the police were good to go. One more attempt was made to get the occupants of the house to answer the door. Sgt. Compton then shouted at the door, "This is Sergeant David Compton of the La Claire Police Department. I have a search warrant for this residence. If you do not open the door, we will open it and will destroy the door in the process. We do not wish to do that, so please open the door."

This brought a response within about a minute. The doorknob turned and Elwood Blues opened the door. The process of identifying, citing, and determining who was too intoxicated to release on their own, and then the search for hidden party-goers began immediately. Additional officers had been called to the scene after Elwood Blues had first slammed the door.

The other Blues Brother had already been transported to the county jail, since he was nineteen years old and had a warrant for his arrest for driving while intoxicated. Most of the kids were polite, scared, and cooperative. They received tickets for underage drinking, and if they were old enough and sober enough, they were released.

After the obvious ones were taken care of, a more thorough search of the house took place. Kids were pulled out of closets and out from under mattresses. The real victims were the three kids dressed in togas hiding in blown insulation. Stammos told McCarthy, "They'll still be scratching when they reach legal drinking age."

After citing the party-goers, the party-givers were given tickets for selling beer without a license, furnishing beer to minors, and a noise violation. Over $20,000 in tickets were given out at the underage drinking party; 101 people were charged, 7 were arrested on warrants, and then came time to collect the evidence.

Compton assigned Stammos to collect it. Stammos was very meticulous, and had the best handwriting. He could write like Thomas Jefferson, if he wanted. There was a fair amount of evidence to take. There were eight half-barrels in the house and the cash box, where admission was charged to enter the party. Stolen street signs were confiscated, beer bongs, which enabled youngsters to drink-to-death, signs indicating "$10.00—all you can drink." One piece of evidence was a "Show your tits for a free shot," which was adorned by candid shots of one young, beautiful lady taking her top off, and another slamming a shot topless. They were both seated at the bar, which the sign hung over. These two young beauties were obviously not the only takers on this offer. A tape in a VCR next to the bar was turned on and it showed many a college and high school beauty from past parties taking their tops off and then drinking the free shot. The shapes and sizes of the breasts varied dramatically, but they shared a similar state of intoxication . . . wasted! The tape was taken as evidence. The work was done so efficiently, because it was business as usual in a college-town. To call these large parties was inaccurate. These houses were residential taverns without licenses. Some kids financed their college education by throwing these parties. They were gold mines. Sometimes the complaints were called in by bar owners, who had to pay for all their licenses and were upset, because these parties would cut into their business. Some drug paraphernalia was taken, but in the time it took to get the warrant, most of the product was disposed of.

Compton had ordered them to open the door, and after 2½ hours, all officers were clear from the house. The chronic party-house would be quiet for two years after this night, to the glee of its neighbors.

After clearing from the call, McCarthy wrote up the thirteen tickets and two arrest reports that he had generated at the party call. He arrested the first fleeing Blues Brother, who had tried to make good his escape. The Elwood wannabe like the real Elwood had an outstanding warrant for his arrest. Carpenter and he also located one other wanted man in the house. He had been hiding between a mattress and a box spring. He was thirty-four-years old and was wanted on a warrant for first degree sexual assault for having sex with a twelve-year-old girl. The low-life had sex with a twelve-year-old and now was attending an underage drinking party to satisfy once again his craving for young girls.

Just as McCarthy was pulling off the police ramp after he had turned in his paperwork from the house party, he received a call, the details of which he would remember the rest of his life. "255. Report of shots fired at 1012 New Berlin Street. The complainant would not give any other details." McCarthy turned on his red lights, but not the siren. As he reached the area, he shut everything off and pulled in, dark and silent. He exited his squad and, slowly and silently, latched his squad door.

At the same time as McCarthy was pulling in, he could see Carpenter parking, lights-out, on the other end of the block. Both officers stayed in the shadows as they approached 1012 quietly.

Ten-twelve was an eight-plex. Everything was quiet and Carpenter had worked his way to the opposite end of the complex. As McCarthy stayed around the corner of the building, a female came to the door of the apartment nearest him. She opened the door, and cautiously looked toward the end of the building that Gary Carpenter was on.

"Ma'am. Police officers. Do you know what's going on here," McCarthy whispered.

Startled, the female brought both her hands to her mouth and spun awkwardly to face McCarthy. "Oh, officer!—I heard them arguing. She screamed and I heard about four loud shots. I haven't heard anything since."

"Who ma'am? And where?" whispered McCarthy in a crouch, with his handgun drawn.

"Ray Draper is the man's name, and his wife's name is Sue. They live in the apartment on the end. I think it's apartment 4."

McCarthy then motioned the female back into her apartment. He also motioned to Carpenter that it was the apartment closest to him, but something at the apartment had already caught Carpenter's attention. He was already slipping up to the side of the doorway. McCarthy moved up to assist, and positioned himself beside the apartment door.

The outside screen door was shut, but the interior door was standing wide open, which was unusual, since it was a chilly night. The lights were on inside the apartment, but no one could be seen initially. To the left of the front door were a kitchenette and a line of cupboards. Beyond that, to the left, was a bathroom, and its door was shut. To the right of the door was a small dining area and, further in, the living room. A chair was tipped over in the dining area. Straight in from the front door was a bedroom, and the light was on. A jumping shadow could be seen in the room, indicating that someone was in the bedroom.

McCarthy looked at Carpenter and whispered, "She heard a woman scream and four shots fired, nothing since."

Carpenter nodded. He also had his handgun out and in a low, ready position. The officers remained silent sentries at the door. Without a word being said, they both knew that the shadow was unaware of their presence and would be coming out shortly.

After less than a minute beside the door, the officers saw the shadow change directions abruptly, and then out the bedroom door came Draper. He was known by both officers. He fancied himself a tough guy, and occasionally he would like to prove it to himself by pounding on a smaller male opponent in a bar, or wait until he came home, and then he would bat around his wife.

As the bully-boy appeared, both officers sucked in a breath simultaneously, as they saw he had changed his MO. He now had a semi-auto shotgun in his right hand. He did not see the officers until they shouted loudly, in one voice, "Police! Don't move! Drop the gun. Do it now!"

The command came out of nowhere, and the shock of it could be read on Draper's face. McCarthy wondered why a man who fired four shots in a city neighborhood would be shocked to see the police at his door. Draper put his hands up and leaned the shotgun against the kitchen counter.

That hand then went up. It looked like the arrest would go without a hitch. McCarthy kept his gun on Draper and then he noticed that Draper would only put his hands to about shoulder-height.

McCarthy took over the commands, shouting, "Put your hands up high! Higher!"

Draper still looked shocked and only marginally followed this order, moving his hands more outward rather than upward. "Turn around and walk backwards toward me."

Instead of doing as he was told, Draper merely kept walking toward the door.

McCarthy sensed something was wrong, because Draper no longer looked shocked. The look was one of determination, and the officer shouted again, "I said put your hands up high and turn around!" yelled McCarthy again, without effect.

Draper ignored the commands. His face now had the look of a punk, itching for a fight. His hands were still at shoulder-height, and he still was facing the officers. As Draper reached the door, his hands dropped down, and he quickly slammed and locked it. The third officer to arrive at the scene was Dooley. He had joined McCarthy and Carpenter at the door, and instinctively he began to kick the door, as it slammed shut.

Then came the sound, which is immediately identifiable to nearly every male raised in the state of Wisconsin. It was the sound of the action of a Remington semi-automatic shotgun, slamming forward, feeding a shell into the chamber. "Back off! yelled McCarthy!" and all three officers moved to the cover of a vehicle parked nearby in the rear parking lot of the complex. The vehicle was about thirty feet from the doorway to the apartment. The standoff began.

As quickly as possible, additional backup units were called to the scene and the exits of the apartment were covered. McCarthy and Dooley orchestrated the evacuation of the apartment complex. Surprisingly everyone was sober, cooperative, and seemed to realize the urgency of the request to leave. Carpenter covered the door, while a sealed perimeter around the complex quickly developed. Nearly the entire shift was occupied with this call.

McCarthy moved to a position covering the front door and watched. While officers remained nervously on the perimeter, Sgt. Compton arrived at the scene of the incident. He dropped what he had been doing to head to the scene. He approved of everything done up to that moment and assigned Brockman to attempt to talk Draper out of the house. Brockman said he knew Draper and could get him to come out. It would be a decision he would regret.

Brockman was able to contact Draper by phone. Draper was definitely intoxicated. McCarthy could hear both sides of the conversation, since Draper was yelling into the phone, and Brockman had chosen the phone in the adjacent apartment with which to communicate with Draper. McCarthy thought this was a foolish position to take, since it was so close and could put Brockman in danger, because shotgun slugs could easily penetrate the apartment wall.

Brockman rambled on with Ray. Ray initially had only one demand. He demanded that everyone leave, because his wife was ok. Then his demands changed. He wanted us to stay, and he would give himself up, if we would have Officer Gary Carpenter and Officer Hemming of the

Horton Police Department stand in front of the door. He would then walk out to them. Horton was the city just to the north of La Claire.

Brockman immediately began to ask to have this arranged. Compton said, "Absolutely not!" Compton explained to him that three months earlier, Hemming had been involved in the shooting of a man by the name of Rick Harper. Harper had come to the door with a shotgun on a noise complaint in Horton, which was answered by Hemming. Harper was very drunk. Whenever Harper got drunk, he was a surly, dangerous drunk, just like Draper.

Harper brought the weapon to bear on Hemming, and Hemming placed three shots into the cardiovascular system of the menacing Harper. Harper staggered, fell and would never intimidate anyone again. Harper had been a close friend of Draper.

Carpenter had arrested Draper recently, and Draper had attempted to try his hand at beating up the wiry, tough, young officer. He lost quickly in front of friends.

Because of this history, it was clear to Compton that even if he was dumb enough to send officers in front of the door in open view of Draper, which he wasn't, he would not send these two officers. Draper had homicide on his mind. He may even have already killed his wife. Compton had decided that there would be no more casualties, if he could help it.

When this demand was not met, Draper slammed the phone down. Brockman continued to try to make contact again, by ringing the phone. McCarthy could hear that Draper had now chosen this moment to do some straightening up in the apartment. McCarthy could hear the constant grinding of the garbage disposal. He thought, Damn!—if only Harper would have given up right away. Not only would I not be freezing right now, but we also would have found the dope that Draper was grinding up right now. By the length of time Draper was grinding away, it was an extremely large quantity.

As McCarthy shivered in his position, he thought maybe it was a good sign, since if Draper was grinding, it meant he was planning for his arrest. He would not worry about destroying evidence, if he planned on going out in a blaze of glory, thought McCarthy.

About this time, McCarthy could see the chief had arrived on the scene. A chief arriving at the scene of any serious situation could be a good thing or a bad thing. If the chief began to take over command from his designees, this was usually a bad thing. If he let his personnel work, and watched, that was a good thing. Tonight the chief would decide to meddle.

Compton explained to the chief what was happening. He explained that it was a waiting game, and it was just a matter of time before Draper came out. "This whole fiasco is costing us money. I do not want this many people left on overtime, standing around waiting for some drunken idiot to give up. He's not going to shoot anyone. Why are we doing nothing."

With that, the chief began walking toward the apartment. "But sir . . . he's dangerous. I think he's a shooter," pleaded Compton, realizing the futility of his effort. He had seen this look on the chief's face before—the look that gave him the appearance he could put his head through a brick wall, and was just about to do it. The chief was filled with what is called "tombstone courage."

It would sometimes get officers results and sometimes get officers seriously hurt . . . or dead.

The chief saw McCarthy covering the door from a cement stairway, which led to the basement of the complex. "Come with me," the chief commanded in a tone that could not be resisted. McCarthy followed. "Get over here!" the chief barked again, calling for Dooley to leave the cover of the parked car in the lot adjacent to the complex.

The chief walked right up to the front door of the apartment. He pounded angrily and impatiently at the door, and then he yelled, "Draper, open the door—this is the Chief of the La Claire Police Department. I want to talk to you right now." His voice was booming and dripping with confidence and authority.

McCarthy stepped away from the door, as did Dooley, and both had their weapons at the ready. McCarthy moved to the window and could see into the apartment through a break between the curtain and the window frame. He could see that Draper was leaning against the door-frame, talking to Brockman again on the phone. He had nothing in his hands. The look on his face showed his immediate rage at the audacity of the chief's approach.

"Chief, get away from the door," said the young officer to his commander.

The chief only pounded louder and repeated his demand. Draper was seen by McCarthy to drop the phone and approach the door, still empty-handed. As he reached the door, he was seen to reach toward the door and disappear from sight, as if he were going to open the door. Instead, he reappeared momentarily pointing the semi-automatic shotgun at the door, and then he was out of sight again to McCarthy.

McCarthy grabbed his chief by the shoulder, screaming, "Gun!" and the chief shrugged off instinctively the grip. Then, all heard the metallic click of the firing pin falling. The gun must have malfunctioned, because Draper was heard to frantically rack one round out of the chamber and then chamber another round.

"He's got a gun!" yelled the chief, as he nearly ran over McCarthy, while running for the cover of the next apartment. McCarthy returned quickly to the basement stairwell. The standoff continued.

Two more hours passed. There was no word of Draper's wife, and finally the chief ordered an entry team make entry to the apartment. In the time that had passed, Brockman had talked continually to Draper. The power had been shut down and returned through negotiations. There were repeated assurances that his wife was all right, but Draper would not put his wife on the phone. The power was put back on, when she was allowed to talk briefly on the phone. She said, "I'm all right," and then the phone was quickly pulled away. Brockman felt it sounded as if she was frightened and possibly injured.

The keys to the apartment were brought to the scene by the landlord, and there were two keys, one for the lock and one for the deadbolt on the door. The plan was simple. Draper was known to be talking on the phone across the front room in the doorway straight in from the front door. His shotgun was leaning against the front door. Brockman would keep him busy on the phone, while McCarthy, Carpenter, and Dooley entered the apartment, after McCarthy keyed the door.

As McCarthy approached the door, he could feel his heart climbing rapidly up his chest, into his throat, and then even pounding in his head. He thought it felt like he was on a very high roller coaster ride and climbing to one of the top peeks, just before the drop.

As he reached the door, he could hear Draper clearly, still talking to Brockman. McCarthy concentrated on Brockman's words, because if something went wrong, he was going to say, "Now, just relax." If possible, the entry would then be aborted.

McCarthy heard no such signal, and he quietly keyed the lock in the door handle and unlocked it. He then went to the key the landlord had said was for the deadbolt, and it did not work. McCarthy then began trying other keys on the ring, attempting to find the one that fit the deadbolt, while controlling his breathing to stay calm. He quietly isolated a shorter key that slid perfectly into the dead bolt.

Draper leaned against the doorway of the bedroom glaring at his intended victim, holding her in place with a stare. He talked on the phone to Brockman and enjoyed his moment of importance immensely. As Brockman asked, "Now no one has been hurt yet. How can we end this thing without someone being hurt?" Draper happened to glance at the dead bolt and saw it beginning to turn.

Draper dropped the phone, just as McCarthy was turning the key in the dead bolt. Draper closed the distance to the door, as McCarthy turned the dead bolt, unlocking the door. McCarthy quickly dropped his grip on the keys and turned the unlocked knob on the door, just as Draper hit the door, with all his weight holding it shut. Draper then adroitly relocked the deadbolt.

McCarthy instinctively kicked the door hard, and his foot almost went through the cheap door, while the deadbolt held fast. McCarthy pivoted out of the way of the door. Just as he did this, shots ripped through the door. McCarthy could feel the spray of the splinters of the door against his leather jacket. He could see by the holes coming through the door that Draper was shooting slugs out of his shotgun.

McCarthy did not need Brockman's signal, and he knew the entry must now be aborted. As the shooting stopped, he heard Carpenter say in a labored voice, "Dan . . . I'm hit." He turned to see that Carpenter must have stepped away from the wall when McCarthy appeared ready to open the door. This put him in the path of two of the deadly rounds. He lay helpless on the ground, tightly clutching his chest.

McCarthy grabbed hold of Carpenter's coat collar, behind the neck, allowing Carpenter's head to rest on McCarthy's wrist. McCarthy holstered his own weapon and picked Carpenter's up, as he quickly slid Carpenter away from the front of the apartment to the cover of the parked car.

McCarthy checked his friend's condition, while Dooley covered the door of the apartment. McCarthy noted a hole blown through Carpenter's left wrist, but all Carpenter was paying attention to was the pain in his chest. McCarthy quickly opened Carpenter's jacket and shirt. He breathed a sigh of relief, when he saw the 20-gauge slug was lodged in Carpenter's vest.

"You're going to be all right, Gary. The round was stopped by your vest," said McCarthy, certain and happy that his friend would survive this terrible night.

McCarthy's attention returned to the wound in the wrist. He concluded that an artery had been hit, by the powerful spurting of blood from the wound. McCarthy found a denim jacket on the seat of the car that they were using for cover. He commandeered the coat and tied it tightly around the gaping hole in Carpenter's wrist. Much to his relief, the bleeding stopped.

McCarthy radioed, "We have shots fired and an officer is down. I need an ambulance now to the north end of the alley, to the east of the 1000 block of New Berlin Street." The ambulance standing by in the area, already was in position, almost immediately. Now McCarthy would have to get Carpenter to the ambulance, which was about one-quarter block away.

"How you doing, Gary?" asked McCarthy.

"Fuckin'-A," Carpenter replied, with a pained look on his face.

"Can you walk?" asked McCarthy.

"No. Man, this hurts like hell," was the pained response of Dan's young friend.

"This is going to hurt some." With that, McCarthy placed Carpenter over his shoulder in a fireman's carry. He could not help but notice that, even though Carpenter and he were the same weight, Gary felt light as a feather. McCarthy ran to a three-foot border fence and jumped it, trying to move quickly to the ambulance, but staying out of the line of fire.

As he landed, after jumping the fence, Carpenter bounced on his shoulder and said, "Fuckin'-A, Dan, that hurts."

"Sorry, Gary. We're almost there."

By the time that sentence was said, Carpenter was in the ambulance and McCarthy yelled, "Don't mess around here! Just get him the hospital—he has a bleeding artery. The jacket around his arm seems to have stopped it for now!" As one of the emergency medical technician's began to assess Carpenter's condition, McCarthy added," He was also hit hard in the chest by a shotgun slug. The round was stopped by his vest."

The neighborhood was three blocks from Mother of Mercy Hospital, and Carpenter was at the hospital within minutes of being shot.

McCarthy moved back to his spot on the perimeter. At this moment in his life, Dan knew that, given the situation and opportunity, he could kill. He prayed to God he would be given the opportunity. He truly wanted to kill Ray Draper. The standoff continued. The stakes were now higher.

Compton had seen what happened. He took command of the scene again, and the chief relinquished it without complaint. He called Sgt. Hopkins to the scene from his home. Hopkins was trained as a negotiator. He told Brockman to set up an area for community services to meet with the press and keep them from coming to the inner perimeter.

Compton called for McCarthy. He said, "Are you all right?"

"Yes, sir. I don't want to leave until this is over," McCarthy said, in a determined voice.

"I'm not sending you anywhere. Do you still have the keys?" asked Compton.

"Yes," came the immediate response.

"You, Dooley, Stammos, and I are going to do the same thing. He won't expect it again.

"Thanks, Sarge. I'm with you all the way."

He then called for Stammos and Dooley to meet with McCarthy and him at a staging area for the entry. Draper did not know he'd hit anyone with the rounds. Sgt. Hopkins convinced him that he was tired, and that if he laid down, they would talk again when he woke up. Draper, who had been drinking continually throughout the incident, was now ready for this. After fifteen minutes of quiet, Compton gave the command to move.

This time, McCarthy knew which key was which, and they quickly entered the apartment. Draper's wife was found unhurt, and Draper was seen lying on his water bed, with both hands empty. McCarthy landed on him first, followed by Compton, and then Stammos.

Draper tried furiously to free himself from the weight of the officers, but it was fruitless. The handcuffing process was seriously complicated by, not only the resistance, but the competing waves, caused by each separate officer landing on the waterbed. The same, relentless motion, which makes making love on a water bed pleasurable, makes fighting on a waterbed an extremely unique experience as far from the pleasures of sex as possible. In any case, Draper was handcuffed and taken into custody, without further injury to anyone else. McCarthy concluded that God answered his prayer to be given the opportunity to kill Ray Draper. God's answer was, "No."

CHAPTER 16
THE AFTERMATH

After clearing the scene nine hours after arriving, Dan McCarthy drove his squad car to the station. As he passed the front desk, he saw the most welcome sight he could have seen. It was his lovely wife, Victoria. She ran to him. She kissed and brushed his cheek. She frantically explained that she heard about an officer being shot on the news, when she woke up. She dropped the children at her mother's and came to the station.

"I'm sorry, but I had a bad feeling about this one. When I heard someone was shot . . . Well, I've never been so afraid in my life," her words being still tinged with fear.

Dan reassured her, "It was Gary. He's going to be all right. He will be mending for a long time. But I have a report to write. Can you wait for me?" He then looked at her, wishing he was home at that moment. He didn't feel strong then. Dan felt as if he somehow failed and wanted to just go home with his best friend, his wife, and never come back to this place again.

"Of course I'll wait." She kissed him one more time. "I love you," were her parting words, which gave him the strength to finish this long and terrible shift.

As McCarthy walked down the hallway to the report-writing room, he passed Capt. Hale. Hale looked like hell. He always looked overworked and stressed-out, even though no one was quite sure what he did. Then Hale called out to McCarthy. "That thing was screwed up from the get-go. If I'd been there, the only one with a bullet in him right now would be Draper," he said in a macho-asshole tone of voice that was, at the very least, unwelcome to McCarthy at this moment in his life. McCarthy felt as if someone had turned a switch that controlled his anger. It built up inside him like the pressure in Vesuvius the day

Pompeii was buried. He actually felt more anger toward Capt. Hale right now than toward Draper. There were so many things he wanted to say to Hale that would have made him feel better, but would have gotten him fired.

In the midst of this anger, McCarthy constructed his words carefully. "Well, Captain, sir, it is too bad with all your skill and experience you have managed to move into a position on this department that ensures you will never have to find yourself going through the door ever again."

McCarthy then continued to walk toward the report-writing room, pushing down the anger he felt toward the fat, arrogant captain, who liked to fantasize that he was still a police officer, when everyone on the department, except he, knew differently. Most officers laughed at Hale's incompetence. Not McCarthy. McCarthy would never find Hale funny again. The shooting of a partner can seriously change an attitude of a young officer. If Hale's supervisory incompetence would have been the last words said to McCarthy that morning, he could have developed into an embittered veteran, who learned to hate his job, his commanders, and eventually even himself. Hale was not to have the last word. McCarthy finished his reports after three hours of writing, and after turning them in to the shift commander, he passed the chief. "Chief, are we going to debrief this incident?"asked McCarthy.

"No. I know where the mistakes were made and who made them. They will never happen again. We do not need to talk about this." He turned slowly and walked away as if the brick wall he thought he could walk through earlier had fallen on him.

As McCarthy turned away from the chief he was confronted by several officers. Stammos was the spokesman.

"McCarthy. We want to tell you thanks for saving our friend. If you wouldn't have acted so quickly, Gary might be . . . well . . . thanks. That's all." Stammos shook his hand, as did the others with him.

McCarthy was speechless. He felt like crying and did not want to do that in front of the guys. He shook their hands and made his way to Victoria, who was seated in the break room area. "Let's go, Sweetheart," he said, as she put her arm around his waist and laid her head on his shoulder.

As Victoria wheeled the car out of the lot and headed for home, Dan said, "Turn around. I have to see Gary. He's at Mother of Mercy." The look she gave Dan almost opened up the floodgate of tears he was holding back with all his emotional might. "Please?" McCarthy added.

When Dan McCarthy walked into Gary's room, he was greeted by Gary's wife, Darlene, who was standing beside her husband's bed. Her eyes were red and glassy from the tears shed earlier upon hearing the news of the shooting of her husband. Now the tears were camouflaged by a brave smile she had chosen to wear.

Darlene Carpenter brought Dan and Vicki McCarthy up to date with Gary's progress. Gary was dozing in his bed, with his left arm heavily lying across his chest. The hospital staff had stopped the arterial bleeding. The doctor said they would need to call in a specialist to rebuild the damaged wrist, which the slug had torn through completely. The doctors were relatively certain he would not lose the arm, but they could not be certain whether or not he could ever return to the department.

Just then, Gary opened his eyes. A smile immediately came across Gary's face. Gary reached out his uninjured hand to McCarthy. "It's good to see you, Gary," McCarthy said, shaking his wounded partner's hand.

"It's good to be here to be seen," replied Carpenter. "My chest feels like I got hit with a sledge hammer, man. It hurts worse than my arm, but I think that's all going to change. Hey, I'm sorry I swore at you when you were carrying me. It really hurt. I didn't even notice the wound in my arm at first, because my chest hurt so bad."

"You don't need to apologize for anything. He shot you with a 20-gauge slug. That would have to feel like a sledge hammer. It must hurt like hell," replied McCarthy.

"Where's Draper?" asked Carpenter, with a cringe caused by pain, as he readjusted himself in his bed.

"The asshole is in jail," answered Dan with disappointment. Dan McCarthy, who had been raised Catholic, did not feel guilty for praying for the opportunity to kill Ray Draper. He would not feel guilty about saying that prayer. God had answered it, no, but McCarthy thought that there was no harm in asking.

"We went in, after he went to sleep. He fought with us some, but did not reach his guns. His wife was ok. She loves him again now," answered McCarthy.

"That's the way it always has been, and that's the way it always will be. He beats her. We save her. We leave. They love each other. They hate us. They have kids who grow up to be the same way. They actually have a term for it now," mused Carpenter.

"What's that?" asked McCarthy, who was familiar with the situation, but not the corresponding professional terminology affixed to the phenomenon.

"Yeah, they call it job security." said Carpenter, laughing at his own joke.

Carpenter then groggily laughed himself back to sleep. He was obviously under the influence of some pretty potent painkillers.

Then, he suddenly opened his eyes again quickly and said with urgency, "Hey, McCarthy. Thanks for getting me here in one piece. Well, almost in one piece. The doctors said that I could have bled to death." Carpenter offered his uninjured hand again.

"I just wish I could have done something to make it turn out differently," said McCarthy, almost overwhelmed by a sudden rush of sadness.

"Don't wish that!" responded Carpenter, with a mysterious burst of energy in his voice. "Different might not have been better." That burst of energy seemed to be the last one young Officer Gary Carpenter had to give, for he slowly closed his eyes once again and drifted back to sleep.

Dan McCarthy rejoined his wife, who had been speaking with Darlene. Gary's wife had her dramatic tale of trauma to tell. She, too, had heard the news of an officer shot and had rushed to the station. She felt instantly that, considering the time of day, Gary had to have been involved. If something serious was happening, she knew Gary would try to be in the middle of it. Her fears were realized, and she was taken to the hospital by one of the day-shift officers. The doctors had explained that there would be a long road to recovery, but he was going to recover.

Gary was already insisting he was coming back to the department. He would not take an early retirement because of the likes of Ray Draper. McCarthy thought, "If there's any way I can help get Gary back into a squad car, I will."

CHAPTER 17
THE RECOVERY

"Flashbacks!"

Everyone has heard of them, and like everything else that is depicted by Hollywood, they are much different in reality than the way they are dramatized on the big screen. At least they were different as far as McCarthy was concerned. McCarthy could be driving his squad, he could be standing at the door of a complainant, or he could be playing with his children, and they would come. They were intense memories. The most common flashback McCarthy would have was a mental picture of the rounds coming through the door, slowly, and deliberately.

McCarthy found that he could change the ending of this intense memory. He found, sometimes, he would kick the door in and shoot Draper; and at other times, he would leap in front of the round headed for Gary, and stop it with his own vest. After the intense, repetitive memory would end, he would be left with a strong sense he had done something wrong. He would feel totally responsible, as if he had done something to cause Carpenter to be gunned down.

One month after the incident, McCarthy was writing up a report on an intoxicated driver whom he had just arrested and processed. The memory came again in all its intensity. He could see the first round coming through the door, followed by the second, and then the third, and finally the fourth. Before he could do anything, he heard, "Dan, I'm hit," and he turned quickly to see Sgt. Compton standing by the door.

"McCarthy, are you all right?" was the question that chased away the memory and left him once again, feeling guilty to be alive and healthy.

"Yes sir, Sergeant. I was just thinking about . . ."

"Carpenter, and the night he was shot," was how Compton, to McCarthy's amazement, finished the sentence for him.

"How did you know?" McCarthy asked.

Compton pulled up a chair next to Dan, and his face ceased for a moment to be the rock-solid veteran that could handle anything. His faced showed the understanding, empathetic compassion that can only come from personal experience. He then recited a litany that would be an elixir for McCarthy.

"I know the look, Dan. You need to know that shit happens. It's not your fault; it just happens. You didn't shoot him. Draper did! The fact is shit happens. Didn't you see that. It was in all the papers. Shit Happens! Teddy Roosevelt said, 'That which doesn't kill you, makes you stronger.' Let it make you stronger, McCarthy! The experience either beats you or becomes a part of who you are. Don't let it beat you."

With that, he held out his hand, and pulled McCarthy closer to him, as he said in a voice much quieter, but with an intensity Compton was known for, "The world needs people like us, who walk through the valley of darkness, and fear no evil. The fact is, we do fear the evil, but we don't let the fear beat us down. Instead, we grit our teeth, stick together, and damn it, we just look the evil straight in the eye and use the fear to win. Otherwise, you never get out of the valley . . . give it time. It will get better. You will get better. I've been where you are. Believe me, McCarthy, when I say, it will get better."

Compton's words were like a tonic. McCarthy thought about what Compton had said. He did not know if it was what Compton said, the way he said it, or just that it was Compton who said it, but it was better than any therapy or medicine. Compton had said what McCarthy needed to hear. McCarthy continued to have the intense memories, but the feeling of guilt never accompanied it again.

Five months after the shooting, McCarthy's phone rang, and it was Gary Carpenter at the other end. "Dan, I need your help."

"Sure. Any way I can," answered McCarthy.

"I told the doctor what you do. I told him that I would not need to be as strong as I used to be to do the job, if I could do what you do, when people resist. Can you teach me that and help me get back to work?" asked Carpenter.

"Fuckin'-A!" McCarthy said, with unmistakable excitement.

"Fuckin'-A!" was Carpenter's reply.

The training took place three days a week. There was a day to recover between each session. Carpenter was an excellent student. He was the perfect student, which is any student that has the ability, coupled with the desire, to learn.

Each session would begin at 7:30 a.m., after McCarthy finished working the night shift. Carpenter became extremely adept at moving in smoothly, and executing any number of holds. His strength was his balance. He had an uncanny sense of balance. As Carpenter took McCarthy to the ground during practice, he had a sense of where he was at all times.

Each session would start with stretches, then techniques would be practiced. They would be practiced by the numbers, and then slowly, for form, attempting to arrive at a smoothness of technique. Then, the two would retire to the weight room for strength building. McCarthy could see his brave friend was fighting through the pain at first; and eventually it either went away, or pain gave up on trying to defeat this worthy adversary.

After one month, Gary began shooting. He had to adjust his grip. At first, the recoil caused him to wince. In a very short time, the Glock looked to be an extension of his arm. It fit him like a glove again. Within a month, he was shooting better than before he was wounded.

One day, after the training had been going on for three months, Carpenter seemed to step it up a notch. He lifted heavier, hit the bag harder, and McCarthy noticed he himself was hitting the mat harder when Gary threw him. It was training, and yet Carpenter had a street-application sincerity about everything he did this day. After the session, both cops were sitting on the mats, sipping cold Gatorade, when Carpenter looked up and declared, as a drop of sweat dripped off his nose, "I'm ready!"

"You're ready!" said McCarthy with sincerity.

"I will see the doctor tomorrow. He wants a report of my progress. Can you give him one?" asked the sweating young warrior, who could not be defeated.

"I will. I will tell him that I would take you into any call with me," said McCarthy.

This comment brought a smile from the Carpenter, who had undergone four surgeries and seven months of recovery, all with the plan of getting back on a beat. Now it was going to happen.

Seven months after the call, Ray Draper was spending time in a state penitentiary, waiting for twenty-seven years to pass. Sue Draper still professed a sincere love for him, but had already been in another abusive relationship to keep the police occupied.

The chief of police had formed a SWAT team to respond to serious calls of this nature in the future. Compton was the officer in charge. Stammos was the team leader. McCarthy was a tactical team member.

As for Carpenter and McCarthy, the experience did not kill them. It became a part of them and made them stronger. They walked into the valley of darkness together, and seven months later, they walked out of it together. They had won the hard-fought battle in all three arenas a cop has to win in.

The first arena they won in was a very close call. This is the true arena. The arena of combat, which is a tough, gritty, unforgiving place, where one side has rules, and the other does not. It was a close call, but they both won physically. McCarthy and Carpenter both came home to their families. It was a long road back for Gary, but the day came when he would once again walk into the line-up room, and smile that thousand-dollar smile, and make the statement everyone longed to hear again, "Fuckin'-A!"—a trademark phrase he shared with Stammos.

Carpenter and McCarthy won legally in the second arena . . . the courts. They had played by the rules. Every action they took was legally upheld. Every statement made by Draper was legally obtained. Every legal hurdle thrown up by the public defender was cleared. Draper was sent to prison for twenty-seven years for his part in the attempted murder of Carpenter and McCarthy. He even got the sentence from Judge Alice. He got only three years less than the maximum. All the cops could say was, "Amazing."

The third arena is sometimes the darkest, most difficult arena to wage combat in. It is usually a private struggle, which cops too often do not call backup for. The third arena is the emotional arena. This was tough for both officers. Carpenter could easily have given up at any time and "pulled the pin" on his career. Many officers do, when they are as seriously wounded as Carpenter was. He could not see it, though. All he ever wanted to be was a cop. He pictured himself going back to school, to learn another profession, and he felt he could do that, if there was no other way. Then, he pictured himself telling someone what he did for a living, and he could not visualize himself saying anything but, "I'm a police officer." He made up his mind and did the work needed to bring himself back.

Carpenter felt that McCarthy had saved his life, by reacting so quickly after Carpenter had been shot. Whether this was true or not did not matter, because Carpenter returned the favor, by living and returning to work. By making the monumental effort to do this, he may have saved McCarthy's emotional life. Seeing his friend walk into the line-up room, as fit as a fiddle, was better for McCarthy than three years of therapy and a whole case of Prozac.

These two cops had gone through a hellish situation together, and they won—physically, legally, and emotionally. They learned that what Teddy Roosevelt had said was absolutely true—"That which does not kill you, makes you stronger."

CHAPTER 18
MARRIED AND WITH CHILDREN

Carpenter and McCarthy were paired together. It would be a busy night. It was warm. It was Saturday, and there was a full moon—a combination experienced cops knew would mean their money would be well-earned. The first call of the night was a domestic on South 32nd Street. There was no need to verify the address when they arrived in the area, because as soon as McCarthy and Carpenter exited their squad, they could hear the screaming.

"You fucking bitch! I am tired of your shit!! I'm going to kill you!!!" followed by a metallic crash, and then shortly after that, a thud.

Carpenter and McCarthy were on a dead-run toward the sounds. They reached a gate to the backyard, where the noise was coming from; and McCarthy fumbled with the latch, hearing a gravelly, choked-out, and barely audible voice say, "You're killing me . . ."

McCarthy's fingers responded to the threat and discovered the combination to the gate-latch mechanism. He swung the seven-foot gate open and burst into the backyard.

"Police Officers!" McCarthy and Carpenter shouted in unison, but their words had no impact on those engaged in the life-and-death struggle before them. A large, balding, middle-aged man was seated on the chest of a female, who appeared about ten years his junior. The man had both hands strongly locked around the throat of the female. Her eyes were bulging and her mouth was open, gasping for air, which was all around her, but unattainable. McCarthy hit the man first, full-body at a crouched run, and peeled him off the female. The man hit hard on the ground and skidded into a barbecue grill lying tipped over on the ground. McCarthy recognized the noise this made as being identical to the metallic crash heard by him when he had been outside the gate. McCarthy was relieved to discover the grill was not in use at the time.

The large, bald man struggled, but could not regain any balance or momentum, after McCarthy's initial impact. Carpenter took hold and control of the left arm, as McCarthy rigorously pried the right arm into a position to handcuff. McCarthy held the arm into position, as the large, angry man struggled to break free. McCarthy reached for his handcuff case and undid the snap.

Before McCarthy could remove his cuffs from their case, he was grabbed forcefully from behind by the shoulder. The female he had just saved from certain death was now trying to pull McCarthy off the large bald man. She screamed, spitting in the startled young policeman's face as she formed her words. "Goddamn it! What are you doing to my husband? Let him go! You're hurting him!"

Having this feminine re-enforcement had an immediate, energizing effect on the large bald man. He began to rise off the ground, lifting the two smaller officers up. Although McCarthy had never ridden an angry bull, he sensed it must feel very much like this. That thought caused the hypothalamus in McCarthy's medulla oblongata to identify this as a life-and-death situation for McCarthy. McCarthy became instantly adrenalized. Carpenter must have been also so inspired, because in unison the two officers pried the raging bull's front legs out from under him, bringing him, face-first, hard into the turf. Like magic, the raging bull became human again and the fight was out of him.

He was handcuffed quickly; it was only then that McCarthy realized the wife was still hanging around his neck, screaming, and trying to tear him away from her husband. McCarthy took her by the arm, shrugged his shoulder, and she flipped over and fell onto the back of her husband. She was a bit easier to handcuff than her husband. Neither the husband nor the wife would explain what the fight was about. They would not even admit there had been a fight. Both officers were "assholes," in the eyes of this "loving" couple. Both were charged with disorderly conduct and resisting arrest. The male was also charged with battery to spouse, but, without her as a witness, the charge would probably be pled away by a district attorney.

Carpenter and McCarthy both left the jail frustrated. They knew they had just saved a woman's life. They were the white knights rescuing the damsel in distress. They even knew they had arrived in the nick of time. Their payoff was to be called assholes and then to have the fair damsel turn into the wicked witch and attack them. This was still new to the young officers; and with time, they would learn the dynamics of domestic abuse and violent controlling relationships. They would even learn to understand it. It would still never be easy.

They had little time to discuss the call, before they were dispatched to a disturbance at Bedrock Catering. This was a large banquet hall, built in the remodeled Power Station Building. They were directed to the rear, where a large group had gathered and were yelling at each other. This was obviously a wedding reception, because the bride and groom were attempting to break up participants.

McCarthy and Carpenter asked for additional units to respond, but dispatch said that all other units were tied up and could not respond. With that said, Carpenter said to McCarthy, "No arrests, unless we have to."

McCarthy agreed and answered, "Peace keepers on this one. If we arrest the wrong one, we'll have a riot."

They pulled to a stop and got out slowly, to let their presence make an impact. It seemed to work; people stopped screaming at each other, though they looked to the officers with the anger and disgust still in their eyes.

The bride was in tears and the groom looked absolutely at wit's end, as if asking, "What happened to the happiest day of my life."

The groups separated naturally, much like the Hatfield's and McCoy's would after a skirmish. Carpenter went to one group and McCarthy the other. It was quickly discovered that the young couple were neighbors. They had found love living close to each other, but the parents had been adversaries for years. The reasons were many and varied. There was a fence built on the lot-line and a car scratched in a minor hit-and-run accident. There was also the issue of one parent working in his shop with that damned saw grinding away all night and the other painting their house the same color as the first. To an insane person, these are all perfectly good reasons to want to kill each other.

What it boiled down to, was that both families had been bad neighbors for years and had grown to hate each other. In the midst of all this hate, both families could not fathom that their children were in love. Tonight's argument had started over a toast given by the brother of the bride. He had hoped that the total love they felt at that moment, would not breed the total contempt that it grew out of.

The battle was on almost immediately after the wedding meal. The groups were separated for now, but it appeared safe to say that this wedding reception would have to be ended. When the group separated, the bride and groom felt that if they went to each other, they would be abandoning their families. They began to walk away from each other. McCarthy called both of them over, under the guise of getting some additional information.

They stood facing each other, on opposite sides of a cyclone fence. This arrangement seemed to satisfy the warring factions. The bride was in tears, and McCarthy thought there was not a much sadder sight than the make-up of a beautiful young bride, smeared by tears of sadness. This is the day that almost every little girl dreams will be her happily-ever-after-day.

By this time, the groom was crying also, but it was the restrained cry of a man who had been raised to believe that a man does not cry. He would brush any tear from his eyes as quickly as it formed.

After McCarthy wrote down the particular information needed for a report, he asked them both, "I was wondering. Why did you two get married? Was it to make your families happy or because you loved each other?"

The lovely, young, dark-haired bride looked at the groom and the groom's eyes locked into hers. The look answered the question. The bride's lip quivered; the groom stopped trying to fight back the tears, and welcomed them as much as he welcomed the feeling of love that swelled in his young heart.

After a short pause, they rushed toward each other, and touched hands through the cyclone fence. Their gaze into each other's eyes never wavered. The groom spoke first, "I am sorry for what my Mom and Dad said to you. I love you."

The bride answered in sobs, "I don't think it will work out. Our parents hate each other, and eventually, it will tear us apart."

"But we have to try. We can't let them tear us apart like this, before we ever . . . Ow . . . Ow . . . OW!" The groom yelled over and over, as he began to jump up and down. He looked down and began to yell even louder, seeing that he unwittingly stood upon the nest of sand bees. The bees were not liking it at all and were attacking his ankles vigorously. "Ow! Ow! Oww! My God, OWWW!!"

McCarthy pulled him off the nest and batted the bees away with his notebook. The groom was quickly taken to his car, which was close-by. He was placed in the passenger seat, and sat with his legs, covered with welts, hanging out of the car. Carpenter ran for ice and returned immediately from the banquet hall's kitchen with a bag of ice and towels.

The bride had come around the fence and was now showering her husband with kisses of sympathy, mixed with love. Officer Carpenter, seeing what was happening between the two young lovers, who could not catch a break from their families, handed the bride the ice, which she tenderly applied to the badly stung ankles of her new husband.

"Are you allergic to bee stings?" asked Carpenter.

"No, I'll be just fine now," said the groom, as he reached for and squeezed the hand of his bride. She looked up at him, and then laid her cheek against his leg, kissing him.

After seeing the bee stings were clearly not life-threatening and the added bond the bees had prompted in the young newlyweds, McCarthy hurriedly suggested, "I don't care what your plans were tonight. Why don't the two of you just leave. Leave now, and begin your lives together. I can see you love each other. You married each other in spite of your families, not because of them. Do not cheat yourselves out of the life you've planned together because of them."

The two looked at each other, smiled, and the bride said, with new-found exuberance, "I'll drive." The groom kissed her and swung his legs slowly into the car, his face alternating between a look of pure joy and of being racked with pain. The bride destroyed the shape of her beautiful gown and without care or concern, got behind the wheel of the car.

As she started the car, she rolled down the window and asked, "What are your names?"

"My name is Officer Dan McCarthy," said McCarthy.

"Gary Carpenter," responded Gary.

She then whispered to her husband. They looked at each other, and then both nodded. "Thank you for everything. Our first boy is going to be named Daniel Garret." With that, she drove off, spinning the wheels on the gravel in her excitement to get on with the rest of their life.

When the car carrying the young couple sped out of the lot, both warring factions ran to the scene and demanded to know what was going on. Carpenter told them, "You've kind of ruined their day. They are going to try and salvage their life together."

McCarthy added, "I hope the line that fits is 'And they lived happily ever after.' Does anyone here want to pursue charges against anyone else?"

The group looked sheepishly back and forth at each other, but there was no response. McCarthy then ended by saying, "Try harder from now on to get along than you have in the past, or you will lose those kids. They deserve better from all of you. They are wonderful children and you should be happy they found each other. Good night, folks."

As Carpenter and McCarthy drove away, Carpenter asked, "Who's going to write up this mess?"

"I will," McCarthy answered, as he reached for the radio, "255 will be 10-8 with a report."

"10-4, 255," answered the dispatcher.

There was a brief, but loud, silence in the squad. Then Gary summed the situation up simply and accurately in a way only Gary could sum it up, "Fuckin'-A!"

"You know it," said McCarthy, "Fuckin'-A."

Chapter 19
Baby Jane

The city of La Claire was noted for its raucous downtown area. The area was filled with a variety of taverns, which came alive each night, giving the area a personality change. Everyone knows a man about whom people say, "He's such a nice guy, until he drinks." That was the way the denizens of downtown La Claire were. It was a nice downtown filled with nice people . . . until they drank, and then the downtown had a very unpleasant personality.

Some said La Claire had more bars per capita than any city in the world. Whether that was true or an urban legend, McCarthy didn't know. He did know it seemed the downtown area had more bars than he had ever seen anywhere in such a small space.

Whenever possible, the La Claire Police Department scheduled foot patrol officers in the downtown area. People behaved better when the foot patrol officers were downtown regularly. When the foot patrol was downtown sporadically, they would be very busy, because the officers were in the middle of action constantly.

McCarthy had been scheduled for several weeks, walking the downtown beat. Early in the evening, he would keep himself busy, busting pot smokers and public urinators in the alleys. Around bar time, he would be in the thick of things, when fights would start. The standard procedure in downtown La Claire was, if an officer had to physically break the fight up, it didn't matter who started the fight, both parties were arrested.

After bar time, McCarthy would follow loud groups walking back toward campus and catch them breaking a window, tossing garbage cans, or harassing females. On this particular night, McCarthy was walking with Stammos. The weather was cool; one of those nights where it was too warm for a jacket, but too cool to go without. The two friends had just hit the street and almost immediately came across two males writing their names on the wall of a business. The ink they were using was urine.

McCarthy walked up to one and stood to the left and rear of the young college-age male, so that he was close, but out of sight. McCarthy informed the young man, "You know, doing that in public is against the law."

The young man was very intent on controlling the release of his bladder, so as to cross the "t" on the name Art; therefore, he did not even look to McCarthy as he replied, "Who the fuck do you think you are, a cop or something?"

"As a matter of fact I am," was McCarthy's answer.

Both young men then attempted to do the impossible. They attempted to stop urinating in full stream and tuck away their "quills," if you will. According to the writing on the wall, one was named Steve and the other was Art. The letters of their last names were badly run together down the front of their pants. Both were ticketed for depositing an unlawful refuse, which was the ordinance for urinating in public.

After citing the boys and turning them loose, the two officers continued walking their beat, at a pace slower than a normal walk. Their steps and pace perfectly matched. After a long silence, McCarthy asked, "Hey, Randy."

"Yeah?"

"Why is it, if a man pulls out his penis in public and stands there with it in his hand, he is charged with the crime of lewd and lascivious conduct? If the same man does all those same things, but pisses all over everything to boot, he is cited with depositing an unlawful refuse. Why is that?"

"Intent. The first time he intends to get his rocks off, and the second time he just needs to tap a kidney. It's not sexual."

"Speaking of sexual, isn't it true that if a man stands outside a window watching a woman inside an apartment taking her clothes off, we charge him with being a voyeur?"

"Yeah. What's your point?" Randy asked, with a hint of annoyance.

"If the same man is standing nude in the window and a woman walks by, looks up, and sees the man in the window nude, we charge the man with indecent exposure, right?! Why is that?"

McCarthy could not grasp the pure dichotomy of reason in these two situations and sincerely wanted to know.

"Again, intent!" said Stammos, once again with a heavy accent on the "tent." "The man wants the woman to see him, so he can get his rocks off in one case, and in the other case, he wants to see the naked woman to get his rocks off. It's the intent that makes the crime."

"Is that always the intent that is assumed . . . that the man is trying to get his rocks off and not the woman?" asked the young McCarthy.

"It's the difference between men and women. Picture Sandy in records in that situation," said Stammos, pausing for McCarthy to conjure up a mental image. Without further prompting, McCarthy pictured the beautiful blonde with her long flowing hair dropping lightly over her shoulders and down her back. She was combing her hair, while wearing a long, silk, red robe, with an elaborate floral design. She had been careless in tying the robe closed, and the knot came loose, forcing those absolutely perfect breasts to free themselves from the confines of the robe . . .

"Time's up!" said Stammos. "Tell me the truth, was Sandy in the window, or on the sidewalk in your little daydream?"

McCarthy felt his face flush, and Stammos, who was a master at body language spotted the embarrassment immediately and started laughing. "I rest my case. You see, that's the way God created men and women. They got it and we want it. That's the way it always has been, and that's the way it always will be."

McCarthy was always amazed at the grasp of the world Stammos had. He had a perspective that McCarthy hoped to achieve someday.

As the two officers had just completed the Peeping Tom versus Peeping Tanya issue, Stammos and McCarthy, in unison, started crossing the street heading toward a parking ramp. Both had seen a balding man in his 30s, following a black female prostitute known as "Baby Jane" into the ramp. McCarthy had arrested Baby Jane on two previous occasions. Once on a warrant and another time for pulling a knife on a "G.I. John," when he failed to pay her for services rendered. She was arrested for the assault, but she wanted to press charges against the G.I. for shoplifting.

The balding man, who was now following the formerly aggrieved merchant, was honed in on Baby Jane like a laser-guided missile. By the look on balding man's face, you could see his "intent" for entering the ramp was something more than to retrieve his parked car. The officers picked up their pace to a fast walk, to gain ground on the man.

Once inside the ramp, they could see the man had gained ground on Baby Jane. He obviously did not see the officers behind him, because he closed to within five feet of Baby Jane, and yelled, "How'd you like to suck on this baby?" He then, in a practiced move, had his coat open and was "cuffing his puppy" feverishly with his right hand.

Baby Jane turned to see what she had seen thousands of times before, and simply raised her eyebrows slightly. If the balding man was looking for a reaction, he had picked the wrong victim. She stopped and took a drag on the cigarette she was holding. She then dispassionately looked down at the man, who was now grunting. McCarthy thought the balding man was doing his best impression of Mount Vesuvius, when it was about to spill hot lava all over Pompeii. Jane sardonically proclaimed, "Honey . . . if I was a man and mine was that small, I wouldn't be showin' it off in public."

By this time, McCarthy and Stammos were on the man, "You, sir, are under arrest!"

The subject attempted to spin away and run, but his momentum was used to direct the embarrassed man to the hood of a nearby car. He was handcuffed, and Stammos called for a car for transport.

Baby Jane was a victim and McCarthy gathered her information for the report. McCarthy was upset to find out there was a probation and parole warrant on file for Baby Jane. Arresting her would just complicate the case, and he knew she would be upset. He had no choice in the matter but wished he did.

When Jane received the news, she was more than a little upset. "Fuck you! Fuck you! Fuck you!" was the only dialog she shared with the officers. After the arrest, McCarthy searched Baby Jane and found a switchblade in her purse, so she was charged also with possession of a switchblade knife.

When they reached the jail, McCarthy took Jane to be booked, while Stammos handled "the weenie-wagger."

Jane was not happy with McCarthy, but at the jail, she no longer was vocal. McCarthy felt she'd calmed down enough to take her handcuffs off. He did so; she stared directly into McCarthy's eyes in what appeared to be an attempt to make him feel the hate she had for him deep in her soul.

The female jailer then said, "Jane, could you please empty your pockets and take off your coat?" This seemed like such a simple request, and it was the first request that Baby Jane appeared anxious to grant. Her eyes changed from a glare in McCarthy's direction, to a sultry look in the jailer's direction. She began dancing in a slow rhythm to music only she could hear. She unbuttoned one button at a time, slowly and deliberately. Abruptly, she dropped her coat to the floor, revealing that she was quite efficiently dressed for a prostitute. She had nothing on under the coat, but her shoes and some black, crotchless pantyhose. She closed her eyes and continued to smoothly and seductively dance.

Sabrina, the jailer on duty, led Baby Jane into the changing room, with a jail uniform in hand. Baby Jane danced all the way into the room, blowing McCarthy kisses all the way.

Back on the street, McCarthy filled Stammos in on what had happened during the booking of Baby Jane. Stammos told McCarthy, "You are going to meet her over and over again. I am surprised she hasn't killed anyone yet. She is one dangerous whore, and she'd use that knife to cut your throat in a heartbeat, if the mood struck her.

McCarthy pictured himself having to shoot a woman. He did not like the idea of shooting anyone at all, much less a woman. Then he visualized what technique he would use to disarm her, if she came at him with a knife. His background in the martial arts would be a hindrance to him, if he was ever attacked with a knife.

McCarthy knew knives were dangerous. They kill silently and quickly. Knives are easily concealed and never run out of ammunition. Some criminals preferred to do their business with knives, because the courts, juries, and prosecutors, truly in their ignorance, did not view the knife in the same way they viewed guns. This attitude existed in spite of the fact that a victim who is attacked with the knife is as traumatized, maybe even more so, than a person attacked by a gun. The criminal attacking with a knife is treated with much less severity than someone making the same deadly assault with a gun.

McCarthy pondered, as he walked quietly with Stammos, that the first thing that he was taught in the first knife defense class, and the same thing that was taught in every knife defense class was, "When you try to disarm a person with a knife, you will most likely be cut. Count on it. Expect to see your own blood. Do not let the sight of your own blood shock you to inaction. If you do, you will lose the fight and you will die."

McCarthy was quite certain that if the attack with a knife came suddenly without warning, he would probably react without thinking, in a manner taught in the martial arts. If the attacker brandished the knife first and he would have time to think, plan, and then react, he would most certainly draw his weapon and shoot rather than risk injury or death at the hands of some psycho slasher.

His silent reverie ended abruptly when a mass of bodies came exploding out the door of Le Cabaret. A very large bouncer in a red polo shirt was sweeping four young males out the door. They were all yelling, threatening, and the two farthest away from the bouncer were swinging at him in unison. The two that were swinging were dressed identically and looked to be identical twins. The blows were not connecting, due to the two screaming men standing between them and the bouncer. The bouncer had done his job. He took it outside, and now McCarthy and Stammos took over.

"255, send us backup and a car for transport to the front of Le Cabaret. We have a 10-10 (fight in progress), five parties involved."

With dispatch notified and help on the way, McCarthy and Stammos waded into the fray, "Police Officers, break it up." Immediately the two that were not swinging, stepped away and began to try to tell the officers their story at once. As the talkers stepped away, the bookends that were swinging, tried to take advantage of the opening and advanced, swinging wildly at the large, but incredibly patient bouncer. The way the twins were swinging, gave them the appearance that they were both being controlled identically by the same puppeteer.

The matched set did not reach the bouncer, whose large, muscular body had established a no-retreat-from-here stance. Luckily for the two drunken, similar siblings, McCarthy and Stammos reached them before they reached the bouncer, and they were "tightened up" by the officers, in wristlocks, and spun away from the bouncer's reach.

They landed over the hood of a Mercedes, parked out front. Both of the identical drunken duelers tried to break free of the rear wristlocks they were in, but found resistance meant pain. "OK, OK, OK, OK, OK," was the answer of both, simultaneously.

The brief, but thorough, investigation revealed that the two young men arrested were brothers. The two men with them were friends of the brothers. The brothers, who were twins, were celebrating their twenty-first birthday. Inside the bar, they'd seen two females, who were also twins. The brothers had felt this was a sign from God, and recognized that God had sent to them this pair of similarly "righteous asses"—they'd walked up to the young ladies and grabbed them in their place of righteousness.

This started the problem. The girls, whose boyfriends were bartenders at Le Cabaret, did not feel that their private parts were willed to these two twins. They told the bouncer, who asked them to leave. The male twins had become belligerent. At the same time, the twins' friends attempted to become street-side lawyers. Everyone was yelling at once. The twins wanted to fight and the street-side lawyers wanted to debate. The bouncer packaged the whole bunch up and ran them out the door.

Statement forms were left for the bouncer, the female twins, and the street-side lawyers. The two male twins spent their twenty-first birthday in jail. They were charged with disorderly conduct and fourth degree sexual assault. The twins were separated and booked individually at the jail.

As the first twin was being booked, he was told by Stammos, "You have been arrested for disorderly conduct and fourth degree sexual assault."

The first twin's face was impassive upon hearing disorderly conduct, but became quite animated when he heard the second charge. He yelled, "Fourth degree sexual assault! No way I raped anyone! What do you mean fourth degree sexual assault?"

Stammos calmly answered, "That means you grabbed a young lady's backside without her consent. That's against the law and is fourth degree sexual assault, sir."

The man's demeanor changed instantly, and he smiled as he nodded his head.

"No way, man. I didn't grab her backside at all, man. That was a righteous ass I grabbed." The first twin smiled, and his eyes drifted skyward as though remembering the soft silkiness of the aggrieved female twin's bottom.

As the second twin was being booked, he was also told of the charge of disorderly conduct and fourth degree sexual assault. "Fourth degree sexual assault!" he exploded. "No way I raped anyone! What do you mean fourth degree sexual assault?"

Once again, as if scripted, Stammos answered, "That means you grabbed a young lady's backside without her consent. That's against the law and is fourth degree sexual assault, sir."

The second twin's demeanor changed instantly, and he smiled as he nodded his head. "No way, man. I didn't grab her backside at all, man. That was a righteous ass I grabbed." The second twin smiled and his eyes drifted skyward, as if also remembering the soft silkiness of the second aggrieved female twin's bottom.

As McCarthy and Stammos walked from the jail, McCarthy said to Stammos, "Booking those guys was kind of like Yogi Berra said."

"You mean it's like deja vu all over again?" replied Stammos.

"Deja vu all over again," repeated McCarthy.

"It was a phenomenon," said Stammos.

"A phenomenon," said McCarthy.

When the officers returned to the downtown area, the streets were barren. Bartime came and went, and all that was left were empty cups, broken bottles, a strong smell of beer, urine, and an assortment of sidewalk pizzas.

This was the part of the night McCarthy liked as much as the busy part. Walking, pulling doors, and peace. The officers would separate, to cover more area. McCarthy would make it a point to reach the area around the riverfront at sunrise. He liked the contrasts of the job. There were the incredibly nice people and the incredibly cruel people. There were times of violent intensity and moments of pure tranquility.

This morning was especially beautiful. Instead of taking a lunch break in a crowded restaurant, McCarthy went down to the river to his spot. It was the cement footing of a bridge long-gone and long since forgotten. He sat there looking at the fog roll over the Mississippi. He watched and listened to the fish jumping.

A turtle popped up in the water in front of McCarthy and looked at McCarthy, as if it was trying to discern what the stationary figure was. The turtle tread water for about a minute and then McCarthy cocked his head. The movement startled the turtle and caused it to dart into the depth of the dark, muddy, powerful river.

As McCarthy looked at his watch and determined that his break time was up, he saw it—majestic, certain, awe-inspiring, and absolutely mythic . . . a bald eagle. La Claire was known for its population of bald eagles that fished the waters and nested in the bluffs along the rivers. McCarthy had seen them many times before, but each time the thrill he felt was as if it was the first time. "Deja vu all over again," he said to himself quietly.

Many great societies have been awestruck by the eagle. The Romans bore standards with the eagle on them. Napoleon's army was led by standard bearers topped by golden eagles. The Native Americans believed that if an eagle flies over your home, your home is blessed. America chose the eagle as its symbol. McCarthy could understand why each time he watched one of these beautiful and powerful birds.

The eagle circled and then dove. The eagle's wings spread wide to slow its decent; and then, perfectly timed and executed, both talons hit the water at once, closed, and just as quickly the eagle was climbing back into the air with what looked to be a hapless perch hanging from its grasp. As the eagle flew out of McCarthy's sight, he sighed, smiled, and climbed off the footing. He walked the slow, steady pace of the foot patrol officer. The young walk man thought, "God, I'm lucky."

CHAPTER 20
WHATEVER HAPPENED TO BABY JANE?

McCarthy loved his job, but even things you love have their downside. In the martial arts, this is described as the balance of nature, or the yin and yang. You cannot appreciate good, if you have not experienced bad. Because there is good, you must have evil. Since there is a heaven, there must be a hell.

At times McCarthy felt as if he was born to be a cop. He could not picture himself doing anything else for the rest of his life. He loved working with Compton, Stammos, Carpenter, Dooley, and the list goes on. He surmised that, since there was a balance that exists in nature, this was why it was necessary for there to be a Stanley Brockman.

McCarthy thought, "If I did not have Stanley Brockman to work with, I would not appreciate working with Randy Stammos, Gary Carpenter, and all the others as much as I do." This was the thought McCarthy had each time he saw his name on the schedule partnered with Brockman.

McCarthy did not hate Brockman. McCarthy could not understand why Brockman had become a cop or why Brockman remained a cop. Since he was a cop, McCarthy was baffled as to why Brockman never tried to improve himself, or even recognize that he needed improvement.

McCarthy was young, and although gaining in experience every day, he still had much to learn. McCarthy knew enough about police work to know Brockman was a putz. He was dangerous to himself. He was dangerous to others. He was also a tenured employee, who would probably manage to hang on to his job for another twenty years, before he could retire. Since Brockman was going to be around, McCarthy would have to work with him. McCarthy once again mentally pledged to be energetic for two, positive for two, courteous for two, empathetic for two, and be cautious for two. Why? Because!

This thought was interrupted by Sgt. Compton, whose line-up was definitely interfering with McCarthy's mental prep for tonight's duties. ". . . Carpenter, you're on Beat Seven, Dooley, you're on Beat Eight, McCarthy and Brockman, you're walking downtown. McCarthy, keep that rookie out of trouble will you?"

"Yes, sir, Sergeant." answered McCarthy.

The rest of the room broke into laughter, and Brockman, who was chewing frantically on some Bazooka bubble gum while he read what Bazooka Joe had to say on the comic, shook his head and laughed insincerely, saying something under his breath.

As they cleared the station on foot, Brockman grunted, "Walking. I hate fucking walking. That asshole Compton is fucking with me. It's bad enough I have to walk, but I have to walk with . . ." He suddenly stopped. Brockman realized that he was actually talking out loud and not just thinking these thoughts.

"What were you saying, Stan?" asked McCarthy.

"I hate fucking walking." grunted Brockman, spitting out his gum onto the sidewalk.

McCarthy thought, as the gum hit the sidewalk, that Brockman was kind of like that chewed up piece of gum. You're walking along having a good day or a bad day, and suddenly, shlop, you step on this piece of gum. It maybe had its use once, for a little while, but now it is no good to anyone, and you're stuck with it. It could be worse—you could have stepped in shit. McCarthy smiled at that thought.

McCarthy noticed the difference between walking with Stammos and walking with Brockman. There was a rhythm to walking with Stammos. Walking with Brockman was like walking with a limp. You can barely walk, but you're not much good for anything else. Brockman wanted to hover in a doorway all night, and do and see as little as possible.

As people passed, McCarthy would say, "Evening, folks. How are you tonight," "Hello," and finally Brockman, who had been ignoring everyone, said, "Would you knock that shit off. These people are not your friends."

"They are not my enemies." said McCarthy, trying to stifle the annoyance he felt toward Brockman. "I cannot help but say hi to people. That's the way I was brought up."

"I'm going to talk to your mother about that, first chance I get," Brockman retorted. "Let's do some bar checks."

McCarthy answered excitedly, "Sure." McCarthy thought that, in the future, when he would walk with Brockman, all he had to do to get him working was to say hi to a lot of people.

Brockman had picked up his pace, and McCarthy, for a moment, felt he was working with a man on a mission. As a team, they were moving in sync. There was no limp about them. McCarthy started scanning the area, feeling that Brockman was now energized and possibly even an able partner. McCarthy thought that maybe he'd said something or done something that rekindled the rookie spirit in Brockman.

All these hopes were dashed against the rocks when McCarthy saw the focus of Brockman's sudden surge of enthusiasm. He had passed bar after bar, and now was obviously heading to the Red Lion. The Red Lion was the most notorious strip joint in La Claire.

"We better stop in here and make our presence known," said Brockman, with an uncharacteristic seriousness.

It was true that the Red Lion was a bar that walk men needed to pay particular attention to. It had more than its share of drug trafficking, fights, rip-offs, and other trouble. McCarthy would not question the intent of any other officer he worked with, but Brockman? Brockman wanted to see some naked ladies, twisting and gyrating on stage. That was Brockman's motivation.

The Red Lion comprised a long, rectangular room. The wall to the left of the door contained a very long bar. In the center of the bar was a round stage, on which an attractive, but very thin, blonde was dancing to the disco song, "Midnight at the Oasis." It was impossible to determine if the blonde was natural, because she had shaved her pubic area.

McCarthy did like coming into this bar. No one hustled to the back door to make good their escape when cops came in the front, because everyone was always focused on the dancers. A cop could move right up on a wanted man and arrest him before he could react, because often they were in a trance from the music and the movements of the nude dancers.

This blonde was pleasing the crowd, because she had about twenty-five dollar bills lying scattered about the stage. McCarthy was always amazed at what a stripper on-stage would do for a dollar. He thought, "If women at home would do what these women did for a dollar, there would be fewer divorces." Then McCarthy mentally chastised himself for not paying attention to the business at hand. Damn it, McCarthy! Pay attention! Tonight you have to be cautious for two.

When McCarthy scanned the bar, he could see the usual crowd. There was also a group of guys obviously there for a bachelor party. One poor schmuck was wearing a ball and chain, a ring in his nose, a brassiere, and was drinking from a bucket instead of a glass. He had a glazed-over look on his face, and McCarthy wondered what was keeping him on his bar stool.

Then McCarthy noticed a familiar face seated to the left of the groom-to-be. It was Baby Jane. Dan leaned to the left and called in a warrant check on Baby Jane. After several minutes, dispatch came back, "There are no wants or warrants." Baby Jane had come to La Claire to get away from the tough life of Chicago's Southside, but she failed to find a new life. She found she could work as a sales clerk at the local K-Mart and not make as much money spending all day on her feet saying, "Did you find what you're looking for? Thank you, have a nice day," as she could in five minutes on her knees saying, 'I gots what you're lookin' for. Oh baby! Oh baby! Oh baby!'"

McCarthy felt sorry for her, and then wondered if he *should* feel sorry for Baby Jane. She did not seem to be the type of person who wanted anyone's sympathy. She was a prostitute, but she was a survivor of a life McCarthy could only imagine.

Jane casually looked in McCarthy's direction and lit up as they made eye contact. She stood up and began to yell to him, "McCarthy. There's my old friend, McCarthy." Her speech was slurred and her balance was unsteady. She was under the influence of at least alcohol. She was trying to introduce McCarthy to everyone in the bar, but no one would listen. That did not matter; she was going to introduce him all the same.

"Hey, Evybody, this be Officer McCarthy. Don't fuck wit him. He's da man. He's mother-fuckin' Chuck Norris. Fuck, he don't want to be no mother-fuckin' Chuck Norris. Mother-fuckin' Chuck Norris wants to be him."

This made her laugh, but she was getting no one's attention but McCarthy's. The thin, nude blonde on the stage now was opening and closing her legs, while she was sucking on the middle finger of her right hand. Everyone was watching intensely. No one more so than Stanley Brockman. Everyone was watching but McCarthy and Baby Jane.

"McCarthy . . . Evytime youse sees me, youse arrests me," she related in the loud, high-pitched tone of a black prostitute born and raised on the hard streets of Chicago's Southside. "Come over here, McCarthy. I gots a present for you."

She turned slightly away from McCarthy, and looked down at the right pocket of her trench coat. Everything slowed down in McCarthy's mind. Everything he had learned up to this point had caused him to move without thought. Smoothly, quickly to anyone watching, but to McCarthy it was happening slowly . . . ever so slowly.

The thin blonde's right hand left her mouth, and slowly moved to the shaved area between her legs, in a mock act of masturbation. Everyone watched her hand, especially Brockman.

Jane's hand slowly slipped into her right pocket, and McCarthy circled around her rear toward her right-side. Jane was focused on her present, which she attempted to jerk out quickly, but it became hung up on her pocket. She jerked a second time and pressed the button on the black handled switchblade. Scnick was the only noise McCarthy heard. He could no longer hear the music, or Jane's words. He could no longer see the crowd, the dancer, or any of it. He saw the knife, her hand, and the movement of both.

Jane brought the knife into a position to kill McCarthy, doing her best *Psycho* impression. She paused. She was confused by the fact that McCarthy was no longer where he had been a moment before.

McCarthy slammed a hammer fist hard down on the precise bundle of nerves in the forearm he was trained to aim for. Jane's hand was forced to open from the impact, causing the knife to fly and clatter the length of the bar. This caught the attention of all in the bar, except Brockman. The blonde dancer had made eye contact with Brockman, and Brockman was moving with the music.

McCarthy put Baby Jane into a tight arm-bar. McCarthy saved this hold for the strong, deadly, and dangerous. Jane was all three. He doubled her over the bar and ordered her, loudly, to give him her other hand.

"Fuck you, Fuck you, Fuck you!" she screamed. This caught Brockman's attention, and he ran over and asked, "What the fuck is going on!"

"Just get her other hand back here. She tried to kill me!" McCarthy ordered.

"Fuck you. If I tried to kill you, your ass'd be dead," screamed Baby Jane, while she wriggled to free herself from McCarthy's hold.

McCarthy handcuffed the struggling prostitute. It was a chore, because the trench coat she wore did not fit her. The coat covered up Jane's wrists and hands, making it difficult to handcuff her. After a momentary delay caused by the coat, McCarthy had her cuffed. He then recovered the knife from in front of the astonished patrons and led Jane outside.

"255, I'll need a car for transport to the front of the Red Lion." McCarthy said "I" and meant "I." He did not want to acknowledge the presence of Brockman, or he would most certainly let Baby Jane go and knock Brockman on his ass. Dan understood Baby Jane, and respected her more than he respected Brockman.

Jane calmed down once she was into the back of the squad car. "McCarthy, I'm hungry. I wants something to eat," said Jane.

"I'll see what I can do for you, when we get to where we are going," said McCarthy, trying to avoid saying the word jail. Jane knew she was going to jail, but McCarthy knew that no one likes to hear the word.

"We're going to jail, not a five-star restaurant," answered Brockman. "You got a right to remain silent, so shut up!"

"Fuck you, fucking fuck!" yelled Jane, ending the statement by spitting onto the floor of the squad.

"Jane, relax. I'm the one you tried to kill, and I'm not angry with you. Just calm down, and like I said, I will see what I can do about getting you something to eat," said McCarthy, in a deliberately quiet tone.

"Promise?" Baby Jane asked, in a girlish tone that made her appearance such that McCarthy could see where she got the street moniker "Baby Jane."

At the jail, Jane was turned over to the female jailer for booking. McCarthy left the room, knowing that the trench coat was probably all she had on. Dan asked Rob Catlin, the steady night shift jailer, if there was anything to eat. He thought for a moment, "Yeah, there are a bunch of lunches made up for the work release prisoners, and they made too many today. Follow me."

Catlin led McCarthy through the labyrinth that is a jail, to the jail kitchen. Inside one of the large refrigerators was a line of bagged lunches made up for the work release prisoners, as if they all were suddenly blessed with a doting wife. McCarthy snatched one and thanked Rob.

When McCarthy returned to the booking room, Baby Jane was just completing the process. She had her trench coat off, and she was in her bright blue, jail jumpsuit. McCarthy asked Doris, the jailer, "Can I have a moment with Jane in the interview room?"

"Sure," said Doris, and she led Jane to the first interview room.

When Jane sat down, McCarthy said, "I would like to get a statement from you, but first I said I would try to get something for you to eat." McCarthy set the sack lunch down on the table in front of Jane.

Jane's eyes opened wide and she looked shocked at first. She then slowly opened the bag and her eyes lit up when she saw the roast beef sandwiches, apple, Twinkie, and carton of milk.

McCarthy had anticipated the pulling of the knife. He'd acted from the training and instincts of a young, burgeoning cop. He did not anticipate what happened next. Jane burst suddenly out of her chair and kissed McCarthy on the cheek.

"You gave me your lunch. Thank you." She said it like a child in a school lunch room. She then sat down, and with perfect manners, she ate the lunch with a smile that never left her face.

Brockman watched the entire thing through the one-way glass outside the interview room. He shook his head and said quietly to himself, "Fuckin' bleeding-heart social worker. That kid won't make the pimple on a good cop's ass." Brockman turned, and walked away, truly disgusted by what he saw.

After Baby Jane finished her lunch, she made a statement. She admitted pulling the knife on McCarthy, but claimed that it was never her intent to kill him. She only wanted to scare the shit out of him. She then gave McCarthy information on a "motherfucker" she didn't like. He was wanted out of Chicago for armed robbery. His name was Joplin Davis. She described the clothes he was wearing and said he is in the "third chair from the front of the bar," at the Red Lion.

After clearing the jail, McCarthy contacted Compton. There was no way McCarthy wanted to go into this situation with only Brockman. In fact, he did not even tell Brockman why he was calling over the sergeant. Brockman's demeanor changed from asshole to worried asshole, until McCarthy filled in Compton about the situation.

Compton, after hearing about the information, asked, "You got a statement from Baby Jane? She actually gave you a statement that had something in it besides 'fuck you'?"

"Yeah, Sarge. We gave her a bagged jail lunch, sucked up to her a little bit, and she caved," said Brockman.

McCarthy ignored his partner and asked Compton, "We've verified the felony warrant out of Chicago. I remember seeing the guy toward the front of the bar. How should we handle it?"

"We'll just go in through the front door. You take the right hand, and I'll take the left. Tie up his hands right away, to keep him from reaching anything. Taking him inside with people around is just as good as taking him outside with people around. He just can't run as easily. Inside, we have the dancers for a distraction."

"What do you want me to do, Sarge?" asked Brockman.

"You go in with us and hang back a little. We'll get him in a position to handcuff, and you put the cuffs on."

Just like most Compton plans, things went without a hitch. Joplin was three seats from the door as Baby Jane had said, wearing clothes just like she'd said. He was watching the dancer, a busty brunette, and just like Sgt. Compton had predicted, Davis did not see the three officers enter. The three cops were on Joplin immediately.

"Police, just relax; you are under arrest Mister Davis." Davis was leaned over the bar and his hands were held back, while Brockman fumbled quite a bit with the handcuffs. He found it difficult to efficiently apply the handcuffs and watch the brunette lightly circle her nipples with her fingertips, at the same time.

Joplin Davis had a Raven .25-caliber semi-automatic in his pocket, and he never had a chance to reach for it. He was in jail with no opportunity to use the weapon in La Claire, all because of a roast beef sandwich and Twinkies. Jane didn't care for the apple.

After that night, McCarthy always remembered that kindness is never inappropriate and can, as observed by William Shakespeare many centuries earlier, tame many an angry shrew.

CHAPTER 21
WHERE'S 255?

"Listen up!" said Compton, as he walked into the line-up room amongst the bantering young officers. The detectives had just taken a statement from Jimmy Baker. He'd admitted to the four robberies in the last three weeks to the Citgo Kwik Marts. They had left him alone in the interview room for a moment and he'd absconded.

"Fuckin' dicks couldn't find a bass fiddle in a broom closet if it had a spotlight on it," chirped Brockman, of all people.

"Since you've never made a mistake, Brockman, I'll let your comment stand," countered Compton. "Here is a picture of Jimmy Baker. The dicks said they have not recovered the Desert Eagle he was using in the robberies. He was last seen wearing a Packer jersey."

"Which Packer, Sarge?" asked Carpenter.

"66. It was one of those vintage Packer jersey's," answered Compton.

"Nitschke?" answered Carpenter. "How dare a dirt ball put Ray Nitschke's number on his back and then commit a crime. Ray would kick his ass, if he was around!"

"Hopefully he's not as tough as Nitschke. Baker is a big boy. He's a white male, 6' 1", 225 pounds. He's pretty stocky," said Compton, as he looked hard at the picture, trying to memorize it for future reference.

McCarthy and the rest left line-up with a mission. Except for Brockman, these guys would do anything Compton asked. If Compton wanted it done, it would get done or they'd exhaust themselves trying.

McCarthy left the ramp, heading in a different direction than everyone else. Some officers headed toward Baker's last known address. Some headed over toward Cabal's Bar, where Baker often drank. Others made a beeline toward Baker's mom's house.

Baker's father had died when Baker was twelve, which signaled the start of Baker's problems with the law. McCarthy knew Baker. Baker had grown up in McCarthy's neighborhood, which was on the Northside of La Claire. He knew that whenever Baker needed money or was in trouble, the first place he would go would be his grandmother's house on Mercy Street. It was on McCarthy's beat, so he headed in that direction.

As McCarthy turned onto the 1200 block of Mercy Street, he immediately noticed a silver Mazda idling directly in front of Grandma Baker's house. The interior lights were on, because the passenger side door was standing open. There was a rather striking blonde behind the wheel, whose face froze with terror as she saw the squad approaching.

The blonde's eyes met Dan's, and he recognized "the look" immediately.

McCarthy got on the radio and cut in excitedly, "255, send me a backup right away. I'm going to attempt to locate Jimmy Baker at . . . ," McCarthy stopped in mid-sentence, stunned to discover how right he was.

At this moment, McCarthy saw Baker stepping out the side door of the house; he was carrying a duffel bag. His back was to the squad, because he was saying goodbye to his beloved granny. He turned, saw McCarthy, and, in an instant, Baker was on a dead-run. "I've got him here. I'll be in foot pursuit!" McCarthy shouted into the mic, and after the transmission, he dropped his mic to the seat.

Every moment wasted was a bigger lead to make up in this foot pursuit he did not want to lose. McCarthy exited his car, making a rookie mistake. He left it parked in the middle of the street, with the door standing open. The blonde hit the gas, causing the wheels to squeal and the passenger door of her car to slam shut.

McCarthy was surprised at how much ground he made up immediately. In his panic, Baker had failed to drop his duffel bag. It was obviously heavy, and Baker had slung it over his shoulder. It appeared to McCarthy that he was chasing the Hunchback himself, come down from the bell tower of Notre Dame. Baker reached a fence and got hung up on it when he went over, and fell hard into the next yard. McCarthy cleared the fence cleanly, and was able to see Baker toss the duffel bag over into the next yard.

With the weight gone, Baker's stride improved considerably. It was all McCarthy could do to not lose ground with Baker. It was just after Baker tossed the bag that McCarthy noticed that Jimmy was still wearing the Ray Nitschke jersey. McCarthy had never pictured this scenario. Dan McCarthy trying to make a tackle on anyone wearing the jersey of the great Ray Nitschke. Nitschke was always the pursuer and rarely the pursued.

Then came McCarthy's opportunity. Baker fell, and fell hard, after failing to see a decorative fence that bordered a garden. McCarthy was on him instantly, and Baker spread out, "OK, I quit!"

McCarthy removed his radio to call in his position, and Baker lurched up and threw the smaller officer off. Baker was up and running again.

It took but a moment for McCarthy to recover, but his radio had been knocked from his hand, into the foliage of the garden, and he would have lost precious time trying to find it. McCarthy was too caught up in the hunt. Nothing was going to slow him down or get in his way. He had Baker in his sights. "Fuck the radio!"

Baker ran out of the yard he was in and doubled back, parallel to his original path. McCarthy thought this was good, because they were headed back to the area that his backup would be heading to. McCarthy began to feel his legs tiring and his lungs telling him to slow down.

Foot pursuits were an unfair contest. A cop had to wear fifteen to twenty pounds of weight around his waist, a vest, duty shoes, and still somehow outrun criminals who were often younger, faster, and in Nikes. Even so, McCarthy could see Baker was wearing out, too. Baker's pace was slowing, and McCarthy could hear that Baker's breath was coming out in gasps and snorts, like a winded quarter horse.

Baker cut back to 1200 Mercy Street and circled toward his grandmother's house. McCarthy could hardly believe it. He was heading right back to Grandma's, as he always did when he was in trouble. Baker ran down the sidewalk heading straight for Granny's. As McCarthy followed down the sidewalk, he saw the blonde beauty behind the wheel of the Mazda driving slowly down the street, watching the outcome of the pursuit. There were still no squads and none could be heard coming.

What McCarthy did not know was that there was no backup coming. He had failed to give his location during any of the transmissions. Officers were frantically looking all over town for McCarthy, but no one could find him. Dooley was checking the area of Cabal's. Carpenter was searching the area of Baker's last known address. Stammos headed over to the house of Becky Harper, who was the blonde driver of the Mazda.

Everyone knew McCarthy needed help and what he needed help with. No one knew where. Everyone was coming up empty.

Stanley Brockman thought, "Fuckin' rookies. They're more trouble than they are worth," as he heard McCarthy's transmission. He had just got a cup of coffee from the Case Street Kwik Mart. Brockman walked to his squad and set up his coffee in the cup-holder.

After Brockman got settled into his squad, he pulled out of the Kwik Mart lot and reached for the radio. He asked Hix the dispatcher, "Where's 255?"

"Channel One is held for emergency traffic only!" barked Hix emphatically, "Take it to Two!"

"Where's 255?" Brockman repeated on Channel Two, in a voice meant to let Hix know that he was pissed at the way he was being talked to.

Hix answered, "255 called out that he was in foot pursuit of Jimmy Baker and now we can't raise him. He did not give a location. We have officers checking the area around Baker's residence, Cabal's, Becky Harper's residence, and we have found nothing yet."

"I'll check out Baker's parents' residence. I'm close," was Brockman's answer.

Brockman was a block away and spotted Mrs. Baker just parking her car. Brockman got out quickly and asked, "Have you seen Jimmy today?"

"No. You are about the fourth cop to ask me," said Mrs. Baker.

"Do you have any idea where he might be? One of our officers is out with him, and we have lost radio contact. What would be your first guess. Where would he go, if he was in trouble?"

Brockman was a good cop, when he wanted to be. He would never want to admit that he ever wanted to be, but right now he had an over-powering urge to find McCarthy. Partly because McCarthy was a cop in trouble, and partly because he liked the kid. The kid had an attitude that Brockman once had and had lost.

Mrs. Baker thought for just a second, then answered, "He is very close with my deceased husband's mother. He might go there. She lives on 1216 Mercy Street. I can't tell you for sure."

Brockman was already back into his car, speeding toward 1216 Mercy Street. It was an address no one had been to yet. Somehow, Brockman knew that was where McCarthy had to be.

Back on Mercy Street, Baker burst through the side door of his grand-mother's house. McCarthy was right behind him, but Baker took the time to slam the interior door back into the young officer's face. This caused the blood to flow from McCarthy's lower lip, but McCarthy did not notice. He merely continued on.

Baker ran into the kitchen, and directly to a silverware drawer. He pulled it open, and McCarthy could see the cutlery set at Baker's dispos-al. As Baker reached into the drawer for one of the knives, McCarthy hit him hard with his whole body, sprawling Baker backwards across the table. He rolled off and fell to the floor. Just as quickly as Baker went down, he was back up onto his feet.

Baker was facing McCarthy now, and he was in an Ali-style boxer's stance. He obviously was not going in without a fight. McCarthy reached instinctively for his radio and remembered he had lost it. This was going to be his fight.

Furniture in the house limited McCarthy's options. He could only maneuver straight forward or straight back. McCarthy then reasoned,

"Come on, Jimmy. Where are you going to go? What you going to do? If you do get away now, how long is that going to last?"

"Fuck you, Dan! I'm not going to prison," Jimmy answered his former neighbor.

"Jimmy, don't!" yelled Grandma Baker. "Stop it right now, Jimmy!"

"Grandma, stay out of this! You don't know. I'm not going to prison. This means prison. I'm not going," he yelled to his grandmother, just glancing away for a moment.

McCarthy saw the opening. As Baker looked away, he reverted back to his high school and college wrestling days. He shot a double leg take down on Baker, and was in as tightly as he ever had been in his competitive days. McCarthy wrapped his arms around both Baker's legs and lifted Jimmy off his feet. McCarthy then turned and brought Baker to the floor. Baker tried to break free, but McCarthy placed him in a reverse-half-nelson. This hold locked up Baker's left arm and McCarthy's right arm was under Baker's head, while McCarthy's right hand was secured in Baker's right armpit, attempting to keep Baker from turning over or getting up.

Baker tried hard to break free, rolling left and right, but McCarthy held him securely. Even though McCarthy had Jimmy secured, he could not handcuff him from this location. Baker knew this and the larger man fought to break free. He reached up with his right hand, and grabbed at the face of McCarthy.

McCarthy responded by punching Baker in the face with his left hand, yelling, "Give it up, Jimmy! Stop resisting!" The struggle continued with no end to the stalemate in sight.

"Stop it, Jimmy! Oh, please, God, stop it, Jimmy!" screamed Grandma Baker, now sobbing.

McCarthy hit Baker three times before he stopped pulling on McCarthy's hair, and then Baker rolled hard in the opposite direction, trying to break the young officer's grip. McCarthy held tight, but felt he was getting tired beyond his abilities to hold this muscular young criminal.

Then the door burst open, "Police Officer!" yelled Brockman.

"Over here. I'm over here!" gasped the out-of-breath Officer McCarthy.

With the arrival of Brockman, Baker laid flat and limp, knowing it was all over. McCarthy and Brockman rolled Baker to his stomach and handcuffed him.

McCarthy could hear the approaching sirens, summoned by Brockman to the scene. Brockman got on his radio, "Slow everyone down. We're 10-95 (subject in custody) here."

"Are you all right, McCarthy? Your mouth is bleeding," asked Brockman.

"Yeah, I'm fine. I don't know how it happened." The whole incident was a Scrabble game of memories. "The bag. I've got to find the bag. He threw a bag."

"I never had any bag!" countered Baker.

"Shut up!" answered Brockman.

"Can you transport him for me?" McCarthy asked Brockman. "I have to find the bag and my radio. He knocked it out of my hand."

"Sure, kid."

Brockman took Baker to his squad, while McCarthy searched the floor area for his flashlight, which had been knocked out of his belt, during the fight.

"I'm sorry for Jimmy's behavior, officer." said Grandma Baker. "He was a wonderful boy until his father died. He needed a strong hand. Too bad you couldn't have come over once a month and kicked his butt. He may have turned out differently. Is Jimmy in a lot of trouble?"

"I'm sorry this had to happen here, Mrs. Baker," replied McCarthy. "Jimmy is in some trouble. He is being charged with multiple counts of robbery, escape, and now resisting arrest. Does he have any things here?"

"Just that bag. I didn't even know it was here until he came over to pick it up. He said he was going on a trip with Becky and needed to pick up some things that he had left here. He went down in the basement and came up with it. He was only here a few minutes, and then you showed up."

Then she asked, as if she was afraid to know, "Do you know what's in the bag?"

"Not for sure, Ma'am, but I am going to find out." replied McCarthy purposefully.

Compton arrived on the scene and told Brockman to take Baker to Central Station. "The detectives are going to want to talk to him . . . and hey, good job, Brockman!"

Stanley Brockman had not heard those two words before his name for some time. He said to himself, "Good job and a dime won't even get you a cup of coffee."

Brockman did not want to admit that he liked those words. He felt good about himself for the first time in a long time.

"I don't know nothing about any bag," yelled Baker from the back seat.

"You got a right to remain silent, so shut up!" yelled Stanley Brockman, as he accelerated rapidly away from the scene, causing Baker's head to snap back.

Compton joined McCarthy, after he'd parked and locked McCarthy's car for him. McCarthy saw Compton and immediately told the story in an adrenalized chatter Compton was barely able to understand.

"We have two things to do. Let's find the bag and radio," said Compton, after hearing how the incident had unfolded.

McCarthy retraced his steps. He found the bag almost immediately. He thought for a moment, before opening the duffel bag, whether he had the authority to do so.

Compton read his mind. "We can look in the bag for two reasons. Number one, it is abandoned property, and the second reason is because Baker had it, you arrested him, and therefore, you can search it incident to the arrest," said Compton, with the confidence that comes from doing something a hundred times before.

"Thanks, Sarge," McCarthy said, fumbling with the zipper while opening the bag.

Immediately, he could see why Baker wanted nothing to do with the bag. There was a stainless steel Desert Eagle handgun inside and a box of ammunition. There was $2,000 in cash and a stack of photographs. The photos were some shots of Becky Harper. The type you would see in the amateur section of *Hustler Magazine*. It was no surprise that Becky was even more attractive naked and provocatively posed than she was with clothes. There, further down the pile, Becky and Baker were in nearly every position McCarthy's young mind could imagine getting into and some positions McCarthy could not imagine they could get out of.

McCarthy had not noticed, but Compton was standing slightly behind him as Dan shuffled through the pile of photos. McCarthy had become mesmerized by the graphic beauty of Becky Harper.

"Multi-talented beauty, don't you agree, McCarthy?"

McCarthy jumped and nearly dropped the photos. "What!? Yes, sir. I-I've never seen . . . well, I've seen, but I've never known anyone who . . . well, I've known, but . . ." stumbled McCarthy.

"She's a pretty girl," said Compton. "How do nice-looking girls like this get hooked up with losers like Jimmy Baker?"

"I don't know, Sarge," answered McCarthy, relieved Compton had rescued him before he killed himself trying to construct one complete sentence after being caught looking at every single photo of Becky Harper. McCarthy then shuffled the pictures back into a neat pile.

"I am guessing that this money and the gun are from the robberies," said McCarthy, bringing them both back to the business at hand.

"Now, let's find your radio." said Compton.

Within a few minutes, they located the yard and the garden in which the radio had been lost. Finding the radio was a more difficult task. McCarthy and Compton scoured the foliage for some time, until Compton started laughing, "I'm so stupid."

He pulled his radio out and told Hix at dispatch, "Do a test count for me, dispatch."

Hix replied instantly, "10-4, testing 1, 2, 3," and at this point Compton turned his radio off. The count continued faintly from the far end of the garden under a large hosta. "4, 5, 6, 7, 8, 9, 10, 10, 9, 8, 7, 6, 5, 4 . . ." Compton and McCarthy moved the green, leafy blanket covering his radio and picked it up . . . "3, 2, 1, end of test, how'd you copy?" asked Hix.

"That's 10-2," said McCarthy, keying the mic on his freshly recovered radio.

"Good to finally hear from you, 255," said Hix, in a sincerely happy tone.

As they walked back to the squad, Compton became serious. "McCarthy, you did a good job tonight—except there is no criminal worth your life. Your feet outran your brain. Do you know what I mean?"

"Yes, sir, I do." answered McCarthy.

"Bad things can happen when you do that. You know, you could get yourself seriously hurt, right?" Compton paused to make sure the young officer was getting the message.

"Yes, sir, Sergeant," answered McCarthy, knowing that Sgt. Compton was absolutely right on this one, but was wishing he wasn't.

"Another bad thing that can happen is someone like Brockman has to come and save your ass, and then you have to go thank him for it." At the end of this comment, McCarthy looked up from his own feet, where he had been concentrating his attention, and saw Compton's mouth curled up on one side in a wry smile.

"Yes, sir, Sergeant," answered McCarthy. "I'm going to do that directly."

McCarthy drove to the station. When he arrived at Central Station, everyone had forgotten the mistakes of the incident, and there were many high-five's all around. As McCarthy arrived, he was met by Det. Sgt. Joe Darnell. He was a competent, but visibly arrogant man, who had a reputation for looking down at patrol officers as the second-class citizens of law enforcement.

"Where's the bag? Let's see the bag," was the first thing he said to McCarthy.

McCarthy had it in his hand and handed it over to the detective. "I'll take it from here, kid. You start working on your report. The first string can handle it from here."

He then walked away from McCarthy, as if McCarthy were less than nothing. More inconsequential than a nobody. Darnell walked away with a look like the bag contained the recipe for turning shit into ice cream and it was his bag.

McCarthy thought, "He's a bigger prick than Brockman. Brockman was a run of the mill prick. Darnell was a first class arrogant prick.

"What an asshole," said a familiar voice behind McCarthy.

It was Stanley Brockman, calling the kettle black. Then, as McCarthy turned to meet the older officer, he remembered what Brockman had done for him.

"I'm glad you're still here, Stanley. I want to thank you. You got there in the nick of time. I was getting tired," McCarthy said in one breath, as he was extending a hand to Brockman.

Brockman had two cups of coffee in one hand, and a cigarette in his other. He put the cigarette in his mouth and shook the young officer's hand as Brockman inhaled on the cigarette. When he had finished the handshake, Brockman removed the cigarette and blew the smoke out into McCarthy's face, saying, "No problem, kid. I'm sure there will be a little something extra in our paychecks for it. Don't ya think so? Maybe not."

Brockman made his quick exit. He was heading down to records. "The detectives want our reports right away. They held Sandy on over-time to type our reports while we dictate them." Brockman disappeared through the exit door, heading downstairs to records.

When McCarthy arrived, he saw that the second cup of coffee Brockman had was for his fantasy girl, Sandy. Brockman did not have a chance with Sandy, but he fawned over her like a sixth-grader with a crush. McCarthy smiled at the sad display of hopeless puppy love. It was the kind of Brockman display that would have disgusted McCarthy just the day before. Then, McCarthy thought that something had happened when Brockman came through Grandma Baker's door. Either McCarthy had learned to dislike Brockman less, or possibly McCarthy just liked him more. One thing was certain—Stanley Brockman had been there for Dan McCarthy tonight. Stanley would undoubtedly fail and fall short in the future, but tonight Brockman had been there for McCarthy.

McCarthy watched as the blushing Brockman said to Sandy, "Is that a new dress? That's a nice dress."

Sandy looked up from her keyboard to answer, "Hmph, what? Oh yeah, it's new. Thanks."

She looked back to the keyboard and continued to type, while Brockman looked at McCarthy and winked. He settled himself back confidently in his chair, thinking himself to be a man who'd scored some major points with the best-looking woman in his world.

McCarthy then noticed the look in Brockman's eyes. It definitely wasn't just lust, the poor schmuck was in love.

On this night, McCarthy had caught the bad guy. What he would remember most about the night was that it was the night he could no longer totally dislike Brockman. He would always long for that pure, simple, clear-cut feeling of loathing he had once felt for Brockman. Now it was all different.

On this night, McCarthy had needed help badly. That help took the form of Stanley Brockman and it had arrived just in time. He had also seen Stanley act like a sixth-grade school kid, with a crush on the beautiful Sandy, who Brockman had *no* chance with. McCarthy snickered at the thought that he was having positive feelings approaching a kinship toward Stanley Brockman. Tonight he had learned something about the world. He learned all people have value . . . even Stanley Brockman.

CHAPTER 22
DEUTSCHE DAYS FRIDAY NIGHT

Each year, a major event was held in La Claire, Wisconsin, that brought tens of thousands of people to the city—an event largely successful, which meant fun for everyone in attendance, except the cops working the event. The event had started in 1960, and was fashioned after the large German festival of Oktoberfest. The event was an instant hit and grew every year thereafter.

La Claire's event had a history of raucous behavior on the opening weekend each year. People would come to downtown La Claire to drink, and engage in bizarre and dangerous behavior. It was Mardi Gras without the costumes. On the two nights of this event, it was not unusual for the officers to make 350 to 500 arrests.

The La Claire Police Department would swear in officers from other jurisdictions, to assist in policing the event. The department would add patrol cars and call in the State Patrol to assist, also. A special booking area was set up in the jail to handle the large influx of arrests.

In the past, the large, mindless, drunken crowds had rioted; and this was always the concern of anyone working the event. Each year prior to the Deutsche Days event, the entire La Claire Police Department would train in crowd control tactics. Officers would bag up their riot gear and leave it at the command center, which was a meeting room in the La Claire Civic Center, about two blocks from the heart of downtown.

As McCarthy entered the command center, twenty minutes early, for briefing on this Friday night of Deutsche Days, he checked his gear one last time. He had his rain gear and heavier coat, in the event the weather changed. He had his long baton with a belt ring, the equivalent of a sheath for the baton. He checked his carrier and could see that his gas mask was in the position to be readily accessed under stress. He checked his helmet and shield, and could see that the screws on the shield were all tight and in place. His mask shield was a bit cloudy. He tried to wipe it clean, but it was evident the cloudiness was permanent.

Checking his riot gear made McCarthy nervous. He knew that this event brought insanity out in people. He never had been in a riot before and did not want to be in one. He wondered how he would behave in a riot. He pictured himself cut off, and surrounded by a hoard of people screaming for his blood; and the daydream made him shudder from a chill, as if the ghost of Deutsche Days past had just flown by.

Then a positive thought entered his mind. It would take a crowd to place McCarthy in peril tonight. He was to be partnered up with an out-of-town officer. His partner was going to be his tae kwon do instructor, Larry Kane. He was eligible to work, because he was a fully-trained, sworn officer. He was a part-time deputy on the La Claire Sheriff's department.

Kane was nearly the same age and size as McCarthy. They were similar, but different. McCarthy devoted his full time to his law enforcement career and was a part-time, but passionate, participant in the martial arts. To Kane, the martial arts was his career, and although passionate about law enforcement, the latter was a part-time endeavor.

McCarthy was a family man, through and through, and loved being with one woman. Kane was just as devoted to maintaining his status as a bachelor, and had difficulty devoting his time to one woman a night. The women he'd been with knew this and seemed to thrive on it. Dan found that Kane, who was as serious as any Oriental Master in the do chang (gym), was a barrel of laughs as a friend. Kane was fun to watch in both environs.

After Dan had checked his equipment, he walked pass the refreshment table. The meal tonight was, what else?—bratwurst. Bratwursts are a big, fat, but tasty German sausage that is usually served on a brown, seeded bun, heaped with sauerkraut and mustard. "Brat und brau mit kraut und mooshtard" would be the traditional German way of ordering this Deutsche Days standard repast.

There was a whole table of donuts and rolls. McCarthy never ate donuts and rolls. He could see it was too many calories available too often for cops. He hated the donut-eating cop jokes that came constantly, also. He chose not to eat donuts and not to drink coffee. He passed on those delicacies and settled for a Pepsi. It was McCarthy's favorite drink. It was all his stomach could handle right now.

As the clock ticked on to 6:50 p.m., the time all street officers were to report for briefing, Kane walked through the door. What a shock. He was on time. Larry came over, sat down next to McCarthy, and shook his hand, "Oy ya, Da, my good friend," said Larry. McCarthy did not know what that meant, other than Larry was happy to see him. It was Kane's standard greeting to Dan.

The briefing to the officers was given by Compton. Everyone listened intently, for two reasons. They all knew the potential danger of this event, and also, Compton was speaking. McCarthy hung on every word Compton had to say. He spoke loudly enough for all to hear, "Good evening, Ladies and Gentlemen. Let's do this one more time. Tonight, we are going to be on the street early enough to try to build a rapport with the crowd. I want you to be friendly, smiling, and shaking hands. Let them stand next to you to take your picture, but do not let them hang on you, disrespect you, or kiss you. I want you to keep moving in your designated areas. Attempt to identify and remove potential problems, while they are small problems. It's easier to put out the cigarette butt than it is to put out a forest fire.

"When you have to make an arrest, do it quickly and efficiently. Stay together with your partners and do not go into the crowd, or any of the taverns, without a team of officers working together. When you do go into a crowd or tavern, have another team stand by, to assist outside.

"Stay together with your partners all night. Do not run in the presence of the crowd. Call ahead, because we have people situated who will be able to cut off anyone running. Remember, there will be cameras everywhere. Don't be afraid of them. The video camera is a professional police officer's best friend. It is a witness that will not lie.

"Keep your breaks short. We need bodies down there. No breaks after midnight. You all know the plan if the situation goes to hell. The squad at the scene of the incident forms a line and holds, while the rest gear up. If we have to pull out, do not leave anyone behind. Remember, you can disappear into a crowd in the blink of an eye. Do not let anyone bait you into moving into that crowd, or out of the line, once we form. We'll accomplish more with ten officers working as a team than we will with a hundred working as individuals. Be safe."

Whenever Compton spoke, everyone felt that they wished they would have taken notes. The man was a leader. He was someone you could follow into hell, because you knew he could kick the devil's ass, rescue someone that didn't belong there, and get you out again.

After Compton spoke, Captain Hale came forward to speak. The officers in the briefing shifted in their seats and made eye contact among each other to communicate telepathically, "What an asshole."

Hale was a captain, head of Community Services. How he'd become head of that bureau, no one really knew. As a cop he did as little as possible, and then he was promoted to sergeant. As a sergeant, he was the opposite of Compton. He was the last person you went to for advice. He was always looking to write someone up for a minor infraction, but two words that were absolutely not in his vocabulary were "good job."

Some people claimed that Brockman was actually a top notch cop, until he delivered a baby one night in the back seat of a car. It had been Brockman's proudest moment as a cop. The young mother would forever after send Stanley a Christmas card with the child's picture in it, so Stanley Brockman, who brought the child into the world, could see his development. Stanley had every picture hung on the inside of his locker door. Stanley could never contain the urge to smile as he opened the card each year. He would read the kind thoughts inside the card and hang the child's picture on his locker door, in neat chronological order, with every other picture he had ever received of the child he had brought into this world in the back seat of a Ford Crown Victoria. Stanley would most certainly never have a child of his own to be proud of, until he got the nerve up to ask a woman out.

Stanley Brockman had received the thanks of the young mother, but never received accolades from the department. Instead, he was called into the office by then Sgt. Hale. Hale did not *talk* to Brockman, who was then only a little older than a rookie. Hale *yelled* as if he were talking to a deaf idiot. He told Brockman that his actions brought the department into jeopardy of civil liability. According to Brockman, he said, "I'll not have you screw up my chance to be a lieutenant because you want to get your goddamned name in the papers."

Hale did make lieutenant, though. Not because of anything he did for the police department. He made lieutenant by making sure the chief's paper was set aside for him each morning. He made lieutenant by making sure there were coffee and donuts at each command meeting. He made lieutenant by lighting up the room with his smile every time the chief entered a room. Hale made lieutenant in Community Services, then was promoted to Captain by applying the same "skills." Hale became a captain in Community Services by knowing who and when to schmooze. Everyone who had no power to advance or promote Hale, saw the real Hale. Hale was a narrow-minded, incompetent, self-centered, small-thinking man.

McCarthy cared not about any of that. McCarthy had his reasons for disliking Captain Hale. Dan McCarthy would never forget Hale's words the night Gary Carpenter was shot by Ray Draper. He could hear those words coming from the jowls of the balding, overweight captain, as if he had just spoken them. "That thing was screwed up from the get-go."

Captain Hale spoke to the officers assembled. "All right. This will be my twentieth Deutsche Days. Remember, just because we give you a gun and a baton doesn't mean you have to use them. Back when I was on the street, we used this," Hale said, pointing at his head. "Too bad they didn't issue him any ammo with that weapon," said Carpenter, under his breath, causing those within earshot to laugh.

Hale was not deterred by the laughter. He thought it was a direct result of his cleverness. "Remember," he continued, "there will be a lot of video cameras out there, and we don't need any Rodney King incidents here in La Claire."

With that comment, everyone was released from briefing. This year, McCarthy was scheduled to walk downtown. As McCarthy and Kane headed toward the downtown area, they decided to make a wide circle on the edge of their assigned area. As they approached Horning's Financial, they could not help but notice an irregularity in the skyline of the building. To represent a bull market, the building had a large statue of a bull erected on the roof. Attached to the back end of the bull was a young man, who was attempting to impregnate the imaginary bull. On the sidewalk below with a video camera was an apparent associate, getting the magic moment on tape.

McCarthy approached and interrupted this scene of filmmaking history by stating, "Good evening, gentlemen." The initial reaction of the bull rider was to pull up his pants and drop flat to the roof of the building. After some coaxing, he climbed off the roof using a fence, which was built to the same height as the roof. This was the third bull rider McCarthy had arrested off this roof in his brief career. He also had interrupted two subjects, who were in the process of tying two bowling balls between the legs of the bull.

The man on the roof was cited for ordinance trespassing and also for indecent behavior. The tape was taken as evidence and McCarthy had his first arrest of this Deutsche Days.

"That was easy," said Kane, as they headed toward River Street. "It took four minutes to make an arrest."

"Dumb people do dumb things. Alcohol makes everyone dumb," explained McCarthy.

McCarthy and Kane continued heading toward River Street. In doing so, they cut through a parking ramp, which was already filled to capacity. As they entered the ramp, a light caught Dan's eye. He hit Kane on the arm and pointed to an occupied van, which was the source of the light. They worked their way closer to the van, staying out of sight. Their stealth paid off when they moved close enough to see what was happening inside the van. There was one person standing outside the open driver's door of the van. He gave a bill to a fuzzy-headed, tall man seated in the rear of the van. In return, the man received a brown vial.

Mr. Fuzzy Head was in a captain's seat in the rear of the van, with a table in front of him. On the table was a mirror with four neatly drawn lines of white powder. Three other men were crouched around the table, and were handing Mr. Fuzzy Head bills.

McCarthy and Kane saw it all. McCarthy radioed, "255. I need a backup to make five arrests for drug sale and possession on the ground level of the Main Street ramp."

"10-4, 255." came the immediate response. The radio immediately began to chatter with volunteers to assist on this call.

Because McCarthy and Kane were close enough to see what was happening, they were close enough for the man outside the van to hear the unmistakable chatter of a police radio in the night air. "Cops!" was all he said, as he turned to run. Out of confusion, he tripped over his own feet and fell. He got back to his feet and was immediately collared by Kane, but he continued to attempt to break away.

McCarthy saw that the evidence was being destroyed and someone had ordered all hands to abandon ship inside the van. McCarthy burst into the van, blocking the exit himself, positioning himself so the people inside would have to go over him to get out. This did not deter anyone for all moved toward him.

The first one to reach him was Mr. Fuzzy Head. McCarthy spun him around and placed him in a lateral vascular restraint. To the layman, this would be a choke-hold. McCarthy was able to use the cluttered condition of the van and the physical stature of Mr. Fuzzy Head to keep everyone inside the van until the swarm of backups arrived. Until they arrived, the inside of the van saw a struggle that sounded and looked vicious, but no one was injured, because there was not enough room to generate any power. McCarthy was able to use Mr. Fuzzy Head to block and parry blows.

As McCarthy saw the welcome faces of Stammos, Carpenter, and their partners, he felt relieved. "Arrest them all. They are all under arrest," shouted McCarthy to the cavalry. The arrival of the additional officers caused the tangled mass of bodies to cease and desist resistance. McCarthy handcuffed Mr. Fuzzy Head where he lay. The rest were handcuffed by Stammos and Carpenter, as they were removed from the van.

Each one of the parties was searched, and the small amounts of cocaine they had on them were taken as evidence. They were all charged with possession of cocaine and resisting arrest. Mr. Fuzzy Head's money was taken and McCarthy recovered the mirror. It had been knocked to the floor of the van, but the trace lines of cocaine were still left on the mirror. A baggie with a little less than an ounce of cocaine was found on the floor, under Mr. Fuzzy Head's captain's chair.

Stammos called for a transport van. When the van pulled up, Stammos handled the transport and booking of the prisoners for McCarthy. The four customers were loaded into the van and two detectives picked up Mr. Fuzzy Head, to attempt to follow-up on the arrest of this drug dealer.

Fuzzy Head was from Chicago and came to town to make some quick bucks. The best place to sell lots of blow fast was at a big party. The Deutsche Days was definitely a big party. He told the detectives that he'd gotten a little careless, because he thought the police were so busy keeping the peace on River Street that the ramps would be safe.

McCarthy finished searching the van, incident to the arrests of the suspects, and brought the evidence to the special booking area. The system for this event was beautiful to behold. The prisoners went one way and were speedily checked for bond. They were shipped in one direction, if they had bond, and another direction for incarceration.

None of this group had enough for bond and had quickly been moved up to the jail for incarceration. McCarthy headed first to the evidence processing area. He field-tested the powder, which was indeed cocaine. He marveled, as always, at what was quickly becoming his favorite color, "robin's egg blue." Bingo! It was a positive test.

The marijuana found was also quickly tested. McCarthy thought the positive test for that was a very pretty violet, with second separation of light gray. As pretty as this colorful display was, it did not have the aesthetic quality of the robin's egg blue. The items were weighed, packaged, and marked by McCarthy, who turned it over to the evidence officer, who was on hand to take charge of the evidence.

McCarthy then walked over to Sandy, who was on hand to immediately type the reports, which could be dictated. "Hi Dan," said Sandy, with her Christie Brinkley smile.

No wonder Brockman and everyone else had a crush on her, thought Dan McCarthy.

"What took you so long? It took you fifteen minutes to find a criminal. That's slow for you," said Sandy, sarcastically.

"Well, we had to arrest two guys before this. They were sexually assaulting Horning's bull," explained McCarthy.

"Tell me about it," said Sandy, with her breathy voice laced with excitement.

"I will. How about you type up the report for me, and I will dictate that while I'm here, also," answered McCarthy, trying to keep a professional demeanor in the presence of Sandy. McCarthy thought, the Good Lord must have had this woman in mind when he spoke the words, "Lead us not into temptation."

Sandy always dressed to show off her womanly attributes. Her perfume was the perfect mix of flowers and sexuality. Her hair was smooth, shiny, and had to be naturally blonde, but no one on the PD knew for sure. She was not married and not dating as far as anyone knew. She was the Bratwurst Queen in the small town she came from, which generated all kinds of disgustingly hilarious locker room banter about what the duties of the Bratwurst Queen are.

Women often resented Sandy. The first thing she was resented for was her beauty. She was a beauty. She could have been a model or a movie star, but she chose to be a secretary. The second thing they hated her for was her efficiency. She could do more work faster than anyone, and everyone knew it. Good employees of any company seem to be resented on all levels. It was a phenomenon that puzzled McCarthy. The third thing was her popularity. She was liked by all the officers, because she was not only the proverbial "10," she was also very nice. The type of humor she liked best were the jokes that were a little risqué. Police work was still dominated by men. In a world that did not allow men to tell sexual jokes around employees, who might be offended, it was a relief to have a woman who allowed it and even demanded it. She gave as good as she got.

McCarthy dictated his reports to Sandy. He started slow and sped up, as he could see that she could type as fast as he spoke. He discovered that he could not speak faster than she could type. When the reports were typed, he read them over and then signed each page.

Sandy then leaned forward with a whisper, "McCarthy. Want to hear a good joke?" McCarthy caught a whiff of her perfume, and could not help but notice as she leaned forward, the hint of cleavage transformed into a little more than a clue to the beauty that lay beneath.

"Sure," McCarthy said, as he pulled his wandering eyes back to eye-level.

"A naked woman walks into the bar and asks the bartender for a drink. The bartender says, 'you don't seem to have any money to pay for the drink.' The woman props her foot up on a bar stool, exposing her womanhood, and says, 'How about I pay with this?'

The bartender pauses, looks, and says, 'Don't you have anything smaller?'"

Sandy then covered her mouth to hold her laugh in. She laughed at the nastiness of it, as well as the fact it was funny.

McCarthy shared the laugh, partly because he thought the joke was funny, as well as for the way it entertained the joke-teller.

"Thanks for doing my report and thanks for the joke, Sandy." said McCarthy, as he headed toward the door.

"Sure. I'll see you later, Dyno. You know I never know whether to call you Dan, or Dyno, or McCarthy. As names and nicknames go, I like them," said Sandy, flashing her prize-winning smile.

"Take your pick. You can call me anything you like," said McCarthy.

"OK. See you later—Late for Supper," said Sandy, pleased with herself once again.

"Don't call me late for supper," answered McCarthy, who had deliberately avoided the cliché unsuccessfully.

As McCarthy and Kane climbed in one of the arrest vans for a ride back downtown, Kane commented, "God, that's a good-looking woman. Can I have her?"

"Don't ask me, ask her. All I know is she's good for my morale," McCarthy said, taking a big breath between sentences.

"Did you get hurt at all in the scuffle with that guy?" asked McCarthy, focusing his mind back on the business at hand.

"No. Me? How about you? It sounds like you were trying to fuck Horning's bull inside that van," said Kane, with a puzzled look on his face. "I almost let my guy go to help you, but then I decided you would ask for help, if you really needed it."

"No, it was too crowded in there for anyone to hurt me. It worked to my advantage, but climbing in that van might not have been the smartest thing I have ever done," said McCarthy quietly, in a moment of self-doubt.

"Fuck that. The bad guys are in jail. We won. Let's find more. This is fun," Kane said, with the exuberance of a young boy who just jumped off a roller-coaster and was headed for the next ride.

McCarthy finally made it to River Street, and Compton contacted him, "Where you been, McCarthy?"

"I just finished up with seven arrests. This is the first time I made it to River Street. How is it going so far?" asked McCarthy.

"We have all the vehicles towed away from the no parking zone. We only had to arrest one, during the towing. He jumped on the car and said, 'Don't tow it, I'll move it.' He said it was his, and we found out it wasn't. He dented the car when he jumped on it, so he went to jail for criminal damage to property and obstructing. We took two more from a fight in front of the Red Lion. That's it so far."

Compton gave out the information with the efficiency of a briefing. "Just keep in this area, and I want you to keep a high profile, McCarthy."

McCarthy knew that when Compton said he wanted a "high profile," that meant arrests. He wanted arrests of troublemakers made, to send a message to all, while we had them outnumbered.

It didn't take long for McCarthy and Kane to make a high profile arrest. On Diamond Street, which connected with River Street, parking was allowed. On the far end of the street was a biker bar called the Drop Inn. Bikes were pulling in and lining up on Diamond Street. The bikers were doing what they do. They were inside drinking, or outside admiring each others' machines. Their numbers were growing.

On the far end of the line, one biker had parked his Harley alone, so it could not be scratched or bumped in the commotion, which was Deutsche Days. It had a shiny apple red paint job, with hand-painted scrolling on the gas tank. It was a work of art.

The tall, hairy, leather-clad biker crossed the street and was immediately met by another equally large companion. McCarthy concluded that the two were both in awe of the beauty of that machine.

This tender moment was interrupted by alcohol-induced stupidity that had to be viewed to be believed. McCarthy saw movement to his right, as he stood on the corner of River and Diamond Streets. A drunken, athletic-looking young man was on a dead sprint down Diamond Street. He cut across River Street, causing the heavy traffic to come to a screeching halt, to avoid turning the smiling, running idiot into a grease spot in the middle of the intersection.

McCarthy started toward the running, smiling idiot. McCarthy could see what the man was about to do, but was helpless to stop it. The man was heading toward the apple-red Harley, and all the running, smiling idiot could see, in the self-inflicted drunken haze that was his current reality, was a pommel horse. He got within about three feet of the motorcycle and jumped, landing with his two hands on the seat of the motorcycle. The machine could not hold the weight of the man and toppled to its side, causing the man to tuck and roll on the pavement on the opposite side of the motorcycle.

Every biker on the street instantly froze and inhaled in shock. The Drop Inn spewed forth bikers, as if some large invisible hand had just squeezed it. Immediately the sudden stillness caused by the audacity of the act transformed to shouts of rage. The wayward gymnast bounded to his feet, uninjured, and threw his hands up in the air, looking for the approval of the crowd. McCarthy, luckily, reached him before any of the bikers did. The gymnast pulled away unable to comprehend why a cop was interrupting his performance, and McCarthy quickly adjusted his grip. He placed the gymnast in the hold made famous by Steven Segal, sankyo. The gymnast's elbow was pointed to the sky and his hand was palm forward, while he went abruptly to his tip-toes, to ease the pressure. His resistance stopped as quickly as the hold was applied.

The bikers were going to kill this gymnast. By "biker law," it had been declared they had the right to kill this man. By "common law," they had the right to kill this man. Common sense would almost dictate that the man should die. No one this stupid should be allowed to live. After all, they hung horse-thieves a mere century earlier. A motorcycle dumped is never the same motorcycle to a biker.

Now the hairy leather-clad group of burly, husky men halted their advance. They seemed in awe of the young officer, who was now controlling the man with three fingers and a thumb. This officer had the crazy, drunken gymnast on his tip-toe, with a grimace on his face, while this cop calmly motioned for the advancing bikers to halt with his free hand. McCarthy chose this hold, because it was not only effective but it was also flashy and entertaining to watch. McCarthy hoped that the bikers, who felt honor-bound to hurt this fool, might allow an arrest of the running, smiling idiot to go on undeterred, if it was entertaining.

"This man is under arrest. He is going to jail. We will get his information, so you can sue the man for damages. I am sorry this had to happen, folks, but this is why we are here." The quickness of the arrest, and the concern in McCarthy's voice, stopped the crowd as surely as the hold, which the bikers would talk about for many Deutsche Days to come.

Larry Kane got the information from the owner of the bike, and several other officers assisted him in picking up his bike. Carpenter, who was a Harley-owner himself, was able to show enough sincere empathy for the large biker's distress to make this incident a win for the police. In talking with the bikers, they soon learned he had been shot. They then all wanted to talk to the cop, who took a bullet and lived. The anger passed quickly.

The gymnast went to jail. The next morning he would wake up in a dark cell. He would be surrounded by metal and stone, and all the sounds that he made would evince a hollow echo. He would never be able to personally remember the night's events. A friend would come and bond him out of jail. The friend would then tell the tale of how he had been a running, smiling idiot one minute and a hapless gymnast the next. His friend would then tell the hapless gymnast how his life was saved by the flashy show put on by a young La Claire cop named McCarthy. The gymnast would always respond by saying, "Sounds cool. I wish I could have been there."

After clearing from the jail, Kane and McCarthy headed back toward River Street once again. The crowd was building and the volume of the environment was on the rise. The polka music could be heard in the night air, floating from the large beer tent on the fest grounds, on the edge of the downtown area.

The air had a heavy odor, which was a combination of odors fighting each other for dominance. It would smell like bratwurst, then beer, then vomit, then urine, and sometimes all of the above.

As McCarthy and Kane approached an alley on Main Street, just one-half block from their destination, an obviously intoxicated young man exited the alley and began crossing the street. Kane and McCarthy could not help but notice that the man's gait was seriously impaired, not only by the alcohol he had on-board, but also by the parking meter he was carrying.

As the officers began jogging toward the drunken meter thief, the man noticed the officers. The man immediately broke in to a hobbled run. McCarthy and Kane picked up their pace, but only a little, because the man was trying to outrun the two officers, while maintaining possession of the parking meter.

The officers caught the man before he entered the opposite alley, and he was immediately handcuffed and advised of his rights. McCarthy asked the man where he'd gotten the meter. The man looked down at the meter lying next to him. A sincere look of horror formed on his face, and he exclaimed, "I have no idea where it came from. As God ish my witnesh, I didn't shteal it."

"255. Send me a van for transport one more time to 300 Main Street at the alley to the north."

The night was picking up considerably. The van was nearly full when it picked up McCarthy, Kane, and Mr. Meter. One arrestee was being held face down on the floor by Officer Dooley. He continually tried to turn his head back toward Dooley and spit in his face, but the position he was held in kept him from successfully achieving his goal. Each time the man spit he would curse, "You fucking pig. Take these handcuffs off, and I'll kick your ass."

Dooley would just calmly respond, "Just relax my friend. You already tried that and look where it got you. Just be nice now." Dooley's eyes met McCarthy and he sighed, "It's only Friday night. What's tomorrow going to bring?"

"Maybe it will be cold," answered McCarthy.

"Seventy degrees and clear is what the weather man said," answered Stammos, from the back of the van.

"Great!" said Dooley with disgust.

At the jail, activity had picked up considerably. Another van was unloading as McCarthy arrived, and a third van was just pulling out to answer another call for River Street. In the holding area, all the benches were taken. One man was crying, and another was vomiting into a garbage can, while the arresting officer kept a hand on his head, to keep him properly aligned. McCarthy thought, as the man vomited, that it was not wise to eat a large pepperoni pizza after drinking two gallons of beer.

"Kane, can you stay with Mr. Meter, while I tag this evidence and do my report?" asked McCarthy.

"You bet, boss," said Kane.

McCarthy hauled the parking meter in to the evidence officer, and completed the slip. Within fifteen minutes, he had the evidence tagged and Sandy had completed the report. McCarthy thought that it would be nice to have such efficient and quick processing of paperwork every night of the week.

After hooking up with Kane, the two hopped into an empty van headed back to the River Street area. "How's it going tonight?" McCarthy asked the driver.

"It's nuts all over town. Forget about the fountain of youth. It's like every beer tapper has magically become the fountain of stupid. I'd guess tonight we are going to go over 200 arrests." The driver completed his prediction, as he pulled quickly into a spot on River Street, where two officers were standing with a prisoner.

As the doors of the van opened, McCarthy and Kane hopped out and said, "See you later."

The driver answered, "I'm afraid so."

It was now nearly midnight and the sidewalks on River Streets were lined with revelers standing shoulder to shoulder. The officers were doing their policing from the curb line. Compton saw McCarthy walking from the van and he immediately approached. As he reached McCarthy, he told him, "Now only take the real troublemakers. We need to keep as many coppers down here as possible, at all times. No more breaks. We're down here until they go home."

"Yes, sir, Sergeant!" was McCarthy's answer. Compton's voice had a serious tone and inspired intensity in McCarthy.

Policing the event from midnight until bar time always presented the same problem. The crowd was too big for the sidewalk. River Street was also State Highway 41, and the mayor, the chief and Captain Hale argued that because it was a state highway, the police could not close it down. "It is a planned event and not an emergency, so legally we can not close it down" was the answer each year for Compton, when he would suggest it once again.

Everyone knew that this was just wrong. All the street-level officers would respond, "We are the police. We can close any street down we want, with reason, and this crowd needs more room."

Compton would always tell the officers to calm down and someone would inevitably say, "They're just wrong!"

Compton would counter by saying, "Son. You have to just relax and do your job. Life will be a lot less stressful when you realize that some people have the authority to be wrong." Whenever Compton made that statement, everyone knew it was time to get back to work. The meaningful exchange was over. In reality he was absolutely right. Some people did have the authority to be wrong.

The bars were full and the sidewalks were full. It was now time for the three-hour dance with the crowd. "Please, sir, could you step up on the curb. Thank you." "Ma'am, could you please step up on the curb. Thank you."

It had to be said hundreds, maybe thousands, of times by each officer. Arrests that were made, had to be made efficiently and quickly. Any prolonged arrest could set a crowd off. It could turn on the police at anytime. Any crowd could.

McCarthy had been taught that in any crowd there are approximately 5 percent leaders, that will always be good. There are 5 percent leaders that will always be bad. Then there are the 90 percent that are followers. They will follow the leaders that are giving the best show. When a large crowd disturbance starts, the followers abandon their own personalities and take on the personality of the crowd. That's why good people can smash windows, loot, burn, and even lynch an innocent man.

Tonight there were enough people to make one hell of a riot, but after what seemed like a thousand "Please step up on the curbs," the crowd started moving on. They spread throughout the city to house parties. The bars closed, the crowd swelled, and then slowly melted away.

The officers were ordered to report back to the civic center. Compton spoke to the assembled group once again, after taking roll. All the officers were accounted for, except Stammos, Dooley, Carpenter, and their partners. They had broken up a true donnybrook and taken the four out-of-town combatants to the "crowbar hotel."

"Good job tonight. Tomorrow night should be very busy. The weather is going to be warm and clear. Load your gear in the vans and walk back to the station. I want the doors, front and back, pulled, on all the businesses from here to the station. See you tomorrow."

McCarthy and Kane started back, pulling the front doors on River Street. The street and sidewalk were littered with beer cups, cans, broken bottles and sidewalk pizzas.

"Boy, the maid is going to earn her money tomorrow," quipped Kane.

Their conversation was suddenly disrupted by the roar of an engine and the squealing of tires as a car was driven wildly off Main onto River Street. It jumped the curb on the far side of the street and smashed into the cement decorative barrier, which contained the garbage can. The driver immediately put the car in reverse and squealed his tires, as be backed feverishly away from the scene of his deed.

Dan stepped into the street and held up his hand to stop the vehicle. McCarthy could see clearly the face of the driver, and it showed a look of startled inebriation. He was not expecting to see a cop standing in front of him at this moment of his life.

The driver paused for a millisecond, as McCarthy walked toward him, but then the look on the driver's face changed to drunken resolve. He hit the gas and drove his car directly at McCarthy. McCarthy pivoted out of the way, and as the car passed him, McCarthy, without giving it a thought, brought his flash light down hard, smashing the corner of the windshield. McCarthy was missed by inches, as the driver accelerated his ugly, little, battered red Chevrolet south on River Street to make good his escape.

McCarthy looked up and down the street for a squad, as he radioed the information, along with the description of the red Chevrolet. "It has right front damage, left front damage, and right rear damage on this vehicle."

"10-4," said the dispatcher.

"Additionally, it has a smashed windshield," added McCarthy, after taking a second to think.

Just then, a biker pulled up. "Can I help you, officer?" were the words the driver spoke, which startled McCarthy. McCarthy recognized the man as the biker who had had his motorcycle tipped earlier by the gymnast.

Without thinking, McCarthy jumped on the back of the motorcycle and said, "Don't break your neck, but just keep that vehicle in sight!"

"You got it, officer," responded the bad-ass-looking biker, and without hesitation he roared after the fleeing drunk.

Kane watched as the motorcycle's taillight got smaller and smaller, then disappeared, as it rounded the bend farther down on River Street. He shook his head and continued to walk back toward the station. "Stay with your partner. That's easier said than done," said Kane, chuckling to himself.

As Kane entered Central Station, he immediately met Compton. Compton asked, "Where's your partner?"

"The last time I saw him he was on the back of a motorcycle driven by Easy Rider, chasing a drunk driver. They were southbound on River Street" was Kane's unconcerned, but quite honest, response.

"Dyno Dan" was Compton's response.

"Dyno Dan," said Kane in agreement.

The driver of the Chevrolet did not notice the cop on the back of the Harley. The biker served as a large, burly, animated camouflage for the determined cop. He did not even seem to notice the motorcycle.

The driver of the Chevrolet doubled back, and was now paralleling River Street, several blocks over on Bluff Street.

McCarthy thought the driver was either an idiot or from out of town, because he was heading right toward the police department. McCarthy was holding onto the cycle driver with one hand and radioing out directions to the dispatcher with the other.

When the "destroyer-of-garbage-cans" saw squad lights coming right at him, he skid his vehicle to a sudden stop, sideways in the middle of Bluff Street. The driver's door on the red Chevrolet swung open and the driver fled on foot. His first ten steps were terribly awkward and he nearly fell, but he managed to regain his balance and he ran.

McCarthy bounced off the motorcycle, while it was coming to a stop, and called to his newfound biker friend, "Stick around in case I need a ride home."

McCarthy gained on the destroyer-of-garbage-cans immediately, because the man still did not know anyone was behind him.

Just before reaching the driver, McCarthy yelled, "Give it up! La Claire Police! You are under arrest!" The driver turned toward McCarthy, and his face had a look that was familiar. It was the same look of startled inebriation that McCarthy recognized from earlier. Once again, he did not expect to see any cop right there, much less the same cop, still on foot.

As he tried to run away, watch McCarthy, and fathom what was happening simultaneously, the .22 grams of alcohol in every 100 milliliters of blood that was in his system took control of the driver's mental helm. The driver found himself skidding across the ground. The fall was unaided and the surrender was complete.

McCarthy handcuffed the suspect and assisted him to his feet. "I wasn't driving. You can't prove nothing. You should have chased the driver. He ran off in the other direction." McCarthy let him talk. To say nothing was his right. To give false information was potentially another charge. At the minimum, it was additional evidence.

At Central Station, the destroyer-of-garbage-cans became very cooperative. He gave a sample of his breath willingly. He was from out of town. He came into town for the weekend from Milwaukee. This was his fourth offense for driving while intoxicated, and he had no valid license. The driver knew he had and now was ready to go to bed. He had been in jail before and would go to jail again. He did so, like the experienced pro he was.

McCarthy was happy to see that Sandy had changed locations, and was still available to do one last report. McCarthy dictated the rather lengthy report.

"You tired, Sandy?" asked McCarthy.

"Yes, I am. Thanks for asking." Then Sandy added, "I really like this, though. The night goes fast, and I get to see all the faces that go with the reports I process all year. It's fun." She continued, "You know I always look forward to entering the information from your reports. They are always entertaining, and when I read your reports, it's almost as if I was there. How do you constantly keep running into the things you do?"

"I don't know. I guess because I look for it. I look real hard. I'm glad someone notices," answered McCarthy.

"Oh, everyone notices, McCarthy. I think you have a gift. Are you married?" asked Sandy.

"Yes. Thanks for asking," answered McCarthy with a smile. "Her name is Victoria. I have two kids too, Nate and Christa." McCarthy said, pulling out pictures of them all, and showing them to Sandy. Here is Nate . . . here is Christa . . . and this is Victoria," McCarthy said, grinning with a pride he could not hide.

"They favor their mother. She is very pretty," said Sandy, glad that McCarthy did not seem to notice that the question about marriage was asked by her for her.

"You are kind of young to be married and have two kids, aren't you?" asked Sandy.

"I was lucky. The first pair of pants I tried on fit. We both decided we would enjoy our kids more if we had them young. So far we have been right," said McCarthy, as he carefully returned his pictures to his wallet, and then his wallet back to his pocket. "The only downside is that we are broke all of the time, but that's everyone's story. "I hope you weren't offended by the joke I told you earlier?" asked Sandy sheepishly.

"No. You have permission to tell me any kind of joke, as long as it is funny. To me jokes are like music. I like all kinds."

McCarthy was now gathering up his paperwork and signing all the forms. It was 5:00 a.m., which meant he would be able to crash into his sleeping bag, set up in the classroom of the police department. At most, he would be able to get one-and-a-half hours of sleep before he had to grab another shower. He would then have to report to his post for parade duty.

"Night, Sandy. Thanks again for typing my reports," said McCarthy.

"That's my job," answered Sandy, with that Christie Brinkley smile.

"You do it very well," said McCarthy.

"Even with my handicap?" said Sandy.

"Handicap?" asked McCarthy.

"I'm blonde," reported Sandy, flipping her hair and cocking her head, letting out a giggle.

"Your wit and competence achieve new heights within blondedom," answered McCarthy. "You don't fit the stereotype at all, except in the category of looks."

"Thanks," said Sandy, blushing, as she straightened up her work area for the night.

As she leaned forward to get her purse, McCarthy could not help but notice the hint of cleavage once again turned into a clue. He tried to look away immediately and almost succeeded. He hoped that Victoria would forgive him for looking. He suspected that she would. Victoria knew that McCarthy was forever hers and no one else's.

As McCarthy crawled into his sleeping bag, his thoughts turned away from work and to his family. He mentally kissed them all good night, and said his little prayer, "Thank you, God, for my life, for my family, and for my wife."

He thought of what Victoria would say if she saw him looking at the lovely Sandy tonight. He knew what she would say. "You can look, but don't touch, Daniel McCarthy! I can't be too hard on you for looking at a pretty woman. You are a man and that's why I married you. I do not know why women get so angry at men for just looking. If they don't look, you'd better check their pulse, because they are either dead or gay."

This made McCarthy chuckle to himself. Then he was asleep. There would be no dreams tonight. He slept the sleep of the exhausted.

CHAPTER 23
COME TO DEUTSCHE DAYS . . . IT'S A RIOT

Dan McCarthy was at his intersection by 8:00 a.m. Working a parade as a cop is a flurry of constant activity. Dan had to set up barricades and close off two intersections. He was at the very starting point of the parade.

The day went fast. It was filled with traffic control, crowd control, lost purses and kids. It was a beautiful day, which always meant problems for the police. Deutsche Days took place during the last weekend of September each year. It was always an incredibly busy weekend for the police. La Claire was a city of about 55,000 people. The city was inundated by over 300,000 visitors for Deutsche Days. Every hotel and house was full, and swilling beer seemed to be the main event of the festival.

The parade was just as good an excuse for people to get drunk as any other, so drunk is what they got. Drunken people watching a parade, next to families with their small children watching a parade, means job security for cops. McCarthy managed to mediate the minor disturbances throughout the day. He was not sure if his successes were because of his people skills or if it was because those involved decided there was just too much drinking-day left to get arrested yet.

McCarthy was done with parade duty at 3:30 p.m. He had to be back at 6:50 p.m. He decided there was no time to sleep, so he went to the department weight room and had a quick workout. He then left the police department for a short run. He thought the run and shower would make it feel like a new day.

As he crossed the street, he ran by a muffler shop. Around the rear was a large parking lot, which was filled, because it was relatively close to the Deutsche Days Fest Grounds. In the first spot closest to the sidewalk, McCarthy noticed a black Nissan with two people in it. The driver's side window was open and McCarthy saw the driver of the vehicle lining cocaine on a mirror in broad daylight. The man in the driver's seat had prepared two lines of the white powder, and he was about to snort it up through the half-sized straw he had in his hand.

McCarthy gave no thought to what he did next. Initially he ran by the Nissan. Then he turned and ran back. McCarthy ran up to the window, reached in, and batted the corner of the mirror up, causing it to spin and spill its contents all over the DARE T-Shirt the driver was wearing. McCarthy, in an angry tone barked, "You're a block from the police department, for God's sake!" McCarthy then jogged off, leaving them stunned. McCarthy looked back and noticed the driver of the car was bugging out of the area as fast as he could.

Dan then thought about what he had just done, as he ran. He came to a conclusion that he probably should not have done it. It was neither illegal, nor was it unethical, but it was stupid and unsafe. It was probably as smart as jumping into a van filled with druggies and hopping onto the back of a motorcycle with a biker, to pursue a fleeing car.

McCarthy thought he might have just outdone himself this time. He had no radio, no weapon, and no handcuffs. He mentally chastised himself, as he ran, for being so impulsive. Then he thought, "Am I acting on bad impulse or good instincts?" He did not know enough about police work yet to know for sure.

He pictured the white powder on the shocked driver's face and DARE T-Shirt. I'll bet I did more to stymie that boy's drug use than his DARE classes, he thought to himself. He did think it was funny; even though he knew he would never handle such a situation like that in the same way in the future, he was glad he did it once. He laughed and enjoyed the beautiful weather, as he ran.

The streets were covered with garbage, left over from the immense crowd that came to watch the parade. This parade was one of the biggest in the Midwest.

When McCarthy got back to the station, he took a shower, shaved, cleaned up, and changed into a fresh uniform for the night. When he was geared up, he caught a one-hour nap in the classroom and woke up incredibly refreshed. He grabbed his gear and hopped in one of the vans for a ride down to the command center in the civic center.

Dan was surprised when he arrived at the civic center, because there was Larry Kane, already there. "What happened to Larry-time?" asked McCarthy.

"Well, just as guys like you are late every once in a while, like a fluke of nature, well, every once in a while guys like me are early." Larry ended his comment with a nod to emphasize the wisdom of his theory. "I will not make it a habit, however. It may upset the balance of yin and yang," added Kane with feigned concern etched across his face and in his voice.

McCarthy grabbed a Pepsi and a sandwich. He had not had an opportunity to eat all day. As he sat down, he noticed everyone was eating immediately.

Randy sat down next to McCarthy and Kane, with a plate of food. He immediately began shoveling it in. "Better eat now!" said Stammos, between bites. "Tonight, we are going to be busy. I think it is going to be a night to remember."

"Why?" asked McCarthy, "Just because of the weather?"

"No. The information everyone working the college area is receiving right now is that, at bar time, the crowd is going to forcibly take the street," Stammos reported, taking a big bite out of a stacked ham sandwich, followed by a scoop of baked beans. His face then had the look of ecstasy on it as he savored the perfect combination of ham and baked beans.

"Do you think they will?" asked McCarthy.

"Most righteously!" answered Stammos, as he took yet another large bite of the stacked ham. The bite he took was large enough to choke a mid-sized hippo.

"No wonder they call us pigs," said Kane.

"You wouldn't dare say that to me, Kane, if you didn't have a black belt. I'd have to come over there and kick your ass," answered Stammos. He continued to devour his sandwich and beans, almost without breathing.

Once again, Compton came to the front of the room. His message was the same as the night before, except he added, "Tonight, at bar time, I want everyone on the street. We have information that the college fraternities are arranging an orchestrated move on the street. If we are all down there, it might discourage it."

Compton then walked over to a flip chart and turned a page. He flipped the top page, and River Street was drawn, showing the primary intersection with Diamond to the south and Main to the north. One block farther north was State Street. Compton continued, "If we pull back, we will form a line at River and Main Street. I will form up an arrest team there. Vans three and four will have already picked up our gear. We will gear up—26" batons, holstered; helmets; and gas masks with carriers. All of you should already have vests, tickets, and card identifiers to affix to your arrests." Compton then pulled out the cards. They were designed to place on the back of the suspects, to make sure the arresting officer and the charges were identified with each arrest."

At this point, Hale stepped to the front of the room and interrupted Compton. "I would like to let you know that I will decide when to get your gear. If we put the helmets on too soon, it could be considered con-frontational. We don't need anyone to jump the gun here." Everyone noticed how Hale looked at Compton, when he spoke the words "jump the gun."

"Respectfully, Captain, if a garbage can bounces off my head, can I just put my helmet on without asking?" Stammos joined in, and then shoved the last bite of a second stacked ham sandwich into his mouth.

Hale's back became erect and his faced showed the anger triggered by the question, which, under the circumstances, was on everyone's mind. "It's that kind of attitude gets us in trouble in the first place. I don't think anything is going to come of this. This is just much ado about nothing. We have so many people working tonight, no one will dare try some-thing. I get paid extra money to make decisions like this. We can't leave decisions like this in the hands of green troops like McCarthy or Carpenter. I'll decide when the helmets go on, not you. Is that clear, Mr. Stammos?"

Stammos answered with a muffled "Yes, sir," because he had a mouth full of stacked ham, mixed with his beloved baked beans. He was not worried about eating the beans tonight, because he would be outside in the night air surrounded by people who would most definitely smell worse than he.

McCarthy pondered why Hale used McCarthy's name in his speech. He wondered if he would ever be considered a "veteran," rather than a "green troop," or a "rookie." He thought he had earned the respect of the other officers, but obviously not of Cpt. Hale. Hale apparently thought it was necessary to embarrass Carpenter and McCarthy in front of every-one, including the out-of-town officers.

"He's a prick, McCarthy," proclaimed Randy, when he cleared his mouth of ham and beans. "There is no one here who would not go into anything with you. On the other hand, there is no one here who would want to have Hale as a backup to a disturbance at a Beenie baby sale. Forget about what he said," counseled Stammos as he wiped some mus-tard from the corner of his mouth with a napkin.

"Thanks, Randy," answered Dan.

"I second that emotion," added Kane.

As McCarthy gathered up his empty plate to toss out, he thought, "When will I hear the words 'veteran officer' in conjunction with my name?"

With that, everyone hit the streets. There was plenty to do. The crews went bar to bar right away and made announcements that any vehicles in the tow-away zone needed to be moved right away, because the wreckers were coming.

People had been drinking all day, and the "7:00 leakers" were located and hauled to detox. Deutsche Days was a drunken beer-drinking bash. Each year, the leakers seemed to start dropping at 7:00 p.m. The next crew began dropping at 11:00 p.m. to 12:00 a.m. From bar time, which was 2:30 a.m., until 8:00 a.m., it was pretty constant. The "leakers" were individuals who did not know their tolerance and would drink massive quantities of alcohol and suddenly drop. They would kill themselves in a variety of ways. They would just overdose: that is, drink a lethal dose of alcohol.

They might do something stupid—like try to balance on a balcony railing and plunge to their death. Sometimes, they would wander to the Mississippi and drown, not realizing that if a drunk person can drown in their own bath tub, they could certainly drown in the most powerful river on earth. Sometimes, they would just walk out into traffic and be run down. Other times, they would get behind the wheel of a car, and take one, two, or more innocent people with them.

There were four officers assigned to each trouble car, running to calls all over the city. These units would haul the intoxicated, to the point of incapacitated, individuals to St. Luke's. The officers would place them in the hospital on an "alcohol hold."

The police were not the only ones busy over this weekend. The emergency rooms at St. Luke's Hospital and La Claire Mercy Hospital looked like there had been a plane crash. The hallways and treatment rooms were filled with a variety of injuries, mostly caused by people who had gone too often to the "fountain of stupid."

When McCarthy finished notifying the bars in the area, he was approached by the biker whose bike had been damaged by the drunken gymnast. He shook McCarthy's hand. Even though the man looked like the stereotypical outlaw biker in dress, McCarthy thanked the man for coming to his aid the night before. McCarthy hadn't gotten the chance that night, to thank him properly.

The two then struck up a conversation, and McCarthy learned that the biker was an investment broker from Chicago. "I'm glad you arrested that guy who dumped my bike. That bike is like my baby. I would have gotten myself into trouble, if I would have gotten there first. Thanks!" said the biker, whose name was Leon.

"I'm glad I could be of help. My name is McCarthy," Dan said, offering a hearty handshake to the large yuppie biker. "Now that you know who he is, you will be able to go after him civilly," answered McCarthy.

"Yeah, I stopped at the police department today and they were real busy, but they gave me a copy of the report. They said normally they don't do that, but the sergeant working has a Harley, too, and he went and got it for me." Leon said, with a big smile, proud of the influence he wielded by riding a Harley. "Hey, McCarthy, what was that hold you put on that guy? Are you in the martial arts or something?" asked Leon.

"It was an aikido hold, which is very painfully effective, but doesn't injure," answered McCarthy. "It's called Sankyo."

"Are you a black belt?" asked Leon.

"Yes, I am, sir," answered McCarthy, trying to be nonchalant.

"I'll bet you like having a partner who is a black belt," Leon said to Kane.

"Why, yes I do," answered Kane.

"Why don't you give him lessons?" Leon asked McCarthy.

"It would not be proper. You see . . . he's my instructor," answered McCarthy.

"Wow. I think I'll hang around and watch you guys kick ass on some of these college idiots. You know, I went to college, but I was never a college idiot," explained Leon.

"I'm sure you weren't. You'll have to excuse us, Leon," McCarthy said, as he began to cross the street to move away from the conversation and toward Lunde's Pub. There was some sort of disturbance inside the front door, moving out onto the sidewalk.

As Kane and McCarthy moved closer, a man in his thirtys had hold of a female by the arm. She was squirming and attempting to break away. She was yelling in a loud, shrill voice, "Let go of me. You're hurting me. You don't fucking own me!"

The male punctuated the last statement with a right cross to the jaw of the skinny, platinum blonde girlfriend. McCarthy reached him right after the punch and took hold of his right wrist and right elbow. McCarthy proclaimed, "Police! Relax! You are under arrest, sir!"

The man attempted to swing at McCarthy with his left arm, and McCarthy placed the man's right arm in an armlock and used the man's own momentum to spin him to the ground. As they reached the ground, Kane was on the other arm and spun it around into a position to handcuff. The man was handcuffed, and Compton, who was calmly arriving at the scene, spoke into his radio, "We'll need a van in front of Lunde's."

After handcuffing, the man began to vehemently deny any wrongdoing. "She is a bitch. I was defending myself. She went off on me inside, and I only hit her in self-defense. I'm sorry I swung on you, guys, but you came up behind me. I didn't even know you were cops."

McCarthy had Kane stand by with the prisoner, while Dan interviewed the female. It appeared her jaw might be broken. "My name is Tammi. My boyfriend is Derek," said Tammi, crying and holding her jaw. She talked, trying to move her jaw as little as possible. "Derek and I were at a table inside the bar, and we were sitting with his best friend, Boyd. Derek got up and went to the bathroom. All I did was try to entertain Boyd until Derek got back. We were laughing when Derek got back, and he got so angry. He wanted to know what was going on. I said nothing was, but Derek didn't believe me."

Tammi cried partially from the pain of the injury and partially from the pain that goes along with falling in love with a violent, jealous abuser. "If I would have ignored his friend, he would have beaten me for that, too. He has never beaten me in public before. This is so humiliating," Tammi said, dropping her eyes in shame. "My jaw hurts so bad."

McCarthy had pulled his roll of cling from his side pants pocket and secured the jaw in place to ease the pain. He was nearly positive it was broken, but he kept his concerns from Tammi.

A La Claire ambulance pulled up and loaded Tammi into the back. Dooley climbed in with the victim and took pictures of the injury. He got a written statement in the hospital from Tammi.

McCarthy and Kane rode to jail with Derek, who now had become silent. At the jail McCarthy advised Derek of his rights. He waived them and made a statement. He shocked Dan and Larry with a sudden turn toward truthfulness. He told the exact story Tammi had told. His explanation, "I can't believe I hit her so hard. I have a problem. My daddy beat my mom. My granddaddy beat my grandmom. I said I would never treat a woman like this, and now I doing the same thing. I'm a piece of shit. I need some help. Is she going to be all right?" Derek asked in apparent sincerity.

"She'll live, but I think you broke her jaw, Derek," answered McCarthy truthfully.

This caused the dam holding the tears back to burst, and Derek started sobbing. Once again, Kane handled the booking of the prisoner and McCarthy dictated his report. There was no time for small talk, since bookings and officers were coming steadily. McCarthy and Kane met again down on the ramp and hopped a van.

On the way back to River Street, McCarthy shouted to the driver, "Let us out here." The driver pulled to the side of the road, and McCarthy and Kane hopped out the side door. "We'll call for a van, if we need it. You can take off," McCarthy told the driver, as he left, obviously on a mission.

"What did you see?" asked Kane.

"Over by the reviewing stand for the parade, there was a guy crouched down. I don't know what he was doing, but it didn't look normal," said McCarthy, as he maneuvered his way to the reviewing stand for a closer look, trying to avoid being seen.

As the two got close enough to see the reviewing stand, it was not possible to see if the crouching figure was still there. The reviewing stand was taken down, and all that was left was the semitrailer flatbed, which held the portable frame for the reviewing stand. During the parade, this stand was where the judges, who gave out awards for the best units, had stationed themselves.

Since the parade, the spot had become a prime spot for parking once again, and a line of drivers had parked their vehicles. To have room to park in the limited space, the drivers had to park the front ends of their vehicles under the flatbed. There was a parked Chevy Camaro between the officers and the spot where McCarthy had last seen the dark figure crouching. As their eyes strained to see in the darkened area, they both heard the noise begin. There was a distinct rusty-metal, squeaking sound coming from the flatbed.

Then it dawned on McCarthy what was happening. He ran toward where he had last seen the figure. As he rounded the parked vehicles, which had obstructed his vision, he saw the figure, who was a long-haired white guy with his back to the officers. His arm was moving furiously in a circle. What he was doing was operating the mechanism that allows truckers to lower the front end of the flatbed and attach it to the tractor. The crouching figure was lowering the flatbed down onto the front ends of the parked vehicles.

McCarthy's voice came out of nowhere for the crouching figure, "La Claire Police—don't move, you are under arrest."

McCarthy felt the man stand straight up and tighten his arm, but McCarthy immediately put the subject in a restraint hold. "Larry, I don't know anything about these things; can you lock it so it doesn't do any damage?"

Kane was on it immediately, being a jack of all trades. He had surmised what the subject had been doing, also, and was able to lock up the flatbed. As it was, the officers arrived in time to stop the massive amount of damage that would have occurred at the hands of the crouching man. They were able to discover that there was damage to the Camaro. There were footprints on the hood, matching the crouching man's shoes. He apparently had jumped up and down on the hood of the Camaro, before he received the brilliant idea to damage the whole line of cars, by crushing them with the flatbed.

McCarthy called for a car with a camera. He then took the information down off the damaged car and left a note for its owner. He took pictures of the damaged vehicle and then walked the crouching man to jail, since they were less than a block away.

"That was the dumbest thing I have ever done. I don't know why I did it. I have never been in trouble in my life," said the crouching man, out of the blue.

"I agree. I don't know why either. You broke your string of days without trouble. You are officially in trouble," said Kane, dryly.

Crouching man was booked for criminal damage to property and attempted criminal damage to property. McCarthy found four baggies of marijuana "crotched" down the front of his pants. He was charged with possession of marijuana with the intent to deliver, because of the multiple packages.

Kane booked him, while McCarthy dictated his report. Then McCarthy packaged the evidence. By the continual flow of officers with their arrests, this had the making of a 500-plus weekend. Kane and McCarthy walked back to River Street. On the way back, they issued four public urination ordinance citations for two men, and two squatting females, who were urinating in an alley behind one of the packed bars.

"The line is too long in the bathrooms" was the excuse/reason all four gave for their sense of urgency.

Kane observed, after leaving the four who put the "p" in pavement, "You know that sounded like a big cow pissing on a flat rock." McCarthy agreed with the comparison.

When McCarthy and Kane reached the 100 block of South River Street, the sidewalks were absolutely packed. It was only 11:30 p.m., and already Compton had spread the word to stay street-side and avoid arrests for minor violations, if at all possible.

McCarthy stood for about fifteen minutes before Kane said, "Watch those two." He pointed at two males, who were apparently oblivious to the police all around them. A blonde-haired, skinny man, who was about 6' 3", handed a bindle to a short white guy with his head shaved. The man passed some folded up bills to the tall guy.

"Looks like probable cause to me," said McCarthy. McCarthy signaled to Compton that he was going into the crowd to make an arrest. Compton came over with four more officers. McCarthy moved toward the tall skinny guy and Kane cut off the short man. Kane had his man immediately, but this alerted Mr. Tall and Skinny, who turned and jumped a wall bordering a parking lot, which was in the middle of the block.

The skinny man hooked his foot going over the wall and fell sprawling to the blacktop. McCarthy did not hook his foot and immediately was on the tall man. McCarthy brought the man's right hand behind him and put him in a compliance hold, which stopped him from squirming.

The man still had the $40 the short man had given him, in his right hand. Compton was with McCarthy in what seemed like a second, and the two handcuffed Mr. Tall and Skinny. McCarthy searched him and found a large baggie containing 40 bindles, plus $2000 in cash in an inner vest pocket.

Compton called for a van to meet with McCarthy and Kane in the alley behind the bars, rather than walk the arrestees through the crowd. As the two suspects were loaded into the van, Compton took McCarthy by the arm and whispered, "Good job. Get clear of jail as soon as you can. We are going to have trouble tonight. I can smell it."

"Yes, sir, Sergeant," answered McCarthy, who then climbed once more into the van. He could hear the crowd on one side of the street chanting "E-I-E-I-E-I-O." The crowd on the other chanted, in return, "E-I-E-I-E-I-O."

This continued, as the van pulled out of the area. When the officers reached the jail, there was a bottleneck. Both prisoners were cooperative, so McCarthy left them to be watched by Kane to await booking. Sgt. Bartz, who was a dayshift detective, was a gray-haired clown, very close to retirement. He was a clown in the sense that he always was looking for a laugh and usually succeeded in getting one.

Bartz was placating the arrested people waiting to be booked by taking their breakfast orders. He would ask, "Do you want coffee, orange juice, or milk?"

The prisoner would think and answer, "Coffee."

"Would you prefer pancakes, waffles, or French toast?"

The prisoner then asked, "What kind of syrup do you have?"

"Hey, don't get ahead of me. What do you think this is a Howard Johnson? Now tell me, is it going to be pancakes, waffles, or French toast." insisted Bartz, with feigned sternness.

"OK. Pancakes. Don't be such a hard ass," was the response.

"That's better, now how do you want your eggs—poached, scrambled, or over easy?" Bartz then looked at McCarthy, winked and smiled.

The rest of the prisoners were listening intently, trying to decide what they wanted for breakfast, also. Right or wrong, it sure kept them quiet. Little did they know that they were all getting a carton of milk, a bowl, a spoon, and a snack-pack-sized box of Cheerios.

McCarthy chuckled and went about his business. This arrest took some time to process, because the officer had to test the cocaine found on both the buyer and the seller. He then weighed and packaged it, and turned it over once again to the evidence officer on duty. McCarthy then sat down next to Sandy, to dictate his report.

"I need to get out there fast. How fast can I go?" asked McCarthy.

"You talk as fast as you can, and I'll slow you down if I need to," answered Sandy, with her fingers at the ready over her keyboard.

McCarthy was done with his arrest report, offense report, evidence report, and the narrative, within ten minutes. "I can't believe it. On any other night, that report would have tied me up for two hours," said McCarthy, thanking Sandy profusely.

"I'm a highly-trained professional," Sandy said with a smile, which even at 12:30 a.m., on the second night of Deutsche Days, still made her look like Christie Brinkley.

McCarthy returned to Kane, and the assembly-line booking had just reached Mr. Tall and Skinny. He was in town from Madison. He was obviously a professional and was fulfilling a demand. "I want to talk to my attorney," were the last words he spoke to McCarthy. That was all right by McCarthy. It would have just taken more time. Tonight Dan just did not have time.

As the officers were leading Mr. Tall and Skinny to the booking counter, he called to Sgt. Bartz, as he passed him, "Hey, Sergeant. Is it too late to change my order to waffles?"

Sgt. Bartz shook his head, his face showing a tempered amount of displeasure, as he paged through his notebook, and made the change. "All right. Waffles it is. But only if you stay cooperative."

"Don't worry. I will. I haven't had waffles in years," said Mr. Tall and Skinny.

It was 1:00 a.m. before Kane and McCarthy were back on River Street. The chanting had stopped and the crowd seemed quieter. McCarthy hoped that was a good sign. Then four people walked by, smiled, and waved, saying in a sing-song voice, "See you later at the riot, officers."

The next pair that walked by added, "Be careful at the riot, officers."

"What the hell?" asked Kane. "See you later at the riot, officers?"

"Be careful at the riot?" asked McCarthy, right back at Kane.

The two officers contacted Compton to let him know they were back and what they had just heard.

Compton said, "I know it. The crowd has been pretty friendly since you left. They started chanting, but some guys came out of the bar and waved their arms, said "Not yet," and they all quit. They have been quiet since."

"What do you think?" asked McCarthy.

"I think we are going to have one hell of a problem at bar time," said Compton, in a matter-of-fact way.

Just then Hale pulled up to Compton and asked, "How's it going?"

"We're going to have a problem tonight. I would like to take half my people and have them gear up to stand by out of sight immediately," said Compton, without hesitation.

"What's this all about?" asked Hale.

"The people that are going to riot are telling us they are going to riot. The people that are not going to riot are leaving and telling us the talk is, there is going to be a riot at bar time. You can see the people lining the parking ramps on both ends of River Street to watch the riot," Compton explained, gesturing to the crowds in the parking ramps, which had been turned into bleacher seats. "The undercover officers in the crowd are telling us there is going to be a riot. I would like to be prepared immediately to respond, when it happens," said Compton in his no-nonsense manner.

"Sergeant Compton, there is not going to be a riot. You are going to believe a bunch of drunken college kids, who have over-inflated egos. At bar time, they will all rush out and find the nearest party, like they always do. We have seventy officers down here in this two block area, and there is no way they will riot with a police presence like this. We are not taking half of them away. Then, we will have a riot. We are not putting helmets on. Then, we will have a riot. You are overreacting, Compton," said Hale, with a smile on his face. He talked to Compton as if he was a confused little boy. "Relax. In another hour, we will be heading home, and you are going to feel pretty silly about all of this."

"Yes, sir, Captain-sir," responded Compton, ever the Marine. "Respectfully, sir, I request that you be present at bar time."

"I'll try, Sergeant, but this is not the only place in the city where police work is being done tonight," answered Hale, as he slid his rotund body into the unmarked unit.

At 1:30 p.m., Compton ordered the equipment vans to pick up the officers' riot gear from the civic center. He contacted Randy Stammos and ordered him to get his gear ready, as if he intended to clear out a crowd of 10,000 rioters. Stammos was a trained grenadier and moved quickly.

Compton contacted each officer and told them the fall-back location would be River Street and Main. "If we have to move, stay together, and do not run."

At 2:05 a.m., it began to happen. The bars normally do not usually empty until 2:15 a.m., but on this night, it happened at 2:05 a.m. McCarthy noticed that a parking ramp near River and Diamond Street was full of people, in lawn chairs or standing as if they were about to watch a football game.

The sidewalks were full immediately, and the crowd surged forward toward the street. Leaders led the chanting, which was so loud that

McCarthy could not hear anything Kane was saying to him. The crowd on one side of the street would shout, "Tastes Great!" and the other would answer, "Less Filling!" With each chant, the crowd would surge another step forward.

After a short time, the chant changed to "Eat shit!" The answer would each time be, "Fuck you!" Then one member of the crowd ran at Officer Dooley and tried to shoot a takedown on him. Dooley spun away, avoiding the drunk, who rolled out into the middle of the street. There was a protracted struggle. The man was built like a running back. McCarthy and Kane held their position, while the man was physically coaxed into handcuffs and taken away. There was a deafening roar of approval from the crowd, and then the verse from the Steam song began, " Na Na Na Na Na Na Na Na-Hey Hey Hey-Go-odbye. The crowd had pushed forward, and the street was down to one lane.

Compton had already ordered traffic cut off to the street. He could see what Hale could not. He could see that no one was going home in one hour, and that the night, if survived, would be remembered by all present.

Compton signaled to everyone to pull back. McCarthy, Kane, Dooley, and about seven other officers with their partners were at Diamond and River Street. As soon as the group of officers started to walk away from the intersection, a roar came from the crowd, and it swept into the street, as if it had one mind. The roar took McCarthy's breath away. He could not grasp how the crowd could have gotten any louder than it was, but it did. It was as if the people in the crowd were of one mind, one personality, one large, dangerous threat.

Compton had managed to close down traffic to the north of the area, preventing all cars from getting caught in the movement of the crowd, except for one taxicab, which had been waiting to pick up a fare. As McCarthy moved northbound, the aggressive front line of the crowd began to attempt to overrun the group of officers.

Compton yelled, "Form a line on me now!" Most of the officers had already obtained their wooden batons by this time, since none were as blind as Captain Hale. The line formed immediately, and Compton yelled, "On . . . Guard!" With this command, the sixteen or so officers snapped their batons into the on-guard position, shouting in unison, "Back!"

This movement caused the crowd's front line to halt momentarily. Then, one man in the middle waved them forward and he moved directly at McCarthy. "We're going to kick your asses tonight, and I'm going to take that badge of yours off your shirt, hotshot."

McCarthy responded with a look that caused people around the man to slow their approach. This man was in his element. This was his moment, and he was going to lead the crowd over the top of this small line of officers and brush them away like so much lint. This man walked right at McCarthy and grabbed hold of the end of McCarthy's baton. McCarthy rotated the baton quickly and expertly snapped it away from the leader, who had continued to attempt to walk right over McCarthy. McCarthy thrust his baton into the leader's solar plexus, knocking him back into the crowd.

The leaders in the crowd saw this and suddenly stopped. All of them wanted to destroy the line of officers, but no one now wanted to be the first to reach the line. The crowd now only moved as far forward as the line of officers moved backward. After the impact, the crowd stayed between five and ten feet away from the line of officers.

McCarthy kept his eyes on the man he had hit. "When the time is right, that man is going to jail," thought McCarthy. McCarthy welcomed having a purpose. It took his mind off the fear in his guts.

At Main Street, Compton re-enforced the line with additional officers. He stationed a number of officers behind the line, to serve as arrest teams. He tapped McCarthy on the line, saying: "Ring that baton, soldier! I want your hands free, handling the arrests."

"Yes, sir, Sergeant," said McCarthy, sliding his baton into its ring and stepping back behind the line.

"Nazis! Nazis! Nazis!" was the chant of the crowd. McCarthy could see his friend, who had tried to take his baton, was pointing at McCarthy as he chanted. He was moving ever closer to the line.

Then came the projectiles. At first it was two-liter plastic bottles filled with water. Shortly after that, glass bottles and garbage cans, rocks and pool balls were sporadically thrown and dodged by the officers.

Compton made contact with Captain Hale. "Sir, can we have our helmets now?" Hale had the blank look on his face seen often in Wisconsin. He had the look of a deer caught in the head lights of a car. This was too much for him. This could not be happening. "No," was his response. Compton looked closely at Hale. He had seen this look before on the face of a young lieutenant in Vietnam after walking into his first firefight. Hale did not have a clue what he was saying no to.

"Sir!" said Compton, trying to snap Hale out it and bring him back to the business at hand. Just then, Compton saw Dooley go down after being hit square on the side of the head with a full garbage can. He shook it off and was back in line, bleeding from a scalp wound.

"That's it!" said Compton, leaving Hale still dazed and as functional as a lawn ornament. He tapped every other person in the line, and they knew what it meant. They fell out and put their gear on. As each officer geared up, he returned to the line. Each would tap someone who did not have their gear on and replace them in the line. Within five minutes, everyone in the line had their helmets on and their gas masks ready on their leg, in their carrier.

McCarthy was busy on the line and one of the last to gear up. The officers were sweeping people through the line for arrest, as certain members of the crowd became emboldened and would physically challenge the line. One of the first to come through was the man who had not learned his lesson when McCarthy had thrust his baton into his solar plexus earlier. The man, who had threatened to take McCarthy's badge off his shirt before the night was over will have to make good his threat from a jail cell. McCarthy tightened him up immediately and handcuffed him.

He was walked back to the van and McCarthy announced to the video operator, holding up the identification card McCarthy had quickly filled out on the arrest, "Miller, Charles B. DOB 1-17-58, arrested by Daniel McCarthy for disorderly conduct, inciting a riot, and resisting arrest."

The tag was placed on the arrested man's back, and he was placed in the van, while he screamed, "You asshole! I want your fucking badge number. You fucking Nazi storm-trooping asshole!" McCarthy put flex cuffs on the individual and removed his personal handcuffs. McCarthy thought, as he walked back to the line, that he wished Mr. Miller, Charles B., could be sent back in time to 1942 and be arrested by the Nazis, so he could know the difference.

By now, windows were being smashed on the southside of the crowd. Information was received that members of the crowd had overturned the cab and were in the process of setting it on fire. McCarthy was amazed that, even though the car and the windows were in the same block he was, the crowd was so dense that nothing could be seen beyond the first line of the crowd. Then came the smoke from the burning car, billowing above the crowd.

Compton came up with Stammos and the loudspeaker. He had the arrest team tap on the shoulder of half the line, so they could step back and put their gas masks on. This being done, this group stepped back into the line, while the other half put their masks on.

The crowd chanted continually, "Ge-sta-po! Ge-sta-po! Ge-sta-po!" McCarthy stepped into the line with his mask on. It hurt him to be called Gestapo. It was the first time that anything said to him on the job had really bothered him. Then McCarthy thought, "Idiot! That's what they want. They want to get to us. The man who angers you, conquers you. I'll not be conquered by this crowd of drunken assholes!" McCarthy looked at the faces of the crowd. They had all changed somehow. The faces looked like masks, and they danced like natives around a fire in a 1950's B safari movie.

Just then, someone in the crowd rushed forward. He grabbed McCarthy's baton and tried to take it away. McCarthy immediately countered. He brought the baton up and around, and snapped down hard. The man who attempted to seize the baton was large and confident in his own strength. He held the baton firmly, which was the worst thing he could do. As McCarthy snapped his baton down to free it from the large man's grip, he sensed the snapping of the man's bone in his hand. The man was still on McCarthy, so McCarthy impacted hard into the man's abdomen, driving him backward. The man was pulled back into the crowd by friends and was never seen by McCarthy again. He would skulk away and seek treatment for his broken hand in another city.

Now that all the officers in the line had their gas masks in place, Compton began shouting commands to the crowd, using a bullhorn. "I am Sergeant Compton of the La Claire Police Department. This is an unlawful assembly, and I am ordering you to disperse immediately or you will face arrest."

Compton gave this command repeatedly, from different points on the line. Each command was followed by a loud "Whoooooa" by the crowd, as they shook their hands to feign fright. One pleasant thing did occur to raise the morale of the male officers on the line. A beautiful blonde, who looked a bit like Kim Basinger through McCarthy's clouded shield, came to the front of the crowd. She was wearing a flowered dress and walked between the crowd and the police-line. She sashayed like a supermodel on a runway. Then she turned to the line and flipped up her dress front and back, revealing she was wearing no panties. Her neatly trimmed pubic area told the fact only her hair dresser knew for sure. She was indeed a natural blonde, gifted with unnatural beauty.

Toward the rear of the crowd, some females were hoisted up by the crowd and some of the well-endowed females were happily exposing their breasts. McCarthy noticed that two girls who looked like twins were hoisted onto the shoulders of some larger men, who held the girls tight, as they struggled vainly to free themselves. The twins held their arms tightly over their breasts, trying to keep their blouses and their pride intact. Their tops were being pulled at by the crowd, while they struggled uselessly to keep their tops on. They came off in threads, and the twin daughters of a Lutheran minister were topless in front of thousands. Their bare breasts would be exposed for years, without their consent, on video monitors in every frat house in the state. The breasts would be noticed by all, the tears would be ignored by most. McCarthy saw the tears.

Then came the flames. They could be seen clearly now behind the crowd. At least one taxicab was on fire. Compton received the order from Field Services Captain Jackson. Hale was now just quietly standing in awe of it all. He had not even put his gas mask on. No one cared to tell him to. Everyone was too busy to tend to Hale's incompetence. Thank God for Compton and Jackson, thought McCarthy.

Compton was given his marching orders. "Clear this crowd, Compton. We need to get the fire truck in to put out those fires," yelled Captain Jackson.

"Yes, sir. Can do. We will need to deploy chemical agents, sir." Compton stated.

"Do it! Move them!" said Jackson.

Compton contacted Stammos, "Get as many going as possible with smoke first. Then CS and CN."

"Burning, sir?"

"Start with the bouncing betties, and then use the burning canisters. We don't want them to come back at us."

Stammos stepped up to the line. He calmly checked the wind and could see it was blowing toward the crowd. Compton had determined this long before, when he had designated the fall-back area. Stammos laid down several canisters of smoke, and this got the members of the crowd running. When the hardcore group realized it was just smoke, they came back and were hit with the CS and CN.

McCarthy watched the haze swirl toward the crowd and the crowd disperse. Suddenly, a person came out of the crowd, who also had a gas mask on. McCarthy instinctively slid his baton into his ring on his belt. The rioter was a pro. She ran at McCarthy and leaped onto his head, in an attempt to rip his mask off.

McCarthy spun the feisty female to the ground, to the rear of the line; and she was quickly handcuffed by the arrest team and taken away. McCarthy motioned that it was his arrest, and they acknowledged him with a thumbs-up. McCarthy readjusted his mask on his face, and he realized it was filled with tear gas. He started to panic, but then calmed himself down. He then remembered what he was to do. He covered his filters and blew hard, burping the mask. He calmly then held his breath while he tightened the straps on his mask.

His next breath was fresh air again, mostly. There was a tinge of pepper in it, but it was just enough to give the event a certain atmosphere. McCarthy then snapped his baton back out into an on-guard position. Compton stepped up the line and yelled, as he gave the corresponding signals for his command, "Moving forward at a step-slide. Now!"

"Back! Back! Back! Back! Back! Back! Back! Back! Back!" the jugger-
naut moved forward. The whole idea was to never catch the crowd. By
now, none of the crowd wanted to challenge this line, this team, this
group of trained professionals—Compton's Commandos. There was no
doubt about who was in command. When Compton ran the show, it was
a show to behold.

The crowd that had not fled from the tear gas was now backing up,
covering up with coats. They were stubborn; a few tried to pick up the
bouncing betties, but they bounced, spit, and spun, and could not be
caught. Others picked up the canisters and tossed them back at the line,
discovering, too late, that they were burned and marked for later arrest.

As the police-line moved up River Street, it was pelted with eggs, bottles, rocks, and, every now and then, a burning canister of tear gas was
returned. In spite of this, the line was undeterred and continued its
advance. The manager at Lunde's ran forward and identified two students, who were huddled in a furniture store doorway. He yelled, "They
were the ones who started the car on fire."

McCarthy, Kane, and Compton moved in and arrested them. They
were taken back to one of the arrest vans, which were following the line.
McCarthy noticed that the vans were filling with arrests and shuttling
back to the jail, to dump their load and return. McCarthy quickly filled
out the arrest tag and attached it to the prisoners. "McCarthy. Criminal
damage to property! Incite to riot! He burned the taxi cab!" McCarthy
shouted to the masked camera man, as he held up his suspect's identification.

McCarthy then rejoined the line, which had continued it slow consis-
tent movement up River Street. One line of four young males and two
females stopped 50 feet in front of the line. They turned and "mooned"
the line of approaching officers, in a last act of defiance. The group then
ran south, to about 100 feet from the police-line. The four males formed
their own line, facing the officers, and urinated toward the officers. They
laughed and ran.

As the line advanced beyond Diamond on River, a group of about
thirty people ran down Diamond Street toward the arrest vans, which
each were nearly full of prisoners. Before they could reach the vans,
Stammos stepped into their path and dropped a canister of tear gas,
which caused them to turn and run.

The last remnants of the crowd gathered at the foot of the parking
ramp, on the south end of River Street. There were also people lining all
levels of the parking ramp. They chanted and tossed rocks from the top
level. Stammos dropped three canisters at the bottom of the ramp; and,
as the white smoke climbed, fingers of the tear gas were sucked into each

level of the ramp, driving the last diehards away. The street belonged once
again to the police.

The damage was substantial. Windows were shattered, cars were hor-
ribly stomped on, and one taxicab was burned and destroyed. After the
crowd had been moved, the fire department units moved in with no time
to lose, since the storefronts nearest to the burning cab, had started to
burn. The fire was put out quickly by the fire department. They had to
wear their self-contained breathing apparatus, since the tear gas had not
completely dissipated.

Compton called the line together. He assigned one squad to report to
the jail. "There have to be over 100 people waiting to be booked there.
That could be a problem. Get there and secure the area," giving the same
command to a squad to secure the police station.

One downtown officer was placed in each trouble car, and sent to
attempt to locate anyone who could be positively identified as those
needing to be charged in this matter. Several were picked up at the hospital, having their burned hands treated. Others were picked up in the
immediate area, while they just laughed and stood around, talking about
the great time they'd had. All of the males that urinated toward the
police-line were picked up. They were also identified as being members
of the crowd who had tossed rocks at the line.

When the numbers were tallied, 175 people had been arrested as a
result of the disturbance. When McCarthy and Kane reached the county jail, there were about 75 prisoners waiting to be booked. They were all
seated, with their legs straight out and crossed, with their backs tight
against the wall. Another temporary booking counter was quickly set up
to facilitate the process. The squad of officers sent by Compton were
keeping the prisoners in line. All were quiet. The long day of partying,
topped off by tear gas, seemed to have a positive effect on their behavior.
They were spent, and ready to be booked.

After McCarthy's prisoners were put to bed for the night, he could see
that Sandy and her associates were swamped. He then walked back to the
station with Kane.

"Was that fun?" Kane asked. It was asked as a genuinely sincere question.

"I don't know if you could qualify it as fun. I think it was one of those
events that you wouldn't want to miss, but would never want to have happen to you again," explained Dan McCarthy.

"Were you afraid?" asked Kane.

"I was afraid for all of us, until the command was taken away
from Hale. When Compton was given the reins by Jackson, I knew
we were going to be all right," said McCarthy. "How about you?
Were you afraid?"

"At first I was. Christ, there had to be 5,000 people in our collective face, who wanted a piece of our collective ass. That all changed when Compton formed the line. I could see they backed off a little. Then when you looked that one asshole in the eye and righteously nailed him with your baton, they all really backed off, and I knew we were going to be all right. They were more afraid of us than we were of them. They never came so close again as they did before you nailed that guy." With that, Kane extended his hand to McCarthy. "Thank you, my friend."

Kane walked to his car, turned, and yelled, "What about that flowered dress?"

"I'll never forget it," answered McCarthy. "Kim Basinger?"

"I thought she looked more like Marilyn," said Kane. With that, he slid into his car and headed home to his small bedroom in the basement of his Martial Arts Studio.

McCarthy headed into the station, where there was a flurry of motion and a buzz of conversations. There were intoxicated drivers waiting to take breath tests. Juveniles lined up, waiting for their parents to pick them up, and officers were at every report-writing station, doing reports. McCarthy went downstairs and bagged up his tear-gassed clothes. He took a long shower. The uncovered areas of skin were burning from exposure to the gas. After his shower, he changed into some clean clothes. McCarthy went back upstairs and arrived as Carpenter was clearing one of the report-writing stations. McCarthy slid into his place.

Dan was able to quickly finish his reports on his arrest, because he did one, long narrative, describing what happened, and copied it for each separate arrest report. He turned in his reports to the sergeant at the desk. He said, "Just throw it on the pile." What a pile it was, too.

McCarthy then packed up his sleeping bag, and the clothes he had used throughout the long weekend, and walked out of the station. He drove through the now-quiet streets to his hometown. As he pulled into his driveway, he felt an overwhelming feeling of relief and exhaustion. He leaned his head back against the headrest and closed his eyes.

He thought he immediately opened his eyes, but discovered his head was leaning forward, with a long, thin, shiny stream of drool hanging from the corner of his mouth to his lap. McCarthy rubbed his eyes, stretched, and then climbed out of his car. The sun was just now peeking up over the bluffs to the east. The birds were once again saying hello to a new day. McCarthy loved this aspect of working night-shift. The shift would start with scream of the siren, but it always ended with the peaceful song of a bird.

McCarthy enjoyed the moment. He took it in like the bouquet of a fine wine. McCarthy savored the moment, exhausted, and wondered how many cops over the years had moments like this. The night was at an end. The violence was over, and they had survived. Then, before they crawled into bed, they took time to savor the contrast in their lives.

He let himself into his quiet home. Everyone was sleeping. He went to his desk and pulled out a pen and pad. The words inspired by the moment poured onto the paper:

The American Policeman

Since 1776, the years have come and passed.
Things have constantly changed, and nothing seems to last.
The uniforms might change, from gray to brown to blue:
We've patrolled by horse, boat, car, and worn out many a shoe.
Throughout all this time, one common thread binds us all:
We've all worked the beat. We've all answered the call.

From bar fights to domestics, homicides to open doors,
We've been here to handle all, through peacetime and world wars.
We've worked first shift, second, but most memorable, third.
It starts with the scream of the siren, but ends with the song of a bird.
We have hoped for the best, but usually see people at their worst,
but through it all . . .
We still work the beat. We still answer the call.

We've been there to listen to the victim's cries;
See their blood, their tears; then listen to their assailant's lies.
A career is a long time to see the things that we do,
And have so few people understand what it's like to wear blue.
Understood or not, come sunshine or snowfall,
We still work the beat. We still answer the call.
We still work the beat. We still answer the call.

McCarthy read his poem, then folded it in half, and slipped it between the pages of his scrapbook. He listened to the soft, breathing noises of his wife and family, as they slept. He went to each one and kissed them with the softest of kisses. The trick was to have them feel the love, without waking them up.

The feelings he felt at this moment were added benefits of working in his chosen profession. There was an overwhelming surge of love felt by the night-shift officer, as he delivered each of these most sincere of kisses to his daughter, his son, and then his beautiful wife . . . the kiss of a night-shift peace officer, who had seen brutal hate and now was overwhelmed with the incredible love of his family.

The night of the riot would end for McCarthy in the most peaceful place in the world for him: his home. McCarthy slid between the clean, cool sheets of his bed. He lay still and quiet. McCarthy listened patiently. Then, he heard what he was waiting for. It was the soulful song of the mourning dove. McCarthy whispered a simple prayer, "And it ends with the song of a bird. Amen."

McCarthy was at peace. As he closed his eyes, he was immediately blissfully asleep.

CHAPTER 24
"KACHINK"

It had been a week since the riot. The violence had brought national attention to the city of La Claire. Captain Hale had been correct. There were video cameras everywhere in the crowd. The actions of the crowd and the police were watched by people all over the world. Soldiers in Germany, who were natives of La Claire, called home to say they'd seen footage of the riots over there.

The footage had been violent and dynamic. What caught viewers' attention and puzzled the news media was that the riot was started purely and simply for the "fun" of it. There were no pressing social issues. There was no poor suspect beaten by police. There was no unpopular war being fought. There was no downtrodden class to be brought up from the ashes. It was a riot for the sake of having a riot.

Although there had been some lag time in decision making, the media did not notice. The La Claire Police were praised for the use of restraint in handling the aggressive and combative rioters. The editorials condemned the rioters and praised the police.

Nearly every officer on the street had reason to be proud. They were on national news, looking like the good guys, in a situation during which anyone could potentially over-react. None of them did. There was even one shot showing the garbage can bouncing off Dooley's head. On the edge of the screen, Hale could be seen with a dazed look on his face and his mouth standing open. Compton was asking him to authorize the use of helmets. The viewing public would only notice the can bouncing off Dooley's head, but everyone with the department knew of the indecision and uselessness that marked Hale's performance.

It was Saturday night in La Claire. McCarthy was feeling pretty good about his assignment tonight. He was scheduled to walk in the bar district with his good buddy Randy Stammos. McCarthy loved working with Randy. In the three and a half years McCarthy had been with the department, Randy had taken McCarthy under his wing and shown him the ropes. He had been responsible for the confident way McCarthy handled himself on the street. Self-confidence is a possession that every successful cop owns. McCarthy possessed it, but it was a gift from Randy.

Randy had decided, when McCarthy saved him from injury at the hands of the Henderson boys, that this young cop was worth his time and effort. He prepared McCarthy for success in the profession the young man had chosen as a vocation. Stammos had discovered in his effort to make this young man a great cop, he had become better, himself. He also discovered that some of the thrill of doing the "job" that McCarthy felt rubbed off on him. In the truest sense of the word, when they worked together, they were "partners" and every other minute of the day they were "friends."

McCarthy's wife, Victoria, and Randy's wife, Jody, had become good friends, also. Jody was a dispatcher at the 911 Center and Victoria was a stay-at-home mother. That is what they had in common. They were both excellent at what they did. They also loved to cross-stitch. They were both working on cross-stitch projects together. Jody was working on a Norman Rockwell painting, depicting a cop at a lunch counter with a kid. Victoria was working on a Sesame Street scene. They would quietly sew for hours together.

After line-up, McCarthy and Stammos checked out their radios and set them up with a collar mic, which was real handy for walk men. While inside the bars, downtown, it was impossible to hear the dispatcher without a collar mic. They also were useful in a foot pursuit, because it was easier to call-in direction and position, without breaking stride, when an officer had a collar mic. A foot pursuit would be inevitable, with McCarthy and Stammos working together. They always managed to find trouble. Tonight would be no different.

After they completed their radio checks, they started walking toward River Street. River Street was close to and ran parallel with the Mississippi River. The Mississippi was what brought the original settlers to La Claire, and it still brought in people. La Claire was a beautiful mid-sized town—a nice place to raise a family.

As they walked leisurely toward River Street, Stammos asked, "Hey, McCarthy. How do you like being a cop here so far? Do you regret not trying to apply in New York?"

"I'm glad I came here. We are busy all the time. I wouldn't have thought that was the case until I started working here. I like the people I work with. I wouldn't have met you, if I wouldn't have come here, and it's a nice place to raise my kids," answered McCarthy. "How about you? Do you ever think about going anywhere else or doing anything else?"

"I don't think I would want to do anything else. Sometimes I think about going other places. We have thought of moving closer to Jody's family . . . or farther away from my family," Randy and Dan laughed.

"Sometimes, when the Brockman's of this world piss me off, or the Hale's force us to buy into their bullshit, I feel like fuck it! I'm out of here," confided Stammos.

"Have you applied other places?" inquired McCarthy.

"No. Never," answered Stammos.

"Why not?" asked McCarthy.

"Well, because I figure no matter where I go, there will always be another asshole like Brockman to deal with. There will always be another dumb shit, obnoxious commander like Hale, who will be telling me what to do; but, you know, I don't think there are too many Comptons out there. There aren't that many Carpenters and Dooleys around. Can you imagine... Carpenter shot, and he comes right back. Dooley gets a can bounced off his head, wipes off the blood, and steps right back in line. Besides there is one other thing I'd better tell you, McCarthy."

"What's that?" asked McCarthy, showing great interest.

"Victoria wants me. We have this thing going . . . and well she's leaving you. Sorry, buddy. There's no hard feelings right, buddy?" said Stammos, offering McCarthy his hand.

"Fuck you. You know how I know that isn't true?" asked McCarthy, with a smile.

"Number one, you are still breathing. Jody would know instantly, and then she would kill you while you slept. Numbers two and three, you have a hairy back and a small dick, and Victoria can't tolerate those characters in a man," answered McCarthy, laughing.

"Hey, that's an absolute lie. Don't be spreading around rumors like that. My back isn't that hairy," Stammos said, with feigned annoyance, which made McCarthy laugh even harder.

As they rounded the corner onto River Street, they could see that things were back to normal. The crowd was a Saturday night crowd, which was large, but usually manageable. The officers moved up the street, walking in and out of bars. They checked identification on anyone who looked too young to be in the bars. McCarthy and Stammos checked each of the bars for trouble and underage patrons. When the bars passed their inspection, the pair stopped to talk with the bouncers and tell them to keep up the good work. It was an effort to let everyone know that walk men were working tonight. The downtown had a better personality when walk men worked the area regularly.

As they entered Lunde's Pub, the officers scanned the bar and noticed a male at the bar, who saw the officers; immediately his eyes darted nervously toward his friend. He got up quickly and headed toward the bathroom. McCarthy and Stammos immediately saw the signs, and headed toward the bathroom.

As the officers entered the bathroom, the male—who had baggie, tan pants, a black leather jacket, and dyed blonde hair with black roots—turned around, and began to leave the bathroom, failing in his attempt to act nonchalant.

Officer Stammos stopped him and said, "Good evening, sir. Could I see some kind of identification?"

"I left it in the car. I don't need it here, because they all know me. I'm twenty-one. Honest!" said Blondie.

"Let's step outside and talk. The music is a little loud in here," said Stammos.

"Sure, officers. No problem," obliged the blonde.

As they walked past the bar on the way out, the blonde man again made eye-contact nervously with the a big man that he had been seated with at the bar. Outside, the blonde was extremely friendly and cooperative with the two officers. He identified himself as Bobby Downs, and gave a date of birth, which made him twenty-two years old. Stammos ran checks through dispatch, and McCarthy motioned that he was going inside Lunde's to find out who this man really was.

McCarthy went into the bar and contacted the big man there. "Good evening, sir. We are looking for a man named Sandy Pettigrew, who is wanted on a warrant. Your friend said that you would be able to verify that he was not lying, and that he is indeed not Pettigrew," said McCarthy.

"Who does he say he is?" asked the big man.

"See, that's the problem. He doesn't have any identification on him, but we think he is this guy named Pettigrew. He looks like Pettigrew, but he says he's someone else. He tells us that you can verify that information for us. So, who is he, sir?" asked McCarthy, sincerely.

"Well, he's not any goddamned Sandy Pettigrew. That's Billy Downs," said the big man.

"Oh, Bobby's brother?" asked McCarthy.

"Yeah, you know Bobby?" asked the big man.

"Yeah. I met him once. You've been a big help," said McCarthy, as he headed back outside the bar.

As McCarthy stepped out of the bar, he walked up toward the blonde man and Stammos, who were having a very friendly conversation. McCarthy then said, "Hi, Billy. Nice to meet you."

The blonde man's smile disappeared immediately. He muscled up, tensed, and ceased all movement, as if the Billy Down's Power and Light Company had just shut down. Then he bolted and ran wildly north on River Street.

McCarthy had anticipated the response, and was on him within twenty-five feet, because the blonde man could not get his full speed up. The baggy pants were a powerful fashion statement but hindered his escape. McCarthy tackled the man, and Stammos was immediately there to assist in handcuffing Downs.

McCarthy then asked dispatch to run a check on Billy Downs. Billy was twenty-one, but he was also wanted for burglary, possession of dangerous drug with intent to deliver and threatening a witness.

After Billy had calmed down, McCarthy told Stammos, "I'm going to check the bathroom to make sure he didn't dump anything. He wasn't in there long enough to flush.

"Sure thing, partner." Stammos said, as he called for a car to transport Billy.

McCarthy walked into the bar and made a bee-line to the men's bathroom. McCarthy stopped and pictured where Billy had been when they had entered the bathroom. He had been right next to a waste can. McCarthy pushed open the swing door of the can and could see on the very top were four rectangular, folded bindles. McCarthy could not help but notice that the bindles were fashioned from the centerfold of a *Hustler* Magazine.

As McCarthy walked by the big man at the bar, the big man yelled to McCarthy, "Hey, what did I tell you? His name is Billy Downs, isn't it?"

"You were absolutely correct, sir. I want to thank you for keeping us from making a big mistake," said McCarthy, shaking the big man's hand.

"Where's Billy?" asked the big man.

"After we found out he was Billy, he had to run," said McCarthy. "Take care. Thanks again." With that, McCarthy left the man at the bar drinking his dark lager, comfortable in his ignorance.

As McCarthy returned to Stammos, Stammos showed McCarthy what he had found slipped into Billy's sock. It was two rectangular bindles of cocaine. It appeared they had come from the same issue of *Hustler* as the bindles McCarthy found.

Later at the station, they would discover that all the bindles fit together like a puzzle. Stammos complained, after they'd pieced together the foldout puzzle, "You know, the only thing that keeps this from being a perfect bust is that Billy sold the bindle that had the centerfold's left nipple on it," quipped Stammos. "You can't have a perfect bust without a left nipple."

"Perfect bust. I get it. You know what. If he would have had one of these bindles in his hat, we would have had to yell, "Stop, Police, you're under a breast!" Both of the officers laughed at their cleverness.

They looked up and saw Compton, who had stepped into the room without them noticing. He was shaking his head. He then left the room. It was Compton's way of saying time to get moving.

In about an hour, the two friends were back out walking on River Street. As they walked up to the corner of River and Main Streets, Stammos said, "You know why I can't leave this place?"

"Why," asked McCarthy.

"Because, Dyno, you and I have too many bad guys left to catch together," said Stammos.

"Yeah. Sometimes, I can't believe I get paid for this," answered McCarthy.

"I like working with you, McCarthy, but I can honestly say I have never thought it was so much fun that I should not be paid. I worry about you sometimes, Dyno," said Stammos, with real concern on his face.

Their conversation was interrupted by the squealing tires of a red Mazda, southbound on River from Main Street. McCarthy was able to get the first three letters on the plate and called for any squad in the area to stop the car. McCarthy then broke into a run, heading east on Main Street.

Stammos started running after him and yelled, "Where are you going?"

"He looks like a cruiser. He didn't see us. I'll bet he'll come around again on Bluff Street.

McCarthy and Stammos reached Bluff and Main Streets, in time to see the approach of the red Mazda. Their luck continued, because the light turned red, and the driver pulled to a stop.

McCarthy walked up to him, smiled, and said, "Good evening, sir. I am Officer Dan McCarthy. May I see your driver's license?"

"Sure, officer." The puzzled driver removed his license from his wallet, and then asked, "What did I do?"

After McCarthy had the license in his hand, he asked him to turn east on Main Street, into an open parking spot, so they could discuss the problem. McCarthy slipped the driver's license into his pocket and advised the dispatcher to send a car over to their location, where they had stopped the vehicle they were looking for. McCarthy ran a check on the Mazda's plate.

As the driver parked, he stepped out of his vehicle and approached the officers, who were on the sidewalk next to a cul de sac, which split two three-story storefronts. The first floor of the two buildings housed

Brown's Jeweler's to the left, and Hatigan's Kitchen Solvers to the right of the cul de sac.

McCarthy removed the driver's license from his uniform shirt pocket and ran a check on the driver with dispatch. McCarthy could smell a pretty obvious odor on the driver's breath and had noticed he had stepped out of the Mazda with enough difficulty to warrant a field test.

"Sir, how much have you had to drink tonight?"

"A couple. Jusht a couple of beers. I'm OK to drive. Beshides, why did you shtop me?" said the driver, slurring his words noticeably.

"Sir, you squealed your tires loudly on River Street earlier. That is why I stopped you. Now I would like to give you a couple tests to make sure you are all right to drive," explained McCarthy.

McCarthy continued, "Now, sir, I would like you to stand with your heels together and your hands at your side. Are you wearing contacts tonight, sir?" asked McCarthy.

"No," answered the driver, and he watched his feet, to make sure his heels were positioned together.

Then . . . "Kachink."

McCarthy and Stammos froze. The noise came from the cul de sac. The cul de sac, where there should be no noise at all, especially not a "Kachink."

McCarthy and Stammos left the driver stand with his heels together, as they both cautiously flanked the cul de sac. As they peered into the darkness, they could see movement on the first landing of the fire escape attached to Brown's Jewelers.

Both officers abandoned the driver and approached the dark figure on the fire escape. As if of one mind, both hit the figure at the same moment with their flashlight beams. It was Billy Mitchell, the perennial burglar, and he had his hand on the bottleneck of a five-gallon decorative glass jug, which was nearly full of quarters. Billy froze, then slowly straightened up, showing both palms, without being asked.

"All right, Billy. Come down from there, slowly," ordered Stammos.

"Sure, officers," answered Billy.

After telling the lie, Billy climbed quickly and smoothly over the rail of the fire escape. He then jumped to the fire escape attached to the Kitchen Solvers building and headed up the stairs toward the roof.

"Damn! I'll head around and cut him off!" yelled Stammos.

"Billy! Stop! Police!" yelled McCarthy, as he ran to the fire escape and then climbed it, two steps at a time, in pursuit.

McCarthy feared little in life when he was adrenalized, except one thing—heights. He hated heights. As he pursued Mitchell, he sensed with every step that he was going higher.

McCarthy could hear the chatter of Stammos calling in the foot pursuit. At that moment, Dooley, who was arriving to back them up on the stop with the Mazda, saw the driver of the Mazda jump into the car and drive away at a high rate of speed.

The driver knew he was drunk and saw his opportunity to get away. He took it. When he drove away, he drove away with no intention of being so foolish as to stop again. He had just enough of a lead on Dooley to give him encouragement, when Dooley hit his red lights and siren. The driver knew what his Mazda RX7 could do and felt confident in making good his escape.

"I'll be in pursuit of a red Mazda from 255's stop!" reported Dooley, in the shrill voice that is owned by every cop, in the first moments of a pursuit.

"We're in foot pursuit!" puffed Stammos, after Dooley's transmission.

The dispatcher was silent. It was the silence which comes from confusion created by two things happening at the same time, to the same people, at opposite ends of a radio transmission. The time does not allow for this kind of confusion to be sorted easily out. McCarthy was oblivious to all of this. On the back side of the second story of the Kitchen Solvers was a line of balconies, which were the rear porch areas of apartments. All the buildings on Main Street were five-story buildings, with storefronts on the bottom floor and apartments occupying the next four floors.

Mitchell was running eastbound, across the second-story porches. When he reached the end of the first porch, he jumped to the next, and then the next. McCarthy followed, never losing the feeling in the pit of his stomach that reminded him he was "way up high."

As Mitchell reached the porch in mid-block, he did the opposite of what McCarthy hoped he would do. He ran up the stairs to the next balcony. McCarthy paused, checked the direction that Mitchell was heading, and McCarthy continued his pursuit.

When Mitchell continued jumping from porch to porch, heading back the way he came from, McCarthy followed, but was losing ground each time he hesitated on the jumps. He could not get the picture of his crumpled body, lying on the ground below, out of his mind.

When Mitchell reached the last porch, he hopped on a metal ladder, which was attached to the building. This led to the roof, five stories up. In the world of ladder climbing, the speed at which Mitchell climbed would have to be categorized as a sprint. McCarthy reached the ladder and went up haltingly at a speed, resembling a crawl. In fact, his body was contorted similarly to a crawl, as he moved up the ladder, higher and slowly higher.

As McCarthy crawled over the edge to the roof, he could see Mitchell was yanking on a roof hatch that would not open. When he saw McCarthy on the roof, Mitchell ran across the roof, jumping over the half-walls separating the buildings. McCarthy gained ground now, because it was more to his liking. He had the feel of open-field running, with no "down" to be concerned with. His carefree moment was just that . . . a moment.

When Mitchell reached the end of the last wall on the last building, next to the alley, he stopped and looked down frantically at the alley below. He looked back at McCarthy, who was about to win the race once again. Billy shoved his hands into his pockets, and McCarthy stopped and drew his weapon.

"Billy, don't move!"

Billy turned away from McCarthy, and began to pull wads of cash out of his pockets, tossing them over the edge of the roof, allowing them to float softly to the ground below. It was raining twenty and hundred dollar bills.

McCarthy seeing this, continued to shout to Billy, "Get down! Down! Billy, Get down on the roof, now!"

Mitchell just continued to lean over the edge, and toss cash to the alley below. McCarthy knew this to be the evidence of whatever crime Billy had committed. McCarthy said again, in a calm, quiet voice, since shouting had not helped, "Billy, you are under arrest. Get down."

Billy looked at McCarthy, and had seen by his uneasiness during the pursuit, that he had discovered McCarthy's weakness. He was afraid of heights in general, and this height that they were currently at, in particular.

"Come get me," said Mitchell, as he moved tight to the edge of the roof, and continued to toss away the money.

McCarthy pictured a crowd of people below, scooping all the money up, then running, leaving McCarthy with no charge. Mitchell was having problems disposing of all the cash, because he had so much of it, and his pockets were stuffed tight with bills, making their removal difficult.

McCarthy said to himself, "Don't look down! Don't look down! Damn it, don't look down!" He then moved quickly to Mitchell, and took him by the arm. The arm tightened, and the struggle was on. Mitchell pulled McCarthy closer toward the edge, and McCarthy tried to forget that he was five stories up and deathly afraid.

Mitchell was, by profession, a burglar, but when he did work to satisfy his parole officer, he worked as a roofer. Heights did not intimidate him in the least.

As the two scuffled awkwardly next to the precipice, McCarthy flashed back to his days as a youth, to Bobby Cochran. Bobby never looked for trouble, except on ice. He was one of the best skaters on the Northside of La Claire, and the only time he "kicked ass" was every winter at the skating rink. No one could beat him on skates. He would absolutely kick anyone's ass on ice, and then would live off his rep the rest of the year, because the ass-whippings he gave on ice were so devastating, no one dared see if he might not be so tough off the ice.

The straight-up grappling continued, with McCarthy's feet against the embrasure on the edge of the roof. McCarthy was holding on to Mitchell, as if his life depended on it. Mitchell continued to break free of McCarthy's grip, knowing if McCarthy went over, he would go, too.

McCarthy then remembered what his plan had been for Bobby Cochran, if Bobby had ever come after him on the ice. He had planned to not fight him standing up. Cochran was superior to everyone standing up, but McCarthy figured, if he could take him down, Cochran would lose the edge he had on ice, and they would be equal. McCarthy never got to test his theory, because Cochran's parents moved to Orlando before he singled out McCarthy for the La Claire performance of "Ice Capades McCarthy's Ass-Whipping on Ice." Then came the thought, "Take him down you idiot!"

McCarthy swept the leg and down went Mitchell on his back. He rolled to his stomach, moving farther away from the edge, and this bolstered McCarthy's confidence. As Mitchell got to his hands and knees, McCarthy was on him, and delivered three quick, accurate, and intense knee-strikes to the lower abdomen of Mitchell, which caused him to crumble back down.

Mitchell immediately recovered, and started to push himself up again. McCarthy then pulled Mitchell toward him, tightening his left arm around Mitchell's waist and breaking down the right arm, which Mitchell was using as a post to push himself back up.

Mitchell went face-first into the tarred roof. McCarthy then just tightened his grip, like an anaconda holding onto its prey. "Randy! I'm on the roof!" he yelled, knowing that he did not want to risk letting any part of Mitchell go, this close to the edge, to handcuff him. McCarthy thought about letting go, and then drawing his weapon to cover him. He decided against letting go. He felt if Billy got away again, McCarthy would have to shoot him. There was desperation in Billy's struggle tonight. Instead, Dan decided to hold on. Besides, thought McCarthy, people who have never fought with someone on the edge of a roof would not understand why McCarthy would need to resort to shooting an unarmed man on a rooftop.

"Randy! I'm on the roof!" yelled Dan. He was now noticing that his arms were feeling like lead.

"I'm right here, buddy," Randy said, as he slid suddenly to the left side of Mitchell and quickly pried Mitchell's free arm back. Mitchell slid further into the tar roof.

At the arrival of Stammos, Mitchell finally surrendered, lying panting and sweating, after giving his all and realizing it had not been enough. Randy handcuffed Mitchell. McCarthy just lay perfectly stationary for a few moments, breathing . . . breathing . . . breathing. He reached for his collar mic and pressed the button, "We're 10-95. McCarthy and Stammos are 10-95 (subject in custody)."

"10-4, 255," answered Hix in dispatch. "Go to Channel Two, and fill me in on who you are 10-95 with. Officers are still pursuing the vehicle you had stopped."

McCarthy then switched to Channel Two. "255, we have a Billy Mitchell in custody. We believe he was leaving the scene of burglary. We do not have the location of the burglary identified yet, but it is probably near our original location. If those pursuing units stop the vehicle, I have a charge of excessive noise with a motor vehicle. He was also possible 10-55 (driving while intoxicated). Advise them I have his driver's license still on me."

Hix then relayed that information to the pursuing vehicles. They had the vehicle stopped on Highway 41, about four miles outside of La Claire. They were also 10-95.

Within a minute, McCarthy got up and recited to Mitchell his constitutional rights.

Mitchell agreed to talk and waived his rights. He said, "I wasn't trying to hurt you, man. I was just trying to get away. Don't hurt me!" with the urgency of a man who had just fought with a cop on a rooftop, after watching an episode of NYPD Blue. He pictured McCarthy and Stammos tossing him off the roof with great relish. It was an easy thought for Mitchell; because, given the opportunity, he would have tossed either or both of these officers off the roof to get away.

McCarthy then explained to Mitchell, in the most concerned voice he could muster, "Now, Billy. You just put up quite a fight. I want you to know, I hope that fight is over, because to continue would just endanger all of us and make the situation worse than it already is for you. I want you to know that, considering it is my job to catch you and your job to get away, I sometimes expect some resistance, within reason, and do not take this personally. I just want you to know, from this point on, we will be getting along just fine, as long as you cooperate and give me no more problems. Do you understand?"

McCarthy had already learned, in his short career, that this line worked like the snake charmer's horn on the deadly cobra.

Mitchell breathed a sigh of relief, and the mental picture of his body, lying five stories below in a crumpled broken heap, disappeared.

"Yes," Mitchell answered.

"By the way, Billy, I want to let you know that, whenever I have arrested you, I have considered it an honor. I consider you to be the Einstein of Burglars," complimented McCarthy, in a sincere voice.

"Gee, thanks," answered Mitchell, in an appreciative tone.

"You have been out of prison just a short time. I can't believe I lucked out with a guy of your caliber and caught you the first time. How many does it make? How many did you slip by us? You are just too good for me to have caught you on your first one," cajoled McCarthy, as he helped Mitchell to his feet.

"Shit, I've hit about 35 places, since I got out in August. Not all of them in the city, though," bragged Billy.

McCarthy began to search Mitchell, and found his pockets were too stuffed with cash to pull out all of it on the roof. McCarthy then checked Mitchell for weapons, and commented to Mitchell, "No wonder you had such problems getting the money out of your pockets. They are full of cash."

"Quite a score tonight," commented Stammos. "Where did this come from? Might as well tell us. We're going to find out; someone will call us."

Mitchell then realized he was being praised for a reason, and no one would call the police. His demeanor changed abruptly. "Nobody's going to call. That's my money. I want my lawyer." Mitchell was cocksure no one would report this burglary. Maybe if he was lucky, these cops wouldn't even find the burglary.

"Randy, how are we getting down from here? We can't take the handcuffs off Billy and he can't climb a ladder with them on." McCarthy was none too excited about climbing down that ladder again, either.

"No problem. Follow me." Sure of himself as always, Stammos walked over to the roof hatch. He adroitly pulled his duty knife out, spun it like he was a drum major and it was his baton, and in one quick movement Stammos was able to slip the hook on the roof hatch with his knife. It was the same hatch that Mitchell could not open in the darkness and panic of his flight. The officers were able to safely negotiate the staircase to the street below.

By now, Carpenter had arrived on the scene. McCarthy asked for some evidence bags, and, after receiving them, he asked Carpenter to attempt to find the cash Mitchell had thrown off the rooftop. McCarthy then conducted a thorough search on Mitchell.

"Hey, what am I under arrest for?" asked Mitchell.

"Right now, you are under arrest for criminal trespass and possession of burglary tools," McCarthy answered, as he pulled gloves, a mini-mag flashlight, and a screwdriver from Mitchell, holding them in front of the suspect, to emphasize his point. "You are also being charged with resisting arrest, and conduct regardless of life." After a brief pause McCarthy added, "My life!" The last two words were said with feeling.

During the search, McCarthy found over $10,000 in cash. Carpenter returned with about $2000 more, that he was able to find. Because the alley was not highly frequented this time of night and the wind was dead calm, the money was lying where it landed.

McCarthy slid Mitchell into the back seat of Carpenter's car, and asked, "Are you all right, Billy? Are you hurt?"

"Fuck no! McCarthy, you can't hurt me. Don't flatter yourself," Billy snapped, having lost the concern, fear, and humility he had acquired on the rooftop.

"Good. I'm happy to hear it. I don't want to hurt you, Billy," answered McCarthy.

Carpenter stayed with Mitchell, while Stammos and McCarthy went back into the cul de sac. They were joined by Sgt. Compton. The pair quickly explained what they had, and Compton said, "You head up there," pointing at the fire escape Mitchell had originally been on. "Find out what he got into. I am going to cover the front, in the event that someone might still be inside."

The officers checked the jewelry store, which was secure. From the sidewalk, McCarthy jumped up and grabbed onto the first landing of the fire escape and pulled himself up onto it. He had to then lower the metal stairs to allow Stammos to join him. The large glass jug of quarters was still setting where Billy Mitchell had set it down, making the original "Kachink" sound that led to his apprehension.

From where they stood, they could see a planked walkway, which crossed the flat roof to the rear of the jewelry store. The building attached to the jewelry store, which fronted on Bluff Street, had apartments on the upper floors. The rear doors to each apartment opened onto a fire escape. On the top level, McCarthy and Stammos could see the rear apartment door was ajar. They left the glass jug of quarters sit, and they worked their way up to the top level. When they reached that level, they moved to either side of the open door and listened for a time. They heard nothing and the apartment was dark.

Stammos pointed at the fresh pry marks on the door, which were Billy's handiwork. The man was good. McCarthy radioed the location of the burglary to Sgt. Compton. Stammos and Dan waited outside, until

Compton acknowledged he was in a position to cover the front exit of the apartment.

"Front's secure. I'm in position," answered Compton.

"We're going in," advised Stammos, quietly.

The officers' search started in a bedroom. The bedroom had a king-sized bed, with an oak frame. It was ornately decorated, as was every room in the apartment. McCarthy was shocked, as he went from room to room. This was a rich man's apartment. Money was no object to this man. The fixtures were top-dollar. The carpet, plus the sound system, and entertainment center were to die for. The bathroom was equipped with a shower, bath, and jacuzzi. McCarthy and Stammos had to remind themselves that they were looking for a possible accomplice, rather than taking a tour of the "Life Styles of the Rich and Shameless."

Then, they entered the office. Mitchell had known where to go and what to look for. This was the only room touched. Drawers were hanging open, as was a large wall safe. McCarthy and Stammos knew now why the apartment was so elaborately decorated. The occupant was obviously an entrepreneur, who could afford such opulence. Some of his merchandise was scattered about the desk and floor. This man was a cocaine dealer. A significant cocaine dealer. When they were certain no one else was in the apartment, they opened the front door for Compton. Compton saw the cocaine and said immediately, "OK, we'll stop right here. We were justified to go this far, to make sure no one else was in here, but now we'll get a search warrant."

Compton called dispatch and asked for a team of detectives to be called out and respond to the scene, as soon as possible.

"Good job, you guys. Your work is done here. Is your prisoner talking?" asked Compton.

"He talked some, and then lawyered up," answered McCarthy. "I think he is counting on the complainant on this one not pressing any charges."

"He'll talk eventually," said Compton confidently. "He'll tell us everything. After pulling this, jail is going to be the safest place for him. This is Ray Dornan's place," he said, flashing his light on an envelope on the desk with Dornan's name on it.

"We suspected he was heavily involved in the cocaine trade, but the drug guys haven't been able to touch him . . . up until tonight. I think tonight we can consider Ray Dornan touched. No, that's not right. This is much more than touched. Touching is just considered foreplay. This is way beyond foreplay. Ray Dornan is truly fucked! In fact he may be pregnant with twins. Good job, you guys!"

"Thanks, Sarge!" Stammos and McCarthy responded, in unison.

"Did Mitchell have any cocaine on him?" asked Compton.

"No. He just was after the cash," answered McCarthy. "About $12,000 worth. There's probably more," McCarthy replied, rubbing his knee, which was starting to pain him.

"Take your prisoner to jail. Take all his clothes from him. Package each item separately. He has to have traces of cocaine all over him. Don't ask him any more questions, and tell the jail not to allow him to make any phone calls for right now. Take care of the evidence you have, and start on your reports. The detective will take it from here. We're passing the ball on this one. I am sure they will call in the State Department of Narcotics Enforcement. DNE will love this case." Compton contacted dispatch, "Contact Captain Jackson. Advise him we need to call in four extra officers on overtime to handle calls the rest of the night. We need four here at the scene, to secure the premises. I want two front and two back. Make sure Detective Captain Severson knows what we have here. He's going to want to call in several detectives on this. He'll decide how many and who."

Compton knew better than to make decisions for Captain Severson. Severson was highly protective of his turf. Compton knew Severson would already take offense that Dornan was going to be reeled in because of the efforts of two patrol officers. He watched, as Stammos and McCarthy headed out of the apartment exchanging a high-five, low-five combination in celebration.

CHAPTER 25
THE VETERAN

As McCarthy sat in the hallway in the La Claire County Courthouse, waiting to testify, he read over his reports thoroughly, trying to refresh in his mind the small details that would be attacked by Mitchell's attorney. Attack was what this hearing was all about. It was a motion to suppress.

What did the attorney want to suppress?

Everything.

Most criminal cases never make it to trial. They are pled out by attorneys and defendants, because the defendants have no chance of winning in front of a jury. What a defense attorney tries to do is chip away at the case, before it gets to a jury. If a good defense attorney can get some of the evidence suppressed, he or she might have a better chance of winning in front of a jury, or of bargaining with the district attorney's office on behalf of his client.

A lot had happened since the arrest of Billy Mitchell. The follow-up investigation by the detective bureau shut down Dornan's operation. They found thousands more in cash and two kilos of cocaine in the apartment on the night of the burglary. This alone was enough to put Dornan away. The investigation snowballed and eight more dealers were taken down in La Claire; and, due to meticulous record-keeping by Dornan, who was truly a businessman, the investigation had moved beyond the state borders. The IRS was also looking at prosecution of Dornan.

Oddly enough, the successful prosecution of Mitchell now hinged on Dornan's testimony. The arrest for possession of burglary tools and resisting arrest would undoubtedly stand. Ironically, Dornan would have to testify that he did not give permission for Mitchell to enter his apartment, or the burglary charge would not stand. Mitchell might not go back to prison without the burglary charge.

Handling the case for the prosecution was a young idealist, chain-smoking crusader named Bob Waters. McCarthy had gotten to know him well over the last four years or so, since McCarthy started on the La Claire Police Department. Everyone wanted Bob handling the case, if it was a big one. He was totally committed to successful prosecution of criminals. He was convinced he was in a partnership with the police, and their job was the health and safety of innocent people on the street. Every cop in La Claire would simply describe Waters as "the best."

McCarthy smiled and stood up to shake Bob's hand, as he walked quickly toward McCarthy. His footsteps echoed loudly through the hall-ways of the courthouse. Bob put his cigarette in his mouth, inhaled, and shook Dan's hand with the vigor of a wrestling opponent just before the start of a match.

As Bob reached the young officer, his words came out like they were being fired by a Gatling gun. "Hey, Dyno. Are you ready? Stupid ques-tion—a guy doesn't get a handle like Dyno Dan without being ready. Always ready! Mitchell's attorney is going to probably leave you be, on the stand. He knows his case stands or falls on Dornan. If Dornan testi-fies against Mitchell, Mitchell is screwed. If he doesn't, he'll be looking at light time on the burglary tools charge."

Dyno was amazed at how quickly and efficiently that information shot out of the bearded face of the stocky little assistant district attorney.

"What about the conduct regardless of life charge?" asked McCarthy.

"Dyno, it's not going to fly. They will argue he never tried to throw you off, and you agree he did not. They will argue that his actual intent was to throw the money off the roof, and you were the one that initiat-ed the contact. Also, like it or not, this system looks at the police like the public pissing post. They expect you to take some lip and some bumps in the line of duty. I know this, because I'm reminded of it every time I prosecute a battery to police officer charge. It's a felony, but I've yet to see anyone go to prison for it. Let some no-mind of a criminal threaten to batter a judge, and the schmuck will do twenty years. McCarthy, most people just do not realize that judges, police, and attorneys are a part of the same team; and attacks on them are attacks on the criminal justice system. Like I said, it all hinges on Dornan's testimony." With that Waters put out his cigarette and quickly disappeared into the court-room.

Waters was right. Mitchell's attorney allowed McCarthy to testify, challenging very little that Dan had to say.

Then Dornan was called to the stand. He was out on $100,000 cash bond. He posted 10 percent of it in cash. He was a tall, dark man, who was dressed in a tailored suit. He raised his hand to swear and stood erect. He was a smart businessman. He made hundreds of thousands of dollars in the distribution of cocaine in the western part of Wisconsin. What made him smart is that he never sampled the product. He knew that cocaine ruins lives, and he was in the business for the good life, and that was why his life was drug-free.

As Dornan took the stand, Waters started the questioning. "State your name please, and for the record could you please spell it?"

"My name is Raymond R. Dornan, D-O-R-N-A-N," said Dornan impartially.

Waters continued, "And where do you live Mr. Dornan?"

Dornan said, "238 South Bluff Street, apartment 501."

"Is that in the City and County of La Claire, and the State of Wisconsin?" Waters asked, establishing the jurisdiction, which is a very important "t" to cross.

Dornan answered, "Yes, sir, it is."

"Could you tell me, in the early morning hours of October 12th of this year, what did you find when you arrived home?" came the next question.

"I found the police were at my apartment, and there had been a burglary there," said Dornan.

"How had the apartment been entered?" followed up the diminutive assistant district attorney.

"Someone had come up the rear fire escape, and then pried the back door and entered my apartment," said Dornan, as he looked contemptuously at Mitchell. Mitchell looked nervously away.

"Were items of yours removed from your apartment?" queried Waters.

"Yes, sir, about $12,000." answered Dornan, shifting nervously in his seat.

"Did you give permission to anyone to enter your apartment by prying on the rear door, and to take anything from your apartment on that date?" asked Waters, dotting the "i" to prove lack of consent and intent to steal.

Waters did not usually clump questions together in this manner, but he thought he would only get one kick at this cat. Dornan waited a long time to answer the question. He took a deep breath and he took on a thoughtful persona. Then he turned to Mitchell. He looked at Mitchell sitting there; hoping against hope that Dornan would give a fellow criminal a break.

Dornan absolutely knew he held the key to Mitchell's prison cell, in his mouth. He could unlock the door or slam it shut for about eight years. Then Dornan's features changed. His lips tightened and his cheek began to quiver. Dornan's eyes became like slits, and his head cocked to the right a bit, as he stared a hole through Mitchell, who had brought all this trouble down on the drug dealer's head.

Mitchell was the man who brought McCarthy and Stammos to his door. Mitchell was the man who called down the wrath of the Drug Enforcement Agency and the Internal Revenue Service. Mitchell was the man who shut down Dornan's business. Mitchell!

Then Dornan looked back at Bob Waters and his words came clear, distinct, and confident, "No, I did not give anyone permission to break into my apartment and steal money from me; but someone did that night, and that's why I am here."

The rest of the questioning served no purpose, because Mitchell was slam-dunked. The most practical present for him this Christmas would be soap on a rope. He would be less likely to drop it in the shower at Waupon State Penitentiary.

The judge ruled all motions to suppress evidence denied. He determined there was probable cause to arrest, and Mitchell would be bound over for trial.

As Dornan left the courtroom, he glanced toward McCarthy, and then walked over toward him. "You are McCarthy?" Dornan asked, but it sounded more like and indictment.

"Yes, sir. Nice to meet you, Mr. Dornan," said McCarthy, extending his hand. "Thanks for testifying today. I know it was tough for you."

"Yeah, well, the guy brought a lot of problems my way. Say, I feel like I should thank you for catching the punk. Now he's going to pay for what he did to me," said Dornan, with his lips tight and his cheek quivering once again, as he watched Mitchell being led to a conference room to speak with his attorney.

Dornan looked back at Mitchell, and their eyes met. Mitchell turned pale instantly, as all of the blood rushed from his face. The look seemed to cause a blood transfusion, because Dornan turned nearly crimson.

"What do you mean by that, Mr Dornan?"

Dornan's face softened, as a smile replaced the look of murder, "Prison, of course. He will most certainly have to pay his debt to society," said Dornan, with a smile. "You've made quite a name for yourself McCarthy. You got people on both sides of the fence talking you. If you don't mind, I won't say "keep up the good work." You'd know I wasn't sincere," said Dornan.

"Thank you, Mr. Dornan. I'll consider that a compliment, coming from you," McCarthy said politely.

Dornan straightened his tie and ran his fingers through his hair, as he looked at his reflection in the shiny acrylic walls of the courthouse hallway.

"Keep your head down, McCarthy," said Dornan, as he simulated shooting into the air with an imaginary gun.

McCarthy watched the hotshot walk out of the courthouse free. Mitchell had a public defender. Billy was about to go to prison. Because of Dornan's money, he would most definitely be able to delay the inevitable; but eventually, he would be joining Mitchell in the prison-yard. McCarthy found solace in a mental fantasy he conjured up in his mind's eye.

He pictured a time one year from this day, after Dornan ran out of delays and appeals. Dornan would be sent to prison, and McCarthy pictured him in the exercise yard with Billy Mitchell. The two of them would be talking about their shared fate, and in the fantasy conversation, Dornan would say, "You know who's responsible for us being here, don't you?"

In this fantasy, Mitchell would answer, "Fucking McCarthy?"

"Fucking McCarthy!" would be Dornan's answer.

This thought brought a smile to Dan's face, as he shifted his bottom on the rock-solid bench he'd sat back down on, after Dornan left the building.

McCarthy's momentary reverie was interrupted by the rapid clicking of heels in the courthouse hallway that could only announce the coming of Bob Waters. Waters quick-stepped up to McCarthy, "Hey, Dyno. Stick around for a bit, will you? If you see Captain Severson and Joe Darnell, have them wait here. I might have some good news for you about those thirty-five burglaries Einstein Mitchell mentioned to you the night the two of you did the rooftop polka. Too bad Stammos isn't here."

Stammos was not at the hearing, because McCarthy was the only officer subpoenaed.

McCarthy stood up in response to Waters' approach, but Waters, who appeared to be on a mission, just blew by him. McCarthy returned to the cold, hard bench he had been seated on. He wondered if the manufacturer of these benches received some special recognition for managing to extract 100 percent of the comfort-giving capacity from these courthouse benches. He wondered how many hours he had spent seated on these benches, whiling away time, waiting, in most cases, to not testify. Many cases were pled out the day of the trial or the day of the hearing.

The approach of Captain Severson and Sgt. Joe Darnell gave McCarthy another excuse to get up from the bench again. McCarthy called to Captain Severson, "Captain, sir. Bob Waters wants you to wait here for a bit. He says he wants to talk to all of us. It's about the Billy Mitchell case."

Captain Severson had just been told to "wait here," by a patrolman. He had very little regard for the patrol force. He had been in the detective bureau for twenty-seven of his thirty years in law enforcement. He had not been a patrolman since officers communicated by the use of call boxes. Patrol officers were a necessary evil in law enforcement. The real police work was done by the detectives. Darnell was good, no doubt about it. He was also as arrogant as one man could be. He was a team player, but the detective bureau was the team, and everyone else was an opponent.

"McCarthy is the name, isn't it?" asked the captain.

"Yes, sir!" said McCarthy.

"Well, McCarthy, how long have you been an officer?" asked the captain.

"Almost four years," answered McCarthy.

"Well, Officer McCarthy, when you are no longer a rookie, and you develop a little more dust on a locker, you will learn not to tell captains where and how long they should wait." Severson's face was tight and red, much in the same configuration of Dornan's, when he had looked at Mitchell.

"McCarthy? That name is Irish," Severson said to Darnell, talking now as if McCarthy was not present.

"Yeah, it's Irish, captain. He'd be a mick," said Darnell to Severson. He then looked at McCarthy, and asked, "What do they call you? Do they call you Mick or Mack or just Rookie?" asked Darnell, making each name sound deliberately like an insult.

"They call me, Dyno. They call me Dan. They call me McCarthy. Respectfully, Sergeant Darnell, no one ever in my whole life called me Mick in that tone of voice more than once." McCarthy said this with a lack of emotion, because the only emotion he could have shown would have been anger and disdain. He carefully filtered out the righteous anger, and all that was left were the words.

"Listen here!" snapped Darnell. "Show your superiors some respect, rookie!"

McCarthy did not get a chance to become insubordinate. It was the direction that his mind was taking him and nothing short of an interruption could keep him from heading down that path.

The door to the conference room swung open, and Bob Waters, the young, enthusiastic, prosecutorial idealist came out clicking his way down the hallway toward McCarthy and his tormentors, Detective Darnell and Captain Severson.

"Oh great! You're all here. I have some good news," proclaimed Waters. "Mitchell has agreed to a plea bargain. He doesn't want to go to Waupon. He wants to do his time in Green Bay. He figures Dornan and his friends will be going to Waupon, and he does not want to be there. I can arrange that, but here's the deal. I told him that I would not do any deals with thirty-five uncleared burglaries to be answered for. He has agreed to help us by claiming all the burglaries he did, by getting back the property he has stashed. He says he will, but he was wrong on thirty-five. He had done many more than thirty-five. He's ready to give a statement right now. What do you think?" Waters smile was so big, it was difficult to notice he had a full beard.

Showing the emotion toward his job of an autistic sewage plant worker, Severson turned to Darnell, and said, "Take Mitchell's statement."

Waters held up a hand, as if to say "Halt." Instead he stated, "Wait a minute. Part of the deal was that he had to give the statement to Stammos and/or McCarthy. It was their arrest, and I felt they deserved to take the statement and clear the cases. Don't you agree?" Waters smiled, truly believing Darnell and Severson would most certainly agree.

Severson bladed himself to Waters, as if the young assistant district attorney had thrown down a gauntlet. He began a diatribe resplendent with motion and emotion.

"Where do you get off, Mister Assistant District Attorney, assigning follow-up investigations to anyone, much less a rookie. Patrolmen do not do follow-up investigations. Detectives do follow-up investigations. No, I do not agree. It is not this rookie's case. It is Darnell's case. Now, Darnell takes the statement or no one takes the statement. He will take the statement when I tell him to take the statement. Do you understand Mr. Waters?" The question was asked with Captain Severson's voice echoing throughout the courthouse and his right index finger tapping sharply against the chest of the young assistant district attorney.

Waters then swallowed deeply. This was not out of fear. This was an attempt to swallow the words he felt like saying, and to take the time to construct some words that were befitting the respect he had for Captain Severson's position. Then, he spoke more slowly and more quietly than McCarthy had ever heard him speak before. Ever!

"Captain Severson, I am sorry to have offended you. It was not my intent. My enthusiasm over the incredibly professional way this case was handled by McCarthy and Stammos, as well as every case that they have handled, distorted my decision-making capability. Of course, you are right. I overstepped my authority. Sergeant Darnell should absolutely take the statement, if that is your decision."

"Darnell, go take the statement from Mitchell," directed Severson.

As Darnell walked away, Waters' eyes followed Darnell, until he was out of earshot. He then turned once again to Captain Severson. "One other thing I would like to say to you, since we are clearing the air here. Officer McCarthy is not a rookie. If you had had the opportunity to follow this man's progress as I have, you would have been as indignant as I was to hear someone call this fine officer a rookie. If I were you, I would be out there looking for a hundred more McCarthys. This man finds real criminals at an amazing rate. He brings them to justice and makes rock-solid cases. He has a stellar reputation with the judges and the defense attorneys. Even the criminals know McCarthy's name and reputation. The district attorneys all want his cases, because they are interesting, complete, and he makes an excellent witness. That you and Sergeant Darnell would allow someone to demean one of the finest officers you have in front of a member of the district attorney's office would be troubling enough; but I find the fact that the *two of you* actually did it, quite shocking." Severson's face once again turned red, and he leaned forward to respond; but Waters turned deliberately away from Severson, toward McCarthy, and continued talking.

"Officer Daniel 'Dyno' McCarthy, I have something to say to you. I may offend Captain Severson, which I do not mean to do, but I feel it necessary. I only have to work with him for another year or two. You are the future of law enforcement in this city, and I want to make something very clear. All the attorneys in the District Attorney's Office have nothing but praise for your performance, your reports, your ability, and your integrity. You have been called a rookie. You are not a rookie. You have been shot at and missed, shit at and hit, and have managed to treat everyone, from asshole attorney to zucchini thief, with the compassion and respect due to every human being. It is a pleasure to work with you and an honor to call you friend. Please let me respectfully disagree with the words that were directed at you earlier. You are not a rookie! In my book you are a professional police officer. The kind of police officer others should strive to be like. A standard. You, Officer Daniel 'Dyno' McCarthy, are a Veteran!" Assistant District Attorney Bob Waters shook Dan's hand and then turned, ignoring Severson, and clicked down the hallway on his next mission, because most certainly for Bob Waters there was another mission dead ahead.

As he marched down the hallway, Waters opened a new pack of cigarettes and lit one up, deftly using only one hand for the entire operation. McCarthy was speechless.

Captain Severson stood quietly for a moment. Severson turned and left McCarthy alone and stunned.

McCarthy stood, silently and alone, in the large, empty courthouse hallway. He then took a few tired steps toward the shiny unforgiving bench and sat down. He wondered if this was how it happened for all cops. The transition, that is, from rookie to veteran. He wondered if captains, sergeants, and attorneys gathered in the hallways of courthouses all over the country, argued the merits of officers, and rendered the verdict. "We find the officer guilty of being a veteran."

McCarthy smiled and thought it doesn't matter much what happened everywhere else. It happened here to him. The case had been argued. All but one vote was in. McCarthy was looked at as a skilled, veteran police officer. He was still unsure. There was one vote to be yet cast. For McCarthy still had one person left that he had to convince, that he was not the same rookie that put on the uniform and strapped on a gun nearly four years ago. The kid Stanley Brockman dubbed "rookie."

The person that had yet to be convinced was . . . Dan McCarthy.

CHAPTER 26
THE END OF THE BEGINNING

It was spring in Wisconsin. The weather was warm and the ground was damp, but all the snow and ice had melted. McCarthy had been a policeman for nearly five years. He was caught somewhere between experienced and inexperienced. In his own mind, he was neither a rookie nor a veteran.

As McCarthy started his shift, he sat down and anticipated another Compton line-up. As he placed his duty-bag on the table, Compton said, "Hey, Dyno. Draper escaped this morning."

"What? Ray Draper?" asked McCarthy.

"Yeah, Ray," said Compton.

"How?" asked McCarthy, who thought it incredible that the man who'd shot his friend Gary Carpenter was out of prison. McCarthy had thought Draper would be in prison until Carpenter and McCarthy were ready to retire.

"He was being transported to a doctor, a specialist, for some tests. Somehow he got a handcuff key, because when the transport officer opened the back door at the hospital in Green Bay, Draper exploded out of the car and hit the officer repeatedly. He took the officer's gun. He's armed with a 9 mm Smith & Wesson," said Compton. "He must have some unfinished business here in La Claire, because he was spotted by second shift in a stolen car. He ditched the car, after a chase, and ran.

"Where was he last seen, and what was his direction of travel?" asked McCarthy.

"He was last seen three hours ago near Bluffview Estates. Second shift saw him run ino the Bluffview Estates addition. They lost him and are still out combing the area. I want you to see what you can do, McCarthy. He's changed out of his prison uniform. He's gotten rid of the cuffs. Grab an unmarked unit, and do what you need to do to find this guy. You are my wild card," said Compton, seriously.

"Thanks for the confidence, Sergeant. I'll try my best," said McCarthy resolutely.

McCarthy jumped into a confiscated Ford Escort. It did not look like a police vehicle. McCarthy wanted to get into the area, without looking like a cop. McCarthy had his full uniform on, but threw on an oversized jacket, which covered everything.

McCarthy headed out on Highway 41. All the way out he tried to picture the area. He felt that the movement of the searching officers probably kept Draper down most of this time. If he had moved, he probably had not moved far. McCarthy had a decision to make. His options were: He could set up by one of the locations Draper was probably heading toward and wait. Or he could take a lucky guess on his path of travel and set up, waiting for him to cross a path. McCarthy could also assume Ray Draper had made it out of the police search area and start making contact at his friends' and family's homes.

McCarthy then said out loud to himself, "Gibbon Park!" Gibbon Park was the best spot. If Draper were to get anywhere out of the search area, he would probably choose Gibbon Park. It was wooded, and he could cover a lot of ground, without crossing a thoroughfare or street.

McCarthy headed to the park to set up. He pulled into the lot, and parked the Escort in a boat landing across the highway from Gibbon Park. He told dispatch, "255 will be in the area of Gibbon Park, on foot." He made this transmission on a secured channel, which is unavailable to all in scanner-land. No one but cops would be able to hear it.

McCarthy used the darkness and went under a bridge, to gain access to the park without being noticed. He checked under the bridge, and found it to be clear. McCarthy was convinced he needed to find a spot that gave him a view of the hiking trail and the riverbank. If Draper was tired, he would use the trail, thinking the search was over. If he was intent on not being caught, he would use the riverbank. This would most definitely be the harder trek to travel. It afforded many opportunities to hide, if Draper crossed paths with another person.

McCarthy worked his way from bush to tree to barricade, quickly and silently working his way toward a spot where the trail nearly met the river. When he reached the spot, he found a large configuration of bushes he used to call a "bush fort," when he was a child. It had paths going in and out among the bushes, allowing movement within. These "bush forts" were all over Gibbon Park, and McCarthy surmised that Draper may have used one to stay hidden so long. McCarthy positioned himself within the bush, to enable him to see the trail and the riverbank below. Now it was time to wait.

McCarthy had obtained a headset for his radio, so he could listen to transmissions silently. In the night, when all is silent, the smallest of sounds travel, seemingly for miles, on the cool, spring, night air. The chatter on the radio was considerable. The search still was going on in earnest. He wondered if Ray Draper was lying low somewhere, listening to the chatter.

Draper had found a spot to hide that had served him well. He had managed to get out of the Bluffview Estates, where he was spotted by the La Claire officer. Too many cops flooded into the area, too quickly, to just make good his total escape. He reached an old farm, just outside Le Claire's city limits. The farm's land was adjacent to Bluffview Estates. It belonged to an elderly man, who'd refused to move, no matter what they offered him for his property, because it was his home.

Ray knew the old man. More importantly he knew the old man's Doberman, Satan. He entered Satan's cage and lifted the roof on the dog-house. The doghouse was a large, two-room facility. Draper crawled into the sleeping quarters and waited.

Officers had been by the cage, on foot, at least three times that Ray knew of, because of the commotion created by Satan. Satan was vicious looking to any stranger, and the searching officers never considered, for a second, looking in the doghouse of this devil dog. Draper was safe from discovery, as long as he stayed in the doghouse.

After an hour of tension, Ray began to relax, in the security of his spot. Draper had the cop's handgun in his hand the entire time, with his mind set on using it on anyone who got in his way, and as a last resort, himself. He had determined he was never going back to prison. It was the one part of the criminal's life he could not take. Ray could handle jail, but not prison.

After lying for over an hour in the doghouse, listening intently to the noises around him, Draper finally relaxed, to the point that he fell asleep. The night before his escape had been a sleepless one, and now sleep came easily. The old man treated Satan well. The blanket was warm, and the room was sufficient for Ray to curl up comfortably. Satan stood guard in the doorway, while Ray slept. The dog seemed aware that his friend Ray Draper needed protection, and protection was this Doberman's vocation in life.

Satan stood guard, then, while the escapee slept. Ray slept soundly for four hours. He was finally awakened by the silence. He was startled, at first, by the silence, and then by the darkness of his surrounding. He was used to the ever-present light in his prison cell and the metallic noises made by the twenty-four hours of movement in a lock-down facility. He could not recall ever having been in such a warm, dark, soundless place.

He had to think, for a moment, to remember where he was. The gun he still held in his hand brought reality back to him. He was startled to realize that, in his sleep, he had put his finger on the trigger and nuzzled the muzzle of the gun up tight under his chin. Draper whispered to himself, "Shit! One good wet dream and I would be whistling out of my neck."

Ray slowly got to his knees and lifted the roof ever so carefully. He realized how stiff he was, when he climbed out of the doghouse. He spent several moments thanking Satan for being his protector, and then he was off. "I'll work my way to the river bank, and then I'm out of here. Thanks pal" were his last words to the devil dog.

McCarthy had been lying in the bush for two hours. The search had dwindled to beat-cars being aware that Ray was on the run. The houses that he might go to had been checked and were being watched; and McCarthy was beginning to wonder if he was not wasting his time, waiting for the noise that didn't belong. McCarthy was not a patient hunter. He did not like to sit and wait. What he lacked in patience, he made up for in determination. He was determined he would find Ray Draper and determined Ray would come this way.

He would much rather hunt on the move. But this time, McCarthy had a feeling he should stay right here. In his four-plus-year career he had learned that every time he did not trust his instincts, he regretted it. Tonight, his instincts led him to the bush-fort and told him to stay put until Draper was caught. It was 1:00 a.m.

McCarthy could hear the river flowing to his left. It sounded like the storied babbling brook, as it passed carelessly on its journey to the sea. In sharp contrast, McCarthy could hear the highway noise to his right, on the outskirts of Gibbon Park. McCarthy began to daydream in his boredom. The park was named after General John Gibbon, who had been the leader of the best brigade in the Union Army during the Civil War. That brigade was known as "The Iron Brigade." La Claire had given many young men to the brigade, and most did not come back. McCarthy's great-great-grandfather had fought with tenacity in the 6th Wisconsin, which was one of the regiments of the Iron Brigade. He had survived Brawner Farm, Second Bull Run, Antietam, Gettysburg, Second Fredericksburg, the battles around Petersburg, and had stood in the front line during the surrender of Lee's Army. McCarthy wondered how many nights like this, his Great-Great-Grandpa McCarthy had sat out on picket-duty, listening to the noises in the night. McCarthy wondered if he could live up to the tenacity of Michael "Mick" McCarthy. He wondered if fear drove Mick on to fight that way, as it spurred on Dan. McCarthy pondered if Mick even felt fear, or if his desire to save the Union and end slavery fueled his furnace to an incredible flame that leant heat to the battle. Joe Darnell had not known that using Dan's ancestor's name "Mick" to insult Dan McCarthy was a good way to get him to fight if a fight was what you wanted. McCarthy wondered if . . . "crack!"

Dan heard it. McCarthy recognized it as the noise that didn't belong. The noise was followed by the rustling of some creature, moving through the brush along the river. McCarthy suddenly could hear another noise that didn't belong. He could hear and feel his heartbeat in his own ears. He knew this was no animal making this noise. It was too slow-moving and large, and it was too late at night for this to be an animal of any size. Raccoons do not make so much noise as this.

McCarthy slid silently through his bush fort, to the path that opened at the edge of the embankment, which led down to the river. The noise in the darkness was still coming toward him. McCarthy removed his weapon from his holster and realized he was by himself. To follow without detection would create the possibility of an armed man, escaping.

The noise was too close to get a backup. He keyed his mic and whispered, "255, I have movement at my location. Head some people this way, silently."

The noise then got louder and closer and nearer, and then McCarthy saw, via the sliver of moonlight below. McCarthy saw Draper. Without thinking, McCarthy brought up his Glock and shouted, "Police, don't move! Drop the gun, Ray! It's Dan McCarthy! You are surrounded!"

Equally without thought, Ray froze for but a moment, but it seemed for both antagonists to be an hour. Ray then spun blindly to his right, toward the shout, brought up the stolen gun, and fired twice. McCarthy sensed the motion and what grave consequences awaited him, if he did not react effectively. McCarthy fired twice, also, so close in time with Draper's shots that a witness hearing the shots from a distance would swear there were only two shots fired.

Silence returned to the park except for the relentless hum of cars on the highway and the rush of the river below. It was over. Peace returned to Gibbon Park. The park named after a man who had witnessed many battles, had just been the scene of a small, desperate battle. One whose stakes for those involved, were just as high.

Would it be life or death? Would it be freedom or the loss of it?

At first, Dan could hear nothing. Then his senses returned. It had taken but moments, but it seemed like a lifetime had passed. In reality, a lifetime had indeed just passed.

He brought his weapon down and saw his life-threatening nemesis lying before him—motionless, helpless, harmless . . . lifeless.

Other officers had heard the transmission, "255, I have movement at my location. Head some people this way, silently." Everyone started converging on Gibbon Park. There was silence for fifteen seconds, and then the crackle of a excited voice came across the air, "255, I have shots fired. The suspect is down. Send me an ambulance and the commander to the scene. I am on the river side of Gibbon Park."

"10-4, 255. What is *your* status?" asked Hix, with concern in his voice that was out of character for this old dinosaur.

"I am uninjured. The suspect appears 10-100 (deceased)," answered McCarthy.

McCarthy stood over the lifeless body of Ray Draper. He could hear the sirens approaching from all directions. McCarthy could detect neither a pulse nor respiration on Ray. Both bullets had found their mark. It would be a closed casket for Ray Draper. If the Native Americans that had lived for centuries in the La Claire area were correct about the afterlife, Ray Draper would be entering the happy hunting ground, blind.

McCarthy suddenly felt an overwhelming surge of absolute elation, for he was alive. He would see his Victoria again. He would be able to dance at Christa's wedding and watch Nathan sing at his senior prom. He would hold his newborn grandchildren. His life that almost wasn't, would be now, thanks to two well-placed shots and two that missed.

Just as suddenly he was overcome with grief, because the price of admission to the rest of his life was the death of another human being. Suddenly, the grief was joined by an immense feeling of guilt. McCarthy remembered the night Gary Carpenter had been shot, that Dan McCarthy had actually prayed to God he would get an opportunity to shoot this man. The guilt was for the act of using a prayer to seek the death of another. The guilt was for feeling such elation at the death of another. There was an emotional cyclone taking place inside McCarthy. It seemed as if he was alone in the darkness, bearing witness to his deed for hours.

McCarthy then remembered something he'd read. "In this world, there are sheep, sheepdogs, wild dogs and wolves." McCarthy realized he had taken the path of the honorable sheepdog. The sheepdog is often unappreciated by the sheep, but sworn to protect them. Ray Draper had chosen the path of the wolf. The honorable, faithful sheepdog did what was expected of the sheepdog. He had protected the sheep, while they slept. Ray Draper would never beat another woman. Ray Draper would never addict another child to his drugs. Ray Draper would never shoot another policeman. The honorable sheepdog had struck down the wolf, while the sheep slept.

McCarthy stood by waiting, as the sirens got closer. He knew his life would not ever be exactly the same again. But it would be life. He would be going home to Victoria, Nate, and Christa at the end of this shift. He looked down at Draper and realized it could have been him lying on the ground, with Ray Draper looking at him. Ray Draper would most certainly not have felt guilt.

McCarthy had faced the ultimate test every warrior and police officer daydreams about, longs for, and yet prays will never happen. He had faced it, and he'd survived the few moments of fury and terror that would live vividly in his memory and dreams the rest of his life.

McCarthy then flashed back to a salesman, who sold him his bullet-resistant vest. The portly and jovial salesman had tossed a vest down on the table in front of McCarthy, and said with a strange exuberance, "Sex and violence! That's what it's all about—sex and violence!"

"What do you mean?" McCarthy asked. "That has to mean something."

"You can't enjoy the one unless you survive the other," was the answer, which was understood now by McCarthy with utter clarity, as pure as fine crystal.

In one flash in the darkness . . . in one explosion of intensity, McCarthy had survived the violence and would live to enjoy all the days Ray Draper had tried to steal from him. No one would ever call McCarthy a rookie again. He would never think of himself as a rookie again. It had been nearly five years since McCarthy had answered "The Calling." The making of a veteran cop had occurred in less than five seconds, when skill and speed decided whether McCarthy went to heaven . . . or Draper went to hell.

Heaven would have to wait for Dan McCarthy—*the veteran.*